USA TODAY bestselling, R critically acclaimed author written more than 130 books and counting. She has a Master's and a PhD in English Literature, thinks everyone should read more category romance, and is always available to discuss her beloved alpha heroes. Just ask! She lives in the Pacific Northwest with her comic book artist husband, is always planning her next trip, and will never, ever, read all the books in her to-be-read pile. Thank goodness.

Bella Mason has been a bookworm from an early age. She has been regaling people with stories from the time she discovered she could hold the dinner table hostage with her reimagined fairy tales. After earning a degree in journalism she rekindled her love of writing, and now writes full time. When she isn't imagining dashing heroes and strong heroines she can be found exploring Melbourne, with her nose in a book, or lusting after fast cars.

Also by Caitlin Crews

Forbidden Royal Vows
Greek's Christmas Heir
Kidnapped for His Revenge

Notorious Mediterranean Marriages miniseries

Greek's Enemy Bride
Carrying a Sicilian Secret

Also by Bella Mason

Secretly Pregnant by the Tycoon
Their Diamond Ring Ruse
His Chosen Queen

The De Luca Legacy miniseries

Strictly Forbidden Boss

Discover more at millsandboon.co.uk.

MEDITERRANEAN HEIRS

CAITLIN CREWS

BELLA MASON

MILLS & BOON

All rights reserved including the right of reproduction in whole or in part in any form. This edition is published by arrangement with Harlequin Enterprises ULC.

This is a work of fiction. Names, characters, places, locations and incidents are purely fictional and bear no relationship to any real life individuals, living or dead, or to any actual places, business establishments, locations, events or incidents. Any resemblance is entirely coincidental.

Without limiting the author's and publisher's exclusive rights, any unauthorized use of this publication to train generative artificial intelligence (AI) technologies is expressly prohibited. HarperCollins also exercise their rights under Article 4(3) of the Digital Single Market Directive 2019/790 and expressly reserve this publication from the text and data mining exception.

® and TM are trademarks owned and used by the trademark owner and/or its licensee. Trademarks marked with ® are registered with the United Kingdom Patent Office and/or the Office for Harmonisation in the Internal Market and in other countries.

First published in Great Britain 2025
by Mills & Boon, an imprint of HarperCollins*Publishers* Ltd,
1 London Bridge Street, London, SE1 9GF

www.harpercollins.co.uk

HarperCollins*Publishers*, Macken House, 39/40 Mayor Street Upper, Dublin 1, D01 C9W8, Ireland

Mediterranean Heirs © 2025 Harlequin Enterprises ULC

Her Accidental Spanish Heir © 2025 Caitlin Crews

Pregnant Before 'I Do' © 2025 Bella Mason

ISBN: 978-0-263-34467-7

06/25

This book contains FSC™ certified paper
and other controlled sources to ensure responsible forest management.

For more information visit www.harpercollins.co.uk/green.

Printed and Bound in the UK using 100% Renewable Electricity
at CPI Group (UK) Ltd, Croydon, CR0 4YY

HER ACCIDENTAL SPANISH HEIR

CAITLIN CREWS

MILLS & BOON

This book is for you.

That I get to write these books at all, much less 100 of them, is one of the greatest joys of my life.

Thank you for letting me tell you these stories, for loving these characters, and for taking this journey with me over the past 15 years—through glorious kingdoms, private islands, glamorous cities, and too many marvelous palazzos to count all over the world. Here's to at least 100 more. I can't wait to see where we go next!

With love and gratitude,

Caitlin

CHAPTER ONE

When I get to the office that summer morning I am already grumpy, thanks to the usual vagaries of the New York City subway system, and it takes me a moment to realize that Tess is not just sitting at her desk, but is *smiling*.

Given that Tess Erdrich, my secretary and office manager, is what I can only call a battle-ax, this is surprising. I'm not sure I've ever seen her smile before in our five years of working together. I'm not sure I like seeing it now.

"It's a marvelous day," she tells me, and now I'm terrified. Tess is a New Jersey native who has never expressed a single iota of enthusiasm about anything, ever. She beams at me, and I pull out my phone to call 911. "He's here."

That is not a sentence that makes any sense. I squint at her. "He who?"

"The only him," she retorts, like I'm being coy. Or deliberately obtuse. Neither of which is in my wheelhouse and she should know that. "The big guy. The boss. *Him*."

"Is this a religious thing?" I ask, lost. I've never pretended to speak Catholic and she's always graciously pretended she doesn't find that baffling.

"It's the closest that I've personally come to God," Tess throws back, and then gives me an exasperated look. "You're slow today, Annagret. I am referring to our boss, the head of the firm, who finally deigned to make an appearance this morning." She smiles then, very cat and canary, and this is no less terrifying. "Mr. Luc Garnier himself has reported for duty."

That name goes through me like an electric current.

Luc Garnier, the owner and much sought-after head investigator at Miravakia Investigations, is so constantly busy that he is never here. Instead, he is forever caught up in the concerns of billionaires, kingdoms, and multinational corporations, dedicated to solving their problems with his keen eye and razor-sharp investigative abilities. He is always rushing from one secret job to the next, too in demand from all quarters to do more than message his instructions from his private plane as he moves from the Côte d'Azur to Saint Barts to Brussels, and back again.

He does not come to New York City office buildings without warning. And he certainly does not appear in *this* one, no matter what.

Something I am absolutely, one hundred percent sure of.

Because I made him up.

Tess studies my face, her overly dramatic eyebrows rising at whatever look she sees there. I honestly can't imagine what it might be as the shock of what she said still reverberates inside me.

"Well, well," she says, drawing the syllables out. "And here I thought you were an ice queen through and through. Frozen solid, never to thaw. Turns out you do have a little spark in there after all. For the boss, no less."

As I laugh that off, I realize I'm playing directly into whatever fantasy she has about me and *the boss*. Because I'm clearly awkward and flustered, but I can't explain *why*. I can't explain any of this, so I do the only thing available to me. I let her see me flustered.

But not too flustered, because even Tess, who is occasionally shockingly romantic beneath her tough Jersey veneer, would find it unbelievable to see me *too* flustered.

"About time he shows his face," I say, because surely that's what someone would say if this was a real boss turning up to his own firm like this. I turn and march past her desk, as if I'm off to slay the dragon in its lair, my mind spinning wildly with every step.

Truth is, the Luc Garnier lie is one that I never expected would or could come back to haunt me like this. Not once I put it into play and was able to see how well it works.

I'd had the best of intentions at the start. When I decided that I could use what my literal wicked stepmother liked to call my *alarming nosiness* to my advantage, and instead of ending up on the streets as I'm sure she intended, I became a full-fledged private investigator.

She always did underestimate me.

I'd thought it would be easy enough. Put up a shingle, get to gumshoeing, and call it a day. But the sad truth of the matter is that people didn't want to entrust their dirty secrets, questionable obsessions, and darkest truths to the overly perky twenty-year-old blonde girl I'd been then.

Looking back from the vantage point of these eight years I've spent acquiring culture, sophistication, and my own sharp-edged veneer to rival anything Tess's Jersey can throw up, I'm not sure I can blame them.

My first few months were dire.

But I was determined to get my footing—because the streets seemed like an upgrade over crawling back to my stepmother and I do not intend to live down to *her* low expectations in this lifetime, thank you—and so one day I took down the sign that hung outside my door with my name on it. I put up a simple one that read *private investigations* instead.

I wanted to see if the immediate disconnect that happened when I told people I was said investigator, or possibly even as soon as they saw my name on my useless shingle, could be handled if I got them in the door first.

And when a man walked in, all furtive eyes and that seriousness about the mouth that indicates *issues*, I prepared to launch into my usual spiel.

I'm here for your boss, sweetheart, he said with curt dismissiveness, looking around like I might have stashed said boss in the requisite dinged-up filing cabinet that came with the rented space.

I didn't mean to do it. But I had a client *in the room* at last and he wanted a boss. And the customer is always right, so I invented that boss on the spot.

I gave my pretend boss the name of the hero from the romance novel I was currently reading to while away the hours no one hired me, and when that worked—beyond my wildest expectations—I named my business after the made-up kingdom in that book, too.

My Luc Garnier is only partly the hero from the book, sure. I refined him to suit my own purposes over the years. He's now a billionaire man of mystery himself, dedicated to ferreting out the truth no matter what it takes. He is elegant yet masterful. Gloriously and unabashedly male yet always exquisitely dressed. No shabbily dressed, seemingly hapless sleuth, our Luc Garnier.

Look closely, I always tell my more suspicious clients while brandishing society rag photographs in their direction. *He is a master of hiding in plain sight.*

Then I claim that we can *almost* see his ear in a paparazzi picture of the most famous person of the hour. Or perhaps we can glimpse his elbow, *just there,* at the sort of outrageously extravagant charity ball normal people can never dream of attending.

Luc Garnier never allows himself to be caught on camera, I tell everyone with great seriousness, and a bit of earnestness and awe, too, for effect. *Such is his commitment to* your *privacy.*

Thanks to Luc Garnier, I went from not being able to book a client to having too many clients to take on. I quickly elevated my office space from the sketchier outer boroughs into Manhattan itself, where I am currently sitting pretty on Fifth Avenue.

I did well, is what I did, and I do better now. And these days I mostly find it funny—and only sometimes bittersweet—that I am *just starting* to be seen as an investigator on my own merits. I have more than a few clients who tell me that if I wanted, I could step out from famous Luc Garnier's shadow.

Though they whisper it, like they expect him to materialize from behind a potted plant and confront them for their daring in making such a suggestion.

Maybe one day, I like to tell them, trying to look

grateful and deeply complimented. *But I'm still learning so much from Mr. Garnier.*

My favorites are the clients who condescend to me and tell me that *they* speak personally to Luc Garnier daily, when, obviously, I know they don't. And then they like to argue that the instructions he never gave them contradict the ones I made up.

I thought that I'd seen it all.

But I did not expect that anyone would wander in the door and pretend to be the man himself.

I charge down the hallway, passing the actual office that I use and continuing on past the little conference room with its view of the city, then on to the grand corner office that stands mostly as a shrine to a man who does not exist. There are client photos on the wall and also, just to entertain myself, I like to frame photographs that seem to suggest that Luc Garnier attended this or that wildly exclusive event—without showing him, of course.

Today, something hitches inside of me as I pass the conference room and can see through the glass that there is, indeed, a man sitting there behind Luc's desk.

My desk, I correct myself.

I stride to the door, throw it open—

And stop dead.

Because the man who sits—*lounges* is a better word—behind the desk I maintain for a completely fictional character of my own devising, looks…

Exactly the way that I imagine Luc Garnier himself *would* look.

If only he was real.

He is so tall that he even looks tall sitting down, and

he *commands* the room somehow, even though all he does is glance up from his laptop—his own laptop, not the prop I leave on the desk, I note—seemingly taking very little notice of me as I stand there.

"Is it office protocol to simply throw open doors instead of waiting to be granted access?" he asks, and his voice is another problem.

I do a sweep of him like he's someone I'm surveilling.

Tall. Commanding. Dark hair and eyes like steeped tea. Chiseled jaw and acrobatic cheekbones. Sensual mouth that's at complete odds with the austerity of the dark, bespoke suit that he wears. That caresses his body as if silkworms and various sheep personally sacrificed themselves for his sartorial splendor.

All that and he sounds like poetry when he speaks.

A kind of distinctly European poetry, I think as I take it in. I can't quite place that accent. His English is perfect, but it is clearly not his first language.

I am not a fan of the way I want to just stand here and *stare* at him.

"Who are you?" I ask.

I am staring at him, but now the staring is with *intention,* I assure myself.

He lifts his head from the laptop screen and stares back at me, and something seems to leap there between us. Somewhere between his inscrutable gaze and the odd sensations chasing around inside me. *Challenge,* I tell myself. That's all.

His mouth does not seem to move, and yet I'm sure there's a hint of a smile there all the same. He lifts a finger and makes a languid circle in the air above his head, taking in not just his office—*my* office, damn it—but the broader Miravakia Investigations office all around.

"Do you lack comprehension skills?" he asks me. "I would think that a surface level requirement for a private investigator, Ms. Alden. How have you managed to remain employed—by me—for so long?"

Once again, I'm certain that I can see some small hint of a smile, not quite there on his face. Some lurking knowledge in those eyes of his that he is fully aware of what he is doing here.

"I'm going to have to ask you to leave," I say, very quietly, because the shocks keep coming and coming inside me, and I'm not certain why I'm finding it hard to breathe.

Temper, I tell myself. It has to be *temper*.

"I beg your pardon?"

He sounds filled with the upper-class affront of a man of means and authority, exactly the way he would if he really was Luc Garnier.

But he's not.

Because despite how real the figurehead seems to *me,* I know he's a figment of my imagination.

I shouldn't have to remind myself of this.

"This office belongs to a very powerful man," I tell him. What I want to say is that I know perfectly well that he's not Luc Garnier, because I made Luc Garnier the way I made everything else in this office, and, indeed, this office itself. I made him up in my own head and I put him onto documents, then put his name above mine everywhere, so that people would finally treat me as if I was more than a secretary. I did these things. He's *mine. This man* is an impostor at best, and I don't want to think what might be worse. "I don't know who you are, but if I were you, I would rethink whatever experiment this is that you're doing and leave before I have to get the authorities involved."

I don't know what I expect from him. Maybe...some acknowledgment of the real situation here? Or at least for him to drop the character he's playing. To show by even a fleeting expression that he knows he's playing a game and that I've caught him doing it.

But instead, the man behind the desk who is absolutely not Luc Garnier pushes back. He takes his time standing, and once again, I am struck by his sheer and astonishing perfection. It really shouldn't be possible. I'm not sure where on earth he could come from, because not even the most gilded reaches of the highest echelons of Hollywood could produce something like *this*.

He looks like a carving of my wildest fantasies, brought to life. Every line, every inch, everything about him is mouthwatering in a way that is so overwhelming that I'm tempted to just...find it funny.

No single human should have *this much* wildfire charisma and that he does *and* is clearly a con man is a sort of whiplash I suspect might take me a very long time to sort through.

But that will have to happen *after* I get rid of him.

Something that's difficult to think how to do when he takes up all the air in this office, and maybe all the air in all of Manhattan, too.

Standing, he's even taller than I imagined. But I notice other things now, like the broadness of his shoulders, that suggest something more than he appears. If

I were to see him anywhere else, I would think that he was aristocratic. It's in the way he holds himself, as if expecting that genuflection might break out at any moment, and it's best to be prepared.

He absently smooths down the front of his lapel, a gesture that I have seen many attempt to ape and only some pull off. It's a gesture born of many, many years of wearing perfectly tailored suits, cut and sewn to the wearer's specific measurements. Men who don't wear suits often, or only wear suits of a lower standard, can forever be found smoothing down the front of them, trying to make them hang correctly.

The way this man smooths his lapel is less about securing a proper fit and more an unconscious confirmation of the excellence of the suit in question, and therefore also of himself.

It is the equivalent of the way a regal woman might minutely adjust her crown, and I doubt he's even aware that he does it.

The moment I think that, it bothers me, because I know it's true of this man. He has that kind of gravitas. And it makes me wonder who on earth this man really is if he can pull that off. This gesture I might normally expect to see on, say, a king.

Con men are good at the suggestion of a gesture, but not all the stateliness and breeding that makes it unconscious.

I hate that I can see the difference.

It makes no sense that a man like this should be here, trying to run a con like this.

He stands by the desk, and studies me as if he has all the time in the world and no fear at all that I might call security. It makes me want to call them immediately, but it also makes me curious.

Why *isn't* he worried?

Who is he?

But I remind myself that what matters is that I know who he's *not*.

"I really must insist," I say, in the calm, sure voice I use when things go awry on a job. "You can't be in here. I think you know that."

That voice usually produces immediate results, but not today. He smiles, then encircles the desk, and watching him move does not help anything at all. It's far too… Liquid, almost. There's an ease to the way he holds himself, and while he doesn't *slouch,* he very much gives the impression that he has high expectations of gravity and expects them to be met.

According to his demands, even.

And I don't know what's happening inside of me. Temper, maybe. That same electric kind of shock, but over and over again. And it's as if something in me is echoing the way he moves, liquid and low.

He rounds the desk and thrusts his hands into the pockets of that suit, marring all those perfect lines and yet somehow making it all…better.

Suddenly I'm aware of his body in a way I'm not sure I've ever been before.

Of anyone's. Not even my own.

I'm suddenly fascinated by things like *sinew*. The interplay of male muscle across a set of shoulders. In the way a man can be almost too beautiful to behold while, individually, all those particular features really ought to be too much.

On him, they make a symphony.

And that's not getting into that long, hard expanse of his chest, his narrow waist. And the way he cuts through space like a deadly, elegant weapon.

He stops directly before me, and I suspect we both know it's so I have to tilt my head back, and look up—and up and up—to meet his gaze.

I can see the glint of something there. But that's all it is. The merest *glint* of what I think is the truth, though I'm not sure I can trust myself to know what it means.

"I," he says, very deliberately in that low voice that brims over with authority—all of it unearned, "am Luc Garnier, the owner and chief investigator of this firm."

I laugh at that. Actually laugh, though it makes my skin feel tight and my whole body even more…*strange* than before. That electricity winds its way around inside of me and gathers weight, as if I might tip over into hysteria, or possibly even tears.

It's the strangest feeling and somehow, I think his knowing gaze is to blame.

"You are not," I retort.

And this impostor leans in close, until I realize that I'm holding my breath. He still comes closer and if I was a fanciful sort of woman, I might imagine that he is leaning in for a kiss—

I can even feel his breath on my face.

But he doesn't kiss me.

Instead, his lips curve into a smile.

"Prove it," he says.

CHAPTER TWO

MY HEART IS RACING. I can feel him—and his words—everywhere. As if those two short syllables are sharp, poisoned spears he's thrust deep into me. I'm afraid that if I look down, I'll see them sticking out of me.

"Prove it?" I repeat, flabbergasted. But there's a thread of trepidation winding through me, too. Because asking me to prove that he is *not* Luc Garnier suggests that he knows I can't, and no one can know that. *No one,* and certainly not some random man who turned up this morning like some kind of nightmare. Because if I'm revealed as a liar, who will trust me again? What will happen to this business I've built so painstakingly over the years? It's not like I have any other skills—or supportive family members—to fall back on. "It's not as if that would be hard. All I need to do is call the *actual* Luc Garnier. And then, I imagine, the police?"

The man standing before me looks entirely too pleased with himself. Those eyes of his in that dark, rich-bodied color, *gleam.*

It all bodes ill.

"Then by all means," he invites me. "Do that."

I realize that I'm holding my breath. But I worry that if I try to do something about it, I'll make it worse. I'll start hyperventilating, maybe, and collapse on the floor, and that's highly unlikely to help me out of this situation that shouldn't be happening in the first place.

And in any case, it won't solve this problem. Neither will working myself up into hysteria.

"Do you think that I won't?" I ask, and try to inject a note of *bemused astonishment* into my tone, as if I can't believe that he would question such a thing. The way I would if he turned up pretending to be Tess.

He only stands there before me for a moment, as if deciding what to do next, and his head tilts slightly to one side.

I tell myself this would be easier if he didn't *look* the way he does. If he didn't make me think of fallen angels, *Paradise Lost,* and all kinds of epic poetry featuring demigods and legends. If the hint of those things didn't seem to gather about him like a thunderstorm and infuse every part of him with that same brooding intensity.

I'm not a fan of how all that thunder and the flashes of lightning echo in me, either.

It shouldn't be possible that any one man can have this effect on me. I detest it. I don't understand it—and part of me doesn't want to.

But he doesn't seem inclined to leave.

And it occurs to me then that I don't know how to make him without causing scenes and forcing questions I don't want to answer.

Or worse yet, risking him telling the world that I'm a fraud.

"Perhaps it's time that you and I come to terms, Annagret," he says quietly.

I decide that another thing I really don't like is my name in his mouth.

"What terms are there to come to?" I demand, but something is happening to me even as I try to pretend otherwise. My pulse is too strange. My blood in my veins feels fluttery and odd, and there's a sort of quickening deep inside of me, seeming to heat me up from within. I am certain I don't want to know what *that* is. "You seem to think you can walk in here and pretend to be a man who everybody already knows, and while I admire the audacity, you must have known it couldn't work."

I try to look *concerned,* like perhaps the reason he didn't know is because he's obviously delusional…but I'm too polite to say such a thing out loud.

He does not look appropriately chastised. "Here's the interesting thing about Luc Garnier. Everyone knows who he is. And everyone can describe him when asked, and always in the most glowing terms." I try not to react to that compliment—because that's what it is. A compliment on my ability to sell a story and watch it take flight. But he's not done. "Except it is never the *person* they describe. It is never what the man himself *looks* like. It is a list of accomplishments. A retelling of feats of detection and investigative prowess."

There's a hint of that brief smile, though I would not call it an expression of joy. Not on him. "I looked all over for a picture of this man. And if you can believe it, none exist."

"Mr. Garnier is famously camera shy, the better to allow him to actually do his work," I say with a slight frown, the way I always do. "It would be difficult to conduct *private* investigations if he couldn't actually be private, wouldn't it?"

This usually gets people to back off, but this man does not look remotely mollified.

He shakes his head. "Not one picture, in all the world, of a man so famous that you need only say his name for people to respond as if he is Poirot. Sherlock Holmes. Remington Steele. Do you know what all of those famous sleuths have in common?"

I know what he's getting at but I have no intention of admitting it.

"None of them do any real-world investigating," I say with a nod as if I think that's what he meant. "The very thing I would be doing right now if I weren't busy trying to peaceably eject a con man from my boss's office."

"Perhaps you can solve this mystery for me," he says as if I haven't spoken. "Given that I have scoured the earth and can find no one who has actually seen the great man in person—"

"Aside from me," I interject.

He inclines his head. "Is it any wonder, if you are the only witness to this man, that some have been forced to conclude that he, too, is a work of fiction?"

"When you've told me you are him?" I ask through my teeth. "This must be a new kind of fiction, with two men playing the same part. I'm not sure I'm familiar with the conventions of the genre, but I have to tell you, I'm not that interested in the premise."

His eyes gleam at that. "Aren't you lucky, Annagret, that despite all the confusion and these many years of remaining out of sight and thus creating comment, I, the great Luc Garnier himself, am not fictional at all?"

And he smiles at me again. Wider this time.

Fatuously, to my mind.

I want to shout at him. Maybe throw something. And the fact I even have the urge is shocking.

I've worked hard these past years to completely divorce myself from the kind of life I had growing up. If not to entirely *forgive* my father's inability to be anything but weak, then to at least stop dwelling on it. And to move past my stepmother's need to forever belittle and demean me because she hated any remnants of my mother, the woman my father loved first, since there was no changing it.

My mother died a few months after giving birth to me. She was told to me in stories, growing up. That was all I had when my stepmother got done purging the house of the pictures and mementos she claimed made my father grumpy and me impossible. My mother became a bedtime story my father told me in a low whisper so no one else would hear.

I became my mother's twin as I grew, looking like her in every way and thereby ensuring that my stepmother would hate me.

And she did.

It had been a loud and fraught childhood home, with rages at the dinner table, shrieked accusations at the slightest provocation, and bitter rants that we were all forced to attend to until my stepmother's temper was satiated. I have long since accepted that there will never be a good reason for the way she made me the target for all of her ire, aside from the cruel jealousy that seemed to rule her, or for my father's inability to defend me from her.

Instead, I spend my life sorting out other people's mysteries, and finding them answers. I couldn't find answers myself, because there is no answer to a problem like my stepmother. She simply is who she is, willing and only too happy to cause damage wherever she goes.

I decided when I left that I would get other answers.

And maybe someday that will feel like healing.

But because of my beginnings and how I left at eighteen—in the middle of the night, with her shrieking behind me to spur me on—I treasure calmness. Serenity. Keeping my cool under any and all circumstances.

It feels like virtue after some fifteen years with a woman like my stepmother.

I've made this virtue my entire personality, in fact. She told me no one could ever love a sneaky, nasty liar like me. I told her that if I was those things, she made me into them. I've spent these years on my own proving that she was always wrong about me, that I do good things, that I *am* good.

I like to think I prove this in my work. That one little white lie doesn't cancel out the questions I've answered and the problems I've solved.

I have no idea why it's so hard to hold onto all that—to *me*—while staring back at this man.

"Tell me how you think this is going to go," I say, and it's a fight to sound *measured* and *even*, but I tell myself that's how I would sound if there really was a Luc Garnier I could raise with a phone call. "You are an impostor. You must know that there's no possible way I'm simply going to…go along with whatever it is you're planning here, do you?"

Again, that smile of his, and every time I see it, it

seems to find new parts of me to bloom in, dark and gold and problematic. "My dear Annagret, you have no choice but to do exactly that. Surely you know this."

I flush, feeling red and angry. And perilously close to breaking some of my longest held vows.

He moves then, and I don't know why I get the impression that he has to force himself into action. As if he's as held tight in this *thing* between us as I am, but thinking such a thing seems to make the *blooming* more intense.

I watch as he crosses the office to stand at the bank of windows and look out at the view. This sparkling sprawl of Manhattan there before us that *I* made possible. Because it's easy enough to have a dingy office somewhere unremarkable.

But a place like this? With a view like *that?*

It's my sweat and tears that he's looking at, and I want to tell him so but it feels too revealing. Too…exposing. He might have taken me by surprise this morning, but that doesn't mean I intend to roll over and show him my belly.

Though rolling around with him, maybe right here on the floor, and showing him my belly is suddenly all I can think about. And it turns out I don't need to breathe for that, because he—

Stop it, I order myself. *He's a con man.*

And he's talking. "You should view this as an opportunity," he tells me, and he sounds…something like serious. "For a little while, your Luc Garnier will be here, in the flesh. I'm certain that you can make use of that."

I'm not sure I like the fact that I was thinking of writhing on the floor while he was thinking in terms of strategy. I feel like I'm letting myself down already.

That might be why I make a scoffing sound that definitely errs on the side of *aggressive*. "So you're doing me a favor?"

"You can call it whatever you like. It will not make a difference. But this myth of yours is now a man."

I might sound aggressive, but inside, I'm too aware it's nothing but panic. How can he possibly know this? Maybe *guessing the truth* isn't wholly surprising, but he's not acting as if this is a guess. He's acting as if he knows the truth as well as I do.

I don't understand how.

Or why he's so confident that he's right, even in the face of my denials.

It's like he can read my mind, and that doesn't help. "Surely there must be a use for that. For you. Perhaps you should stop fighting the inevitable and think about what that use might be, Annagret."

He turns back as he says that. This myth turned man, and I hate myself immediately for thinking of him in such terms. But how can I not?

Firstly, if ever a man looked like a myth, it's him. Everything about him suggests that shrines should be constructed, statues carved of the finest bronze and marble, and all necessary sacrifices made to win his favor.

And secondly, he's not wrong. But I deeply dislike being put in this position. And I hate that he's made me feel helpless when I haven't felt like that in years. Ten years, to be exact, since the night of my eighteenth birthday when my stepmother told me my birthday gift was that I had two weeks' notice to leave and I said, *why wait?*

I decided, then and there, that the only way I would return to that house was in a coffin.

Just like I decide, here and now, that the last thing I need is to give this man more ammunition against me.

I blink at him. "I still can't imagine why you think I'm going to just…go along with this delusion of yours."

His face changes again, and I have the impression of that regal authority once more. As if he is not used to his dictates being challenged in the slightest regard, but it's not the baffled rage that my stepmother used to show me. This is something else. As if it's not a narcissistic wound of some kind that he wants to give voice to, but rather something he truly has no experience with.

As if he is used to reverence, not pushback.

I am intrigued despite myself, but then he simply looks at me seriously and I feel…breathless once again.

"I do not have any choice," he says, and there is a quiet sort of heft to the way the words land. To the way he looks at me, steady and sure and something I might have called sorrowed, if this was another situation. "And I am sorry if that upsets you. Truly I am, but nothing can be done."

"I can think of something that could be done. Right now, in fact." I lift a brow and try to fill up with enough breath and bluster to ride this out. "You could leave."

"I have already told you how and roughly when that will happen." He shakes his head, and his expression changes again. "Come now. There is no need to dwell on these things. Why don't you and I put our heads together and come up with ways that you can use the appearance of Luc Garnier to bolster your position."

The last thing I need is a figment of my imagination patronizing me.

"You're bribing me with your body?" I ask, my voice dry.

I don't think it through. I just say it.

But then it is said.

And it seems to hang there between us in the space of this office. This gleaming, bright office that is all Manhattan skyline and the hustle of the street below. Inside these walls of glass, it is hushed. Intimate.

And it is very clear that he is taking what I said in a very specific way.

A way I don't mean.

A way I don't *think* I mean, but then again, I think of us rolling together on the floor, of *blooming* and breathlessness, and I am not so sure.

"There are other ways that I could use my body to please you, Annagret," he tells me, his voice gone dark and low.

I hate myself for the heat that washes over me. I hate myself for the fact that I want to fidget. That I am perilously close to a betraying *giggle*. That I want to be immune to him, if not actively repulsed...yet can't.

"I see," he says, this dangerous, impossible man who should not be here. And what I worry is that he really can see, all of me, all the places I am soft and hot and want things I don't want to admit. "You'd like a little bit of talk and some mythmaking, is that it? But reality, it seems, confounds you. I will keep that in mind."

I become aware of a pain in my chest and it takes my palm pressed hard against the ache of it to realize it's my heart. *Pounding.* Jackhammering against my ribs as if it's trying to claw its way out.

At the same time, something seems to shift in the man before me. It's as if he's come to some kind of resolution and I can see him straighten his shoulders, just slightly, as he faces me fully.

"I took the liberty of looking at the office calendar," he says, and it is a completely different tone from the one he was using before. Gone are any hints of *mythmaking,* or *apology,* or any recognition that I mentioned his body.

Gone, too, though slower, is the heat in my cheeks.

It feels like a relief. As if he's released his grip on me and I can *breathe*—

But then his words penetrate. "Why on earth would you imagine you had access to proprietary information?" I demand.

Even as I say it, I realize how foolish it is. He doesn't even need to aim that smile at me.

After all, if he is prepared to assume an identity not his own, how shocking can it really be that he intends to rifle through everything he finds, private or not?

"I will have to have a word with Tess," I say coolly.

"What will you instruct her?" he asks, as if this is a matter of great interest to him. "You will perhaps tell her not to obey…her boss? The name on all her pay stubs? What reason will you give for such an extraordinary instruction?"

There is nothing to say to that, so I do not attempt it.

He only nods, as if he expects nothing else. As if that is close enough to obedience. "There is a charity event tonight, is there not? The sort of place, I imagine, that people in our line of work can easily pick up new clients. New clients with deep pockets to fund ongoing retainers, yes?"

There is a particularly challenging sort of gleam in his gaze, now. I feel vulnerable and naked about all of this. I don't want him to see the vulnerability and I certainly don't intend to use the word *naked* in his presence. But in all these years, no one has strayed close to the truth. No one has even questioned it, not really. At most, clients might question what they consider my gatekeeping of the great man himself. Luckily, in today's world of technology, it is not so difficult to send people on endless loops without ever getting anywhere.

And without ever having to meet the people we're speaking to.

I can't say I like the fact that someone called my bluff. Yet what I *really* don't like is feeling as if this man has peeled me open. As a child I learned that any hint of the real me was a weapon used to hurt me. Any whisper of my real feelings an invitation to attack me. I've made certain never to let anyone in, ever. No one gets to see inside. Not ever.

That this man even knows the way I operate at charity events in New York City that I know he has never attended with me makes me feel things I vowed I would never feel again.

I don't like any of it.

It's one thing to slide in and take over the role of a fictional person, surely. That's a con man move, there's no doubt about it, but it's not...*this*. It feels as if he's trying to get inside me, too, and I really, truly don't like it.

I tell myself I don't like it, again and again, because

it seems as if that flush on my face has found its way inside, winding its way down deep.

I don't like *that,* either.

"What I do or don't do to drum up clients for this firm could not be less your business," I tell him. "And are you going to tell me your name?"

His gaze heats a bit as he regards me. And I do too, in a response I can't seem to control—and worse, I think he knows it. "You know my name. Feel free to use it."

I don't want to. Everything in me revolts at the very idea, but then again, as he keeps pointing out, I don't have a lot of options.

Or really any options.

It occurs to me then, as it must surely have already occurred to him, that if he really wanted to he could fire me from my own firm.

I'm not sure why that didn't occur to me immediately. But now it's all I can think about.

"It seems to me that it is exactly the sort of event at which I should make my first appearance in New York," he is saying, sounding perfectly unconcerned, as if he's wholly unaware of the riot going on inside me. And if it were any other man, I might think he really didn't know. Or care.

And I can't say that I think he *cares.* But I feel certain that he knows.

That in some way, it's deliberate.

It's that thought that gets through the haze.

If it's deliberate, then it means that he wants me unsettled and chaotic and veering from disbelief to temper and back again. And that's good information to have. Because that means what he wants is to direct my attention elsewhere. He wants me to be constantly on the wrong foot, worrying about what next bomb will drop.

You're actually good at this, I remind myself. *If he wants to be a mystery, well, let him. Mysteries are what you do.*

So I smile at him. And I must get it close enough to my usual level of professionalism, because his head tips back slightly. I've surprised him, and this, I like. I like it a lot.

"I disagree," I tell him with a shrug. "It's a tiny little charity event, all things considered. Local to New York and really more of a trade thing, despite the fancy dresses and wildly expensive tables. I can't think of a single reason why the great Luc Garnier would grace it with his presence." And I lift a hand when he looks as if he's going to speak. "No need to get yourself in a lather. I'm not saying that the idea is a bad one, I'm saying the event isn't worthy of hard launching Luc Garnier in the flesh to the world."

"First," he says with a certain silken menace that I feel all over me like a shivery weight, "you can be certain that I'm never *in a lather,* whatever that might mean. Second, it would surely seem like a stroke of eccentricity, which seems to be the hallmark of the man." He inclines his head at that, as if anticipating my next words. "Me, I mean."

I take the opportunity to study him, now. I take a breath, as deep as I can manage. Then I let it out slowly.

And I remind myself that I am only as unsettled as I allow myself to be. That he does not control this. It's true that he's called my bluff in a way I didn't expect and, yes, find astonishingly shocking. It's hard to imagine what kind of man he must be when he's not here, to even conceive of such a thing.

Much less attempt it.

Then to pull it off with such ease. But the fact that he did tells me a great many things.

About him, that is.

He must have researched this extensively. He has to have been absolutely certain that Luc Garnier was a construct, not a person. And the only way that's possible is if he's been following me for a long while.

Following me. Tracking the firm. More than that, he's had to talk frankly with those who use our services.

He's been investigating us, in other words. Investigating *me*. Building a picture, then striking with such precision that the only possible response was this.

Me. Reeling.

But this suggests, I can only think, that he means it when he says that he intends to inhabit this role and then disappear again. That tells me something, too. He wants anonymity. Or at least, he wants to be Luc Garnier—not the person who found out Luc Garnier is a lie.

I don't recognize him on sight, so he can't be famous in the celebrity culture of the day. He doesn't even look familiar.

Except, something in me whispers, *he does look precisely as you imagined he would. If he was really Luc Garnier.*

I think again about that unstudied gesture he made with his suit. I think about how he inhabits this room. He has a different kind of authority, that much is clear. He's a man who is used to getting what he wants, and who expects his needs to be anticipated. He holds himself with the kind of confidence that I have never seen a man who didn't truly possess it manage to broadcast in this way. Even though I know him to be a liar, and even though I know that he's running a scam here, something like *integrity* and *certainty* exudes from him.

He holds himself like he matters, even when he's said something that should keep me focused on me, not him.

"In two weeks there is a particularly exclusive gathering in Cap Ferrat," I tell him. Then add, "that's in France," because I have the notion it will annoy him, the suggestion he doesn't know where Cap Ferrat—that monied retreat in the South of France—is located. I see that it does, and smile. "Mr. Garnier has declined the invitation year after year, citing work conflicts."

I could have had Mr. Garnier send me in his place, of course, but I've always worried that appearing alone at this particular event would require a lot of very careful maneuvering around the sort of haughty, impossibly wealthy men—in a *group*—who are the reason I invented Luc Garnier in the first place. Better, I've always thought, to find them in other places, where they are not in a famously wealthy throng of offhanded affluence and might compare notes.

It's easy to flatter a man alone. It's harder to flatter a group of them at once. It's my experience that they prefer to think of themselves as singularities.

"Perhaps this is the year he will make his appearance," I say now. "My understanding is that it is a desperately chic sort of dinner party and ball, impossibly sophisticated in every regard, and the sort of gathering that is only whispered about afterward. In hushed tones of awe, naturally, when faced with this sort of wealth and power on display." I purse my lips. "Though not *quite* on display, of course. As I believe the ball and all the rest of it is masked."

He nods. And we are still standing there, on either side of the expanse of this office, facing off like it's high noon.

"I suppose that will do," he says after a pause.

But it's the kind of pause that thrums with unspoken certainties and wild eddies of understanding just beyond my reach.

"Wonderful," I reply in as cheerful a voice as I can manage at the moment. "I can't wait to read about the reaction the world has to its first sight of such a man of myth and legend. In the prosaic flesh, at last."

I expect him to react to the word *prosaic*. I might even have said it deliberately, to force that reaction.

But he is not responding to what I said. Or at least not that part.

Instead, suddenly, it's entirely too easy to read the look in his eyes.

It's triumph. Sheer triumph.

As if this particular masked ball was what he was after all along. That tells me something, too—and not only that I walked into whatever trap this is. But that he likely never wanted to go to the charity event tonight at all. That he got me to offer what he wanted from the start, and I didn't even notice he was doing it.

It would be tempting to conclude that I'm an idiot, but I know perfectly well I'm not.

He's that dangerous. I need to remember that.

And he doesn't need to smile when he replies.

But he does. "I'm sure it will be nothing short of epic."

"You have perhaps overestimated the allure of an investigation, I think," I say, and it's my turn to hint at matters beyond his comprehension. "Unless you find thinking about things an epic battle, that is."

His gaze darkens in a way I tell myself I don't understand. No matter how it feels, deep inside.

But he ignores me. And drops the bomb I knew was coming, so I guess I haven't completely lost my touch. "You will be there, of course, Annagret. Right by my side. For every Sherlock Holmes needs his Watson, does he not?"

CHAPTER THREE

I EXPECT THE other shoe to drop, but it doesn't.

I don't want to leave the office that first day, certain that when I return I'll be locked out and *persona non grata* in the place I built, but that doesn't happen. I get in early the next day—a bit psychotically early, I will admit—and everything is as it should be. I make it in so early that I beat Tess in and that's a good thing, because I don't have to run the gauntlet of her innuendos or speculation.

I don't think I can control my facial expressions. Not yet.

I see that Luc is not in his office—and I am deeply ashamed of myself for thinking of him by that name, but I can't seem to help it—so I duck into mine instead.

I have always liked it. It sits along the hall on the way to the big office, and I've always liked to think of it as the power behind the throne. I happen to be both the power *and* the throne, but no one knows it but me. So why not sit in a little internal office that has no windows of its own, but commands every window in this place?

I've always liked being underestimated. I learned that in my stepmother's house, too.

And that first day after the appearance of Luc, I'm

grateful for the fact that I can sit with my back to a wall, my door closed, and will therefore see anyone coming. That there will be no sneaking up on me in my delightful cave of an office.

I spent all last night digging around online, looking for clues to this man's identity, but I came up with nothing.

This man showed up in the most sacred place I have, my beautiful office that runs precisely the way I want it to, where I am never questioned or demeaned or attacked by anyone. He clearly studied me without my knowing it, and this makes me feel even more exposed.

I feel like the kid I haven't been in years, trapped in a house I hated with a family that—it was made abundantly clear—wasn't mine. If I didn't stay out of the way, I paid for it. Sometimes I paid for it even when I did stay scarce. My stepmother's goal was to get rid of me and she accomplished it.

Will the fake Luc Garnier do the same thing to me now?

The very idea makes my entire body ache. Like a vicious bout of a sudden flu—the kind that can kill a person if they're not careful.

This man did all these things already to place himself in the middle of this life I built, he is *doing them* even now, and I can't find anything on him, anywhere.

It makes me feel even smaller and more precarious.

This morning I decide instead to switch my focus to the upcoming masked ball in Cap Ferrat. I put in a long morning of digging, trying to figure out the highly exclusive and not at all public guest list.

Because once I have it, I can try to cross-reference

the sort of people who would want entry to a place like that—enough to, say, pose as a fictional character—and what they might do there if they got it.

It's slow going. Absurdly wealthy people can afford privacy and the security to go with it.

I look up at the knock on my door and call out a quick, "Come in," assuming it's Tess finally coming to see what's become of me today.

I have to school my expression when Luc appears there instead, filling up the whole of the doorframe in a way that instantly reminds me—so much so that my stomach seems to drop—of how big he is.

Enormous and yet elegant. It's a dizzying combination.

But I swore to myself that I was not going to let him get to me today.

"It's an unusual name," he says, nodding at the name on the door. "Annagret Alden."

"It is only unusual in some cultures," I correct him. "In others, it is very common."

I focus in on him and notice that he is wearing a completely different suit from the day before. Yet it achieves, in all its particulars, the same level of perfection as the one I already saw.

This solidifies some things for me. A person might be able to find, purchase, and inhabit one such suit but two? That feels like a lifestyle. A style to which one has long since become accustomed, even. I make a note.

And then I continue. "The story I have been told that my mother was of royal Danish blood, though a great many generations removed. That was what my father always said when I was small and asked about her." I can see the next question in his gaze, and forestall it. "I personally cannot remember her. She died when I was only a few months old and there are no pictures of her anywhere in my father's home, because my stepmother objected. But as he is a small, brown-haired man, I have always assumed that the story was true."

I wave a hand in my own direction, encompassing all six feet of me sitting there behind my desk. Complete with the blue eyes and blond hair that mean I resemble nothing so much as a shield maiden. Or a Valkyrie.

The latter of which is where I got the logo for Miravakia Investigations.

"As you can see," I say, "I look as if I ought to be at the helm of a Viking ship in a terrible storm, cleaving my way through the North Sea. Instead, I'm afraid my origins are rather more ordinary. I grew up in the unremarkable suburbs of a midsize city in Pennsylvania, nowhere near any ocean of any kind, and the closest thing I ever did to going Viking was to take the train to New York City on my eighteenth birthday. I've been here ever since."

I sit back in my seat and look at him, standing there so deceptively casually in my doorway. "What about you?"

He smiles at that and I almost think it looks genuine.

"No one has ever confused me for a Viking," he says.

We both know he's avoiding personal questions, but I have to like—again, against my will—how easily he does it. As if we are both involved, now, in some grand joke. Just the two of us and this secret of ours.

"I was up most of the night thinking about all of this," I say.

"Oh, dear," he murmurs, his voice a dark knowing.

There's a golden sort of gleam in his gaze, and nothing like an apology on his face as he moves into my office, making me suddenly and irrevocably aware of how small it is. Almost claustrophobic, really. Maybe it's simply that his shoulders seem to take over the space, even when I can see that they don't. They don't *actually* brush the walls.

Still, it feels that way as he comes and sits in one of the chairs on the other side of my desk, where the clients normally perch themselves. And in so doing, he somehow makes it seem as if *I'm* the one begging for an audience with *him*.

And that dark knowing is in his gaze now, too. "Did I keep you awake at night, Annagret?"

I feel the heat of that and I don't want to. I resent it.

I tell myself that I resent it *deeply* as it winds its way inside me, but that is not the point of this. It doesn't matter what I feel. It can't.

It can only matter what I *do*.

"You must be here for a reason," I say, and though it's a struggle to keep my voice light, I manage it. "Given that this is a private investigation firm, I have to assume that the reason is that you're looking for something. Or someone. Why don't we look for answers together?"

"What a generous offer." His tone is sardonic.

"Not at all." I make sure my smile is pointed. "It's entirely selfish. I want you gone. It seems to me that solving whatever mystery it is you're here to solve will get you on your way sooner rather than later."

He looks as if he wants to laugh at that, but he doesn't. He sits back in that chair that is nearly too small for him. The chair that I suddenly realize he could easily smash with a fist, if he wished. I study him with more intensity, trying to understand how a man who can look elegant enough that he could grace the cover of an Italian fashion magazine with ease can also seem as if he is *only just* keeping the true power inside of him under control.

I'm fascinated.

And I'm aware of an alarm that rings at that fascination, deep and long within me, but I ignore it.

Luc is not exactly leaning into the hand he has propped up on the arm of the chair, but he taps his index finger against the side of his face as he regards me. As if contemplating his next move in a chess match.

"I'm looking for a woman," he tells me after a moment or two pass us by.

And there is a terrible clarity in the disappointment that runs through me at that.

A terrible, revealing clarity and one I could do without—because it tells me far too much about the various sensations I feel in this man's presence. Sensations I've been calling by other names because I don't want to admit what they really are.

When surely I ought to know better. I *do* know better.

I'm disgusted with myself, but all I do is sit forward and flip open my notebook as if this is any client intake meeting. "I'm listening," I say.

I can feel his gaze on the side of my face, as if I've thrown open one of the windows I don't have in this room to let the summer sun in. "If she exists, this woman might have emigrated here from somewhere in Europe. That would have been some thirty-five years ago. Give or take."

I put down my pen. "You do realize that you've described a vast number of people."

"I do indeed realize that."

"Do you have any other details?" I look up at him. "Any actual details, that is?"

"She was known by the name Mariana," he says, as if it costs him something to say that. I remind myself this could be an act, even though, somehow, I don't think it is. "But, of course, I cannot say if she kept that name. Or ever used it."

"Of course." I sit back and look at him. "Surely a man of your means has other ways to go about finding this sort of information."

His eyebrows rise into an expression of such sheer arrogance that I am once again certain that I'm right about him. That this is no con man in the classic sense. This man has never known a moment of life that does not pay homage to his great consequence. I can feel this in my bones.

"Do you mean as the head of an internationally renowned private investigation firm?" he asks.

I roll my eyes and have the distinct impression that he is not used to seeing such insolence. So I do it again, and for longer, *and* I add a long-suffering sigh, for good measure. "I think you know that I do not."

He stands at that and I watch him perform that same gesture that I'm certain is unconscious, a simple touch to his lapel, because when he sees me tracking it, he stops.

"You asked and I told you," he says, and his tone does not match the intensity in his gaze. "I am an open book, Annagret. You may read it or not as you wish."

And I read a great deal over the next few days, but

most of it involves toggling between my active cases, the guest list for that masked ball, and a barrage of information on random women entering the country some thirty-five years ago.

My active cases begin to feel like a refuge.

"We are so lucky," Tess sighs at me a handful of days into the firm's occupation by an impostor.

She catches me racing in after a fruitless morning meeting spent with one of our more overwrought clients. We are forever following her boyfriends around the city, looking for evidence that they are after her rather modest inheritance. When mostly what they are is nothing more than the same low caliber of man—that is, barflies who I am never certain realize she has money to begin with, much less have any designs on it.

I tried my best to convince her, over crepes and coffee, that her latest boyfriend should be kicked to the curb. Not because he's cheating on her—though he is—or even because he's out for her money—which he could be, but I doubt he's bright enough to notice she has some—but because he resembles nothing so much as a rat. Physically, I mean. And his attempts at musicianship in dive bars do not give him the patina of success that she seems to think.

But if she listened to me or my advice, she wouldn't be a repeat customer.

I stop in the outer office and focus on Tess. "I have no idea what you mean," I say. "What luck? I'd like some of it, if it's available."

"I've spent all my years here impressed with Mr. Garnier's abilities," she says, which I feel like a sharp betrayal. As if she should know who the real Luc Garnier is, even though I've hidden it. Deliberately. From her, specifically, as well as the world outside these walls. "And then when he finally turns up, he exceeds every expectation I could possibly have of him. Isn't it marvelous?"

That is not the word I would use. But I can't share the word I'd like to use with her. She'll read things into it. She'll make assumptions and build a narrative.

She'll get too close to the truth, something in me whispers, and I don't much care for being called out from within.

It feels like more of that unwelcome vulnerability.

"I'm glad that you're enjoying his presence here," I say, trying to be careful while also not *sounding* careful, and I don't think I quite land it. "I don't know how long we can depend on his being in the office. But yes, it's just delightful while it happens."

The phone rings, saving me from that look of speculation on her face, and I'm certain that I've saved myself from an interrogation as she goes to answer it.

I march back to my office, already coming up with devastating remarks that I can use to lay into him when I see him—

But his office is empty.

And once again, I find myself forced to contend with the fact that I am more invested in this man, this lie of mine brought to gloriously impossible life—than I ought to be.

A few more days pass, and things almost begin to feel like a routine. Sometimes I see him in the office, always on that laptop of his. Sometimes we pass in the hallway and he inclines his head as if he is made entirely of carefully cultivated manners. There's something about him that makes me want to respond in kind, though it would be completely ridiculous in a setting like this. Not to mention… I don't actually know who he is.

I don't need to curtsy to this man.

I spent a lot of time interrogating myself about why I feel I should.

One night, I run into the office after a long night of surveillance, thinking that I can get a few hours of sleep on the couch in my office before a midmorning meeting without having to go all the way back home—where I am much more likely to sleep too long.

I'm surprised to find all the lights on when I arrive, and even more surprised that when I walk back toward the offices, the lights are coming from his office.

And more, he's there.

Not simply tapping away at his laptop while dressed to impress, as usual.

Tonight not-Luc-Garnier is spread out on the sleek leather couch in the big office, wearing nothing but a pair of lounging trousers.

That's the only thing I can think of to call them, because they are not the sweats a lesser man might don. They are the kind of gray that suggests cashmere and the trousers themselves seem to be involved in a complicated hagiography of their wearer.

Though as far as I can see, he is entirely *proportional*…and it occurs to me that the tailoring of his perfect suits is about minimizing his assets, not enhancing them.

This notion leaves me breathless.

Inside, everything in me urges me to turn and leave

before he sees me. To get out of here, because it doesn't matter what he's doing. Or wearing. What matters is that I can't seem to get a handle on what's happening inside me.

In my head, I turn and move silently back down the hall, let myself out of the office, and grab a car to take me home.

The truth is, I don't move.

At all.

I stand there for a long moment, aware of entirely too many things. Not simply Luc. *He is not Luc,* I correct myself, but the corrections don't matter. He is like a portrait of the perfect man, and I have never imagined myself the kind of woman who would be rendered helpless at this sort of thing.

At the sight of all that male beauty, just there, on the other side of a wall of glass.

His head is propped up on the arm of the sofa, and he is holding his phone in his hand, frowning at it as he scrolls.

And everything else is just…hot.

I think that my head is spinning and I'm losing control, but in another moment I realize that actually, what I'm hearing is his music. It's sweeping and classical, and something about that seems to grip me in a tight fist.

I tell myself, desperately, that it's information. More information, that's all. But I know better.

He doesn't know I'm here and he can't have expected me. I didn't know I'd be here tonight either.

So this feels like a window into whoever he really is. At his ease, and this classic, wildly emotional piano music playing all around him.

I feel as if I'm seeing into his secrets.

As if this is his moment of vulnerability, yet instead of feeling powerful for seeing it, it makes me feel stripped bare too.

And all I can think is… *I want more.*

It's as if I'm compelled by something outside myself.

I move closer, drifting down that hallway as if I'm in a dream. And I know the precise moment he lifts his gaze from his phone to me.

I feel it, like a touch.

Like a caress, something in me whispers, as the sensation washes over me, a sweet, scalding heat, marking me from the very top of my head down to the tip of my toes.

Then pulsing everywhere in between.

What I want to do is go and press my overheated face to the cool glass.

But I realize that's a lie even as I think it. It's not that I don't want to do that, it's that I don't want to do *only* that.

Glass is not the only place I'd like to put my face.

I want, more than I can put into words, to move inside that room. To open that door, walk across that office, and press my body against his.

Of all the truths that his appearance here has brought to light, this one feels as if it might tear me to shreds. As if it might actually be the end of me.

Because I have never wanted anyone. Not like this.

Not at all, if I'm honest.

It has never been for lack of offers. But somehow, no matter how soulful the gaze or entertaining the conversation, I can never see my way through to what might be expected on the other side of such social niceties. I can never understand how a person looks at another, comes to some agreement, and starts systematically removing clothes. And then they go and press their bodies together, flailing about until pleasure is achieved.

It's not that I think that there's anything wrong with these things. It's only that each step along the path seems so outside my comprehension. I can't see the connection between the conversation and the desire to strip.

Or why I would ever allow someone to see me do such a thing, baring myself entirely before them.

Until now.

Because I realize that conversation is completely unnecessary. If he crooks his finger, I am terribly afraid, I would happily strip where I stand and then go to him without question.

I can feel my yearning for him as a physical thing. I don't care who he is.

Or rather, my body doesn't care who he is. It doesn't care what he's hiding, or what he's doing here.

Everything inside me wants him, that's all. That's everything.

It is as if all those sensations and longings in me are a song, and he is the only one who can sing it, and all I want to do is sing along.

It's as if everything in me is already his.

I watch as he sets his phone aside. There's something stark in his expression, austere in a completely different way. There is a knowing there—

And everything in me wants it. Even as somewhere deep inside, something in me shivers, too.

I'm aware of so many things at once. That music, all around me. That look in that steeped-tea gaze of his, highly caffeinated tonight though it seems. Dark but with that gold swirled through it.

And there's so much of his body on display. That perfect chiseled chest, all ridges and planes, and I have never felt softer, smaller, or more feminine.

When I have never thought of myself as any of those things.

It's as if looking at him makes me want to be some version of femininity I never quite grasped before now.

As if he is a decoder ring, and now, finally, I understand the entirety of a secret language that was lost to me before.

I can't tell if I'm holding my breath, or breathing too heavily, because it all seems to be part and parcel of the same thing.

He stares at me, this man of myth that I made up and yet is all too real. This version of Luc Garnier that exceeds anything I could have imagined on my own—and yet, at the same time, is everything I imagined.

I stand there, frozen in place in the hallway.

My hallway, but right now, that isn't how it feels.

And even though I can feel the floor beneath my feet and I know that this is not a cliff, but an office, I feel as if I'm poised on a precipice. As if at any moment, I might look down to find nothing but a steep, endless drop into God only knows what.

As if I can feel the wind up here, shuddering on this edge.

It's as if all it would take is a breath. His or mine, I do not know.

But in the end, there is no wind, no cliff.

The song he's listening to ends and in the interval before the new one begins, reality asserts itself.

I feel as if I've been released from a tight fist.

I suck in a breath, and it hurts.

His gaze is locked to mine, and there's something there. Something that almost looks…stricken?

But I'll never know. Because I turn and duck into my office, and for good measure, I lock the door behind me.

And I don't come out again until morning.

CHAPTER FOUR

Neither one of us speaks of that night.

Neither one of us really speaks at all, for that matter, which I decide is just as well. And soon enough it is time to head over to France and enter what I've been thinking of as the endgame in this little pretense of ours.

It has only been two weeks. This is a good thing. He cannot have done too much damage in that time—and I know that aside from Tess, he has seen very few people who will connect his face to the mysterious *Luc Garnier*. I assume that when he gets what he wants from this party he will disappear.

I am *hoping* he will.

I have dug up as much information as possible on the expected guests, and I have some names, but no idea what it is I should be looking for. And more to the point, no idea what *he* is looking for, either.

He is unreadable in every regard.

What I can't understand is why I remain...fascinated.

Much more fascinated than I ought to be with a con man who's taken over the firm I built and the figurehead I've created.

I can't make sense of it. I want to tell myself I feel the same sense of paralysis I did when I realized he could expose me to the world as the liar my stepmother always called me, back in those days when I told only truths. I want to assure myself that I'm only going along with this because he claimed this would only last a short while. I want to believe that this is me white-knuckling it through until he disappears.

But that fascination lingers in me like smoke, making me a liar all over again.

Making me wonder if even I should trust me.

But it is not until we are both sitting in a town car, heading for the airport, that he informs me that we will not be taking the commercial flight I've been expecting.

"What do you mean? Tess booked the tickets—"

"Luc Garnier does not travel commercial," he says dismissively.

He does not even look at me as he says it. And I want to argue—about a great many things—but I stop myself. Because he is not wrong about the way Luc Garnier travels. I have always made it seem as if he has his own *fleet* of jets.

How is it possible that this man can know a character I made up better than I do?

The car takes us to a private airfield that I have been to before, not far from Manhattan. And though I am beginning to feel something like trepidation—I tell myself it's just the lingering *unsettled* feeling of being schooled on my own creation by the person pretending he *is* him—but I refuse to let him see any of it. So I follow Not Luc as he crosses the tarmac and climbs the waiting steps to a sleek, unmarked plane that waits there for us.

It is clearly not the kind of plane that a person can

charter. I see that at once as we board. It is privately owned. The devil is in the details, as ever. The hints here and there that this is not a craft that needs to project a certain neutral elegance, accessible to anyone who can meet the going rate. This plane is *opulent.* Fewer of the nautical wood and brass flourishes that scream *finance bro.* From the moment we step inside, everything is bright and gold and hushed, like the lobby of a fine hotel. We move through a dining area—complete with a dining table that looks like it seats twelve—then into a lounge area that is set up to give the impression of more space than there ought to be on a plane, with crescent-shaped couches and tables that could seat four.

This is definitely not a charter.

And my impression is confirmed when I see Luc lift a brow at the flight attendant who has led us through this quiet, gorgeous, sleekly designed plane. She turns to me and smiles.

"Welcome aboard," she says in scrupulous English, though she has much the same accent as he does. "Mr. Garnier—" and she doesn't stumble over the name, but still "—we expect to take off within fifteen minutes."

"Good," he says, and nods, which is apparently enough of an order for her to turn and stride off with purpose.

I am certain that this is his own private plane, whoever he is, but any identifying details have been removed. Meaning that if I knew more about jet interiors, maybe there would be clues in the silk coverings on the couches and chairs, or the recessed lighting that makes it feel like we're outside. But otherwise, there is nothing in plain sight that I can use to triangulate his identity.

There is a hallway that extends beyond the lounge we're in, but Luc waves me to one of the tables. I sit where he directs me, because I want to exude *calm serenity.*

What I *feel* is…on edge.

We are not even alone, Luc and I, as the plane rolls down the runway and takes off. I know that his staff is here, but it feels perilous, somehow, to leave New York in the company of this man.

To follow him into the unfamiliar when I already can't quite trust myself around him.

I would like to pretend that nothing occurred that night in the office, but I know better. I know better, and more—I know that he experienced the same thing that I did.

Maybe even in the same way. Our eyes met. I couldn't breathe. He was there.

He knew.

Much as I want to pretend, it's always there, shimmering in the space between us. I'd like to deny that—and have, in fact, denied it to myself repeatedly—but I can't quite manage it on this plane where there are no ringing phones to distract me, or Tess just down the hall.

I watch him pull out that slim, metallic laptop of his. I pull out mine.

Then, for some while, as the plane soars high into the sky and leaves New York far behind, there's nothing but the sound of the air and the engines and the *tap tap tap* of our keys as we type away on our respective laptops. It's almost peaceful…until I remember where I am.

And who's with me.

It's like I keep jerking myself back from the edge of some daydream where I'm imagining he really is Luc

Garnier and this is our life, jetting about to solve mysteries together—

My God. I am astounded at myself. *You need to pull it together, kid.*

I return to my work with a vengeance.

And I can't tell if she is acting on a signal from Luc when one of his staff members appears some while later, but if so, I miss it. She glides up to our seating area with silver trays on each arm, each one filled with the sort of five-star delicacies that are not usually on offer on any flight I've been on.

Even in recent years when I've treated myself to more comfortable air travel—as a business expense—it has never been anything like this.

The finest linens and cutlery that would not be out of place in a Michelin-starred restaurant. Plates of fine cheeses and meats, the fruit so fresh it looks almost tropical, a soup and a salad that are inviting and smell delicious—no plastic or processed or microwaved food to be seen.

A glance at Luc makes it clear that none of this is new to him. This is only more evidence to suggest that whoever he really is, he is so used to such niceties that they barely register. Once again, I am left to wonder what rung of the social ladder could possibly lead to such unconscious elegance without stripping away the ability to function. I find myself thinking about a prince I once worked for who was unable to dress himself without assistance.

That is not this man, I am certain.

His tray is set before him and he nods his thanks. His

gaze sweeps to me as a matching tray is set beside me, and then he returns his attention to his laptop.

I finish the email I'm writing, summing up case findings and recommendations of next steps for a client, and send it off. Then I sit there, looking from the tray filled with crystal and gold-plated treats set before me to Luc himself.

Every day I look for more information about who this man really is. And every day, I come up empty. I've had a similar run of bad luck when it comes to the woman he seeks.

And it occurs to me then, as I watch him type, that I have absolutely no reason to believe that what he told me about that woman is true.

He might not be looking for a woman at all. He might not be looking for anyone. How can I possibly tell?

Following an urge I'm not sure I entirely understand—but I think, deep down, that it's a gut feeling or even a hunch, and in my line of business as well as in life the smart move is to follow those—I open up the camera option on my laptop and take a picture of him. We are sitting opposite each other. I can get his full features in the shot, almost full on.

I take three.

More than enough for facial recognition, I tell myself.

In an abundance of caution, I email the pictures to myself. Then delete the outgoing email before I shut down the program entirely.

Just a little safety measure or two. Just in case.

In case of *what,* I don't know.

"You are looking at me as if I am a piece of veal," he

tells me in that low voice of his that sounds wry to me, though his expression remains unreadable.

I wonder, briefly, if he knows that I took a picture of him—and more than one at that—but I quickly shake that off. Somehow I have the feeling that if he did know, he would not be sitting there so calmly.

Because I know that this man does not want pictures of himself. Not in my hands. Not anywhere.

And the moment *that* thought penetrates, I realize further that this is likely the reason that he is so interested in the masked ball we'll be attending.

I don't know why it took me so long to get there.

Because what this tells me is that he expects that if he attends a party like this with no mask, he'll be recognized. I start flipping through what I know of the guest list in my head.

"Veal is cruel," I make myself reply, just in time to make it seem like a reasonable pause since he spoke instead of me drifting off somewhere. "Though perhaps you're a bit too high in the instep to have gotten that message."

"Is that what you were doing the other night?" he asks, so mildly, though that voice of his is nothing but silken temptation. "Measuring my instep?"

I'm shocked that he's referencing that night in the office. Willingly. And seemingly out of nowhere.

But then, after a moment, I'm not so shocked. If he's trying to divert my attention from a conversation regarding his origins, however obliquely, that means that I'm correct.

Fake Luc is *someone* with a capital *S*.

This is why I smile at him. "I wasn't studying your

instep at all, actually. I was wondering why it was that the magnificent Luc Garnier, known far and wide for his wealth, taste, and commitment to luxury that apparently includes private jets like this one, is homeless. Sleeping in an office instead of in one of the numerous investment properties that make up his portfolio." I pick up the heavy silver fork on my tray. "Given the opulence that is available to him, you can understand my confusion."

But he only smiles back and applies himself to his laptop. I know he won't answer.

Some part of me would be disappointed, at this point, if he did. Because I am good at finding my own answers and solving my own puzzles. It's only a matter of time before I solve the mystery of him, too.

I'm less certain I can solve the mystery of my reaction to him, sadly.

"I have an idea," I say then, perhaps a bit too brightly. "Why don't you tell me one thing? One true thing." Then I laugh. "Between you and me, I don't think you're capable of it."

"I am fascinated," he says after a moment, almost musingly, "that you have such an apparent commitment to honesty, Annagret." He looks up then and his dark eyes seem to spear me where I sit. "When your entire life is built on a lie. I think some people would consider that hypocrisy, yet you seem to think it imbues you with some kind of moral superiority."

Ouch.

But I only shrug. "Women have to do what they must do to make it in this world," I say flippantly, even though I do not feel *flippant* at all. "I'm not apologetic."

"Why would you be apologetic? You haven't exactly been found out. No one knows the liar you are but me."

It turns out I really dislike being called a liar. More than I disliked it as a child, but I suspect that has a lot to do with how *warm* I feel in this man's presence.

"Because you're not a liar?" I manage to ask, softly enough.

Which is maybe not *soft* at all.

His gaze cuts to mine and there is something so stark, then, all over his face that I know I will never have to consult those photos I took to remember him. Not when the way he looks at me now seems to burn its way into me, as if he is branding my bones.

"You have no idea how much I wish this was not necessary," he says, and he manages a quiet in his tone I couldn't.

"Then make it not necessary," I say, but I don't know if I mean I want him to go away or…tell me the *why* of this. And it feels like a kind of ache in me that I can't tell the difference.

"There are greater things at play than—" He shakes his head.

"Than what?" I'm leaning forward then, my gaze trained on his. "My life?"

That hits him. I see the force of the blow.

"Annagret." And I don't want my name in his mouth. Not when he says it like that. "I did not understand, I think, what this would ask of you."

My heart is a driving, terrible force, a threat in my chest. "You didn't? That's astonishing. What did you think it would be like to insert yourself into the middle of a stranger's life like you have a right to it? What did you imagine would come of simply taking over what isn't yours? I don't even know why I'm surprised. Men like you always take what they want and care not at all for the consequences, don't you. That's what makes the world go round."

He looks stricken. As if I've sunk a knife deep into the center of his chest.

If I squint I can almost see it, and I tell myself that what I feel is a surge of something like victory, not the far more concerning pulse of…distress. On his behalf.

"If I could tell you the reasons I am here, I would," he says. "I am exploiting a loophole, not exposing you." He swallows. That starkness recedes and he is unreadable again. He inclines his head slightly. "You might want to find your way to more gratitude."

I feel many things then, but none of them are *gratitude*. Some of them veer worryingly close to *homicidal*, actually. "I suppose I'm glad we're admitting that you're a con man now, instead of pretending that a fictional character is real. Progress?"

If I want him to respond to that—to actually *admit, out loud,* that this is a game we both know full well he's playing, no matter his reasons—I'm disappointed.

Luc returns his attention to his laptop again and we do not speak for the remainder of the flight.

Though from time to time I see a muscle in his jaw tense, as if he is not as calm as he wishes to appear. I try to take a bit of comfort in that.

We land in Nice. And it occurs to me, as the car sweeps us away from the airport and we are soon nearly blinded by the intensity of the blue sky and sparkling waters of the Côte d'Azur, that I've lost control.

This is not my car. These are not my arrangements. I don't even know where he's taking me, and the strangest thing is, it's something I should have been paying attention to all this time. Yet I wasn't.

It's as if I was lulled into some false sense of security…why? Because I could perform Olympic gymnastic events on his cheekbones?

I can't even take in the normally restorative views of Nice, the dome of La Negresco beckoning, because it has occurred to me only now that after all these years of cheerful immunity to men, it turns out that I am decidedly basic after all.

Because I know that if this man was not gorgeous, I would have waved him off at the airfield outside New York and found my own way here, then stayed in my own accommodations. If he wasn't absurdly beautiful in the *exact* way that gets under my skin, when I thought no one could, I would not be in this vehicle. I would not be hugging the coastal road as the car winds its way out of Nice and on into Villefranche-sur-Mer, which clings to its hillsides and basks in the light.

I tell myself I'm perfectly capable of handling whatever he throws my way. And that may or may not be true—I don't really want to find out.

The real truth is, I want to see where he's going with this.

Still, as I sit in the car beside him, I do a quick check-in to make sure I'm not being *too* foolish. I decide that I'm not. This man had initial access to every single part of my business and did not block me from it, lock me out, or help himself to the bank accounts before I quietly changed all the passwords.

He has not exploited anything more than the loophole.

More importantly, he has not behaved in a way that I would describe as inappropriate at all.

To my own dismay, if I'm being brutally honest.

Not just because he's stunningly beautiful, with that gravitas to what ought to be pretty features that make him impossible to look away from. But because it would all be a lot easier if he would cross those lines. It would make things clear.

But he never does.

And I know it would be easier to dismiss him if he did.

Besides, I assure myself as I continue checking in with my rational brain, now that the golden glow of his plane isn't addling my senses, I'm not exactly helpless. I've been in questionable situations before—that's part of the job.

People get angry when you start poking around in their lives. Sometimes they get blustery about it, too. I've always been good at talking them down.

It helps to be a six-foot-tall woman who looks like a Valkyrie. Most of the men who've gotten a little too aggressive were smaller than me.

Nonetheless, I do not drift off as we take the turn and head into the peninsula that is Cap Ferrat, one of the most expensive places to live on the planet. I pay attention to my surroundings as they become immediately more impressive and harder to see from the narrow, winding streets. I pay attention to *him*.

And there's something about his total lack of concern that is comforting.

A person bent on harming me would have done so

already. I was isolated at the moment I stepped on that plane. Besides, there's no point taking me all the way to the South of France to do something that could have been easily achieved in an office building in Manhattan.

Especially when what he wants from this is not me, in any form, but Luc Garnier. The image. The name.

I am determined to find out why, and being here in France on the day of the masked ball only makes me feel more pressured to do so.

Because I'm almost positive that after tonight, I won't see this man again.

We make our way along streets that are all walls and gates and hedges, and what look like houses rearing up into the street—but are only garages, a carriage house, and possibly a security detail or two. This is not the playground of the wealthy. This is several cuts above.

The wealthy play in their yachts out in the sea. Here on land, the villas house only the most elite. Some are so private that their names can only be guessed at, so I suppose that in that sense, this man is in good company.

We pull through a set of gates to a villa that is set behind a wall of thick vegetation so that no one can see it from the road, and we are greeted by staff members who do not bow and scrape, but somehow manage to give the impression of doing so all the same.

And all of them speak the same English as Luc, with the same cultured accent.

I grow more fascinated by this man by the minute.

I tell myself that it's his *mystery* that intrigues me, nothing more.

Maybe that's the real reason I feel not a single twinge as I follow him inside.

"I have some matters that require my attention," he tells me as we stand in the center of a great, airy foyer through which it would not seem out of place to hear a *hosanna* or two. "You are in good hands here. My staff is ready and waiting to assist you with anything you need."

"Like, to pick something at random, your genealogical information?" I ask, feigning great innocence.

"I would think you already know the Garnier family genealogy," he replies smoothly, but there's a hint of something like a smile in his tea-steeped gaze. "As you are such a trusted lieutenant to the great man himself."

We are standing too close, I think, but I don't step away. "You do know that speaking of yourself in the third person makes you seem deeply affected, don't you? Real people don't do that."

"I am pleased that you still cling to that belief," he replies, his eyes glittering. "You have obviously encountered a far better class of people."

And then he stops.

I have the sense that he's given something away. Though I can't think what.

Maybe, something in me suggests, *he simply forgot himself for a moment.*

And for a man pretending to be someone else, forgetting his role is as good as handing over his passport.

I like to think that maybe I'm pushing his buttons, too. I think of that stark look on his face as we flew, that sense that he was *this close* to revealing himself...

There's no reason at all that my pulse should be rocketing around the way it is, making me feel weak. And silly.

We are staring at each other, the sun from high above

spilling between us and seeming to dance its way inside me, too. A *hosanna* all its own. I have the strangest urge to reach across the light and touch him, almost like I want to assure myself he's real—

But he steps back, out of the light. And keeps going until he's in the shadows again.

I tell myself this is a relief, though the humming in me suggests otherwise.

It doesn't ebb. Not even when he murmurs something that I only realize is an order when he hands me over to a waiting woman, dressed in a uniform that I do not have to have seen before now to understand indicates a certain status as a member of staff.

Because clearly he has not just staff, but *levels* of staff.

The woman does not offer me her name. She leads me up through the villa and into a lavish suite of rooms that could put a five-star hotel to shame. There are sweeping views from the window, a jumble of the sea and more of these famous French coastal towns in the distance.

"Feel free to make yourself at home," the woman tells me. "And should you need anything at all, you need only call."

She indicates a button on the wall, not the bell pull of my favorite old movies, and I feel a hint of disappointment as she leaves, closing the door behind her.

When I turn, I can see that my suitcase has preceded me here. It is already here waiting for me, but when I go over to it and pick it up, it's empty. It takes me a few moments to find my way through the serene set of rooms to my very own dressing room, where my clothes have been hung and folded.

The dressing room is bigger than my first New York apartment. If these are guest rooms, it is clear that the people who stay here come with trunk upon trunk and are expected to attend wildly fancy parties that require endless costume changes.

"Then again," I remind myself, "that is exactly what you're doing here, too."

That strikes me as funny, and I laugh—but the laugh goes on too long. I laugh too hard. I laugh until my chest hurts, and for a moment there I'm strung out in the midst of my own overreaction.

I take a breath. A deep one, because I'm alone. The door is shut behind me. I have nothing to prove and no one to see me react.

So that's what I do. I stop plotting and puzzling. I stop worrying.

I *react*.

I kick off my shoes and let down my hair from the tight twist I keep it in for work. And then, barefoot and feeling free for the first time since I walked into the office and found a figment of my imagination made flesh, I wander around these absurdly lush rooms and simply... let myself enjoy it.

I have been adjacent to great wealth over these last years and have enjoyed that level of hospitality before. It is all quietly understated in these places. The wealth and consequence on display does not require explanation. Experiencing it, I realize, is meant to indicate who and what it represents. It is in the details.

A Texas oilman's bearskin rugs and enormous antlers, decidedly not purchased from a store. A Belgian heiress's seeming nonchalance about everything in her surprisingly down-to-earth home in the Hollywood Hills...save the collection of vintage Chanel that rated its own cottage.

I want to go creep around the house and see what other clues I can find, but something stops me. Somehow, I doubt I've actually been left to my devices here. If I step outside this room, I feel certain I'll have an escort within moments.

But there's more to it than that. It feels like a strategy. If I'm caught snooping, he'll know that I'm looking for him. Or pieces I can assemble to find out who he is. And maybe not snooping might lull him into a false sense of security.

Either way, I take advantage of these hours I have to myself. My office is across an ocean. My laptop needs a charge. I draw a bath in a freestanding tub that could fit a dozen of me and sink into it, laughing a little as I look out at the exquisite view. Terra-cotta rooftops. The sea in a shade of blue that defies description. The hills and cliffs that lead to Monaco in the distance.

I find myself thinking about where I came from. Where I grew up and was always treated like some kind of discount Cinderella. My stepsisters were coddled and beloved. I was the target. And my father, because he was and remains fundamentally weak, apologized for my stepmother when he and I were alone but never did anything to change it.

I spent years thinking there was something I could do to change this. I modeled my stepsisters' behavior. I dressed like them. Sometimes I copied them down to the tones in their voices.

But it made no difference what I did or how I did it. They were adored. I was despised.

Eventually I understood that the problem was me. No matter what, my stepmother could not love *me*. She never had and she never, ever would.

My father could, or so he claimed, but only in secret.

What my stepmother did love was telling me, in detail, that no one ever would or could love me at all, and I believed her. She never understood that this was not a point of shame or upset for me, not really. Oh, certainly there were moments that stung and some that kept younger versions up at night or in tears, but it was all I knew.

Once I comprehended that it was not a problem that could be solved, that there was no answer that I could find to change it, I adapted.

You can't truly miss what you never had.

There's a liberation in that, I've always thought.

But I realize now, surrounded by a level of magnificence that I never thought I'd experience in my lifetime, that I am pettier than I realized before this very moment. Because a part of me really does wish I could reach out and show them all where I've ended up on an evening in one of the most beautiful places in the world. Because I know that they have not done the same.

I know exactly where all of my stepsisters are, what sort of men they're married to, and how clear it is that they're never going to get out of that town where we were raised. I know that my father grows weaker by the day, and fights it even less.

And while I will never lower myself to reach out to them—because tracking them is easier and requires no interaction—I hope that somewhere, in that sad little suburb they all claimed they'd leave as soon as they could, they all feel a twinge. That they all wish, somehow, that they'd made better choices when it came to me.

That sometimes, the wondering if I'm okay keeps at least one of them up in the night.

But I don't *need* that, and so I let the pettiness go and I stop thinking about them altogether.

I luxuriate in my bath. When I'm done, I enjoy myself in the well-equipped bathroom that might as well be its own spa. I try on lotions, scents, and creams. I make myself sneeze when I lay on too many, and so I eventually rinse off in a glass-and-stone enclosure that bears no resemblance whatsoever to any other shower stall I've ever used in my life.

It's not as if I've done badly over the years. But what I make, I put back into the business. That's what I've been doing for years now. That's how I've made it to the place that I have. I thought it was smooth sailing before *he* turned up.

It only occurs to me now, playing latter-day Cinderella-at-the-ball games in this villa, that I have perhaps neglected myself and my self-care for a little too long.

I eat a perfectly presented dinner by myself out on a little terrace, letting the sea breezes wash over me. And when I go inside, prepared to dress at last, the same woman is waiting for me.

She smiles at me when I only stare at her without comprehension. "I thought perhaps I could help you dress for the event tonight," she says.

I open my mouth to laugh a little bit and send her away, but I stop myself halfway through.

Because this is all taking on the hue of a fantasy, so why not take it all the way? It will all be just as mysterious if I get dressed and primped into a version of myself I've never met before. *He* will be just as unknowable no matter if I do this by myself or not.

"Why not?" I ask.

It is not until she inclines her head that I understand that it was not actually a request.

And so I sit down at the little vanity in the dressing room, and surrender.

She does my makeup, but what she does bears no resemblance to the kind of makeup that I've learned how to do for myself, and that I've considered the perfect blend of practical and sophisticated all these years.

What she does is make me look like a dream.

And then she does my hair to match, twisting it up and adding accents—sparkly things to catch the light and give the impression of some kind of tiara without actually putting any kind of crown on my head.

I look like a blonde goddess, a Nordic queen, in nothing but a silk robe.

I hardly see myself in the reflection.

Then she produces a gown.

Not the dress I brought with me. This is the kind of gown that is never sold in a store or available for anyone to shop and find. This is the kind of gown that appears only by invitation and only in the finest ateliers in places like Milan or Paris, or perhaps in magazines like *Vogue,* and is otherwise a collector's item.

Tonight I am wearing art.

I feel something like breathless, but I know it's not the gown itself. It's that he picked out this gown. It's that he wants to see me in it.

That humming in me takes hold.

When my nameless fairy godmother is done, I look at myself in a full-length glass and I'm not certain that I will be able to remember my own name.

It doesn't feel like much of a loss when I look *edible*.

"Here," the woman says, sounding as if she very much approves of her own work.

She fits a diamond-studded mask to my face. It covers only my eyes, but somehow, it seems as if it's the final straw in this Cap Ferrat transformation.

Whoever that woman in the mirror is, exquisite and glamorous, she is no longer Annagret Alden. Not the Annagret Alden I know.

This woman would have no idea at all where a certain gritty Pennsylvania suburb lies. I doubt she could locate Pennsylvania on a map.

She is someone else entirely.

I am someone else.

I am *magnificent*.

And *that* is the chic, refined, breathtaking woman who glides down the stairs to the ground floor of this quietly perfect villa. *That* is the work of art who sees the man who calls himself Luc Garnier standing there in black tie with his own domino mask to cover his eyes and make him that much more mysterious.

That is the woman who smiles at him, like she's finally got him where she wants him.

And for that wild, giddy moment, I believe I do.

CHAPTER FIVE

THE PARTY IS being held in a villa set far behind high walls, set up above its own, private cove. Some of the guests arrive by water, ferried in from the grand yachts that clutter the harbors all along the South of France. I can see them coming in, the running lights of the smaller crafts like sleek lanterns on the water, as I walk with my mysterious not-date in the silence—hushed and complicated—that has sat with us the whole way here from his villa.

Though, of course, it might not be his villa at all. It is entirely possible that nothing he's showing me actually reflects who he *really* is.

I don't know why I'm so sure that's not true. That it *is* his villa and it *does* reflect him and that I somehow know more about the cipher of this man than I should.

Because this is what foolish women do, I tell myself sternly. *They make up a man in their head and then expect a living, breathing,* actual *man to be the man they made up.*

Except in my case, I never expected the living, breathing, actual man. I never *wanted* a living, breathing, actual man—I just wanted the idea of him.

I'm not sure why his unexpected appearance has made me foolish all the same.

And yet somehow, walking along the path marked with candlelight to beckon us in from the dark, I cannot bring myself to parse the mysteries within mysteries that make up the man playing Luc Garnier. Not any more than I already have.

Every step feels like surrender. Or maybe it's the gown I'm wearing and the way it flirts with me as I walk, teasing and taunting me, reminding me that all this time that I've been playing the private detective... I've been a woman, too.

I am a woman, and he is a man, and as we walk together in the sultry night, I find I am less and less interested in what other things we might be.

It's something about the night itself, I think. The bright, golden burn of the day has faded and I can feel the press of the night against my skin, weaving in and around the mask I wear. Both feel more like sensual caresses. The mask is like a reminder, with every breath, that this is all a game.

And that maybe I should consider *playing,* for a change.

We do not touch, this man and me, but we walk side by side, and I'm certain that I can feel a kind of humming heat from his body. To match the humming in me. As if being this close to him is like straying into some sort of electromagnetic field.

As if he does not simply have expectations about the role of gravity in his life, but exerts his own gravitational pull.

I can feel it pull at me, the same way this gown I'm wearing moves over my skin.

It feels like a *becoming*.

As we approach the villa, all its doors and windows thrown open wide and the softest, most golden light beaming from within, I understand in a flash that I have fundamentally misunderstood all the glamour I thought I'd been adjacent to before now.

Or perhaps it's just that this is simply a higher level. Maybe the highest level possible.

We walk into a kind of atrium, open to the stars above. Staff move like dancers, anticipating needs and meeting them before they can be expressed. Everything is exquisitely wrought, but the effect is comfort and ease.

If cozy shopped at Chanel.

And it is immediately apparent that everyone in the room exists on the same level that Luc does. They are all instantly recognizable, not by name or face—as those are hidden—but by the way they hold themselves. The way they move. Even the timbre of their laughter and how it rolls around them, and up into the night.

"You look as wide-eyed as a sacrificial lamb," Luc says from beside me, and there's no pretending now that there is not that sardonic note in his voice. Or that it does not work in me like fire and longing. "Why not simply offer yourself up as prey and be done with it?"

Without meaning to—or, possibly, fully meaning to, what with the *humming* and the dress and his exquisite, arrogant beauty—I move closer to him. "Prey?" I laugh. "In what way am I *prey?*"

"You must know that you are far safer the more bored and nonchalant you act."

He looks down at me and I can see something glittering there, wild and yet still unreadable in the depths of that gaze. As if there really are things he wants to tell me, but can't.

You are delusional, I chide myself—but I still see it.

"With you?" I dare to ask.

"You are never safe with me," he shoots back, but then he catches himself. Or maybe the roughness in his voice and that stark look in his eyes once again makes his stomach drop the way mine does.

Straight into the heat that blooms lower down.

"And yet," I say quietly, "I am not afraid. Should I be?"

"Never afraid." Again, that roughness in his voice. Again, that look so stark it hurts. "God help us both, but never that, I hope."

And for a moment we both look at the scene all around us, all that is bright and shining and there to be marveled at. Though all I see is that look in his eyes.

All I feel is that heat.

"These are the sort of people who like shiny new things," he tells me after a moment, and there is no reason that it should sound like he is murmuring sweet nothings. Or why my body should respond as if we are alone somewhere—though I am fairly sure that his does, too. That I am not in this alone. It's a heady sensation, one I can't make sense of. "What they like most is to get their fingerprints all over them."

I remind myself that I can't stand here, staring up at him even in the heels they gave me, because he's so tall and commanding that a lesser woman would simply swoon. "Spoken by someone who sounds as if he's spent a great deal of time in the villa much like this one. Where did you leave your fingerprints, I wonder?"

Next to me, Luc seems to vibrate with what I would call a kind of fury if he were a different man. Or possibly concern, if he was a *completely* different kind of man. And the way he looks down at me, I have absolutely no doubt that it's concern for *me*.

But that makes no sense. That is not at all the sort of thing I inspire. Not in anyone.

Not ever.

And besides, I remind myself, I don't actually know what kind of man he is. No matter what I might feel. No matter what I might have imagined in that glorious freestanding tub, with only the quiet around me and the Mediterranean gleaming in the distance.

No matter what the dress tries to whisper to me as I move, as I breathe. As the domino mask presses into my skin just enough to feel like a touch.

Maybe his touch.

"Stay close," he tells me, forbiddingly, and yet it is somehow compelling.

Then he forestalls any commentary I might possibly have by reaching over and taking my hand.

Our fingers lace together as if we've held hands a thousand times before and it's a muscle memory. His hand is so big that mine almost seems to disappear in his grasp, but with every breath, I can feel the tug of the places where our fingers intertwine.

And I can feel that tug *everywhere*.

In my breasts, my nipples hardening. Between my legs, not only in the sensuous way my thighs brush when I walk but deep between them, where I can feel the heat of his palm against mine.

I'm too hot, though the night is cool. I get hotter with

every breath, until it feels as if I'm breathing into a corset when I know the bodice of this gown is not nearly that restrictive.

And when he hands me a glass of champagne from the tray of a passing staff member, I know I ought to refuse. I never drink on the job, and despite the Cinderella games I let myself run away with earlier, this is a job.

He is the job whether he hired me or not.

And besides, I already feel as if I might be internally carbonated already.

But I take the glass anyway and I click it to his, our eyes seeming to meet and cling the way our hands still do. I take that first sip, not sure why the simple fact of him watching me do it makes me feel as if that stern mouth of his is all over my body.

Maybe it's right at this moment that I finally accept it. This thing I've tried so hard to pretend hasn't been happening all along.

Maybe it's finally time for me to face facts.

Whoever this man is, and it matters less the harder my heart beats against my ribs, I want him.

"Annagret." My name is like a song on his lips. "Annagret, this is not the kind of place that wants its mysteries solved."

I suspect that's true. But what I say, in a tone like his, is, "I think you are the one who does not want his mysteries solved."

His eyes look anguished behind his mask. I forget that we are in a crowd. I see the ache in them. I feel it in me. I feel it where our hands touch, like we are connected by so much more than a mere clutch of fingers.

"Me most of all," he agrees.

And my breath gets tangled somewhere in my throat.

But the moment ends in an abrupt shower of laughter that comes too close and turns into coy introductions from people with shrewd eyes behind masks and very familiar silhouettes. They pretend to ask questions, but are really just playing games.

Because that is what people like this do. It is all they do. They dress up in masks and laugh as if they care for nothing.

I remind myself that the man beside me, who dropped my hand when we were swept up into their orbit, is one of them.

I am sure of it.

And I like the comfortable life I've built for myself. Every bit of it comes as a result of my own hard work, and I take pleasure in both the work itself and the life it affords me. We had none of this growing up, and I had the smallest slice of anything we did have.

I couldn't have imagined a place like this back then.

Or a *day* like this.

Yet still, in my head, I try hard to make a distinction between him and them. Something he helps along by seeming to find what's going on around us somehow distasteful himself.

And it is not until much later—as the party spills recklessly all throughout the villa and I find myself in the atrium once more—that I accept that the music and the splendor and yes, the bubbly, have all gone to my head.

Then again, I correct myself, the night and the gown and the man who held my hand so briefly did that, too. I can still feel it.

As I flex my hand, remembering that touch, I feel a kind of prickly heat move down the length of my spine. I shiver, then repress it.

Then I turn my head to find Luc watching me from across the atrium floor.

And it is something more potent than any wine or pretty house filled with pretty, careless people. It is something more complicated than the rise and soaring fall of the music that plays all around us. Something more dangerous than the way water tumbles out of that endless fountain in the center of the atrium, and something infinitely more treacherous than all these people who move like shadows around us, caught up in their kingmaking, and their scandals, and their bright, glittery party.

I should have spent the night making inroads here, like the businesswoman I am. Yet somehow, I couldn't bring myself to do it. I almost wanted to be someone else for a change.

Maybe, the woman I've been made over into tonight. That woman I glimpsed so briefly while walking down the stairs toward Luc earlier.

The woman who has no thought in her head but to be this man's arm candy.

Because a bright and frothy piece of candy knows exactly where she's ending up tonight. And exactly how he will enjoy her.

But these are not the smartest things to be thinking as Luc cuts his way through the crowd and comes to stand before me.

I open my mouth to tell him that I think we should go, or that I should, but he holds out his hand.

There is something simmering in those dark, nearly bitter depths. And it feels like gold inside of me.

And the kind of *helpless* I feel right now moves through me a little too much like joy.

I reach out and put my hand in his, again.

When I say nothing at all, when I make no argument and state no case, he draws me out onto the atrium floor to join the other dancers.

We still have our masks on. I tell myself that it's safe, being held against his body like this. This is perfectly appropriate, I assure myself as he twirls me around and around and his hand at the small of my back sends fire cascading through me.

I tip my head back, so I can look in his eyes.

So it feels as if he is already inside me.

When the music ends, he does not let go. He still holds me, looking down at me with a scowl on his face, as if fighting some kind of desperate battle…

I do nothing to help him.

On the contrary, what I want to do is dare him. To figure this out. To *do* something. To make this one thing or the other—

He mutters a curse in a language I don't quite catch. Then he takes me by the arm and pulls me with him, leaving the glitter and noise behind. He leads me through the hallways and breezeways of this place, inside and out, until I realize belatedly that this place makes his villa seem snug and intimate.

I'm happier once we step out onto a path that leads away from the sprawling place, the light seeming less like gold and more like something tricked up to be gold instead.

Outside, that clutching sensation in my chest eases a little. The sea air feels deliciously cold all over my overheated skin, and I make no comment as he leads me farther into the dark.

It takes me a few moments to understand that he has found us a path that winds its way along the cliffside. We walk in silence, listening to the waves caress the rocks far below. I feel the breeze like it's a part of the spell he's weaving, as he leads me through the dark, the only light from the stars above and across the water.

We keep walking until the villa is out of sight, meandering around until the path delivers us to a cottage.

I want to ask him how he knew this was here. The lights are out but this does not deter him. He opens the door with a certain hesitancy, but not without familiarity, and I remember—almost against my will—that my running theory is that he wanted to come here because he could come masked. Not as himself.

Not as the man who has clearly been here before.

I want to ask him a thousand questions, but when he leads me with him into this secret cottage by the sea that feels worlds away from the mad whirl of the party in the villa, I say nothing.

And when he pulls me into his arms once more, and murmurs something that sounds like *have mercy,* I melt.

Then *ignite* when he takes my mouth with his.

Because everything is pure fire.

It is white-hot, and scalding, and I understand as we move together that my whole life will be divided, forever, on either side of this kiss.

That I will never be the same.

That nothing will ever be the same, as long as I live, because he tastes like fate.

And together, we move like glory.

We kiss and we kiss—moving closer, pulling back. Testing, learning, indulging.

I think I could do this forever, but he sweeps me up against him, holding me high against his chest in the darkness of the cottage. There are no lights on. I don't care if half the party is hiding here in the dark, because all I can think about is how to angle myself down to keep kissing him.

I figure it out, and throw myself into that kiss again. His stern mouth. The silken flame of his tongue. The way it feels, shivery and intense, when he rubs it against mine.

I don't care who he is, I think. *As long as he's mine.*

I have a vague, jumbled sense of our surroundings. Some sort of living room space, but then he's carrying me through a doorway to tumble me down onto something soft. I have a scant second to register that it's a bed behind me, but then, better still, there is that huge, hard immensity that is him on top of me.

I can't seem to fit in my own skin.

"I cannot bear this," he tells me in a deep growl, dark against my throat. "You're the one temptation I cannot resist."

"Why would you want to?" I ask.

"There are matters at play here that you cannot understand," he tells me with some urgency. "I am not the sort of man who indulges in parties like this, or nights like this, or…"

He trails off. He does not say *or you,* but I hear it.

"Stop resisting," I whisper. "Indulge. Just this once."

And when he groans, everything inside of me seems to quake.

"I never wanted to hurt you," he tells me in a low, intense voice. "I never wanted to cause you any kind of pain, Annagret. You must know this."

What I know is the feel of him against me, our bodies flush in the dark. What I feel is that urge that never made sense to me before. To strip off all my clothes, and his. To press our naked bodies against each other and see what happens. To be closer still.

I want these things as if my next breath depends upon them.

"I know it," I tell him.

I would have told him anything.

And at first, everything seems like a rush.

He shoves off his coat and something flutters out from his pocket. I mean to point it out to him, but I have other things to think about.

So many astonishing other things.

Like that almost sharp, starkly sensual look on his face.

"You are so beautiful," he tells me. "It should not be permitted."

"I will take it up with the creator the next time we meet," I say with a laugh.

But if I imagine that might inject some levity into the situation, I am mistaken.

He does not laugh. He shrugs out of the rest of those impossibly beautiful clothes and tosses them aside with a carelessness that, once again, offers me a clue.

Except that, for the first time in a long, long while, I don't want clues. Not now. I just want him.

He has fire in his eyes, but he is gentle with me. He turns me over on the bed so I am face down, and then he moves behind me. I sigh as he presses those shimmering, terrible, marvelous kisses down the back of my neck, between my shoulder blades, and then I feel a kind of tugging, and then the dress is peeled away.

"I knew how you would look in this dress," he tells me in that same voice that sounds like some kind of agony, but makes a deep, hard thrill rush through me. *"I knew.* I did this to myself."

He moves as he speaks, rolling me one way and then the other to pull the dress off, so that when he tosses it aside I am lying there in nothing at all but a pair of lace panties.

He breathes out, hard, as he turns me back toward him.

And then, taking on the look of a man at his devotions, he pulls me toward him again and settles me beside him on the bed. For a long moment he only gazes at me, something that feels almost too intense in his gaze.

I gaze back, though I feel the hint of moisture threatens.

He reaches over and brushes the back of his hand over one cheek. I feel him breathe. I catch my own breath.

"Annagret," he says. "I wish…"

But he doesn't finish. And I put out my own hand and trace the shape of his mouth, then find my way to those impossible cheekbones.

I try not to think about the fact that none of this feels

like the mad rush of lust. Not that I don't feel that rush. But this feels like something else.

This feels golden and quiet. This hovers in a space I can't seem to look at directly.

As if this is sacred.

As if what happens here, between us, is its own kind of holy.

My hand moves over his jaw and we stay there, possibly forever, lost and found. He takes my hand from his face and presses a kiss into my palm, then smiles as I curl my fingers around it.

And when he kisses me this time, the whole world changes. Again.

He kisses me until we're both groaning, and then he shifts, moving me to my back. Then he wastes not a single inch of my skin. He trails his way down my neck and all the way to my breasts, until I'm arching up to give him my nipples as he teases them both, making twin points of aching.

I think I might actually die when he pulls one, then the other, deep into his mouth. He sucks, hard.

And I think it's possible that I explode.

He laughs, testing their weight with his hands, and then does it again.

Everything is champagne and heat. Fire and a long, slow simmer into golden, so sweet it hurts.

And I don't know if I'm the one who's glimmering, or if it's him, but it becomes all the same bright heat. He finds ways to make parts of me I've never considered all that much feel beautiful and sexy and *his*.

He does this with every part of me he touches.

Lower and lower he goes until he finds its way to the crease of my thighs, and then in between them.

I don't even have time to think about this. Or maybe it's that I can't think past all the sensation that only seems to build in me with every touch, every scrape of his jaw against my soft skin, every breath across my body.

He pushes one thigh out of his way, then settles in.

I hold my breath again. He laughs as if he knows, then lifts me up and spreads me open wide.

Then he licks deep into me.

And I lose my senses entirely.

It is all heat. *Him*.

I'm aware of what he's doing, and *who* is doing it, and that it is *his* mouth—

But there is nothing but the way he tastes me. The way he feasts on me and I arch into him, again and again, noises spilling out of me that I didn't know I could make.

And then the pleasure, sharp and growing, surging and expanding.

So hot and so intense it's almost scary. Maybe it really would be scary if I could do anything at all but surrender to it.

It hits me like a punch, a detonation, exploding inside and then shooting everywhere, leaving nothing behind.

I am obliterated.

I am outside myself. In pieces.

He laughs and I can *feel* it, there against the tenderest part of me, and then he begins again.

And again.

I quickly lose track of how many times I come apart.

How many times he takes me to the precipice and flings me out to that bright, hot flight into glory.

I hear a sobbing sound, and realize it's my voice. I hear a low, hot murmur, and I know it's his.

There is nothing, now, but the dark of the cottage around us, the softness of the bed beneath us, and all the sparks we light as we roll and taste and bite and moan.

He teaches me how to take him deep in my own mouth, and when I have difficulty with his thickness, his length, he runs a hand over the side of my face. As if he knows I need the touch. The reminder of softness while he is so hard in my mouth. He moves his hand in a soothing way that makes me want nothing more than to open wider and take him deeper.

And I do.

But he does not give me the release I want. He pulls himself out, despite my protests. And then, murmuring words that sound somewhere between prayers and apologies, he switches our positions once again and settles himself between my legs.

And I feel so dizzy, so gloriously new, that it takes me too long to remember the one little thing I should have told him from the start.

"Luc—" I begin.

His gaze flashes to mine and I realize we're both still wearing those masks over our eyes. Something about the eroticism of that, and the fact I can feel that blunt, hard part of him nudging up against the softness of my center, makes me shiver.

"Don't call me that," he says, as if it hurts him.

And then he slams his way inside me.

Then, immediately, freezes.

And for a moment, I cannot tell the difference between pain and pleasure. For a moment, we are both strung out there in that single mad thrust—

"*Cosita*, I did not know," he is saying against my ear.

When I pull in a breath, not sure if I want to stop or shout or cry, something else happens instead.

It's as if the breath floods through me, and that hot place where we're joined…shifts. One moment it's a tight, hot pain, and then the next it becomes something else. Something like a white-hot heat, not comfortable, not sweet, but addictive.

I move my hips. He sighs, but I want more.

"So be it," he says.

He pulls me to him, so it feels as if we are one.

And then slowly, almost tenderly, he begins to move.

But I don't want slow and I don't want tender. I want all of him.

I realize I said that out loud, growling it like some kind of wild thing, when his gaze finds mine once more.

And I can see the laughter there.

Masks and bittersweet tea and laughter, and a bolt of something like lightning goes through me, hard.

He rolls us over so I sit astride him, and when I look around in concern, not certain what to do in this new position, he settles me with his hands on my hips. He moves me experimentally, and I get it. Then I meet it.

Soon enough, I am the one lifting myself up, sliding down, and learning the rhythms that make him groan, too.

And when I feel that precipice coming, I try to hold it off, but he really does laugh at me then. He pulls me down so that our faces are close as he takes my mouth with his, and kisses me with such dark passion that it's hard to tell which part of him is doing the most damage.

Beautiful, life-altering damage.

It comes on slow at first. A winding heat, moving inexorably out of my control. Then like an avalanche, rolling faster and faster and taking me with it, until I'm sobbing and jerking and slamming myself against him.

Then he's rolling over and surging into me with none of that careful restraint, and it's beautiful. It's glorious.

And then it's happening for both of us, wild and hot and ours—

Until he roars out my name in the crook of my neck as we fall.

He does the same more times that night than I can count.

But in the morning, he's gone.

Just as I knew he would be when I never dreamed I would get naked with him, in more ways than one.

I wake up with that damned mask still on my face, but askew. I know he's not in the bed before I open my eyes. I know things about him, about me, that would sound delusional if I put them into words.

Things that only come from an intimacy that shouldn't be possible between people who are playing games and hiding in plain sight—but that's the thing. Last night there were no barriers.

Last night I knew him.

Last night I gave him me.

It was so intense and so perfectly ours that I can't even regret it as I sit up and confirm that he is not here.

He is *not here*. As expected, the man who was never Luc Garnier disappeared with the dawn.

Leaving nothing at all behind but the card that fell out of his coat pocket to the floor. When I pick it up and frown at it there is the name of an attorney on the front, with offices in Nice.

And there is a name written across the back of it in slashing script. *Amara Mariana Vizcaya.*

But all I can think about is the fact that in this Cinderella story, it's Prince Charming who isn't who he pretended to be and ran away anyway, leaving me here to figure out how to take my poor heart and shove it back into my body.

When I already know it won't fit.

CHAPTER SIX

ONE MONTH PASSES. Then two more.

I go from crushed to furious to something more like banked coals waiting for reason to blaze. It feels as carbonated as that champagne, but painfully so. It's wedged under my ribs in that misshapen place that isn't mine anymore.

A heart that only beats for a man who was never here, not really.

It hurts.

That's the long and the short of it. *It hurts.*

I never wanted to hurt you, he said.

On that night I was mad enough to think nothing ever could if only he touched me.

Sometimes I think it would be easier if he'd left me to perform a bedraggled walk of shame all the way across the South of France—diamond-studded mask still welded to my face to make it that much more embarrassing—but he thought about that. He planned for that.

And I can't decide if he did it because he's simply that conscientious, or because he didn't want me tracking down that villa and pounding on the door. Sometimes I just get caught up in the fact that he *thought it through,* and I can't decide if that means I imagined the whole part where we found each other in that cottage…or if he was playing me all along.

I'll never know, because when I finally emerged from the bedroom of the cottage, the woman who dressed me the night before was there in the living room with that same iron smile welded to her face.

I don't mean to rush you, madam, she said in that soothing voice of hers that talked me into dressing up in the first place. *But we will need to get you to the plane sooner rather than later.*

And then, as I stood there, dumbfounded while wearing last night's dress haphazardly, she'd taken charge. She turned on the water in the bath, all but herding me in to take a shower. When I came out, squeaky clean in a body that didn't feel at all like mine, every remnant of the night before was gone. When I looked in the mirror there were no goddesses looking back, it was only me.

The me without him, and that felt like grief.

When I wrapped a towel around me and walked out into the bedroom, the bed was made and looked as if it had never been touched. The dress and shoes and mask were gone. She had even laid out clothes for me on the bed.

My clothes that I'd last seen in a dressing room in a different villa.

Is this a cottage of requirement? I asked her dryly when I dressed and tried to make myself feel anything but the pain in my chest and the absence of a man who'd never existed.

This is not a place that anyone can access without an invitation, she replied, with that cool gaze of hers.

But it's part of the villa where the party was last night.

I watched her face, but it was smooth and gave away nothing. *It is considered a part of the estate but I believe that technically, it belongs to a previous owner of the property and can only be used with that owner's permission.*

But—I began.

Madam. Her voice was as impenetrable as her expression. *The plane.*

And it was my intention to stay awake the whole flight home and pepper the crew with incisive questions before conducting an in-depth investigation of all the parts of the plane I didn't see before, but the events of the night before caught up with me, and I slept.

Deeply.

Then, like a terrible magic, I was back in New York as if nothing had happened.

Back in my life, where I realized after only a few days, that he was not going to appear again. He was well and truly gone.

He had done exactly what he'd told me he would. He'd assumed the Luc Garnier persona, held it for a short while, and then disappeared.

I wonder if he found that woman. I wonder who she is to him. I wonder if she was worth all of this. If finding her was worth burning so bright and then leaving all that flame to sputter out and die.

I wonder how I let this all happen in the first place.

How I let him hurt me when no one ever has, not since I left my childhood home behind.

I should have leaped into action immediately, the moment I got back to New York, but I didn't.

It was almost like I wanted to sit with that night. Hold

on to it for a while before I forced myself into unraveling the mystery.

Because part of the mystery was why I'd fallen so hard for him when I *knew* he was nothing but a lie.

Tomorrow, I kept telling myself.

I would start tomorrow, but tomorrow never came.

In the meantime, I took myself to the office each day. I performed for Tess and all of my existing clients. Hints of Luc Garnier were sprinkled all over the papers, tales of sightings and rumors of his many glorious deeds, fueling a surge of new clients.

I didn't have anything to do with it, which meant he had. He must have.

I had to sit with that.

I didn't only sit with it. I *felt* it. And I didn't like feelings, so I decided the best thing to do was to eat mine.

I dedicated myself to finding the perfect treats. But what I thought about was him.

The calls kept coming as time went on. Tess and I talked very seriously about hiring another investigator, and began taking interviews to find someone who fit. I should have been jubilant that this dream of mine was going so well that it was hitting new milestones… But I wasn't.

It was like I couldn't feel anything unless it was a sugar rush. I became fixated on toast. I had my job to perform and this lovely little life that I built, and sugar and toast could not keep things running the way they should. I had to throw myself into my role the way I'd always done, and I did, but that meant that it was only at home that I could face the things that were really bothering me.

Like, say, the fact that I had sex for the first time in my life with a man who didn't exist.

And who had abandoned me without a backward look the morning after anyway.

More time passes than I like to admit to myself before I shake that off.

Well. I don't *shake it off,* exactly. But I stop spending my time aimlessly doomscrolling on social media. I stop staring at the ceiling in my apartment when I should be sleeping. I become deeply revolted with toast and crave burritos from a particular restaurant across the city from my apartment, and make sure I get at least one a day. Usually more.

Plus there's a chocolate peanut butter truffle situation. Don't ask. They taste like love should feel.

It's going on four months by the time I stop moping and do the only thing I know how to do.

Solve the damn mystery. Or try.

I have the name he left behind, and part of it is the name he gave me. This makes me think that it might actually be a real lead so I throw everything I have into figuring out who this woman is. Or was.

In between my other jobs, I dig. Late at night in my apartment, I hunt through records and trace faint hints.

I build a picture—well, not a picture. A sketch at best.

Amara Mariana Vizcaya existed. She was real.

It's amazing how relieved I am when I discover that. Like it makes up for the whole man I slept with who… maybe isn't real at all no matter what he calls herself. She was a servant, originally from Basque Country, who left a great house in Spain some three decades ago. She entered the United States on a tourist visa in New York City, and like many, promptly disappeared.

I can find nothing in any US papers to tell me why she should be of interest to anyone. Much less of such interest that a man like *him* had gone to the trouble of assuming a fictional identity just to find her.

Assuming that's what he was doing.

I'm thinking about this one morning while sitting in my little cave of an office, wishing I hadn't let Tess talk me into breakfast sandwiches—that beloved New Jersey staple, a Taylor ham, egg, and cheese on a Kaiser roll—shortly after we arrived at work. It isn't sitting well with me, but then, I'm convinced that might simply be more of the same temper that's been gripping me since I flew back from France, because I'm fairly certain I've had indigestion ever since.

Four and a half months and counting.

I rub my belly—which, I can admit, is a lot thicker after months of eating my feelings around the clock—and glare at the screen in front of me. The truth is, I don't actually know what he was doing here. He told me he was looking for this woman, and something in me really wants to believe that's true, but I don't know that it is. Or even if that was what he was doing. Or what reasons he had for doing *anything*.

Including all the things he did that night—

"You really have to stop thinking about that," I mutter to myself.

I never wanted to hurt you, I hear him say again and again in my head.

I researched that law firm in Nice and identified the people who worked there months back. Several attorneys and a fair number of support staff, I believe. I remember that now and check the clock, pleased to see it's only four o'clock in the afternoon over in France.

I look at the remains of my breakfast and feel gross. I feel thick and strange, the way I have for months now. I decide only answers will save me, so I call one of the lower-level assistants and lay a breathless sob story all over her. Complete with vocal fry.

"I know this is outrageous," I say in the kind of broad American accent that makes every French person I have ever met roll their eyes, especially after no attempt at all at French, "but my boss gave me a list of tasks and I thought I wrote them down exactly as they needed to be done. Except there's this one name on the list and I don't know *why*."

The woman on the other end of the phone laughs. "We have all had these days," she says, in perfect English. The rebuke is implied, but also feels automatic, not personal. This is what I was hoping might happen. "What was the name? Perhaps I can help."

I try to sound like I'm reading it out to her. As if I don't have it memorized. "Amara Mariana Vizcaya. That's all I have."

I hear the tapping of keys, but all I can see is the face of a man who is certainly not Luc Garnier. The Luc Garnier who Tess asks me about every morning. As if she thinks I might have gone off to France with him for the express purpose of chopping him up and leaving him by the side of the road somewhere.

Luc Garnier, who everyone seems to believe in even more now than they did before. Just because of the *hint* of his presence. Just because it was whispered in the right ears and passed on by the right sources that he was actually at that party. That people met him and interacted with him, so any concern about his identity or indeed his existence is gone as if it never was.

Whispers of his presence, his prowess, are everywhere these days.

That I was also at that party is never mentioned.

"Luc Garnier," the voice with that French accent says on the other side of the phone.

My heart thumps in my chest again, so jagged and so hard it hurts. "Excuse me?"

"Your boss," the woman says with a laugh. "He has been looking for this woman, who was a client of our firm, for many years. He was not certain of her name, or how to track her. It took him some time to come along and find us. Did he not tell you this?"

"He doesn't tell me anything," I say, hoping I sound like every overwhelmed intern who ever lived.

She makes a clucking sound that I interpret as victory. "So I see this is the same everywhere, *t'sais?* Well. Apparently he heard the story at the beginning of his career and always wanted to get to the bottom of it. So, finally, he found our firm and they were able to tell him not only her full name, but the sad news that she passed away not long after she left Spain."

But I looked up that name. I tracked her here. "I don't think I realized she was from Spain," I say, making myself sound bewildered. "I'm sure that we were talking about his French projects."

"*C'est vrai, mais* she went from Spain to Nice, and then from Nice to the United States." The woman sighs. "I suppose the mystery will endure forever."

"I will tell my boss that," I say.

"He is a very nice man, your boss," the woman tells me, but this is not exactly what I wish to hear about the man in question. "When Monsieur Du Hamel came back to the office after meeting him, he was filled with praise. Too many people have been chasing Amara Mariana Vizcaya over the years, but none were as thoughtful as Luc Garnier. He told Monsieur Du Hamel that he became interested in the case because he could not believe the story as he heard it."

She lets out that sigh again, as if she is being swept away in some sort of romantic daydream, and while I am pleased that she's the one I reached, I find myself doubtful that she has a long career ahead of her in her law firm.

Not that I stop her when she continues. "I think it's a shame that he could not definitively conclude one way or the other that she did not, in fact, give birth to the marquess."

Everything in me shifts a bit at that. I sit a little straighter in my chair. I'm used to this feeling by now. It's what happens when a set of hunches and theories come together, and I just *know*.

If I could tell you the reasons I am here, I would, he told me once.

There are matters at play here that you cannot understand, he told me.

And, *I am not the sort of man who indulges in parties like this, or nights like this...*

She says that word, *Marquess,* and I feel it. I *know*.

"Then again, no one can prove that she didn't," my new contact says merrily. "So I suppose we will never know."

"Thank you so much for telling me," I gush at her. "Now I will sound knowledgeable in the extreme when he calls me on the carpet. I can't thank you enough."

We exchange pleasantries and bond over the baffling behavior of our superiors, and then after the calls end, I sit there for a long moment. I stare at the computer screen before me.

My heart is thumping and thumping, as if it's trying to batter its own hole through my ribs.

My stomach hurts. I feel on the verge of pale and clammy—likely because it's been all feelings and very little fitness these last few months. My clothes don't even fit well any longer.

But I type the words into the search bar. The name, and then the key bit of new information. That title. *Marquess*.

Just to make certain, I add Spain, too.

And the screen fills with his face.

I feel the contents of my stomach decide that it's high time to vacate, and I only manage to grab my wastebasket at the last minute. I think I'm about to be thoroughly sick, but all I do is heave, which feels like a final indignity.

When I swivel back to the screen I see that I have neither woken up from this nightmare nor hallucinated the face I see on my screen.

It's him.

I wait to see if there will be any more heaving, but there isn't. I feel fine. So fine that any thought that I might be coming down with a stomach flu deserts me immediately.

Apparently, my reaction to him has not waned. I fish

out the Goldfish crackers that have always been soothing to me and are basically comfort food at this point, and then, at last, I turn back to the screen.

To him.

The man who was inside my body.

Who had his mouth...everywhere.

The man who I knew perfectly well was never Luc Garnier.

But I see that my other suspicions about him were correct. He is no circus carney on the loose, some two-bit con man.

That isn't to say he *isn't* a con man, given that he did, in fact, run a con.

Yet what the screen tells me, after I hit the translate button, is that he is also Taio de Luz, Eighteenth Marquess of Patrias, an ancient bit of land in Spain.

My throat feels tight. I feel frozen solid, but I make myself scroll past the picture of Taio—not Luc, because he was never Luc—and read the article.

It takes me longer than it should to realize that it is not exactly a piece of high-quality journalism. It is a tabloid and it is reveling in what it calls *The great scandal of the once noble house of de Luz*.

There's no reason at all that I should be holding my breath.

I read on.

It appears that some ten years ago, following the death of the Seventeenth Marquess, an unnamed source released a purported diary that made the bombshell claim that the current Marquess was, in fact, illegitimate. That rather than being the product of his father and supposed mother, he had instead been gotten as a by-blow on a serving girl who had been banished for her trouble.

And the rules of inheritance for this ancient title stated that the Marquess could not be illegitimate.

The diary could not be proven to be real. It could not be proven to be false, either.

So the Marquess had existed ever since with a cloud over his name that was matched only by the scrupulous excellence of his behavior.

Even the tabloid lauded him for it. He was a study in excellence of character, the article gushed. As if he had decided that the only way to combat the things said about him was to set an example of hereditary perfection that no one could argue against.

Except, of course, *I* know all too well that he's a liar.

I sit back in my chair, panting as if I've run some kind of marathon. He came here for information, I understand. But not from us. Not from *me*.

He wanted to use the persona of Luc Garnier so that he could find out once and for all if he was actually illegitimate.

And it was a brilliant plan. It would have worked either way.

So what I don't understand is why that night happened.

I don't understand why he acted as if he was swept up in it as I was, when that can't be true.

I knew from the start that he had that kind of regal bearing about him. I shouldn't have let myself be swept away in all that magic that I tell myself I can barely remember now. It must have been the champagne, and anyway, he should have moved right on, disappeared into the ether, and never, ever touched me.

Maybe someday he can be a funny story I tell at parties. One regrettable night with the gentry.

But nothing about this seems funny just now. I feel something like hollow. And I find myself going over every single interaction I had with *Taio de Luz* over the course of those two weeks.

As I think back, I find myself rubbing my belly again. The way I do a lot these days.

And something else occurs to me. Like a concrete block falling on me.

Something that should have occurred to me a long time ago.

I count back, one month, another. All the way back to that night in Cap Ferrat.

And then, with a dawning sense of something like horror, I think about how many times I've eaten my feelings in these months and kept thinking I was *about* to feel better when my period came.

But it never did.

And I was so busy I forgot about it.

I can hear my own breathing now. Because in all my years, I have never, ever missed a period. I've never been so much as a day late. If it weren't for that night, and that man, and how lost I was in him, I would have realized this sooner.

Wouldn't I?

I stand up abruptly, gather my things, and stride toward the front office. I smile at Tess, mouthing that I have to go do something. She waves me off, clearly talking to some kind of salesperson on the phone. I can tell because her Jersey accent is even more prominent than usual.

My mind is whirling on the elevator down and I practically sprint out the front of the building, then down a few blocks until I find a drugstore. I give thanks for the total disinterest of cashiers in New York City, purchase the test, and then make myself walk all the way home, to see if that calms me.

It does not.

I love my little apartment not far from the Metropolitan Museum of Art, where I happily pay for the neighborhood and not anything like space. But then, I'm rarely here. I've made sure that when I am, it's as welcoming as possible.

Though today it doesn't feel welcoming at all. I'm not sure what would.

I throw my bag on the counter in my kitchen and tear open the box, scowling at the instructions. It suggests first thing in the morning for the best results—well. I'm not waiting.

I perform the necessary tasks, set up the test, and set a timer on my phone.

Then I wait through the longest few minutes of my entire life.

When my phone starts bleating at me, I blow out a breath. I walk back into my tiny bathroom with its prewar black and white tiles.

Then I stare down at the two blue lines that blaze there on my test.

Unmistakably.

For a long time, I do nothing.

I simply stand there. Maybe breathing, maybe not.

I straighten, rub my eyes, and look again, but nothing changes.

The truth is as unmistakable as those two blue lines.

I'm pregnant.

With *his* child.

With the *Marquess of Patrias's* baby.

"I can't wait to go to Spain and tell him," I tell my reflection in the mirror, when I can speak. Though I have to hold myself up against the sink. "I hope he's pleased. Right before I kill him."

CHAPTER SEVEN

It takes me longer to get to Spain than it should, and not only because I fly commercial the way I usually do. Or even because I wait to see my doctor before I go. It's almost as if there's a part of me that's dragging her feet, in no rush to leap into the confrontation I know is coming.

Or possibly I prefer my fictional versions of the man who came into my life as abruptly as he left it.

An observation about myself that does not thrill me.

But I am not getting any less pregnant, and it will soon be impossible to pretend it's just random weight I've gained, so in the second week of November I invent a job in Spain, leave the firm in Tess's capable hands, and go.

I land in Seville, hole up in a lovely hotel that feels like a private hacienda, and dedicate myself to working out how, exactly, I'm going to get to the Marquess himself.

If it could be as easy as showing up on his doorstep, I would—but all my research tells me that the Marquess lives on a grand, old estate in the rolling hills of Andalucia that comes complete with a name and its own history.

The gates to keep the unwanted and uninvited out are implied.

And also visible when I look it up online.

I've been to Spain before. I had a client based in Madrid, and another in Bilbao. But I have never been to this particular part of Spain with its whitewashed houses and dreamy hills. A few days after arriving in Seville, and adjusting to the new time zone, I drive myself out into the countryside in my rental car.

Because I determined that the de Luz estate is open to the public at certain times each month. And lucky me, I make it over to Spain just in time for one of the house's open weekends.

I've spent my few days in my lovely, airy hotel room fuming.

Mostly at myself. It's true that I was a virgin that night. But I was not a young virgin straight out of the schoolroom, some trembling little fawn being taken down by the big, bad wolf.

Quite the contrary. I might have deliberately chosen not to get that close to another person over the years, but in the meantime, I didn't exactly live a sheltered life.

I know perfectly well that I should have used birth control. I should have discussed it, at the very least. Then insisted upon it.

I can't forgive myself for forgetting. For somehow being so swept away in the magic of that night and that man that I...became someone else. Someone reckless and irresponsible, when I've never had the luxury to be either.

But the funny thing is, no matter how annoyed I am with my own failures, now that I know I'm pregnant it's as if my stomach is settling into the truth of it.

And so do I.

Because I find myself rubbing my belly, but not because it feels weird any longer. These days I'm talking to the baby that's growing inside.

"Just you wait," I whisper. "We're going to have a great life, you and me."

Because as I drive myself along the winding roads that lead the way to the bit of countryside where the man I know and yet don't know at all lives—in and out of picturesque whitewashed villages clinging to hillsides, through olive tree alleys, through vineyards, past bell towers and haciendas, *cortijos* and fields, all the way to a set of huge, imposing gates that look as if they've stood *just so* since medieval times—I know one thing with deep certainty.

I will not be weak. I will not be my father. I will always protect this child, no matter what happens. If that means from my baby's own father, then so be it.

But before I give birth and all the days after, I will make certain that my baby knows that it is loved.

These are the things that sustain me across the ocean, through my handful of days in Seville, and out into the lands known as a part of the Patrias estate.

But none of this, I remind myself as I drive, excuses *him*.

He should have been more concerned about protection against exactly this result, given that he is the one with these apparently vast lands and a title already in question.

At the very least, he should not have disappeared the way he did—without a trace, if I'd been someone else—knowing perfectly well that no steps were taken to ensure this *didn't* happen.

Not, I can acknowledge, that I was in any fit state to negotiate such things myself.

The massive gates are open today, which does not make them any less imposing. I drive through them at the requested slow pace and I don't really want to admit that everything inside of me is jittery and strange and something like...

But I don't want to think that word. I'm not *excited*. This is a business call, nothing more.

Because I've done a lot of furious thinking on the way here. And I've had three days to sit in a hotel room, asking myself what I really want from this. From him.

It's not apologies, not really. I can already sense how insulted I might be if he attempts to apologize for this child within me.

What I do want, and will insist upon, is that we come to some agreement about how this child will never want for a thing. Not one thing, ever. No matter what happens to me. So that if my business disappears tomorrow, the child will be just fine.

My child will never find itself on a train to New York City, hoping for the best.

No way is this kid going to live like I have.

I feel so jittery by the time I catch up with the group that's assembled for the house tour that I'm half-afraid that they're not going to let me walk inside with them. I park and walk toward the assembled throng slowly, breathing in the sweet scent of flowers on the mild breeze. This is nothing like November in New York, dark and bitter. Here it's a bright, blue day, the sun golden and warm. It has to be seventy degrees here in front of the grand, sprawling house.

Paradise, I think.

Maybe I would pretend I was someone else, too, so no one would chase me here.

When I reach the group I brace myself to be turned away, though that wouldn't be a hardship here. We're standing on a sloping lawn that stretches lazily toward a lake and a tangle of trees, and there are the sounds of happy bells in the distance. I have the odd thought that I could be happy here, too—

But that's not why I'm here. And none of the other tourists really look at me, so it looks like I get to go inside.

I've gone to the trouble of haphazardly disguising myself, which wasn't really any trouble at all. No masks or heavy stage makeup or prosthetics or any of the rest of the tools of my odd trade. But I have braided my hair on one side, which is unusual for me, and crammed a baseball cap with a sports team logo on it on top of my head, which is unheard of. I'm wearing jeans and a long-sleeved T-shirt and a pair of sneakers, like any other American tourist.

Which is, I suppose, what I am today.

What I should not look like is the sharp, sophisticated Manhattan businesswoman he met just over four months ago.

Much less that wannabe Cinderella he took to a ball, and then left behind.

So I guess that makes me the shoe.

I stick to the back of the group, my mind going a thousand miles a minute as the docent leads us up to the grand, Moorish arch that rises at the front of the house, then beckons us to follow her into the grand courtyard that waits on the other side.

There is a fountain, and beyond it, a grand set of stairs, and that's where we're led. Then inside to a foyer that has clearly been created solely to impress.

And I'm indoors, something else seems to take me over, sweeping me up in a tight, hard grip that reminds me of his.

I know it's not him. It's this house. *His* house.

I feel like Elizabeth Bennet when she first sees where Mr. Darcy lives.

It's the inescapable weight of his history, and ancestry, and all the things it means to be the *eighteenth* of anything. All the generations that led to him. Much less a name like his, that according to the internet and our tour guide stretches back across time and marks him as a Grandee of Spain.

Whatever that is.

All I could tell is that it is a designation that is spoken in tones of reverence, at least here.

What I know for certain is that *my* family's ancestry reaches back to a boat from somewhere far to the north of here. And not one of the boats with a name that's taught in schools. Just any old boat, unremarkable and unremembered, that delivered a load of weathered peasants from one hardscrabble land to another.

And in all the time since, we might have pulled ourselves out of abject poverty but we would never, no matter what we did, turn into *this*.

I thought the plane he took me to France on was pretty special. I thought that first villa was lovely and gracious in every regard. The house where the ball was held, on the other hand, was nothing short of remarkable. Extraordinary, even.

But this is not a house, grand or otherwise. This is a *palace*.

And even that is too tame a word to describe it.

I'm only catching snatches of the tour guide's lectures on the art and history, issues and politics, that are intertwined with this family, this house, and the story of Spain itself. There are stories of kings and queens, court intrigue, political upheavals, and ancient scandals.

But what I can't help thinking is that this is the kind of wealth and consequence that doesn't have to shout. Because it *is* a shout. In and of itself.

Its continued existence is its own bullhorn, sounding down through the centuries.

The very fact of this place, built as a fortress and prettied up a bit more each generation. As a gift to this or that Marquess to his wife. Or as a mark of ego. Or simply because it was fashionable to have fewer battlements and more ballrooms.

At the end of the day, I realize, these grand old homes are record keepers. Storytellers, room by room, stone by stone. And they bear the marks of all the history they've weathered, just as they whisper of the futures they'll contain.

And this is where the man who spent that night with me comes from.

I've spent a lot of time thinking about him already, but all in terms of the role he inhabited: Luc Garnier, private investigator writ large.

It never occurred to me that he might have shrunk himself down to play that part.

Just as it never crossed my mind that when I dreamed up Luc Garnier in the first place, I was dreaming small.

Tiny, comparatively speaking.

I feel as if the blood inside my body is moving foolishly. Sluggishly. I am too hot, then too cold. I trail along, farther and farther behind the group, because every piece of art I look at feels like an indictment. Every glimpse of the rolling fields and hills through the windows feels like a slap.

It's as if I'm walking through that beautiful body of his, rediscovering him with every room.

Every statue is a clue. Every antique rug or piece of lovely furniture is a hint.

And it doesn't help that as I think that, I remember the way I explored his actual, physical body, crawling all over him there in that perfect little cottage. Rolling around and around in that bed.

I drift off, my feet taking direction from that insistent beat of my heart, and I'm helpless to do anything at all but follow where they lead me.

I walk and walk, awed by the fact the house all around me is more like a museum. I take in all the art on the walls, and more, the way it's arranged in a style that seems haphazard, but isn't. After all, when a person has a selection of masterpieces, there is no need to place one in its own space, like a shrine.

When a person is a Marquess, it's acceptable to pile them all onto walls next to each other in what might be called a *collage* if a person happens to be poor.

Here, I'm only too aware, this is an expression of breathtaking good taste.

But I become far more interested when I take a turn into the portrait gallery.

I feel as if I'm finally on a scavenger hunt that matters, tracking the evolution of Taio de Luz's features through time. It's immediately apparent that this is the family wing, because the walls are filled with eyes like steeped tea and stern mouths that look cruel in some generations and something a bit more kind in others.

And then, finally, I turn a corner, and see that at last I've made it into the modern era. There are portraits, but there are also photographs. First black and white, then full color.

The story of Taio is *right here*.

A portrait of the round-cheeked baby he was, scowling at the artist. The dreamy-eyed boy he became. Then, too soon, a somber-looking adolescent standing stiffly behind an older man who looks remarkably like Taio himself does now, and a woman with such stark, strong features that she ought to be off-putting. But the effect of all those features together somehow works itself out into a striking beauty.

I stand before that one for a long while.

It takes me a moment to understand why. That it's a family, and as posed and formal as they look, they also look like they…go together.

I sigh at that, and smooth my hand over my belly. "We'll have this, too. One way or another. I promise we'll be a family."

After the portraits come the photographs of a man I recognize. The man who I first met in that gleaming office in Manhattan. The man who took my hand in Cap Ferrat, led me down a path by the sea, and changed everything.

The man who is the father of my child.

I blow out a breath, standing there staring at a face

that I have dreamed of every night since the day I met him, my hands resting on the thickness of my belly. I haven't thought about it *quite* like that. Not in this place brimming with family in a way my own relatives never could, or would.

But they don't matter now.

Taio is the father of this baby. I am the mother.

I have to fight a bit, all of a sudden, to keep my breathing even.

I've reached the end of this section, but there's a door at the end of the hall. I look back over my shoulder, but I can't even hear my tour group. I have no idea where they went. So rather than retracing my steps, I go to the door and open it.

Immediately, there's so much light that I'm dazzled, and it takes me a moment to realize that I'm standing in some kind of music room. The ceiling is high and arched, like a cathedral. There are delicate settees set here and there.

But most importantly, there is an antique piano in the center. And a man sitting on its bench, ferocious in his focus, playing a melody that I recognize immediately.

It is that same soaring, freewheeling piece of music that I last heard in the Miravakia Investigation offices. That night I nearly pressed my face to the glass so I could continue to look at the beautiful man lounging there on the sofa.

It takes me a long, stunned moment to realize that it is the same man playing that same song. And I feel like I might break wide open.

Because he plays with an intensity, a creative flair,

and a brooding specificity that reminds me of nothing so much as being in bed with him. Naked. Wild with desire.

And him so deep inside me that it's like he made himself a part of me, forever.

I can still feel him now.

The music stops. And I jolt a little at the silence that follows, seeming stretched wide to fit the space the music left behind it.

He stands up from the piano, and I know who he is now. Taio de Luz. The Eighteenth Marquess of this place, these lands.

I know what he was hiding from. I even have a few guesses as to why.

But mostly, I realize that part of me never expected to be in the same room with him again. I can feel that ache inside me, sharper now. And everything else hums, the way it seems I always will when in his presence.

"I'm afraid you have strayed from the public part of the house," he says, in that voice of his, low and deep and so welcome—so missed—that I almost feel as if I might cry.

Hormones, I tell myself flatly. *It must be hormones.*

I want to say something suitably cutting. I want to start this off by ripping into him the way he richly deserves.

But I can't seem to say a word. I watched as his gaze sharpens. He tilts his head to one side in a show of arrogant astonishment, and I understand that even though I have seen that particular gesture before, what I am seeing now is *the Marquess*.

Not the Marquess playing the role of a lesser man.

As if on cue, he moves his hand to his lapel. And I

have seen the entire march of his personal history out in the gallery. Generation after generation of men with precisely this stature and sense of themselves.

It is all right there.

He allows his mouth to curve, another gesture. This time toward courtesy. "I will call a member of staff to come and collect you, shall I?"

I realize that he has not yet realized who I am.

I wait.

He takes a step in the direction of another graceful arch in the opposite direction of where I came from, then stops.

Dead.

My heart picks up speed.

He turns back and I watch as recognition dawns. I watch the expressions that move in rapid succession over his face.

Shock. Bewilderment. Something that looks far too much like a lightning bolt of joy, one that I can feel echo in me—

But maybe I'm imagining that, because too quickly, he scowls.

"What are you doing here?" he demands, his voice low and raw, and nothing like that aristocratic hauteur he used only moments ago. "You can't be here."

"It's nice to see you, too," I replied, impressed with the coolness of my own tone.

I wait for a beat. Then I take my time looking around, taking in this room, and the enormous palace directed all around. I look back at him.

Then I use what I discovered is his proper address, complete with a deliberately awkward curtsy. "*Excelentísimo Señor.*"

And I'm sure that I see him pale.

"You really cannot be here," he says, and he is moving again, coming toward me with a frown on his face, and still I wait.

Because surely, any moment now—

And I watch this happen, too. The way his gaze moves over me, almost greedily, something I recognize because I feel it too.

But I can see when his eyes move over my belly, and then back.

And it is just as satisfying as I hoped. As I imagined. As I dreamed. He stops walking, almost as if he slams into an invisible wall.

He is staring at my belly. I lift my hand and smooth it over the jut of my belly, outlining its shape. He makes the faintest sound. A groan or a prayer, I can't tell.

Slowly, almost painfully, he raises his gaze to mine.

"Oh, yes," I say with a soft kind of intensity that isn't quite malice, but isn't *not* malice, either. "We have many things to discuss. Your real name is the least of it."

CHAPTER EIGHT

He ushers me out of that room and the music he played seems to hang about us in the bright sunlight that pours in through the arches and paints the courtyards we pass in gold. There is something thunderous about the way he strides through the house, though I get the impression that he is keeping an eye out for something as we go.

Perhaps *someone*.

A terrible suspicion begins to take root inside of me.

I read about him. I read every article I could find, though many were in translation. One thing I'm certain was never mentioned in any of them was a wife.

But then, this man is not like some other noble families I've encountered. They come complete with PR teams, social media managers, and a robust internet presence. Everything I read about Taio suggests that he prefers the family name to carry the weight.

Meaning, I realize with a sickening feeling of dread deep inside of me, he could absolutely be married. With twenty children, for all I know.

For the first time in a long, long while—since I lived in my stepmother's house, to be precise—I feel something like shame wash over me.

And I am more shaken than I would like as he leads

me into a book-lined study and shuts the door behind us. Tightly.

"You should be off your feet," he mutters at me, and herds me into a deep leather chair.

I would object, but I can't seem to find the words.

"Are you married?" I demand instead, before the wondering eats me alive.

He stops still in the center of the room, halfway to the seat opposite me. He turns and stares down at me with something like amazement. "Am I *married*?"

There is a kind of fury in his tone. It feels like a lash, but I can't let that deter me.

"You heard me. Are you married? Do you have children?" That one hurts, but I don't back down. "Are you a cheater in addition to being a liar and a con man?"

Taio lets out a sound that is technically a laugh, but I do not mistake the bitterness in it for anything like humor.

"No." He bites off the word. "I am not *married*. How could you think—"

He slashes a hand through the air, cutting himself off, and I find myself holding my breath at the look of *outrage* on his face. And something in his eyes that almost makes me think that I've deeply offended him.

I don't understand, but I can taste the urge to apologize on the tip of my tongue. I don't know how I keep myself from it.

He continues to the chair across from me and throws himself into it, and I'm convinced that he looks… wounded, somehow. For there is something hollow and raw in the way he looks at me, and it fuses with that ache inside me, and I worry for a wild moment that I might actually burst into tears.

I don't. Somehow I don't.

Taio slumps in his chair, as if my appearance here has taken the starch out of his spine.

I can't decide if I should feel jubilant or sad, but what I find I can't bear is the silence that seems to get wider and heavier by the moment.

"Well." I clear my throat. "I suppose it's nice to meet you at last."

He has the grace to wince at that. "Yes," he says after a moment, his gaze too dark as he regards me. "I am Taio de Luz. I have a great many other names, but they are all for show. And I'm afraid that the deception was necessary."

"You're trying to find out whether or not you are the legitimate heir to all of this," I say coolly, and there's something satisfying in watching him take on board that I discovered his secret.

He doesn't look surprised. It's something more like resigned. "You found that card."

"You left it," I reply. "Perhaps if you hadn't gone sneaking around in the dark and then run away like a coward, you could have retained your secrets. *Mr. Garnier.*"

And he inclines his head at that, but there's a different sort of gleam in his gaze now. As if I extended a challenge and he intends to meet it.

"I'm happy to say that the time for fiction has passed," he tells me, and he no longer looks as if his spine has given up on him. He stretches out his legs and suddenly, he is every inch the aristocrat. As if even his bones dare not defy him. As if his expectation is that I won't, either. "What else have you discovered?"

I quash the urge to sit straighter, because that might tell him that he's getting to me and I can't have that. "Is it not enough that I found you? And know why you foisted yourself upon me in the first place?"

"That all depends, Annagret."

Before I can jump on that, he shakes his head and pulls his mobile from his pocket. He taps on it, puts it to his ear, and then begins speaking in a stream of what I realize at once is smooth, upper-class Spanish. It sounds not unlike the music he played, and it has the same effect on me. It seems to wrap all around me, like gossamer and heat, so I'm almost tempted to slide off this chair and roll around in it…

Somehow, I control myself. But it's close.

"You must be famished," he says, his eyes hot as he slips the mobile back into his pocket.

As if he knows exactly what I'm imagining. My cheeks feel red, and I can only hope they are not bright with that heat—though something about the way he studies me tells me they are.

"I'm actually relieved to discover that I'm pregnant," I tell him. "For some while I simply thought that I was fattening myself up as if I planned to sacrifice myself at the first opportunity. To what, I can only imagine."

He takes his time shifting his gaze from the heat on my cheeks. "How fortunate that such a grizzly end was averted."

And then we just…sit there. In the silence that seems to shimmer between us like its own light, its own heat.

I have spent months not only thinking of things I'd like to say to this man, but practicing them in mirrors. In my head. In my dreams.

I have shouted at him. I have delivered stinging monologues. I've torn him apart in every possible way, over and over again.

Yet here, now, sitting in this lovely little room with him, I can't seem to remember a single word.

Because something about being near him feels like a balm for my poor battered heart, and I might hate that something like this can be true, given what has happened between us so far. But that doesn't make it any less real.

When his gaze moves from mine I follow it, and realize that I am pressing a hand against my heart.

If I drop it now I feel like that will give too much away, so I don't.

And I can feel the heat of my own palm there, now. I think instead of his, and this is not remotely helpful.

Gradually, I become aware of a ticking clock. At first I think it's my heart, overtaking not just me but the whole room. But then I spy the grandfather clock against one wall, counting out the time. Filling this silence for us.

And somehow, that, too, makes me feel easier.

The look on Taio's face is not easy at all.

"Annagret," he begins, in as anguished a voice as I've ever heard, I'm sure of it—

But the same woman who dressed me, who hustled me onto that plane to go home, is here. She inclines her head in my direction, nods at Taio, and then pulls a trolley inside, laden with food.

"I believe you know my *mayordomo*, Salma," Taio says.

"A pleasure to see you again, Madam," the woman says in that same voice, so calm and unruffled I can't tell if I'm soothed or triggered.

"Yes," I agree. "An absolute delight. This time, will you drug me and throw me in the back of a car before you whisk me off somewhere else?"

Triggered it is.

Salma the *mayordomo* does not respond. But Taio has that thread of laughter in his gaze again. "Only if I decide you've become too mouthy," he says.

The two of them exchange a look. Then he nods, and she bows out of the room.

And I watch, something like amazed, as this man who has taken on a number of roles already in my presence, takes on a new one. This time, of a nurturer.

He transfers the plates from the gleaming trolley to the low table between us. And I can only stare as he does it, because it is getting harder and harder to believe this is real. I think of everything that's happened. What these past four and a half months have been like, and now we are just... Here?

Having a snack?

Though in fairness, it's really more of a banquet of small plates.

I want to refuse any sustenance at all, like some kind of Victorian heroine, but pregnancy really gets in the way of sustained theatrics. Because I'm hungry. Really hungry, and the baby comes first.

"This is very kind of you," I say. I lean forward and load up my plate with savory tapas and bright pieces of fruit. "But maybe you can take this opportunity to tell me what, exactly, all of this was about."

"It seems you know already. Since you, after all, are the real Luc Garnier."

I have wanted to have this conversation for a long

time. I dreamed of having this conversation. Of the two of us admitting what is fact and what is fiction. Of saying these things out loud.

But the reality of *this* moment, of him saying such a thing to me with his whole chest, is another humming inside of me. I can't tell if it is agony or relief to have it out there, in the air between us, at last.

"I had to create Luc Garnier," I tell him, as I have told no one, ever. I tell him the story of how I started, how no one would hire me, how they only came to me when they thought I had male oversight. "It was that or crawl back to my stepmother's house, hat in hand, and that was not possible. It is still not possible. Even if she would let me in, it would kill me."

He studies me for a moment. "Is she your only family?"

"She is married to my father." I try to smile. "But I would not call either one of them family. I'm not sure either one would call me that, either."

And there is something about the way he frowns at that, as if he cannot comprehend what I'm telling him. As if it makes no sense. "Your own father does not consider you family?"

He sounds…baffled.

So baffled that it makes me feel a kind of warmth, everywhere.

"He might. But my stepmother does not like it. She was actively opposed to it from the moment we met." I force a smile when he lifts a brow. "I was three."

Taio mutters something I cannot understand, dark and low.

This, too, is warming. Almost soothing.

"I have never told anyone these things because there was no one to tell," I find myself saying. "If I am honest, I suppose I have long suspected that there is something about me that caused it all, so it was better to keep myself at a distance from others. In case they all felt the same." His eyes widen at that. I laugh. "It sounds sad when I say that out loud, but it doesn't *feel* sad. It's just how it is."

"This, Annagret," he says quietly, "is the greatest lie you have ever told."

"Taio."

Our gazes slam together, then. And I know why. This is the first time I say his name. Out loud. *To* him.

And I know how that must feel, because I know how it feels when he says *my* name.

Every time he says it.

Once again, I remember lying side by side in that dark cottage with that tapestry of recognition and awe wrapped all around us, in ways I could never explain to anyone else. In ways that seemed made up even to me, afterward. One more case of a jilted lover pretending it all meant more than it did.

But I can feel it again now.

I watch him breathe, low and steadying, like he's as off-balance as I am.

How can I feel what he feels and have made this all up in my head?

For a moment I think he won't continue. That he will maintain his enigmatic silence the way he has all along.

I realize I don't have any idea what I will do if he does.

But I hear a scrape of sound, a breath released. He sits

back in his chair and props his head up on one hand, as if he's trying to think of the best way to say what must be said.

I continue to eat, chasing one extraordinary flavor with the next, not exactly surprised that everything tastes so good. Everything about this place seems to demand excellence. Maybe that's what they spent eighteen generations perfecting.

"My parents had a very cordial marriage," he tells me after what seems like a very long while, very much as if the words are being torn from him. I think that if I look at him directly he might stop, so I keep my eyes on the array of plates before me. "This was my impression when I was young and it did not change once I was older and understood more. When I was eighteen, my father sat me down and explained that a relationship based on mutual interests rather than emotions was preferable for men in our position. That indulging the passions too often leads to disaster and is best avoided. He chose my mother with great deliberation, he told me, because she came from a grand old French family with its own legacy and could therefore understand what was required. I never saw them fight. I never heard a harsh word exchanged between them."

He shakes his head, slightly, as if attempting to come to grips with something. I want to leap in and say... I don't know what I want to say. Anything that might help.

But I don't. Because I already know what I think about what happened. I've already put together any number of potential scenarios to explain all of this. I want to hear what *he* thinks. What he did.

Taio looks over at me. "I tell you all this because it

came as such a deep shock to me when that diary was released. It described my parents' marriage in terms I could not understand. It suggested that they were people that I had never met. I assumed that everyone would laugh it off, but that was not what happened." He shifts his chair and frowns, though he does not appear to be looking at anything in particular. "I also expected it all to blow over quickly, but it has not."

It occurs to me that it's possible that he has never spoken about these things before either. That maybe this is a conversation of firsts for the both of us. I'm certain of it when he rises, but with none of that habitual elegance that I expect from him. He simply pushes himself out of his seat and then begins to pace back and forth along the study floor.

I would have said he could never be this agitated. I am riveted.

But I don't want him to see *how* riveted. I'm afraid he'll stop.

Though he shows no signs of stopping. "I was always raised to respect my title and this family's legacy above all things, and I did." He shakes his head. "I went to the finest universities in Spain. I did graduate work at Harvard and the London School of Economics, so I could better steward the estate into the future. I have always been mindful of my behavior, knowing since I was small that it does not merely reflect on me."

Taio lets out that bitter laugh. "I was a paragon, in other words. And I was comfortable in the knowledge that my father was a man of honor before me. Only to find out that the whole world easily and fully believed the opposite of both of us."

He paces some more, and I can feel the outrage pouring off of him. "Because if that diary is to be believed, not only am I not worthy to be the heir to the de Luz legacy but my father was not a man of integrity. If the diary is true, he not only seduced a servant but did so with the full knowledge that she was his wife's closest confidante. And then he compounded these sins by allowing her to give birth to his child, passing it off as having come from his own marriage, and then banished the poor girl for her trouble."

I want to jump in then, to soothe him. To try to comfort him. I want to tell him that it's the most normal thing in the world for families to be prickly and uncomfortable and sometimes downright destructive.

But somehow, I still can't seem to speak.

"Years upon years have passed, Annagret." Taio's voice is raw, now. Harsh with the years of suppressed emotion. "And still the rumors persist. Yet at the same time I am of an age where I must look to securing the future of this place, if indeed it is mine to secure."

I watch him rake a hand through his thick, dark hair, an expression of something like agony on his face that makes everything in me...something like itchy.

I have never seen him *undone*. I'm not certain I like it.

Or maybe what I mean is, it makes me want to rush to his side and soothe him any way I can.

"And what does your mother have to say?" I ask, past that lump in my throat. "Surely she could put an end to all of this."

He shoots me a look that I can't quite read. "Asking my mother to submit to some kind of blood test to prove that she is not a part of some intricate lie is the same as accusing her of participating in the squalid affair."

"What you mean, I think, is that she has not offered to clean this up for you."

Taio frowns at me. "You have not met my mother. She is an extraordinarily dignified woman. There is no scenario in which I will be the one to take that dignity from her."

And I realize as I hear him say this that I'm unfamiliar with the emotion that underpins it.

Love.

He loves his mother. He doesn't want to hurt her and, in fact, wishes to protect her. He will shoulder this forever if it will keep her from harm.

I smooth my palm over my belly again, but this time I can feel the way my own hand trembles.

"I decided I would go about getting to the bottom of this in a more roundabout way," he tells me, and I do not ask again why he doesn't ask his mother to take a simple test to find out the truth. How can I? What do I know about mothers? I suppose my life has been marked by the absence of mine, but until I got pregnant, I'm not sure I could even begin to glimpse the enormity of the loss.

But he is telling me his story. I focus on that, and not the pressure behind my eyes. "I happened to be at an event where an acquaintance was bragging quite loudly about the benefits of having his very own private investigator on retainer so that he could immediately look into anyone who approached him. Whether it was a new lover, a business connection, or even a neighbor at one of his properties. Whatever the situation, he told me, he could always dig into their backgrounds and know precisely with whom he was dealing."

Taio seems several degrees less agitated now, though he still paces. He thrusts his hands into the pockets of yet another perfectly cut suit. So perfectly cut, in fact, that putting his hands in his pockets in no way mars its lines.

It's a true sartorial feat.

I tell myself that this is neither the time nor the place to admire the elegant, deeply masculine lines of his body. Much less to sit here and remember exactly how I navigated my way around those lines and licked my way—

Focus, I order myself.

"It had never occurred to me to hire an investigator," he is saying. "On the contrary, I rather thought that doing so would be an admission of guilt. That has not changed. I knew that if I were to be seen digging into this question, that would be seen as an answer all its own. And so I spent a lot of time researching various investigation firms, hoping that a solution might present itself to me. But all roads seemed to lead back to Miravakia Investigations. And Luc Garnier."

"We have an excellent reputation," I manage to say.

His gleaming gaze touches mine and then moves away, but I feel it all the same. All over me, like fire.

"You do," he agrees, his voice intent. "I thought that what I would do is arrange to meet this Luc Garnier. Not in his offices. Not officially. But all rumors suggested that sooner or later, we would cross paths at some or other gala. Except we never did."

"This is what made you suspicious?" I ask. "Did it

never occur to you that perhaps you were simply at different events?"

He studies me then, and it makes me feel hot, and not only because of the things I've been imagining. It's as if he can see straight into me, and I'm not sure I like it.

I know I don't. But I also know it goes both ways. I remind myself of that as he regards me for yet another moment, and it does not feel like a *two-way* anything.

"It is a smaller world than I think you realize," he tells me. Eventually. I get the strangest notion that he is trying to…protect me from understanding what I can't have known—especially back when I started—about the kind of clientele I wanted to attract. "For some, who could never dream of attending any such event, it might seem that there are too many of them to count. But the truth is that there are only so many that count at all. And everything else is filler, or focused on outward-facing celebrities. These are not the same kind of events and everyone who belongs in these circles knows it."

He *is* trying to protect me. From my own ignorance of the very, very wealthy. After all this time.

A great tide of warmth rises in me, but I don't think this is the time or place to show it.

I clear my throat, carefully, and hope my eyes aren't too bright as I gaze up at him. "So what you're saying, I think, is that you have a secret club."

I'm certain his lips curve in one corner, but he turns before I can confirm it. "The club isn't secret but what it is, I'm afraid, is tediously exclusive. And so I began to wonder how it was that everyone seemed to think that this famous detective was at all the same events that I went to over the course of several determined years, yet was never present when I was. And once the idea took hold of me, I could not let it go."

"I would accuse you of being obsessive," I say. "But that is actually a compliment in my line of work."

Taio inclines his head. "I began to look into the actual agency itself. And there you were."

Something runs through me as he says that, another kind of electricity, maybe. It's that look on his face—

But he turns again. He paces until he is standing on the other side of this small study, filled with so many books and cozy places to read them. He has his back to a set of doors that, given the brightness pressing in from the other side, I suspect lead outside.

I ought to feel trapped. But I don't.

Because looking at him reminds me of the way we exploded into the universe together, far-flung and yet stitched together like a spell the stars cast themselves.

I do not feel trapped at all.

"I watched you," he tells me, with that same intensity. "For some time."

I sit up straighter, a different sort of shivery thing working its way all over me. I'm fairly certain it is *delight*. "You are the Most Excellent Taio de Luz, Eighteenth Marquess of Patrias," I say in mock astonishment. "Are you saying that you are also a stalker?"

"I believe that in your parlance it would be called surveillance," he replies. When I only lift a brow, he continues. "I only saw you and your secretary. And so, eventually, I decided to risk it. You know the rest."

It's tempting to linger here. More than tempting. "But your timing was specifically planned to get us to that masked ball," I say instead. "That was the point of the whole thing."

"Not entirely." Something shifts in his expression, though I can't read it. He begins to look almost angry. "There were also things I needed to do in New York."

"I tracked her there, too." He looks almost...*relieved* when I say it. I don't understand, but I keep going. "I can tell you when she arrived in New York, but I don't know what happened to her afterward. The law firm in Nice is certain she died. They didn't tell me how they came to that conclusion."

He considers me for a moment. "I do not believe she died. I believe she married, changed her name, and made sure she could not be tracked. And I do not blame her." His expression darkens. "Much as I take pride in this family and all the things I believe the de Luz name means, I think that she was clever indeed to put it all behind her."

"But you talked to that law firm yourself, didn't you?" I ask. "Did they share your suspicions?"

"They had a great many theories, but mostly, they don't know. They performed a very specific task." When I stare back at him, he blinks. "I thought you knew. They helped her emigrate to the United States."

"That makes sense." And it does.

Meaning, it makes sense that someone would use a law firm like that to do such work. What doesn't make sense is how the apparently lowly servant girl managed to hire that kind of high-level firm to do it.

But I don't ask him about that, because he rubs a hand over his face. And when he pulls the hand away he looks as weary as I've ever seen him.

And when his gaze meets mine, it is something like... torn. Sad, even.

It makes my heart break all over again.

"In the end," Taio says quietly, "I could not come to any kind of definitive conclusion. So I remain in the same limbo. I live under a shadow. No one can prove that I am not the heir that I was raised to be. But they can still question it all they like. My existence has become a stain on my family's name."

Too many things seem to be whirling around inside of me. I can hardly catch a single one of them. But I can feel the weight of my belly, solid and real.

And I know that some things are true no matter if there are stains or not.

My child will not be a scandal. *My* child will not be caught in a trap not of its own making. Not like I was. Not like Taio still is.

I will not be the kind of parent who lets my child suffer.

I will not create that kind of suffering in another person, no matter how little I like to think my childhood affects me now.

But by the same token, I don't want either this child—or me—to add to Taio's suffering now, caught in this spiral he can't seem to escape.

I can see only one way forward. "I came here because I wanted you to know that what happened between us resulted in this baby," I tell him, and it hurts to keep my voice even, but I manage it. He wanted to protect me, and about something so small. I can protect him, too. "Now you know, Taio. But this does not have to complicate your life. This does not have to add to the stain."

His eyes darken near enough to midnight. He doesn't move, and yet it seems as if he *expands*. Until it's as if he's taken up all the space in this tiny little study, and all the air, too. His eyes *blaze* at me.

"I beg your pardon?" he asks, very quietly.

Possibly too quietly, because the question seems to sneak over my skin like a lick of a new flame, but I ignore it.

"I'll sign whatever you like," I assure him. "I'm obviously perfectly capable of taking care of this child on my own. You don't have to be involved." I hold my hands out, though I'm not entirely sure why I feel the need to act the part of the supplicant. "No need for any further stains on your name. *My* name is completely unremarkable. No one cares if it's tattered or torn."

I can't tell if what I hear now is the blood in my ears or that clock, still ticking away while we stay where we are. Too still when it feels as if we're sitting on some kind of volcano.

It's hard to swallow. My throat hurts.

I can't look away from him.

"I think you have mistaken my meaning," Taio says, and I realize that the only way to describe his voice is *dangerous*. "I do not believe that I am illegitimate, Annagret. I do not accept it. What I do know is that no child of mine will be born without the protection of my name. This I can assure you."

My lips feel chapped. "What are you talking about?"

"It is very simple." He lifts a brow, every inch of him the Spanish aristocrat, lord of all he surveys, including me. Maybe especially me. "We must marry at once."

CHAPTER NINE

Obviously, I say no.

I say no repeatedly, but Taio mounts one argument after the next.

"Surely," I say in some desperation after this has gone on for a long while, "the fact that I'm an ignorant American should disqualify me already from any possible consideration that I might become your wife."

"None of that matters," he says now, gruffly. "You are carrying my child. That is the beginning and the end of it."

"Taio—" I begin, with renewed determination in my voice.

But he cuts me off this time by coming and kneeling down before me. So we are eye to eye. His gaze stays on my face for a long, simmering moment and then, perhaps inevitably, his hand moves to cover my belly.

It might be inevitable but I feel it.

Everywhere.

And it is complicated now, or perhaps I mean layered, with all that's happened between us since the last time we really touched each other. The lies and separation. The truths discovered and told. This urge we seem to both have to protect each other.

The baby he now holds beneath his palms.

Inside me, yes. But ours.

I can remember, with perfect clarity, every single touch we shared between us. And now there is this.

The warmth of his hands. The wonder all over his face.

And the slickness between my legs that connects to that winding, humming, insatiable need deep inside me that is never far from the surface.

All of it makes my heart seem to swell and grow, and this time there doesn't seem to be a single thing that I can do to keep the tears from falling. I tell myself it's because I've never understood the lure of families, not until this moment.

Not until this man touched me like this, because now, suddenly, I feel as if I finally get it. He and I made this child together. What magic would it be to raise it together, too? And this does not feel like an intellectual question. It feels primal and raw, like it is coming from a part of me I've never encountered before.

"Annagret," he says urgently. "You are the mother of this child already. Do not deny me the right to be its father. To be a family."

And I am not prepared to argue that one away with my cheeks wet and his hands on me, that intensely raw look on his face. How could I? How could anyone?

I think of my own father, stooped by the weight of his inability to stand up for anything, especially me. I think of the times I cried while he held me over another cruelty or dismissal from my stepmother, yet nothing changed. And how I learned to stop crying.

I gaze at Taio, who has already stood up for our baby more than my father ever did for his.

I think of how the word *family* feels in me when he says it.

The way he's looking at me seems to jar my heart wide open, so wide open it ought to hurt, and I don't have it in me to deny him anything, it seems. "Okay," I manage to say, wiping at my eyes with the backs of my hands.

"Okay?" he repeats, and I am certain it is not that he does not comprehend the word.

He wants me to say it. He wants me to make it real. So I do. "I will marry you," I tell him, though saying those words out loud makes me feel shaky inside. Not precarious. Just...awed by my own temerity to let myself believe in something like this. Like him. I try to soften it. "If you think that I must."

"I know that you must," he replies.

I expect him to stand, then, and start issuing commands, or whatever it is that Marquesses do. But he doesn't move.

Taio stays where he is, those warm, heavy palms molded to the curve of my belly. His thumbs move almost absently, stroking my bump and the baby within.

It's a tender moment, but it also sends a wildfire sensation spiraling through me and I wonder if I ought to be this immediately electrified by him when the baby is *right here*. Surely I ought to have been taken over by some maternal instinct by now that would protect me from seductions like this.

Like him.

But instead, I feel myself go soft and hot.

I can see that gleam in his dark gaze now, and I remember the last time I saw it. When he was so deep inside me and it was all that delirious pleasure, the moments of pain barely a memory—

"Very well, then," he says, though his voice is gruff. And that fire is clear to see in his gaze. "Consider it done, *cosita*. I will see to everything."

And he does. He pulls back from that chair, leaves me shivering where I sit, and does exactly what he promises.

I am swept off, once again by the impenetrable Salma, to yet another astonishing suite of rooms. I'm fed, clothed, indulged.

But not by Taio.

I don't mind. I'm going to marry this man. I've decided that this is the best thing for the baby. That makes all this perfectly rational. Even smart.

By this point, I can barely remember that I *might* have cried *slightly* in that study.

I allow Tess to think that I'm still off somewhere on a job. On the third day we video conference with each other and I applaud her choice of new investigator and I agree that she ought to hire the two others who impress us both.

"Maybe it's time to level up," she says.

"I agree." I look at her, the first person who really believed in me, and smile. "And I trust you to put it together, Tess."

It doesn't occur to me until after the call is over that it's almost like I'm letting go of Miravakia Investigations…but I dismiss that.

This is a strange little break, that's all. It can't be *reality*.

Reality, as I know all too well, does not often turn up in a *palace*.

And when, on the fourth day, it is time for the wedding that Taio has arranged, I let Salma and a fleet of aides dress me. They fuss and they sigh and they turn me into the perfect bride in a white dress that looks like it was made of dreams. My hair is braided around my crown, then curled as it hangs down, with flowers woven in. The dress itself manages to make me look like the very best version of myself, feminine and strong at once.

"It's beautiful," I whisper before I can stop myself.

"The Marquess had a specific vision, Madam," Salma tells me, but she's the closest to smiling I've ever seen her.

When I look in the mirror, it's not that I can't recognize myself this time. It's that I do. I look like a version of me I stopped believing in a long, long time ago. A version of me I left in the ashes of the life I left behind in Pennsylvania.

I look *hopeful*. I glow.

I find myself wishing we could wear those masks again.

"Are you ready, Madam?" Salma asks me.

I blink and realize that all the other aides have left. It's only me standing before a mirror, wishing for the first time in a very long time that my mother was around. This seems like a day that calls for mothers.

I blow out a breath, press a hand to my belly, and remind myself that I am one now. And that has to be enough.

Salma walks with me down a set of stairs I didn't know were in this part of the house, to a courtyard that's bursting with flowers and bathed in the midday light. And when we reach the bottom, Taio is there, wearing a top hat and tails the way other men wear baseball hats and sweats. It is that level of ease, wrapped up in all that masculine grandeur of his.

"Annagret."

He says my name as if he did not really expect to see me. Or maybe he didn't think he would see me like *this,* in a bridal gown with curls in my hair, the sun on my face, and this bizarre urge to go and *hold* him like we're—

But we're not, I caution myself. We're not anything. We're getting married for the baby. That's the reason this is happening.

If I wasn't pregnant, we would never have met again.

I want to say something funny or cutting to reset this mood. To wipe away that look of reverence in his gaze and make myself feel...well. Not better, but less likely to dissolve into floods of tears here at the bottom of this ancient stair.

Instead, all I can seem to do is smile.

Taio escorts me from the grand house, down a winding path to a sweet little chapel tucked into the hills. Once we are there, we are greeted by a priest who knows Taio by name. Salma comes in behind us, accompanied by a man I am fairly sure I last saw doing something of great importance involving the displays of flowers all over the house.

The ceremony is swift, which I am grateful for, despite the reading of Taio's many formal names and titles. And lovely, which I did not expect. The vows are spoken in English and Spanish, and I find myself laughing, as if this is an act of joy.

I remind myself that it can't be.

Even though he looks like a dream come true, again. Still.

It was bad enough in that courtyard, but now, in this small chapel, he's all I can see. His wedding suit is a feat of sartorial splendor, and I know, now, that it's not only the cuts of fabric that exalt him, but the simple fact of his own magnificence. He is so beautiful that it hurts, and he holds my hands in his so that I hurt, too.

He slides two rings of exquisite beauty onto my finger when it is time, but I can hardly bear to look at them. Because I cannot bear to look away from him.

I feel the weight of his gaze inside of me, as if he is turning me inside out. As if he can see every last part of me, like some kind of searchlight.

"You may kiss your bride, *Excelentísimo Señor*," the priest says, with an encouraging nod.

And Taio does.

He gathers me into his arms. He tilts me back and I find this unforgivable. His hands on me. That simmering gleam in his gaze, his stern mouth. If I didn't know better, I would think he is something like possessive.

But the true issue is that it feels too much like that night, and this is meant to be reality—

His mouth finds mine, and it's as if we spiral right back to that enchanted little cottage sitting there on a cliff in France.

Where everything is possible, and we are connected, naked and vulnerable and wide open.

As if I didn't imagine those things.

As if they are always right here, available to us, if we want them—

I kiss him back.

I put my hands on his lapels and hold on, while he does things with his tongue that light me up, everywhere.

But we are in the presence of a holy man, in a sacred place. Taio pulls away. I try not to let my shockingly weak knees go out from beneath me as the ceremony concludes and we turn to walk back out into the sunshine.

"There," he says when we stop just outside the chapel's doors. "It's done now."

And again I see that hard gleam on his face, as if this is a victory, but I can't make that make any sense.

"I don't know why we needed a whole bridal display," I say, frowning at him. "We could as easily have filed a few papers down at—"

But I lapse off into silence when he slides his hand over to hold my face.

He just…holds me.

And I can feel the metal of the ring he now wears, warming against my skin. I can feel the heat and strength of his hand. His gaze seems like it's *inside* me.

I can feel myself struggle to get a breath in.

"It's nice to meet you at last, wife," he says, his voice gruff and the strangest look in his gaze. Possessive, yes. But also something like tender.

I want to say, *you have known me forever,* because it feels true. But I know it isn't.

"Hello," I say, because I can't seem to help myself. I move my face to nestle my cheek in his palm. "Husband."

And then, together, we walk back up to the house. He twines his fingers with mine, and I remember the first time he did this. I feel the wash of heat and longing.

Only now, I cannot seem to stop thinking, *we are husband and wife*.

And how a white dress and his hand on me makes me want, desperately, for that to mean something more than simply a legal arrangement for our child.

I swallow hard as we walk closer and closer to the house, such a sprawling collection of red-roofed wings and whitewashed newer builds that somehow work together. It should be a monstrosity but instead it becomes the whole of the horizon.

I decide I have never seen anything more beautiful, unless it is him.

The Marquess. My husband.

I can feel my heartbeat in the crease of my elbows, the back of my knees, and deep in the soft center of me.

"You are now a de Luz," he tells me, and I can see that smile in his gaze. "Annagret Alden de Luz, Marchioness of Patrias."

I wonder, then, if I am the only one who sees that smile. Every other part of his life is so serious, and I can feel something in me become immediately protective at that thought.

What I know is that I would fight to make sure that he keeps looking at me, just like this.

I do not intend to let him know that. I focus on what he said, and not on how the sound of that title seems to land on me, hard. "I don't know what on earth makes you think I'll be changing my name."

"It is tradition, of course," he tells me. "There is no

such thing as the wife of de Luz who does not take on the mantle of the family name." Again, that smile is in his dark eyes and I want to lose myself there. "Indeed, it is considered an honor in some circles."

"I warned you," I tell him, unable to keep myself from smiling, too. "I told you that I am American and would inevitably bring with me my own deep stain. Perhaps that is the retention of my *actual* name."

"But my dear *cosita*," he says, and he is openly smiling now, and it makes everything inside me dance wildly, "you are the marchioness now. No matter what names you call yourself privately. And the Marchioness of Patrias cannot be anything but perfect. It is the law."

He adjusts his hold on my hand. The hand where he slipped those rings earlier, and I can feel the weight of them on my fingers now, gleaming platinum reminders that this is real. That I married him.

That he gave me a title and expects me to use it.

I'm not sure I can process it.

And I suspect he knows it, because I can hear the low rumble of his laughter as he leads me into the private wing of the house.

Once again, he leads and I follow, wondering why it is that he is the only man alive who can compel me to do so.

He leads me back into that courtyard that I've never seen before today. There is a covered bit, wrapped round with flowering vines, and it all looks a bit wild. Beneath it, the staff has set up a table and two chairs, and I can see another meal laid out for us.

It looks like we're about to have a wedding feast in a perfectly lush garden.

"My mother was supposedly a marvelous gardener," I tell him as he takes me over to a chair and helps me into it, as if I am not fragile, but precious. It makes me feel something like teary. "When I was little, sometimes my father told me stories about gardens she kept. I always hoped that I inherited her green thumb, but I'm not home enough to keep a plant alive. So I still haven't had the opportunity to dash my own hopes."

"Here we have many gardens you can play in, if you like," Taio tells me. He sits in the other seat, more next to me than across from me. "Or you may simply admire the work of the gardens as they are. Whatever you prefer."

And still, I feel that sensation like a sob deep inside of me. That ache that has plagued me for months now. That *thing* that some nights I wished I could dig out with my hands.

Today I have an inkling of what it is.

"Taio—" I begin.

But someone clears their throat. And whatever spell this is breaks. I can feel it fall apart around us, crumbling into ash.

Or maybe it's simply that Taio's demeanor changes at once.

"Mother," he says in a formal voice I have never heard from him before as he gets to his feet.

I don't know why it hasn't hit me until this very moment that it's strange I haven't met his mother. And stranger still that she was not at the wedding ceremony.

I follow Taio's gaze, and there she is. Francette du Luz, the previous Marchioness. She looks exactly as she appeared in that portrait I saw in the gallery here, with discordant features that are somehow stunning, although she's older now. Her dark hair has become an elegant gray. She is tall and the sort of slim that makes her seem even taller and more forbidding. She is dressed to perfection in what I imagine she considers a casual outfit. It is only that the trousers and jacket she wears are quite evidently from one of the most exclusive fashion houses in the world, the epitome of understated elegance.

She looks at her son. Then she looks at me, and I, who have stood tall in far more difficult moments than this one, feel the very strong urge to quiver in my seat. I repress it, but her eyes are a fierce and pitiless hazel, her lips do not even twitch in the corners, and I think she knows.

"Mother," Taio says again. "It is my honor to present to you my wife, the new Marchioness of Patrias."

I note he neatly sidesteps the issue of my name and have the unruly urge to laugh. Loudly.

I repress that, too.

Taio glances at me, then back to his mother. "Annagret, this is the dowager Marchioness, my mother, Francette Arceneaux de Luz."

I decide that it is the better part of valor to repress the head bob that nearly takes me over.

"So it is true," his mother says. She does not look at me. "You have gone and done it, and quickly, so that no objection could be raised."

"What objection could there be?" Taio asks in reply, his tone cool. "I have made my decision."

"And what a decision it is, to do this thing. I mean no offense to you, of course," Francette says, looking at me. It is at this moment that I understand that she is speaking English deliberately. That she wants me to understand what she is saying, when surely she and Taio more regularly speak in Spanish or French. "But surely you understand what my son does not—or cannot. You are American. My understanding is that you come from a family of no great name, have no education to speak of, and have thus far lived…" She pauses, delicately. "By your wits?"

"The interesting thing about living by one's wits," I say before I can stop myself, because I'm not sure if she's insulting him or me but I don't like it, "is that it becomes obvious when the people around one are unequipped."

But I smile winningly, just in case she's having a laugh. This is a strategy that has often worked with self-important clients who aren't used to any pushback. It never occurs to them that they *could* be insulted, so they laugh and all is well.

I think I hear Taio sigh. His mother merely raises her perfect brows. There is no hint of anything like laughter.

"And you are, as expected, disrespectful on top of all the rest," she says. "How delightful."

This is giving the shades of Pemberley being polluted and so I stand, too, because I feel like a target just sitting there. "I apologize if I'm adding to the stain upon your family name," I say, with great insincerity.

"Annagret," Taio warns, but I keep my eyes on his mother.

"My name is unstained in every regard," she replies crisply. "And can be traced back to the Norman Conquest. Or thereabouts."

"A pity, then, that you can't see your way clear to sorting out the matter of the current stain on Taio's family's name," I say, hoping that I look as unimpressed with her lineage as I feel. When she could help her son, yet hasn't, who cares about a bloodline? "I wonder why that is."

His mother frowns as if she doesn't understand. I can't believe she doesn't.

"This is an odd way to offer your congratulations, Mother," Taio is saying. "But perhaps we can all get together for family discussions at another time."

"The time for family discussions is past," Francette says with a bleak wave of her hand. "Honestly, Taio. I expected better from you."

"Unfortunately, he knocked me up," I say brightly, because I don't care if this woman comes for me. But I can't bear her swinging at him, and I decide not to interrogate myself about why that is, because I had my chance to tell him and I didn't. "So it was marrying me or contributing to the illegitimacy issue currently clouding the family legacy. We wouldn't want that, would we?"

Francette stares at me in a kind of frozen astonishment that I suspect is meant to shrivel me down to size.

Instead, I stand my full six feet, complete with the two-inch heels I'm wearing today, that put me right at Taio's shoulder.

"I thank you both," Taio says sardonically, "for making this as seamless transition as possible." He glares at his mother. "You know exactly why I didn't tell you about this. For precisely this reason. Annagret is my wife. That's the end of the discussion. You will notice that I did not ask for your commentary." He turns to me. "And this is my mother. You do not have to like her. But I must ask that you respect her."

I feel immediately chastened, and a little bit like a child, which is not a pleasant place for me to be. But I suck that up, because what matters here is that he loves her. I don't need to get in the way of that.

"My apologies," I murmur.

He and his mother exchange a few more frozen sentences—in French this time—and then she glides away, back to where she came from.

And we stand there at our pretty garden table, dressed in our wedding clothes, and stare at each other.

"I'm sorry," I say while she's gone. To him, directly. "I don't know what came over me."

"The thing about my mother," Taio says, his gaze dark as he looks back at me, "is that she is not necessarily a warm woman. If forced, I would describe her as frozen solid. I do not know if she was always this way or if she became this way. But she is my mother." He shrugs then, and looks something like helpless. "And she is the only parent I have left."

"I understand." I go with an urge and reach over, then, to take his hand. "Even now, I love my father. Even though I know that he cannot love me back in any way that's meaningful to me. He chose my stepmother and my stepsisters again and again, and I'm certain that if I gave him the opportunity he would do the same thing again. I've always considered him a weak man. I think he is one." I squeeze Taio's hand and lean in closer. "But that doesn't mean I don't love him. It just means I can't subject myself to the way he loves me."

And after a moment, that dark stare of his changes. I see the gleam of that smile in those tea-steeped depths. I feel my shoulders sink down from my ears.

"You will notice that this is a very big estate," Taio tells me, and when his mouth curves, I smile back at him. "It is very easy to go a great many days at a time without encountering my mother at all. This is how we prefer it."

"Who does she want you to marry?" I asked.

"It may surprise you to learn that she feels that the gene pool would be improved if we added more Frenchwomen to it."

"And does she therefore throw them in your path?" I try to imagine a pack of *soigné* French girls, all jutting cheekbones and slim hips, smoking their cigarettes *at* Taio. And how much he would hate it.

"She would never lower herself to do such a thing. She must always be above such petty considerations." He flips our intertwined hands over and plays with the rings he put on my finger, wiggling them this way and that. It makes me feel…*cared for,* I think. It's difficult to name when I have never experienced its like before. I don't know how to categorize it. "She makes her wishes known in other ways, but believe me, I am never in any doubt."

I think about my father, and how his body has reflected his choices over time, stooped and tired. I think about my stepmother's harsh words and insults and the grooves they've left in her once-lovely face. I think about the deep chill that Francette seems to exude with so little effort.

"I think we will have to decide, you and me, what kind of parents we will be," I say, the words spilling out of me heedlessly. "Because I promise you, I will not be cold. I will not be…like your mother. At all."

"And I assure you that I will not be weak," Taio tells me in the same fierce way, his eyes on mine. "I will never, ever choose anyone over you, Annagret. This I promise."

That electric connection we've had since the start sizzles, then. It snaps inside me, crackling with intensity. I can see it has the same effect on him.

So I go up on my toes and tilt my face back so I can look him in the eye.

"Taio," I say quietly. "What if I'm not hungry for food?"

And when he sweeps me up in his arms this time, he carries me back up the stairs and through this grand, sprawling palace of the house, taking me into a part of it I haven't seen. His part, I understand immediately.

He lays me down on yet another bed, and once again, meets me there.

And as our mouths find each other again, and our hands follow, I acknowledge that I never thought that I would get to taste him again.

It's like coming home. It's like being made new.

It's possible that I've never lived until now. That coming back to him is what makes me whole at last.

When he slides his hand up beneath my smooth white gown and finds my soft heat, I believe it.

And everything between us explodes quicker this time. We are wilder. Bolder.

We are *married* and it makes us desperate. We tear at each other's clothes. Our mouths fuse together, and it's feverish.

Even more glorious than I remember.

We are naked flame and we burn bright—again and

again—and when we are done, we lie in a panting heap, together. His hand rests upon my belly. I feel him, deep in my soul.

In every breath I take.

And I understand a deep and irrevocable truth.

I am in love with this man I married, despite my best intentions.

But this marriage is precarious, and I know better than to believe in it, because I know where I came from. And I know where I am.

I don't see how these things can ever go together.

And no matter the glory we find together in this bed or any other, I do not intend to live a lie, ever again.

Especially not with him.

CHAPTER TEN

Taio handles the upset of his mother's appearance—and our nightly experiments in vulnerability and true nakedness—by doing what men always do. He hides behind business.

Though in fairness, I would do it too, if I could.

But my business is back in New York, and I haven't yet worked out how to tell Tess about my change in circumstance, so no hiding in convenient jobs for me.

"There are matters I must attend to," he tells me each morning with what seems like stiff and strange courtesy to me.

Because every night, he loses himself in my arms. Every night, we find new ways to tear each other apart.

Every night I am more in love. Every night it's as if there is less and less that separates us. As if these different bodies we wear are entirely beside the point.

I am beginning to loathe the dawn, like some kind of emotional vampire.

Because no matter how early I wake, by the time I make it to the breakfast table, Taio has retreated once more behind his aristocratic veneer. Perfect suit. Perfectly shaved and showered. A hint of that spicy scent of his to haunt me as he sits and reads the newspaper with his bit of toast and olive oil, and his coffee black.

I eat churros and chocolate and try not to *gaze* at him too much. I want to confront him. I want to parse what his mother said and interrogate the difference in his nighttime and daytime behavior. I want to crawl in his lap and give him something to think about besides the dry financial news.

But I have never been a wife before. Much less a *marchioness*.

Maybe these *staid* and *proper* daytimes are par for the course. Maybe that's why this house has separate bedrooms for the Marquess and his wife.

Maybe these rich people aren't allowed to act as if they like getting naked with each other and this is one more obvious rule I can't figure out, coming from my lowly beginnings the way I do.

I decide to try something completely new to me as a person.

I become *accommodating*.

"Where are you again?" Tess asks me over the phone after one such breakfast. I've had hours to brood about it after Taio took himself off to his offices with a stern look and the ever-so-slightly chiding *I will see you,* cosita. *Later.* In case I am tempted to get any *ideas*. "I've never known you to stay away from New York for so long."

"I know," I say. I look around these new, separate rooms they moved me to, adjacent to Taio's. I might end up every night in his bed, but we must maintain the pretense that sleeping in my own bed *could* occur at any time. "Attending that ball really upped our profile."

"Oh, it did. We're getting more calls than we can handle."

But she laughs, because she loves a challenge, which is only one of the reasons I love her.

And I discover that I am something like ashamed to tell her the truth. Not the whole truth—since that would involve both Taio and my *wedding* and the fact that the man she thinks is our boss not only is *not,* but we have no boss either because I made him up—but the fact that I'm on something of a holiday.

Because I never take a break. I haven't had a vacation in ten years.

It's always been a point of pride. If I tell Tess I'm relaxing, she'll assume that's a cry for help and alert the local authorities.

I can't tell her that. I can't. "If you need to hire support staff, the budget can support that," I say instead.

"Finally," Tess breathes. "I've always wanted my very own minions."

The truth is, I hardly know what to do with myself. I spend the first few days as Taio's wife wafting about like a lady of leisure. A real *marchioness,* I tell myself.

I take walks through olive groves and vineyards. I try to read books in languages I only wish I spoke. I flip through European magazines. I swim in the heated pools, curl up in the cozy armchairs in a variety of salons, and gaze out the window.

By the third day, I am deeply bored.

By the seventh, I am considering building a tree fort in the olive groves with the various bits of wood I've found littered about the place, but I suspect that this is the sort of lowbrow, non-aristocratic urge that his mother is concerned about.

I wander around the absurdly gigantic house until I find my husband. He is tucked away in what I assume is his office suite—this, too, looks like it could double as a throne room with no file cabinets or copiers in sight—looking through stacks of documents.

He glances up when I enter and once again I watch his face run the gamut of expressions. First, and I don't think I flatter myself, I see pure delight. Then something more like *consternation*.

And now this, the stern gaze he reserves for me.

"I need something to do," I announce without preamble. "I'm not used to not working. I'm becoming nonfunctional."

A frown appears between his dark brows. "The role of marchioness is in and of itself a job."

"Then you will have to tell me what that job entails. Because I have done all the wafting about that I can bear, and will soon start attempting scientific experiments in the garden sheds that might or might not involve an explosion or two." I don't know how to make things blow up, but surely that's what the internet is for. I smile sweetly at him. "What *will* the neighbors say?"

"We have no neighbors in any real sense." Of course his tone is *repressive*. "There are a great many kilometers between this house and the next."

I have taken to wearing the absurd *lounging pajamas* that are set out for me, because I take immersion in a role seriously, and lean one *silken hip* against his doorjamb. "That sounds like a challenge."

"I assure you, it is not."

But if I hope that he will be the one to take me by the hand and teach me how to bear his title, I'm disappointed. He passes me off to his stone-faced *mayordomo,* who looks me up and down as if she doubts very much that I have what it takes.

"Let me guess," I say as she walks me into yet another part of the house I haven't seen before—the kitchens and, beyond them, a hall of what seems to be offices. Hers being the first and largest. "You too believe that I am a stain upon the family name."

Salma pauses as she goes to sit behind her desk and I realize she's waiting for me to sit first. When I do, she follows, and delicately clears her throat.

"You are the Marchioness of Patrias, Madam," she says in her matter-of-fact way. Her gaze meets mine, steady and knowing at once. "Save the Marquess himself, whose opinion about this family could possibly matter more than yours?"

And that introduces me to life as a grand lady of a grand house.

And I like solving mysteries. It's all about collecting and sorting through details. Deciding how to weight them, how to interpret them, and how to use them to build a picture.

Running a house like this is much the same.

Especially because the house spends part of each month being open to the public, which requires a whole different set of details to follow and keep on top of.

By the end of the second week, I can admit to myself that it would be possible to live like this after all. Because an estate like this is made up not simply of the people who own the house, but all of the great many people who work here. The land. The rentals. The tours. There are relationships with locals to maintain, regulations to follow, and an endless variety of ways to handle these things depending on the goals of different months and seasons. Is it a harvest period? Is it a heavy tourist period? Are there repairs that cannot be delayed? Is there outreach that can be undertaken with the locals to try to lower any animosity about the resources a huge house like this consumes?

No two days are ever the same and I discover I like being good at something else.

As if there's more to me than the thing I decided I'd be good at when I was eighteen and scared.

I tell my husband this later that same night when I meet him out on one of the balconies before dinner, a nightly custom I have also come to love.

"Don't tell your mother," I say as he hands me a drink, something fizzy and nonalcoholic, "but I think I will be an *excellent* marchioness."

"I would prefer that we not discuss my mother," he replies, and his face looks almost tortured as he pulls me closer, setting his mouth to mine.

I make a note to wear this particular red dress—another magical addition to my *grand lady* wardrobe—more often.

And when we finally get to our dinner, we eat it cold, wrapped up in blankets and each other before the fireplace in his room.

But the next day, after I wake naked in my husband's bed, still giddy from the things he did to me the night before, and then another stern and silent breakfast, I realize that I'm into my third week of handling *grand estate* affairs. And my fifth month of pregnancy.

I stop halfway through getting dressed—because lounging pajamas are for ladies of leisure, not competent marchionesses, as Salma did not dare say directly but I feel she *implied*—and let those facts press into me.

Particularly the latter.

My baby will be here soon. Very soon.

And there is one matter that needs to be addressed directly before that happens.

So after I dress as impeccably as possible—something that is not hard when my wardrobe expands on its own, every piece a work of art—I do not go to the little sitting room attached to these quarters that Salma indicated was the marchioness's office. I seek out his mother instead.

Francette lives in one of the newer parts of the house. Salma, who finally took me on a real tour of the entire house and all the ground, told me that the wing that once stood here burned down in the nineteen-twenties and they only rebuilt it twenty years or so ago, to modern standards.

It is kept out of the tours, the *mayordomo* told me.

Because it does not give that historical punch that the punters want? I asked. *No coats of armor and random masterpieces?*

And I swear I saw her lips curve.

There are yet more offices and storerooms here, I see now. It is not until I climb to the second floor—something that is a lot harder than it used to be with a pregnant belly—that I see more of what I expected to find if Taio's mother actually lives here. Private drawing rooms, a gloriously appointed dining room, a long gallery with the expected art displayed as if this is a museum.

I suppose, like the rest of the house, it is.

I find Francette herself sitting in a bright room that has built-in bookshelves, exquisite floral arrangements, and extraordinarily antique chairs and tables—all gilded and gleaming—that nonetheless look comfortable.

My mother-in-law sits at a delicate wood secretary, apparently attending to her correspondence like a heroine from a historical novel.

She gazes at me when I appear before her, without warning, and only lifts one silvery eyebrow. "I do not have a meeting with you in my diary."

"I'm dropping in unannounced," I tell her cheerfully. I walk into the room, find a seat on the sofa, and take my time lowering my heavy body into it. It's as comfortable as it looks. "Only to be expected with uncouth Americans like me."

Francette's expression goes wry and she inclines her head. The way her son likes to do.

"I do not wish to offend you," she tells me in her calm, lovely voice. "My son has taken great pains to inform me that I behaved badly. I forget that Americans can be so sensitive about these things. For me, you understand, it is always better to call a thing what it is."

She reminds me of my stepmother then, always managing to get in that dig—

But I stop myself. Francette Arceneaux de Luz is not the same as mean little Cayleen Alden, tucked up with her blind pets, cowed husband, and spoiled daughters in a Pennsylvania town that no one ever visits *by choice*.

For a great many reasons, not all of them involving my mother-in-law's blue-blooded hauteur and selection of everyday jewels.

There's also the most important reason. This woman in front of me will be *my* child's grandmother. My husband might find her problematic, but he loves her.

I'm not a child. I get to choose what kind of relationship I have with this woman. No one is forcing it on me and telling me that if I could only shape up and get with the program, maybe I'd be worthy of love.

Something, I vow then and there, no one will ever make *my* child feel. Not if I have anything to say about it.

"I understand completely," I say to Francette, not the ghosts inside of me. "And that's what I came here to do." She eyes me. I smile. "I want to call the thing what it is, actually." I lean in, as far as I can with my belly in the way. "But first I have a question. Do you love your son at all?"

She blinks. She pulls back, the very picture of French horror. "What kind of question is this?"

"A real one," I say quietly. "Because my baby isn't even born yet and I already know that I love it. More than that, I would protect this child with every last breath in my body, and I would never put it through the agony of a scandal I could end myself. So I ask again. Do you love Taio?"

She pulls herself up a bit taller in her seat, which should not be possible with her already ballet-straight back. I expect her to denounce me and send me away. She looks as if she's considering it.

"Because I do love him," I tell her, and I don't mean for my voice to thicken. I don't mean to sound so raw.

But I can't take it back. Maybe I don't want to. "And I cannot bear to see him sink any further beneath the weight of this."

And only then, as I gaze back at her, does she relent.

"You do not understand," she says after a moment. "The way I was raised, one never comments on the baseless imaginings of others. It gives them legitimacy, does it not? When it should be beneath notice. Beneath contempt."

"It isn't going away. And it would be one thing if it didn't bother him." I lean forward again, keeping my eyes on her. "But you must see that it does."

Francette frowns and sits back in her seat, her spine somewhat less straight. When she looks at me again, I can see Taio in her features. In that stern expression on her face.

"Amara Mariana was my friend," she says, just when I'm starting to imagine that she's going to freeze me out or send me away. She doesn't look at me. She keeps her eyes trained out the window, toward the lake, her gaze troubled. "She was my servant, so I know that in these enlightened times, people will claim we had no friendship. But we did. We were both young girls thrown into circumstances beyond our control. We both made the best of it."

I think she almost smiles then, as if remembering, but it fades before it takes hold. "I was lucky in many ways," she says. "My marriage was, at times, a heavy weight, but it was not cruel. The trouble for Amara Mariana is that she was a servant. And so, when my husband's friends came to visit, as they did often in those days, there was one companion of his in particular who took a shine to her. Too much of a shine."

Francette presses her lips together. She stays like that for a moment, then looks at me directly. "I hated him."

She shakes her head, and I do not dare do anything but hold her piercing gaze. "He was the sort to act one way when my husband was around, when other men could see how he was. But alone, when there were only women—and especially women who could not openly defy him for fear that they would be thrown out of the house—well. That was when his real face could be seen."

Again, she presses her lips tight together, and I know she's remembering that real face. "Things are very different now. Back then it was still very traditional in this house. I required my husband's permission to do most anything, and my wish did not always translate into his acquiescence." She folds her hands in her lap. Then rearranges them. "If I did not care to wait for my husband's permission, the only thing I could do was rely on what was only mine."

It seems as though she's waiting so I nod encouragingly, hoping she'll go on.

And she does. "My grandmother owns a great deal of property in France. Or I should say, she did. Some of it has been sold off. Some of it is mine. So I sent my friend to a little cottage where no one would think to look for her."

"In Cap Ferrat," I guess.

"But that was not far enough. Not for a man like my husband's friend." Francette lets out a small sound, like remembered frustration. "When he got too close, I set her up with a lawyer who had been a family friend of my grandmother's. He helped Amara Mariana to leave Europe. And I have never seen her since." Her gaze crosses back to mine once more. "So perhaps we were not the friends I thought we were, after all."

"Or," I say quietly, "perhaps you were both girls stuck in bad situations who had to make the best of what they had, and decided not to look back."

I'm startled when I see something warm in my mother-in-law's eyes. "There are many such girls."

"Indeed there are."

And as we gaze at each other in this quiet, lovely room, I think we come to a place of understanding. It feels as close to a hug as I imagine a woman like Francette ever gets.

"When that so-called diary leaked," she says after a moment, "I was incensed, of course. To imagine that I would scribble such things into a diary at all, then leave it to fall into the wrong hands… The *insult*." She presses her lips together again. "I assumed that a dignified silence would make it go away, as it should have. But it didn't. And I will tell you, since I am told you are good at finding the truth of things, that I have always supposed that this was an act of revenge by that same friend of my late husband's."

I make a noise at that. She nods, slowly. "He is precisely the sort who would wait. And look what he's accomplished. He has made me look like a bleating fool. He has thrown Amara Mariana's name all over the papers, hunting her all over again. He has even managed to question my son's legitimacy. Mark my words, it's he who is responsible for all of this."

"Do you wish you could have stopped him then?"

She lets out a bitter sort of laugh, telling exactly where Taio gets his. *"évidemment."*

I lean forward in my chair. I hold her gaze, this woman who I understand better than perhaps I should. "Then, Francette, why don't you be responsible for fixing it?"

Then I hold my breath. She stares at me in astonishment no less arrogant than her distaste.

But this time, she nods her head. "Do you know," she murmurs, a gleam in her eyes, "I believe that I will."

Later that evening, I stand out on the usual terrace before dinner, sipping on my drink as I watch Taio and his mother walk through one of the late fall gardens below. She holds his arm. He leans down slightly, giving her his full attention.

I know what she's telling him.

I see him stop.

I hear his voice on the breeze, raised—but clearly not at her.

And when they embrace, out beneath the wild Spanish sky as the sun goes down, I know exactly what I must do.

I stay where I am. I wait until he comes.

When he does, he looks like a different man, and it makes my heart glad. Or maybe it simply aches for him the way it always does, I can no longer tell.

"My mother is going to take a blood test," he tells me as he comes toward me. "She intends to settle the matter of the scandal once and for all."

He comes to me, turning me toward him from where I've been standing at the terrace rail, gazing out across this ancient land as the sun drips into orange, then gold. "Are you listening to me, Annagret? At last the cloud will be lifted from the De Luz name. The friend of my father's who perpetuated this indignity will be held to account, one way or another. You are a magic worker indeed."

Taio leans in to kiss me, and I should stop him. I know I should, but it turns out that I am perhaps as weak as my father ever was, after all.

It's a sobering thought.

And it makes my heart hurt even more.

We separate, but I put my hand on the side of his face. He lifts a hand and places it over mine.

And it would be so easy to stay like this. Just like this.

But I love him. And my staying here can only diminish him. The fact that I don't want that to be true doesn't make it any less so.

"I've been thinking a lot about your family legacy," I tell him, gazing up at that perfect face. Those etched cheekbones. That deliciously stern mouth. "I understand now, in a way I never could have before. I have no legacies. Only convenient fictions." I breathe in, hard, then make myself say it on the exhale. "And that is why I will set you free."

He looks down at me without comprehension. "Set me free? What do you mean?"

"I'll wait for the baby to be born, so there can be no confusion. No more scandals. No question, ever, about legitimacy." I take another deep breath, because this hurts. But I'm certain it's the right thing to do. "We can divorce quietly. Then you can pick the appropriate wife that you deserve. A wife who will honor this legacy and enhance it. That's what you deserve, Taio."

I expect him to react. To do…something.

But he only stares down at me as if I have grown

several extra heads, or perhaps started spouting off in a different language than the ones he speaks. He blinks, but there is no other reaction.

"This isn't a trap," I assure him, in case that's what's fueling him here. "I've so enjoyed my time here. I find this estate fascinating." *I love you,* I think inside, but I can't say it. I promised myself I wouldn't say it. "But it made me deeply aware of what's required here. And I am definitely not it."

He steps back, something like thunder gathering on his face, as if a storm has swept in. A dark and dangerous storm. "Have you taken leave of your senses?"

I blink as I look at him. Then I frown. "What kind of question is that?"

And as I watch, it's as if he...*implodes*.

As if everything is thunder, crashing and rolling.

He grips my shoulders, not tight enough to hurt, but in a firm way that calls me immediately to attention.

"What are you—" I begin. I can't breathe. "I'm setting you free, Taio. It's a *gift*."

"I don't want an appropriate wife, Annagret," he roars at me, his fingers gripping me tight, his eyes pure fire. "I want *you*. You little fool, I have only and ever wanted *you*."

CHAPTER ELEVEN

I STARE UP at him, aware that my mouth has dropped open, but it's as if he transforms before my eyes as I look at him.

At first, I think he doesn't look like himself at all.

But then I realize... It's that nothing about this man is cold now.

His eyes are *ablaze* and only getting hotter. It's as if the bones of his face have rearranged before me as I look at him, as if I'm watching as he sheds his skin.

Or a mask.

It feels as if my heart might explode inside my chest.

Maybe it already has.

"I don't understand..." I whisper.

"What I told you about finding your firm is true," he seethes at me. "But it's only part of the truth. Your picture is right there on that website for anyone to see, Annagret."

I feel his hands tighten again on my shoulders, just briefly, and then he lets go. He steps back. And I feel winded.

But it looks as if he finally feels...like himself. There's something majestic in how *alive* he seems. Nothing cold. Nothing *stern*.

Somehow it makes me think of that night in the cottage, both of us stripped so bare, and not only of our clothes.

Tonight it feels like we're standing on a cliff, waiting for a wind to come and not knowing whether it will push me back to safety or send me spiraling off into the unknown.

"I couldn't get that picture of you out of my head," he is telling me, this extraordinarily beautiful man, who must have any number of women toss themselves upon him wherever he goes. "It was something about you. Something about the way you held yourself. You know the picture I mean."

"I do." I shake my head. "I had Tess take it on a sidewalk to the tune of an entire irritated construction crew shouting at us to move. Not exactly a glamour shoot, Taio."

The picture on the website, last I checked, is nothing special. We picked the particular building because it was brick. I stood in front of it, and tried to exude *Luc Garnier* energy into the camera.

I decide not to tell him that. It's already weird.

"I found myself in New York for work. I need you to know that." That, then, is stern. Or maybe solemn. "I did not fly there for the express purpose of locating you. But I was there. And I still had you in my head. So I went to the agency, thinking that I might make an appointment, though I was worried about exposure."

He shakes his head, his eyes actually seeming to change color, and it isn't the sunset. It's that he's lost in his memories, like he's seeing it all over again. "I was standing outside. It had rained earlier that day and it was still cold and moody, even for March. You came out of a taxi at the curb and walked straight past me, then inside."

Taio focuses in on me and I've never seen a look like this on his face before. Not *soft*, not really...but open.

Vulnerable, I think.

"I find it hard to believe that I could walk past you and not see you," I tell him, not exactly surprised that my voice sounds so raw.

"I saw you move," he tells me. "I saw the way you take up space in the world. You have a specific electricity around you, Annagret. A particular heat. Like a summer storm."

I want to tell him that he must mean someone else, but I suddenly find that my knees do not wish to support me the way I would like. I go and sit in one of the chairs set back from the railing, feeling shaken straight down to my core.

Taio studies me, and I have no idea what he's looking for. "You can imagine the temperature of things around here when I was growing up."

"Chilly, I would imagine."

"A long, cold ice age, Annagret. It is all I knew."

He stays where he is, at the rail. I stay where I am, because I'm not sure I could move if I wanted to. But I know that I'm not the only one fully aware of that heat and need that blazes between us, as if any space we even dream to put between us is imaginary.

I was so sure he felt it, too, but hearing him say so feels like a revolution inside of me.

"I have never felt anything like it before," he tells me. "You were like a bright blast of sun after a cold winter and, at first, I hated it. I tried to stay away. Instead, I kept finding myself back in New York, catching glimpses of you when I could. And I knew that if anyone were to discover what I was doing it would all be ruined. Because how could anyone learn about it and not insist that I stop?" He shakes his head almost ruefully, but there is still that fire in him. "But that was when I began to think harder about the *Luc Garnier* of it all. I deliberately attempted to track him, this man in your life, or so I thought."

"You said that took years."

His dark eyes gleam. "It did."

"Taio," I manage to get out. "Do you mean to say…?"

"Yes," he says swiftly, so there can be no mistake. "It took me three years to decide that the man wasn't real, and then to plot out a course of action. I walked into your office that morning five months ago knowing full well that you weren't there. I thought Tess would be easier to get past, and I was right. So I did. Then I waited. And soon enough, there you were."

He says that almost…reverently.

"There I was." I can only repeat that. I can't process it. It doesn't make sense. None of this does. "But you… You were…"

"You were magnificent," he tells me. "You did not back down, even though both of us knew there was no such person as this boss of yours."

I think for a moment that his tone suggests that this is a good thing—for poor, fictional Luc Garnier.

But he goes on. "I was shaken. Perhaps there was some part of me that hoped that once we interacted, this madness would lose its grip upon me. But if anything, it got worse."

He moves then, something edgy seeming to inhabit him. He stalks toward me and crouches down before my chair.

"That night. You know the one. I thought that I'd fallen asleep. That I was dreaming. That you were a figment of my wildest, most fervent fantasies." He reaches out and I shiver, then melt, but all he does is tuck a stray hank of my hair behind my ear. "But in my fantasies, you do not stop. You do not stare at me through glass. In my fantasies, you come to me, put your hands on me, and we both burn and burn."

I can remember that night distinctly. It lives in me, like its own, low drumbeat.

"I wanted to," I whisper.

"And then we went to France." He traces the curve of my ear with a finger. "I thought that the masked ball would set things right. That it would be immediately clear that you were the sort to get caught up in the game of it. Who knows, maybe even find some other masked man to play with. Then again, I suppose I set myself up for disaster." He smiles. "That dress was a mistake."

"It was a beautiful dress." I can't seem to tear my gaze from his. "It made me feel like a fairy tale."

"I think that the sight of you in that dress will be burned into me forever. And to think that when I first saw you come down those stairs, I thought that nothing could be better. But then we went to my mother's cottage."

"I don't understand how she's connected to that villa. To that party."

"It is all her land. My cousin lives in that villa now."

The light dawns. "That was who you didn't want to recognize you."

"There were many people there that night that I did not wish to be known to," he agrees, that gaze still steady on me. "It is as I told you. Any indication that I take the allegations about that diary seriously is as good as announcing my own doubt in my position."

"That won't matter now. Your mother will take the test. Soon enough, no one will mention your legitimacy ever again." That reminds me of what I was trying to do before he started making all of these extraordinary comments. "And once that happens, I think you're really going to want a more appropriate—"

"Annagret," he says, his voice raw and intent, his eyes so bright they are setting me afire, "I'm in love with you. I am deeply, madly, irreversibly in love with you. You are the only thing I think of, night and day. This obsession has not waned. If anything, it has gotten worse."

But this is exactly what I most want to hear, and I can't allow it. I can't *believe* it.

"You left me in that cottage!" I burst out. "How can you say all these things and expect me to believe you when your actions point to something else entirely?"

"How could I tell you who I was?" he demands. "I could not tell anyone. I was pretending to be someone I am not. It seemed not entirely unreasonable that I should finally get to touch you while playing that role and then have to leave."

I lean forward in my chair. "I had no idea you were such a martyr."

When he speaks again his voice is something like

flat. Stripped of anything but the hardest truth. "Those were the worst months of my life."

"Taio…"

"And then, one day, as I sat in the fallout of my own choices, playing a melody on a piano that reminded me of you, there you were." That gaze of his is bright again. Wild and hot. "First I thought that I was dreaming again. And then, when I realized that you were carrying my child, I will admit it. I got greedy. Selfish. I wanted you for myself, and I was willing to do anything to make that happen."

I frown at him. "But you had to rush it, because you are terribly afraid of your own mother and what she might do—"

"To *you,* Annagret," he thunders at me. "I love my mother. I listen to her opinions about my life and my choices out of respect, and then I continue to do as I wish. My concern about her was that she would turn all of that iciness on you and I could not bear it. To extinguish your fire would be nothing short of a crime."

My pulse hurts in my veins. My heart aches as it pounds. I can feel every part of me, and it is all a *riot,* and his gaze is like light. Life.

He leans forward then, his hands moving to hold my legs as he crouches there. "Look how successful she is. Do you doubt her power? It took her two conversations to convince you that you should leave me. *For my good.* What will be next?"

"She had nothing to do with it." I belt that out, because it stings. "I've seen your life here. You might have tried to hide me away, but I can tell what it's like all the same. Running a place like this requires a head for all those details, but it also requires *you* to be the face of it. Someone steady and calm to while the years away, one generation to the next. That would be a great deal easier to do if you did not have an American wife who everyone will assume is an embarrassment without my having to do anything."

"I'm not the least bit embarrassed by my American wife," Taio tells me gruffly. "And I would very much like anyone who feels differently to take that up with me directly. I look forward to it, in fact."

"Taio." And my heart is pounding so hard again that I feel almost dizzy. It hurts. I hurt. *This hurts*. "We come from two different worlds."

"That's not the issue here, I think."

He moves back and then he pulls me up to my feet so he can hold me in his arms. Then he looks down at me, and there are no masks between us. There is only that heat. That glory.

This, I think. *Us.*

"You don't believe that anyone could love you," Taio says.

And then stands there, looking down at me with a kind of intense patience all over his beautiful face.

When what he's done is blow me to smithereens.

"…what?" I manage to get out, though my throat is tight. My chest is constricted. I feel as if I'm about to break, and that's before I can feel the wetness on my cheeks.

I do nothing to stop it. I can't seem to move.

"You're not the only one who is good at looking into other people's lives," he tells me, very quietly. Very intently. "Your father should have loved you better, Annagret. That's the beginning and the end of it."

I hear a sound, but it makes no sense. It reminds me of some kind of wounded animal, and then he's holding me closer, my face is tipped into his chest, and I realize it's me.

But it can't be me, because I don't cry, give or take a tear or two. I don't cry like *this*—hard, howling sobs.

It takes me a long while to hear the things he's murmuring, but they seem to hang in the air as he holds me. As he rocks me, slightly, side to side. As his hand smooths down over my hair.

All I can do is sob. Again and again.

"The most charitable interpretation I can come up with is that he loved your mother so much that her loss destroyed him," Taio says. Maybe he has said it before, but this time I hear it. "That doesn't excuse him. It only offers some kind of explanation. Maybe he simply gave his heart away once and couldn't again. I don't know."

Still I sob.

"Look at me."

He tilts my chin up as he looks down at me, and I watch those dark eyes of his soften. He makes a low noise and then his thumbs are brushing away the moisture beneath my eyes.

Then he kisses me. One cheek and then the other. My forehead. The tip of my nose.

I'm used to wildfires and explosions, but this soft, tender heat is new. It moves through me like warmth. Like sweetness.

It's beautiful.

"You have dedicated your entire adult life to solving

problems, answering questions, telling truths." Again his thumbs move beneath my eyes. "And there is no doubt that you are the best."

I make a snuffling sound that would embarrass me at any other point. But somehow, it doesn't now. Not with him.

"As long as I'm the best," I say. "I like that to be acknowledged."

And he smiles, this man who has been with me far longer than I imagined. Isn't it funny how his confession makes me love him more? Because it isn't a momentary lapse of reason. It isn't a flash in the pan.

When he says he loves me, I think then, he means it.

And I feel something deep inside shiver, but this time, as if it's finding its way into settling. Clicking softly into place.

"But I can't help but notice that the way you do this thing that you're so good at, the very best at," he adds, his eyes glinting, "means you must always play a part. You must always be alone. You dig around in human relationships, yet have few of your own."

"I think the same could be said for the Eighteenth Marquess of Patrias," I point out. "Long may he prosper, etcetera."

"It absolutely could be said," he agrees at once. "I have often said it. You investigated me, did you not?" Because he's smiling, I nod. "One might even call that… stalking, yes?"

And somehow, even though I feel as if I might still like to sob a bit more, I smile. Maybe because with him, I don't have to be one thing or another. I can be… whatever I am.

Whatever that looks like.

"I'm actually a licensed private investigator," I tell him loftily. "So, no. Not a stalker."

"You and I are the same," he tells me, and he is serious. I can see it all over him. "And I do not understand how this can be so, but it is. I love you, Annagret. I have been in love with you for years, though the version of you I made up in my head is a cardboard cutout in comparison to who you really are. The mother of my child. The lover of my fantasies. Everything I have ever wanted in a woman, a partner, a wife. A marchioness." He slides his hand around to cup the nape of my neck, giving me his heat. "I feel as if I tricked you into marrying me, and yet I can't even claim that I'm sorry for it."

"If it's a trick, it's a good one," I tell him, and that thing inside me clicks again, like this is the lock. Like he is the key. "I tried so hard to keep from losing myself on our wedding day. When really that was all I wanted. The way you kissed me. The way you held my hands. Taio, I love you. I have been yours from the start."

He moans a little at that, or maybe I do, and our lips touch.

And it's a kiss but it feels like magic. Like a new beginning.

Like us made fresh and new.

"Cosita," he murmurs. *"Te amo tanto. Eres mi sol, mi luna y todas mis estrellas.* You are my sun and moon and all my stars. I love you so much."

He puts his arms around me and I slide mine around his neck, and then we hold each other there, almost like we're dancing.

But the only music is the way our hearts beat for each other.

Together. As one.

"You always call me that," I say. *"Cosita.* I don't know what it means."

He shifts back, slightly, and his eyes are almost golden now, bright with luck. With hope. With us.

"Little thing," he says. "That's what it means."

"But I'm not little. I'm six feet and some consider me a Valkyrie, which does not exactly imply sweet and soft and feminine—"

Taio kisses me soundly, then smiles down at me when I sigh.

"First," he says sternly, "you are littler than me. Second, there is not one square centimeter on your entire, perfect body that is not feminine and alluring, and I know, because I have tasted every bit of you." He kisses me again, deeper this time. "And third, *cosita mia,* anyone who has ever told you that Valkyries are not attractive is weak. Foolish. And, frankly, unworthy of such a woman in the first place. Remember that."

"Bold words for a man who has been icy in the extreme all day every day," I say, my head tipped back as I look up at him. "Almost as if he's embarrassed—"

I don't realize that I'm not joking, that there is some little kernel of shame inside me, until his eyes widen at that.

"Embarrassed?"

And he laughs. For the first time in as long as I've known him, Taio de Luz throws back his beautiful head and laughs until he has to wipe at his own eyes.

Then he fixes me with a look that has everything inside me…shimmering.

"My beautiful wife," he says, laughter threaded into his voice, his smile, his eyes, "I did not wish to scare you off. If it were up to me, we would never get out of bed at all. I could not be *less* embarrassed by you, for there is not one part of you I do not love. Not one. Not ever."

And then, as if he wants to prove exactly how tiny I am to him, how feminine, how *electric,* he picks me up, carries me to the bed, and kisses me silly.

Until movement in my belly makes us stop.

We look at each other, both of us filled with wonder.

"Is that…?" he asks, hushed.

"I think it must be," I say, and as I guide his hand to my belly there's another kick.

And I know.

"Taio," I whisper his name like a prayer as he bends to kiss the little soul who kicks at him, like the baby already knows its father. "We're going to be a family."

"My only love," he replies, kissing his way up the length of my body so our eyes can shine together, and our smiles can match. "We already are."

CHAPTER TWELVE

Everything changes with love.

For the better.

This is what I tell myself at the start, and this is how I feel as the years roll by.

Taio and I go back to New York. We sit down with Tess and tell her the truth.

Part of me expects that she will storm out, call me names, and decide she wants nothing more to do with Miravakia Investigations.

What she does instead is laugh.

"I knew it," she cries. She waves her hand. "Oh, not the Luc Garnier part. That's very Remington Steele, isn't it? But I knew the two of you belonged together. It was obvious."

To my astonishment, that's the end of the matter. She takes on an even more expanded role, becoming in many ways the new Luc Garnier. She takes charge of the agency and sends out our new pool of investigators to work at her direction.

She loves every minute of it. She tells me so all the time.

As for me, I become a consultant on the really fun cases, the thorniest puzzles.

But mostly what I do is have babies.

Together, Taio and I make our own family. Our first son is born in the spring and we know that he is magic from the start. I know it before he comes into this world, because he brought me home to Taio. I know it when I watched his father hold him in his hands first as the doctors check him, and then lay him on my chest. I know it as Taio and I become parents, lying down in that bed with the baby between us so we can share his first moments together.

I know it for sure when I watch the effect his flashing eyes and melting smile have on Francette.

She does not get less icy. But I learn not to take it personally. And even if I did, it wouldn't matter, because she is the best grandmother imaginable.

Taio and I decide that there's no such thing as too much love, or too much chaos, or maybe it's simply that we're not any good at impulse control or using appropriate protection.

"We can afford to be reckless," he tells me, usually when he's deep inside me. "I mean that literally."

And he does.

But it's only after our sixth child is born, the loudest of them all and our only girl, that we hold each other as we like to do—with our newborn between us—and understand that she is the last.

"It is a shame," my beautiful husband tells me, "because the only time you are more beautiful than usual is when you are pregnant. Ripe and sweet."

Just because it feels bittersweet, we find, it doesn't make it any less the right decision, and we stick to it.

And our six children change more than just me, or

him. They bring laughter and hope to the stately old house and these ancient lands. They make Salma laugh and play games with them. They make their grandmother sing silly songs in French from her own childhood Taio claims she always told him she forgot.

She is the one who releases the results of her blood tests to the media.

In complete defiance of how she lived her life up until that moment, the Most Excellent Francette Arceneaux de Luz calls a press conference, and, in a voice dripping with aristocratic disdain, announces that she is descending to the revolting level of proving that she gave birth to her own child because she is revolted at the speculation.

"My own reputation is, I'm quite certain, impeccable," she says icily. So icily I am shocked that winter does not descend over Europe on the spot. "My son is widely known as a paragon of virtue. These things alone should be enough. But in case anyone is inclined to believe the juvenile witterings of an individual who clearly feels overwhelmed in the presence of his betters, I give you this. Indisputable proof that the Eighteenth Marquess of Patrias is exactly who he says he is. As should have been obvious from the start."

She takes no questions. She leaves no crumbs.

She is iconic, and I tell her—in time—that I want to be her when I grow up.

"Don't be silly," she says, and I think the ice has thawed by then, but she does like to pretend. "You are still an American, *mi hija.*"

I don't know when she starts calling me *daughter*. I only know I love that she does.

And over time, that certain friend of Taio's father suffers innumerable setbacks and lawsuits, until, by the time our sixth child is walking, he is of no importance or interest to anyone.

Which is only what he deserved.

But something far more beautiful comes out of that. Because once I know the full story, I redouble my efforts to find Amara Mariana. And one day I have the distinct pleasure of bringing her back to Spain, with her husband and family, so that she and her old friend can link arms in the gardens and walk together, their heads pressed close.

If I squint, I can almost see them as the girls they'd been once, clinging to each other in a sea of men's choices.

As for my own father, I reach out to him once.

I tell him that I am happy. That I have all the things I am certain my own mother would have wished for me. Love. Support.

And a beautiful family that loves me back. Six complicated, delightful, gorgeous monsters—my children who never doubt for a single moment that they are adored.

Completely and utterly and always.

I do not expect the response some months later, long after I've stopped thinking about it. Or him.

It has two things written on it.

The first, *you deserve it*.

And then, at the bottom, *I'm sorry*.

And I realize that I don't need anything more. Not from him.

Because I have everything. Almost more than my heart can bear.

But the best of these things is Taio.

And every year we take a holiday, away from the children and the estate that I take delight in running, and we go back to that little seaside cottage in Cap Ferrat.

We remind ourselves of who we are.

Thunder and light. Sweet heat.

Two hearts made one.

Every year we go back and love each other, without masks. And we stay tangled up together when the mornings come, remaining there until it's hard to remember that we could ever be anything but this.

Us.

"Read me my favorite story," he tells me on one such morning, a long way into our happy years. "The man who brought us together."

I laugh and pull out the small book, white and red, with *Pure Princess, Bartered Bride* on the cover. Above a diamond solitaire set in gold, and a cameo that encircles a couple we like to tell each other looks like us.

And I read to my love, as I always do.

"Luc Garnier did not believe in love," I read out loud into the warmth and sun of the cottage. *"Love was madness. Agony, despair, and crockery hurled against walls. Luc believed in facts. In proof. In ironclad contracts and the implacable truth of money. He had been relentless and focused all his life and as a result, wildly successful. He did not believe that this was a matter of luck or chance. Emotion played no part in it. Just—"*

And I stop, smiling at my husband the way I always do at this part. *"Just as emotion played no part in picking out his future bride."*

"Poor Luc," Taio says with a grin, as he always does. "Love will claim him all the same."

And we read the rest of the book together, until it does.

Because love doesn't require belief to be true. It only requires love.

As we are living proof.

* * * * *

If you were captivated by
Her Accidental Spanish Heir,
then be sure to check out these other passion-fueled stories from Caitlin Crews!

Forbidden Royal Vows
Greek's Christmas Heir
Greek's Enemy Bride
Carrying a Sicilian Secret
Kidnapped for His Revenge

Available now!

PREGNANT BEFORE 'I DO'

BELLA MASON

MILLS & BOON

For Felicety.

You introduced me to Sleep Token, so I don't know if this is quite enough, but for all the music, the inspo, the unending support, two books' worth of questions about Italy and years of friendship…
this one's for you!

PROLOGUE

Two months ago

BEEP...BEEP...BEEP.

The constant sound of the hospital monitor greeted Emilio De Luca as he entered his mother's bedroom. It might not be the master suite of the generations-old estate that had been passed down from *conte* to *conte*, but it still had an uninterrupted view of the vineyard-covered hills Perlano was known for.

The sound was a comfort to him. His mother lay in the large bed, machines all around her. She was quite still—sleeping, most likely. Emilio moved into the room as quietly as possible.

'Don't hover, *piccolo re*,' Valentina said in a small voice.

Emilio chuckled as he took a seat beside her bed. Though they weren't blooming locally at this time of year, a bouquet of pink oleander sat on her bedside table: her favourite flower. And, even though she was too frail to move around on her own, her make-up was applied as impeccably as ever. She was dressed in a soft warm blouse, looking as good as she could despite how ill she was. It was a small thing, but he knew that it made her still feel like herself.

'I thought you were asleep.'

His mother gave a small shake of her head. 'It's cold,' she

said, looking out of the window. A leather-bound book shut with a clasp lay beside her on the covers.

Emilio knew what she really meant. He didn't want to think about it, but the truth was that Valentina was unlikely to see the vineyards in all their glory again. No amount of hope could change winter to summer.

There was nothing he could say. Emilio De Luca was CEO of the American division of De Luca and Co, a man with so much influence and power he could control the world's elite with a word…and yet that was all so utterly useless now. It couldn't save his mother. So, instead of saying anything, he pulled up the throw from the foot of the bed, fussing until he was satisfied that she was comfortably tucked in.

'Stop fussing. I am fine.' But she wasn't. Otherwise she wouldn't have a nasal cannula to help her breathe, or a monitor attached to her index finger. She took Emilio's hand; he adjusted their hold to make sure he avoided the drip attached to her mottled skin. 'I worry about you,' his mother said.

'Me?' he asked in confusion. Emilio was the picture of health and wealth. If there was anything he wanted, he could simply buy it, regardless of cost.

Except Mamma's health.

The one thing he wanted most of all. But all the money in the world couldn't restore her.

'Yes,' Valentina continued. 'I worry about what will happen to both my sons when I'm gone. But I especially worry about you.'

'Mamma.' Again, Emilio knew what his mother was getting at, but he didn't want to talk about his brother.

'You made a mistake.'

Yes, he had—a drunken mistake, an impulsive one. Emilio had never intended to sleep with his brother's fiancée, and he had never forgiven himself for doing so. For the wound he had inflicted.

'He will forgive you one day,' his mother said. 'You can make up for it, *mio figlio*.'

I have been trying. Emilio couldn't say the words out loud but every single day he fought that impulsive side of himself. Every day he tried to be better, every decision driven by a desire to repent for the worst thing he had ever done.

His mother, in contrast, was driven by hope. And, with her condition deteriorating from one moment to the next, he couldn't bring himself to tell her the simple facts. Not only would Enzo never forgive him, Emilio didn't *want* Enzo in his life.

'I want you to know, *piccolo re*,' Valentina went on, 'that even when I'm gone, I will still be with you.'

'Mamma, please…don't.' Even though Emilio had spent the last few weeks at his mother's side, he refused to think about her death. All he wanted when he was with her was to hold onto the moment for as long as he could.

But Valentina was insistent. 'I will take care of you.'

This time Emilio had no idea what she meant. 'Don't speak like this, Mamma. You need to save your strength.'

'Nonsense.' She batted away his concern.

Despite everything, he couldn't help laughing. 'Always so stubborn.'

'Just like my boys.'

'Ah, it must be a good thing, then,' Emilio said, living for the small smile on his mother's face.

'My son, the charmer.' Valentina gave a wheezy laugh that had her wincing.

'Mamma!' Emilio scolded.

'You are hovering. Go to work. I am tired after all.'

'Okay.' He smiled and stood, placing a small kiss on her forehead. 'I will see you later. Isabella is close, and I can call your nurse in if you wish.'

'Emilio!' Valentina scolded, sounding so much like her

old self that Emilio raised his hands in surrender. 'Before you go, there is something I want to tell you.'

'It can wait until you wake, Mamma. Get some rest.'

'I love you, *mio figlio*.'

'I love you too, Mamma.'

Just as he'd thought, she was far more exhausted than she wanted him to believe. It didn't take long for her eyes to flutter closed. Even once she was clearly and peacefully asleep, Emilio couldn't bring himself to leave. He stood where he was and watched his mother sleep, the beeps of her monitor constant and predictable. The sweetest beat. A rhythm that assured him his mother was still with him. Once she had rested, he could return, and she would lovingly scold him for fussing. And then he would listen to whatever she wanted to tell him.

With one more look, paying attention to the expression on her face, the rise and fall of her chest, Emilio turned to leave the room.

It was just as his foot crossed the threshold that the constant, comforting beep turned into a long, continuous, monotonous wail—a sound that would haunt him for ever. The sound that meant his mother had gone.

CHAPTER ONE

Two months later

THE NUMBING GLIDE of alcohol was exactly what Emilio needed. He crossed his leg, ankle over knee, as he sat on a plush, scalloped couch in blue and gold. The striking vibrance of its colours dipped into near invisibility and back again as the lights overhead danced to the beat of blaring music.

The club, Boulevard, was situated on the top floor of one of New York's most expensive hotels, and was *highly* exclusive. The guest list was notoriously hard to get on, with a months-long wait even for the few who made the cut.

Emilio's name was always on it.

He took a sip from his rust-coloured drink, then placed his glass on the brushed gold table and dropped his head back against the back rest. The fragrant negroni ran a smooth hand over the knot of feelings within him he was trying to ignore. That tightness in his chest that hadn't eased in two months.

A woman had sat down next to him, uninvited, and was trying to chat. He focussed instead on the hypnotising patterns drawn by the lights and the beat pulsing through his body, letting it submerge him and drown her out. With a deep breath, he tried to let go of the stress of his day at De Luca and Co—and everything else.

The woman next to Emilio shifted. He felt it, but didn't look. She might have been beautiful: he wouldn't have known. He could hear none of her words and he didn't care to. He didn't care for anything about her. He had no intention of attracting company tonight.

He went to Boulevard so that he could drink in peace, enjoy the crush of bodies. It was a place where, unlike in his daily life, no one expected anything of him except a good time—and that was only if *he* felt like it. Often, he did. For just a night, he could indulge in his need for pleasure. There were no emotions involved. It was pure carnal release.

Emilio had no interest in the risk emotions posed. Not since Gia—his brother's fiancée. He'd let his emotions get the better of him then, and that situation had been a disaster for everyone. Sure, his feelings for her had been genuine, but in hindsight their decision to act on them had been impulsive. Emilio had been young and hadn't thought about what being with Gia would mean long-term. He could see now that even the best-case scenario would have led to family strife; his being ostracised.

Of course, that had happened anyway.

'It was a fantasy, Emilio. I deserve more. It's over.'

He hadn't been enough for Gia to choose to be with him when Enzo had left her. Emilio would never forget the words: *deserve more*. More than him, because he hadn't been enough. He would have had to give her fame and fortune. Keep her in the spotlight, as Enzo had. Maybe more than that.

Now, when Emilio thought of the future, he couldn't see himself growing old with anyone. He didn't see any possibility of having a family or a healing, nurturing love. That wasn't for him. All the evidence proved as much: Gia leaving; his father's constant rejection. There must be something about him that was inherently unlovable.

Perhaps that wasn't fair. There was one person who loved him beyond all else—*had* loved him. His heart constricted painfully at the thought of his mother. She was dead. She had trusted him so much that she had left all that was hers to him—well, apart from the vineyards. Those had always been meant to go to his brother. Now there was no one left with a shred of affection for him.

So, no, there would be no love, no relationships. Those were off the menu for him. The one-night affairs were far simpler and safer. He risked nothing. His heart was barred, and yet he didn't have to be alone either.

He picked up his glass, swirling around the alcohol, orange peel and ice as he watched the people on the dance floor. He spotted more than a handful of famous faces among the heaving bodies. He smiled inwardly at the many whose movements mimicked actions that he was certain they wished they could do elsewhere: a bedroom, maybe, if they even made it that far. This was what he needed, this surge of energy and carnality—overwhelming, drowning. This was his medication. It meant he never had to be alone with himself, with Emilio De Luca.

After all, who would want that? The only person he could think of was dead. The grief from losing his mother was choking. Boulevard was the one place he didn't have to feel it.

Still toying with his glass, Emilio pulled himself from his swirling thoughts in time to see a woman cut a path to the bar with bouncing blonde curls in a devastating, blue sequin dress that reminded him of sparkling Mediterranean waters. He couldn't fully see her face, but he couldn't look away either.

Jasmine held her head high as she made her way through the cavernous space of the glossy club. Dancing bodies thronged around her, barely a hair's breadth between them. She couldn't hear the clack of her four-inch heels on the shiny dance floor. Her height meant that her head rose above most others, making her feel as if she were floating through the tide, taken by the current towards the bar. There weren't very many seats open, but she snagged one at the end beside the black mirrored wall.

Her long legs crossed, with stiletto sandals on her feet. Her dress, short and sparkling, with thin bands tracing around her neck. Her back, entirely exposed. It was the most daring thing Jasmine had ever worn. She turned away from her reflection and called the handsome bar tender over.

'What will it be?' he asked, leaning closer to hear her better.

'A Pinot Gris, please.'

He nodded and moved away, giving Jasmine a chance to scope the crowd. There wasn't a single face she recognised—as planned—but there was one watching her, a man lounging on a scalloped couch. His arm was draped along the back rest, and in his fingers dangled a drink. As she stared, a spotlight flashed over him, giving her a proper glimpse. Perfectly cut dark hair, a little long on top. A fitted suit, his shirt button undone at the base of his throat. Neat, well put-together.

A civilised costume for a ravening beast. A flutter passed in the depths of Jasmine's belly.

She consciously replaced the flutter with a flash of annoyance and turned back to find her wine had arrived. She didn't want to feel a flutter after the way her day had gone. Jasmine reached for the glass then stopped, staring at her ring finger. Her *bare* finger.

God, this day was supposed to have gone so differently. She was supposed to be wearing a diamond ring and a sparkling wedding band. She was supposed to be here on the top floor of New York's hottest hotel *with her husband* having a celebratory drink before they left on their honeymoon. It was supposed to have been her wedding day. If everything had gone to plan, she and Richard would have danced for hours here before getting on a plane destined for the Maldives.

But none of that had happened because her fiancé had run

off with Zara, her maid of honour, just before Jasmine could walk down the aisle. Neither of them had even had the decency to tell her. Instead, they had snuck off and left a letter.

Jasmine scrunched her hand up in a fist, took a breath and let it out. It did little to quell her anger and hurt. She took a large sip of her wine instead.

How had it all gone so wrong? She'd had a plan. One she had formed as a child, watching her single mother trying to make ends meet alone and still be everything Jasmine needed in a parent. A plan she had stuck to, with hard work and determination. She'd wanted to graduate by twenty-one, make management by twenty-six, be married by thirty and have a child at thirty-five. That would have given her enough time to ensure the foundations of her life were solid before starting a family and she would have had the financial freedom to take care of her mother.

She was twenty-eight now, and had been ahead of her milestones—until today.

Today was a catastrophic failure. And now any future hopes of marriage and family had gone out of the window. By leaving her at the altar, Richard had definitively proven to her that she could not trust men, ever. No exceptions.

Her father had been the first to teach her that lesson, by walking out on her mother and her when she'd been five. Jasmine had been viciously independent and untrusting ever since. That was until Richard had come along.

'You can try to push me away but I'm always going to stand by you, Jasmine. I'm not your father.'

Words like that had thawed her heart, brought her walls down. But today he had shown her that she'd been right the first time. And as for her maid of honour, her so-called best friend... Well, Zara had just taken a sledgehammer to what little trust remained in Jasmine. And, if she couldn't trust, she couldn't have a marriage, and no marriage meant no family. She wouldn't be a single parent like her mother had been.

Suddenly Zara's teasing jokes made so much sense. *'You're so lucky to have Richard. I wish I'd found him first!'*

Or Richard's little comments. *'Promise me you'll always keep Zara around. She's good for you. We all need a Zara in our lives.'*

They hadn't been well-meaning as she had first thought. They'd been a prelude to the infidelity she was enduring now.

God, what a mess!

An unexpected buzz startled Jasmine back to the club with its pounding music and flashing lights. She reached into her bag and pulled out her phone. It was another missed call from her mother. She'd already tried several times. Even Richard had called twice. Jasmine didn't want to speak to anyone, especially not the man who had wrecked all her plans. The man who had hurt her even more than her father had.

The man who had said she was too controlling. Stifling.

Well, she'd show him.

Tonight Jasmine was out to forget. Forget about her plans, her ruined wedding, the years of careful control, the betrayal...everything.

Tonight, she was letting her hair down.

There was something about the woman at the bar that called to Emilio. That made her shine as if a spotlight had been cast only on her, despite the still-strobing lights of the club. Emilio hadn't gone out seeking company, but this woman blew straight through that. He hadn't been able to look away since she'd walked in.

She kept twirling a lock of her curly, blonde hair. Emilio's hand itched with the need to feel it for himself. He watched her drink the last of her wine and place the glass down, drawing patterns in the condensation.

He could take it no more. On impulse, he drained what was left of his negroni and walked to the bar. Standing beside her, he silently hailed the bar tender.

'A negroni for me and a wine for her.'

The barman nodded but a cleared throat made both men turn.

'Excuse me?' The woman cocked her brow. Emilio felt her appraising gaze rake over his body from head to toe and back. Normally it was the kind of look that gave him satisfaction. An indicator of exactly what was to come right after: no-strings sex. This time he felt something else, his heart hammering at the sight of her: the perfect corkscrew curls that hung below her shoulders, framing a face that took his breath away; hazel eyes that were a nearly even mix of green and brown. And that mouth… Full, pillowy lips that beckoned him closer. When she licked them, he almost fell to his knees.

Emilio had seen beautiful women before, but he'd never reacted to them quite like this.

Then she spoke, breaking his reverie. 'I'll have a martini,' she said, her eyes never leaving his.

Emilio smiled. He liked a challenge. And pleasure was always a welcome distraction.

'You know, it's a crime for a woman as beautiful as yourself to be drinking alone.'

She laughed, a vibrant and carefree sound that Emilio wanted to hear again. How long had it been since he'd had genuine laughter in his life? He couldn't think of much to be happy about lately.

'Is that the best you can do?'

'No,' Emilio replied, leaning his elbow on the bar, the picture of casual confidence. 'I just told you the truth. I don't need pick-up lines.'

'You're awfully sure of yourself,' she said with a smile

that was entirely contagious. Emilio could feel one spreading across his own face.

He shrugged in response, pleased to see her swivel on her stool to face him.

'You look familiar,' she said. 'But I'm not sure we've met.'

'You don't know who I am?' Emilio asked, quietly hopeful that she didn't and that she would still want to join him, nevertheless. Still want to choose him, even if he were just another person and not a De Luca.

Like Gia wanted?

'I can't say that I do,' she replied.

'Let's keep it that way. You can just call me Emilio.' He held out a hand.

'Jasmine,' she said, taking it.

Emilio brought her hand to his lips, placing a gentle kiss on her knuckles. 'Nice to meet you, Jasmine.'

'And you, Emilio.'

The way she said his name did something to him. Suddenly, he wanted to make this night last as long as possible. He wanted time to bask in this connection with the most beautiful woman he had ever seen. 'Would you care to join me at my table?'

CHAPTER TWO

ALL JASMINE HAD really known when she had got dressed and left her apartment was that she was determined to have a good time. At no point had she thought that 'good time' would include joining the most attractive man she had ever encountered for drinks but, now that she was faced with Emilio, she couldn't say no. Something inside her wouldn't let her. She always let her head make decisions. Logic was her guiding principle; it was how she managed to achieve her goals. But tonight a gut feeling told her that being in Emilio's company was imperative. That she couldn't pass up this opportunity.

She picked up her martini, catching the bar tender's smirk, and turned to face Emilio.

'Well, lead the way.'

He reached past her to grab his own drink. His arm lightly brushed against Jasmine's as he did so, igniting a flurry of sparks in her belly that decimated all thought in her head.

She followed Emilio to his table, surprised that it was still empty. She was almost positive she'd seen someone beside him earlier, but with so many people in the club she couldn't be sure. Really, that fact made it *more* surprising. In a club this busy, a vacated table would usually be occupied again immediately. Unless it belonged to a VIP… Who exactly was Emilio?

Jasmine was tempted to look him up discreetly on her phone, but she ignored the idea. She was meant to be taking a break from 'uptight' Jasmine. She was going to go with the flow and see where the night took her. A little bit of mystery would only make things more fun.

Emilio pulled out her chair. Her first instinct was to tell him she could do it herself, but she managed not to. Chivalry was rare in her day-to-day life. Running a successful online boutique meant Jasmine usually had to be the power in the room. When she wasn't, it was because she was meeting with other high-powered executives and investors, and she would never allow any action that could possibly have them perceive her as weak, or anything less than an equal. It was nice to let herself enjoy a chivalrous gesture for once.

She watched Emilio move round the table and pour himself into the scalloped couch. A passing strobe momentarily illuminated his dark-brown eyes, making her think of rich coffee. He leaned across and snagged the cocktail stick out of her drink. Perfect white teeth gripped onto the first of the three olives and slid it off before he deposited the stick back into her glass. His Adam's apple bobbed appealingly as he swallowed the stolen garnish.

She bit her lip. He was presumptuous. Why was this so erotic?

'So, Jasmine,' he said. 'Alone at the club?' His words pulled her attention to his lips, pink and full. Images of biting into them filled her mind, and she had to force herself to stop short of physically shaking her head to clear it enough to answer.

'What about it?' She had no intention of talking about her failed wedding with this handsome stranger. This close, she could see his hair was ever so slightly curly and her fingers itched to run through the silky strands.

'I think there's a story there,' Emilio said, leaning forward to place his elbows on the table.

'And what makes you think that I'm going to tell you what

that is?' she replied, mirroring his movements. His unmistakeable Italian accent was like music to her.

'You might find it helpful to unburden yourself to an interesting stranger.'

Jasmine could see his eyes dance with mischief, and she was certain in that moment that a man like this would never be short of company. He probably never experienced rejection.

'I think you're curious,' she said, running her finger round the brim of her glass. 'And you know what they say about curiosity.' She sipped her drink and watched his eyes darken. Everything below her waist clenched at the sight. How curious she should experience attraction like this today of all days, when she hadn't felt anything close to this in months.

Jasmine shut down that line of thinking. She wasn't going to entertain another thought about Richard, or her former best friend, except to acknowledge the lesson they'd taught her. Of course she shouldn't confide in this stranger. She could trust no one. She needed no one.

What she did need was a distraction.

'I think I have enough lives,' Emilio said.

She smiled. 'Hmm, tom cat.'

Emilio simply shrugged, no denial on his lips. For some reason, that appealed to her. Maybe it was because he was honest about what he was. There were two kinds of men: those who pretended to be a white knight, who inevitably disappointed, and those who didn't care about being a knight at all. They were cads and wore the badge proudly. Tonight, Jasmine preferred the latter. They provided honest fun with no strings attached and had no reason to feel threatened by her intelligence and control.

'You know, I'm not the only one alone here tonight,' she ventured.

'What makes you think I intended the night to end that way?'

'On the prowl, are we?'

'Not any more,' Emilio said, smirking.

'Very smooth,' Jasmine said. She crossed her legs under the table, her stiletto-clad foot brushing against his leg as she did so. It was an accident, but an exhilarating rush flooded through her.

'Likewise.'

'Not every touch equates to flirting, Emilio.'

'No, not every touch, but yours certainly do.'

'And how do you figure that?'

'I can see it in the way your breath sped up. I can see it in the flush of your skin. I can see it in the way you look at me.'

'And just how, exactly, have I been looking at you?'

'Like you're undressing me with your eyes.'

'It's dark in here; there's no way you could see all that,' Jasmine said in a half-hearted denial.

'Oh, I definitely can. But, most of all, it's in the way your body keeps trying to move closer to mine.'

It was only then that Jasmine realised just how far forward she was leaning. His face was inches from hers. 'So does yours.'

'I never denied it,' he retorted. His low voice sent goose bumps skittering across her skin.

Jasmine could barely think. Breathing his air was intoxicating. If she wanted to forget everything for a night, then meeting Emilio was the answer to her prayer. In that moment she could scarcely remember why she was even at the club. But she could remember how to be bold. 'So, what do you want to do about it?'

'I want to kiss you,' Emilio said, cupping her cheek. He ran his thumb lightly over her lips, smearing her lipstick on his skin. 'I want to kiss you until you forget where you are and what you're called. I want to kiss you until you're completely consumed by me and, then I want to kiss you some more, until you're writhing and panting and wanting.'

And that was when Jasmine threw caution to the wind. She wanted exactly what he was offering. She wasn't considering tomorrow. She wanted to forget today. 'So then, what are you waiting for?'

'The word.'

'Kiss me.'

'Those are two words. And not what I'm looking for.'

'Please.'

'There you go.'

She expected him to crush his lips to hers in violent passion, because that was exactly what stirred within her. Instead, he took her mouth in a slow, deliberate dance, allowing her to feel every brush and glide of his own. And it made her hunger for more. She wanted to be taunted and taken on a ride.

Somehow seeming to know that, he ran his tongue over her bottom lip and, when she parted them on a sigh, she expected, *wanted*, his tongue on hers, but he wouldn't give that to her. Not yet. He playfully bit at her lip, taking his time, making her want to push through the table so she could settle over him and feel this all over her body. Except the edge of the table dug uncomfortably at her middle. Jasmine didn't care. All that existed was this frustrating, intoxicating kiss, so she reached out and grabbed onto the lapels of his jacket, bringing him closer.

Give me more! she wanted to scream. Every bit of her had turned molten. She needed a release. She needed to press up against him.

'What's your name?' He breathed against her lips.

But, just as he had taunted, she couldn't respond. In utter want, she breathed his instead. 'Emilio, *please.*'

She felt his self-satisfied chuckle first, then his hand hook around her nape. That was when he finally caressed her tongue with his. She felt it everywhere, like fire cutting paths through her body and moisture collecting in her core. She squeezed her thighs together, desperate for some relief from this consuming, clawing need, and kissed him back, returning the inferno to him. The kiss morphed, becoming desperate. Urgent.

Emilio pulled away and Jasmine was about to protest. She was drunk on this kiss. It couldn't end here. But then she opened her eyes and met his darkened gaze.

'Come with me,' he said. His accent was somehow thicker in this state. 'Please.'

Still incapable of words, Jasmine just nodded and placed her hand in his.

CHAPTER THREE

Emilio was shaken by the kiss, by the power of it. He had wanted Jasmine to be the one desiring him, but he was the one hopelessly consumed. It couldn't end here. He needed more of her.

Every day Emilio fought the siren's call to be impulsive. He hated himself for that part of his nature. He'd strengthened his resolve against it. He only ever made calculated, logical decisions. Now? Afflicted with a grief he couldn't escape, and an attraction so powerful it overwhelmed him, clouding his impeccably honed judgement, he finally lost that battle. He could think of nothing but Jasmine. No woman had affected him like this.

He led her wordlessly out of the thumping, noisy club, heading to the lifts that would take them to the rest of the hotel. It was only once they left that he realised just how loud it had been inside. He had heard nothing, noticed nothing, while they'd been speaking. While they'd kissed.

'Where are we going?' Jasmine asked as they reached the lift. She was flushed and breathless. As breathless as Emilio felt. It was satisfying to know she was just as affected as he was.

'You'll see,' he said.

The doors slid open and he hit the button for the ground floor, praying no one else would stop the lift.

In the enclosed space, a haze of lust settled over them. The air was thick with it.

'Are we going to your place?' she asked.

Definitely not. Emilio didn't entertain in his home. A home was for a family, and he didn't have that—would never have that.

'It's too far,' he answered. Judging by that kiss, she was as impatient as he was. Before they could fall into another, the doors opened, letting them out on the ground floor. He took Jasmine's hand—the thought of not having any contact with her electric skin was too much to bear—and walked them to the hotel reception.

'Mr D—'

'I need a suite,' Emilio said, before the hotel receptionist could give his name away.

'Yes, sir. Overnight stay or longer?'

'Overnight is fine.'

Despite the receptionist's efficiency, it felt like an age while he typed on his keyboard. Especially when Emilio looked into Jasmine's eyes and found himself leaning towards her. It took all his willpower to tear his gaze away and thank the man behind the desk when he handed over the keycard.

As soon as they were once again ensconced in the lift, Emilio's resistance ran out. With one arm wrapped around her waist, he pulled her against his body, his entirety pulsing with need.

She kissed him, hard and full, surprising Emilio with her fervency. His back thumped against the golden wall as he pulled her with him, their mouths never parting. Every slide of their lips making them desperate, turning the kiss ever wilder. Her lips were as frantic as his. He felt the scrape of sequins against his palm as he fisted her dress, wishing he could tear it right off her; her hands were digging at his side, his chest just as desperately.

Emilio had been with many women but none quite as tall as Jasmine. In her heels she was only just shorter than him. And he loved it. Loved the fact that every part of his body pressed against her. She would be able to feel his arousal exactly where she would be craving it most. He craved her too. He was utterly lost to this maddening chemistry and only barely heard the ding of the lift.

They moved together down the corridor in a frenetic dance, lips locked. Emilio only managed to pause long enough to swipe the keycard that allowed them entry into the swanky suite. Lights flickered on as they stumbled through the door. It had barely clicked shut before lips and hands were everywhere—pushing, shoving, tearing at each other's clothes, laying a trail of fabric breadcrumbs leading to a spectacular bedroom. Emilio didn't take notice of a single detail. All that mattered was the bed.

He picked Jasmine up and laid her down gently on the soft covers. His lips trailed along her jaw, down her neck, over her chest. Taking her nipple into his mouth, he made her back arch in a gasp, but he didn't linger there, continuing his path of kisses down her body until he caught the band of her panties in his teeth.

'Emilio,' she whined.

He wanted to take his time teasing her. Wanted to drive her completely mad. But he would only be doing the same to himself, and he had very little patience left. He didn't know what it was about this woman, but she affected him like a drug. He ripped away her panties. The sound that escaped her was part-laugh, part-moan as he let the scrap of lace fall to the floor and dropped to his knees.

When he pulled her to the edge of the bed, Jasmine let out a sound of shock.

'Eyes on me,' he instructed and, holding her gaze, he lowered his mouth to the heart of her. Licking, sucking, teasing. Tormenting. And relishing every heaved breath, every moan, every nonsensical utterance. Every one of them drove his arousal higher and higher, until he was so hard it was nearly painful. But still he wouldn't let up, not when she was writhing in pleasure so pure, and he could tell she was getting close. So, he banded his arms over her hips, keeping her still, forcing her to absorb every ounce of pleasure—until she was shattering on his tongue.

And he kept going until she sunk her fingers into his hair, pulling on it. Only then did he climb over her and give her exactly what she wanted: a kiss so wild, so untamed, that it cast every thought from his head. In this moment, sharing with Jasmine her own honeyed taste and feeling her body undulating against his—*wanting* his—Emilio was nameless. He had no history and no future. He existed solely in this void where passion was soul-consuming. There was only now.

'*Belleza,*' Emilio said lowly. 'I want you.'

'I want you too,' Jasmine replied.

'But—'

'But this is just for tonight. No last names.' It was as though she'd read his mind.

'No talking about the past or future.'

'No strings.'

'Just pleasure.'

'Now take me, Emilio.'

Jasmine had never quite experienced anything like this. Emilio had given her one of the best releases of her life, but she wanted more. She was insatiable and something told her the moment they were done, she would want more yet again. *Emilio made her insatiable.*

He'd answered her plea by rolling them both, allowing Jasmine to straddle him, his back against the covers. Now her hips began to move of their own accord. 'It's my turn,' she said, feeling utterly wicked.

Emilio casually folded his arms under his head, but he didn't fool her—not with the pupils of his coffee-coloured eyes blown wide, his muscles cording from his restraint. She wanted to see that restraint snap. So she peeled his underwear away, watching as his chest rose and fell and his eyelids fluttered closed. She took a moment to admire him in his perfect nudity, to trail a finger between the valley of his abs all the way down, where the muscle arrowed towards his hardness. What an incredible specimen of a man he was. What a perfect partner she had chosen with whom to let loose for the night.

'You don't get to close your eyes,' she said as she grasped his length.

'Tentatrice.' His voice was hoarse. His breathing sped up as she lowered her head and when she took him in her mouth his groan was guttural. It all made pride swell within Jasmine. She teased him mercilessly until she felt his fingers in her hair pulling her off him.

'Belleza.' He swallowed thickly. 'You're torturing me. I need to have you.'

Jasmine wanted that too, so she let him go enough to reach for the foil packet that sat on the bedside table. He must have pulled it out of his pocket when she was too preoccupied tearing at his clothes to notice. She took the square from him, tearing it open with her teeth and rolling the latex down his length. It made him curse and, before she knew it, she was on her back and panting as his fingers ran through her slickness.

'Please, Emilio. Stop teasing me,' she begged. It hadn't escaped her just how easily he had taken control, but she decided she didn't care as long as he delivered on this taunting promise of pleasure.

He hooked her leg around his hip and slowly pushed into her, a string of curses falling from his lips, setting a storm of lightning flashing in her core. The intensity was nearly more than she could bear, and yet she chased that feeling. She wanted more.

And Emilio delivered, setting a punishing rhythm that had sweat beading on his brow. Driving them both to the edge of sanity. All rational thought annihilated. Her body existed only in this plane of pleasure.

Just as she was about to lose herself altogether, she heard Emilio curse.

'Merda!'

Everything came to a grinding halt.

'What's wrong?' she asked. She was barely able to think. All she wanted was for Emilio to resume, to continue driving them to euphoric heights.

'The condom broke.'

'It's fine. Just don't stop!' she begged, thinking of the release that waited just out of reach. Her hips bucked, trying to gain any bit of friction she could find. 'Please!'

'Jasmine…' Emilio panted. She could feel the tremble in his body.

'I'm on birth control. Please, Emilio. Please don't stop!' They both needed this. *'Please.'*

And he finally listened, picking up right where they'd left off. Their moans were a melody floating in the air. Their bodies provided the rhythm.

Jasmine wrapped her arms around his neck, wanting to get even closer. Higher. She wanted everything. And that was when she felt every thread in her body grow taut, then snap free in a violent release that erased all sound and sight. But she still felt Emilio. Felt the pulse of his release, the tensing of his body. And the very first thing that penetrated the deafening haze of pleasure was the sound of him growling her name.

Jasmine had always enjoyed sex, but she had never felt anything like this—such utter intensity. Her whole body was sensitized and yet she was completely limp. Spent. Her eyelids were already growing heavy. She heard Emilio murmur her name again, but he so sounded far away…

The first thing Jasmine became aware of as she stirred awake was a warm weight against her back. The unfamiliar room around her was nearly black, the only light filtering through cracks around the doors. She blinked away the cobwebs of sleep and realised she was in a hotel room. One she had slept in...with a stranger.

Her heart began to race. What the hell had she done? Memories of the intoxicating passion from the night before came rushing back. She turned to look at the man soundly asleep on the pillows beside hers. Emilio. No last name. Sleep did nothing to dull his beauty or bring any relief from her attraction to him, but he was still a stranger. She never lost control of herself like she had last night.

With as much care as she could muster, limbs still loose with sleep, she climbed out of bed and began her search for her clothes. She didn't take her eyes off the man in between the sheets, even as she was shoving her legs into her recovered panties.

It's fine, she thought to herself. *We're consenting adults. We needed a release.* But rational thought did nothing to ease the butterflies in her belly when she looked at him, nor the anxiety from having acted so out of character. With one last look at him, she quietly crept out of the bedroom, locating her garments in a trail that led to the entrance of the suite. Once her second stiletto was on her foot, she slowly opened the door and softly closed it behind her.

It was still dark outside. And maybe this encounter could remain there, in that darkness. There need be no guilt for leaving so quietly, because Emilio had wanted this to be a night without strings as much as she had.

No past, no future, Jasmine reminded herself as she made her way to the bank of lifts and hit the down arrow. *We went out looking for fun and we found it. But now we put this night behind us and move on.*

And, as if the lift had heard her, the doors slid open to carry her away.

CHAPTER FOUR

Two months later

A SLIDESHOW OF models in various garments travelled across Jasmine's computer screen as she sat at her desk in a glass-walled office in Style on Point's loft-style workspace in Manhattan. She was supposed to be looking through the proofs the art department had sent her for their upcoming season catalogue, but she couldn't concentrate. Not when she was ravenous and exhausted. And when every dark, curly haired model made her think of the man she had met two months ago in a hectic club, who had taken her breath away with hours of toe-curling pleasure.

Pleasure so vivid that even its ghost—the memory of his touch, of his breath on her neck—had her squeezing her thighs together to relieve the ache of want. The same ache that had haunted her since she'd left the hotel.

She hadn't even looked back as her cab had driven away that morning. It had been a moment to let her hair down, and then it became the past. But her memory of that night stubbornly refused to fade.

Damn it, Jasmine. Concentrate!

She pushed thoughts of Emilio to the back of her mind. She had to be focussed for her meeting—not something she usually needed to berate herself to achieve. Ever since high school, she'd kept careful control over every aspect of her life; it was necessary to attain the strict goals she'd designed for herself.

She'd never faltered before, winning a scholarship to college and coming up with the idea for Style On Point—'SOP'—before she'd even graduated. From there she'd climbed the corporate ladder, all the while saving the start-up capital and attracting investors for her passion project, until she'd been able to take the plunge and launch the boutique. Despite being such a young company, it had already seen exponential growth: she'd had numerous purchase offers from bigger conglomerates, but she'd turned them all down, and would keep doing so. Jasmine had started SOP with Zara, but after the wedding debacle Jasmine had bought her 'best friend' out and forced her to leave. There was no way she would trust her life's work to someone who had already betrayed her. SOP was *hers* and she was determined to see it grow into a powerhouse in the industry.

If something arbitrary wasn't causing her to remember a specimen of a man she should forget, there was a bone crushing exhaustion ever present to distract her. It didn't help that her breakfast had ended up in her bin that morning after she'd discovered her yoghurt had spoiled.

Still, she needed to push through. Her goals wouldn't achieve themselves. In the last two months, they'd undergone some re-alignment. Jasmine was no longer looking to get married, or raise a family. Her sole focus would be on SOP. All the time she had once wasted with Richard and Zara would now be poured into the only thing that mattered: her work.

A knock on her open office door had her looking up.

'Ten-minute warning, Jasmine,' her PA said.

'Thanks, Jenna. Take these files to the meeting room. I'll be right there.'

Jenna was looking closely at her. 'You look exhausted. I can reschedule?'

'That won't be necessary. Close the door on your way out, please.'

Jenna nodded and did as she was told. As soon as she was out of sight, Jasmine pressed her fingers to her eyes. One more meeting—a meeting with her buyers about stocking a young, up-and-coming designer that Jasmine had been looking forward to for weeks.

Everyone had already gathered when Jasmine entered and sat at the head of the table in the biggest conference room on the floor. She called the meeting to order and tried to listen to the input of everyone around her. Her head was pounding.

'The samples Paris Elham sent over are amazing,' one of her buyers was saying. 'The quality is great.'

'What about the fit?' Jasmine said. 'People trust us to provide clothing that's inclusive. It's not enough that the quality is good. She needs to fall in line with our ethos as a company.'

'Well, she did send samples in several sizes, plus we asked her to send over pictures of them on variously proportioned models.'

'And do we have those pictures yet?' Jasmine asked, twirling her engraved Montblanc pen in her hand. It had been a gift from her mother after SOP celebrated its first birthday. Jasmine knew it would have taken months of saving for her mother to afford it and it was always close at hand.

'We do.' The Head of Buying pressed a button on a remote and a new slide appeared on the screen, showcasing the dress.

'It looks good,' Jasmine said.

'It looks *great*, Jasmine!' the woman presenting said. 'I would love something like that when I'm bloated.'

'Yes!' another buyer agreed. 'That time of the month is the worst.'

At the words, Jasmine felt the breath leave her lungs. She

picked up her phone and opened her cycle-tracking app. There were no entries for this month. Nor were there any for the previous month. Jasmine's heart began to race. Her mouth had gone dry.

She'd been so busy that she hadn't noticed her missed periods. She had thought nothing of her skipped breakfast, the yoghurt she'd tossed out that morning. Because it was spoiled. But she'd only thought so because the scent of it had had her gagging. Just as the scent of her favourite shower gel had suddenly started turning her stomach. After the wedding debacle, she had thrown herself into her work and thought of little else. She ate, slept and breathed SOP—that had been the only possible explanation for her exhaustion.

'The designs look good,' she heard herself say through a constricted throat. 'I'm happy to sign off on this. Jenna, finish up here.' Then she was out the door without another word, working to keep her breathing even as she half-walked, half-ran to her office and shut the door. She couldn't panic in front of her employees.

Keep it together, Jasmine, she told herself as she lowered the blinds on the glass panels of her office, her hand shaking round the remote. She dropped it and her phone with a thud onto the stack of papers on her desk.

'This can't be happening!' she whispered to herself, pacing the length of her office. She couldn't be pregnant. She hadn't had sex in five months...apart from that one night when she had been vulnerable and letting her hair down. Trying to escape being her for a night. And she had...with Emilio.

I can't be pregnant with the child of a man whose first name is the only thing I know about him! I just can't!

What happened that night?

Her pacing became more frantic.

We used a condom. Yes, it broke, and yes I asked him to continue. But I was on the pill!

She grabbed her phone—the one tool she had to rely on in an emergency—off the table and opened her health app, scrolling back to the night in question and all the days of the week leading up to it. She had been religious about recording everything she did. Just as she had thought, she hadn't made any mistakes with her birth control.

God, how can this be happening? One time! I let go one time and it comes back to bite me in the ass!

She was very nearly hyperventilating. 'Think, Jasmine!' she said out loud, and took a deep breath, then another. And another, until the haze clouding her judgement lifted enough for her to get control.

Okay. I don't know that I'm pregnant yet. Either way, I need to see a doctor.

For the first time in an age, Jasmine called to make her own appointment. Jenna didn't need to do this for her. No one needed to know anything yet.

CHAPTER FIVE

DOCTOR BASU'S OFFICE had remained unchanged for all the years that Jasmine had been going there. As a child, she'd appreciated the doctor's maternal warmth; as an adult, she respected her no-nonsense approach. Now Jasmine sat opposite her, the air thick with tension.

The doctor was the first to break the stilted silence. 'From your silence, I take it this is a surprise.'

Pregnant.

Every thought in Jasmine's head had been wiped clean by that one word.

'We need to establish how far along you are.'

'I know when it happened,' Jasmine said, her throat dry. She opened her app and showed the doctor the date. While she had been taking a break from her usual self-control the night she'd slept with Emilio, she had been back to normal the next morning and had recorded the encounter, keeping track like she did with everything in her life. It was proof that things only worked out when she had control. There would be no letting her hair down again.

'Based on that, we should be doing your ten-week ultrasound,' Dr Basu said. 'And you need to stop your birth control immediately.'

The thought of her birth control nearly had Jasmine in tears. 'I don't understand why it failed.'

The doctor frowned. 'Were you on any medications leading up to that night?'

'No, nothing.'

'Any natural supplements—any at all?'

'No. I didn't— Wait…' Jasmine paled, thinking back to the weeks before the wedding. How stressed she'd been. She had arranged everything. Richard hadn't helped at all.

'Relax,' he'd said. *'It's not that important. We can get married in the court house, for all it matters.'*

'My mother gave me St John's Wort tea to help with my anxiety about the wedding. Do you think that's what caused it?'

'That could explain it,' Dr Basu said sympathetically. 'I'm going to write you a prescription for some supplements you need to take and two referrals: one for your ultrasound and the other for a great OB/GYN.'

'Can I get the ultrasound done today?'

'Yes, I'll call ahead for you.' Dr Basu reached over the desk and took Jasmine's hand. 'It will be fine, Jasmine. If you need anything, you call me.'

Jasmine was about to say that she would, but then she remembered Zara—the best friend to whom she had been so much closer than Dr Basu. A person she had trusted implicitly. A person who had betrayed and humiliated her.

No matter how much Jasmine liked the good doctor, she was determined not to need anything at all.

'Thank you.'

She left the doctor's office and went to her car in the car park. Too quick for her driver to get to the door, she let herself into the back seat and pulled out her phone.

That night Emilio had asked if Jasmine knew him. At the club, his seat hadn't been touched, and even getting a suite had been no problem. He had to be someone of importance. She opened up her browser and typed 'Emilio'. Her finger hovered over the search button. How many Emilios must there be in the world? Thinking, she added 'New York' and 'Boulevard' next to his name—all that she knew about him—and hit enter.

Hundreds of hits landed.

And yet, when she opened the images tab, she immediately saw him. Neat, curly brown hair. Sharply tailored suits. Paparazzi pictures of him dressed a little more casually. Those coffee-coloured eyes. There was no mistaking him.

Jasmine cursed under her breath. He wasn't just a VIP. He was Emilio De Luca.

Emilio sat behind his desk. He'd just ended yet another virtual conference call, and had only a handful of minutes before the next one. Some days were just like that. It was one meeting after another until late into the evening. And to recover, he wouldn't go home to rest; he would go to Boulevard. A tired mind had the tendency to wander, and Emilio didn't want to be alone with his thoughts at the best of times.

And yet, once he got there, he couldn't bring himself to seek out company for the night. He hadn't for two months. Not since he had been with a tall, curly haired beauty. Just as he was about to call for Rachel, his PA—and a strong espresso—the door swung open and in she walked, holding a large manilla envelope.

'Sorry to disturb, Emilio,' she said. 'A messenger dropped this off you.'

'Did they say what it was?'

His PA shook her head. 'No. Just that it was urgent.'

'Thank you, Rachel.'

He watched her close the door before he opened it. When he pulled out the document, he stopped breathing.

The last will and testament of Valentina Adriana De Luca.

Just like that, the pressure in his chest that had slowly

been easing over the past four weeks was back, like boulder making it hard to breathe. The will had been read months ago. Why was he receiving a copy now? He was already in the process of receiving everything that had belonged to his mother—everything apart from the vineyards, that was, because his father had ensured that even in death his mother obeyed him and left *those* to Enzo. His heir, the favoured son. But Emilio didn't want to think about his father. It would only leave him bitter and facing all that was wrong with him. All that wasn't worthy.

He shook out the envelope in the hope there would be something to ease his confusion. A handwritten note fell out. He picked it up, a lump forming in his throat. He would recognise his mother's handwriting anywhere. He read the note written in Italian and had to force himself to remain calm. To keep the grief that was back in full force from dragging him under.

'I will always take care of you.'

Emilio remembered that last day when he'd sat by her bedside and tucked her in before she'd died. He would never forget it. He still had nightmares about it. The moment he'd lost the only person who had ever loved him. He remembered her saying those same words. She had wanted to say something else to him then, but he'd stopped her, and she'd never said another word again.

Was it about this? With a lump in his throat and his chest cracking open, Emilio turned the page and began reading the document. His eyes skimmed each line. So far, it was exactly the same...

Until it wasn't. There was a difference—a monumental difference. All breath left Emilio and he slowly sank into his seat.

The vineyards had been left to *him*. Not just the ones in Perlano that had been passed down for centuries, but also the ones in the other family estate in Piemonte: Vozzano. Vozzano had been started by his great grandfather at a time when Calabrians had been leaving the area in great numbers. It hadn't mattered that the people of Perlano had ultimately been happy and had chosen to remain; the acquisition of Vozzano had been an opportunity to expand the *conte's* portfolio to the north, ensuring the family wealth would increase in a time of uncertainty. And so another wine estate had been added, one which created some of the finest grappa in the world.

'Mamma...' he whispered in the dead quiet of his office.

He stared at the line, reading and re-reading it, as if by magic it would suddenly change. He wasn't sure how long he had been looking at the will, but the faraway sound of a phone ringing made him realise that he was short on time. He had another meeting in minutes, but he would never be able to focus on it. Not after the bombshell that had been dropped into his hands.

He picked up his office phone. 'Rachel, move my meeting.' He hung up without waiting for her to confirm the instruction. He must have sounded robotic, but right now his body was on autopilot. His mind was stuck on what his mother had left him.

He picked the envelope back up, looking for the return address. He recognised the law firm. It wasn't the one that handled all the business of the De Luca family but the firm that his mother had used for her own affairs. He had to call them. Two wills, two different sets of lawyers... Before he went any further, Emilio needed to know this wasn't some sort of cruel joke.

It would be pretty late in the afternoon in Italy, but this was urgent, and he needed answers. Luckily for him, his mother's lawyer had never turned away his call.

'I wondered when I would hear from you, Emilio,' he said by way of greeting.

'Is this will real?' Emilio asked, cutting to the chase.

'Yes. Your mother instructed us to wait four months before sending it to you.'

'Why?' It surprised Emilio how steady he sounded when his throat had gone dry and his heart wouldn't stop pounding in his chest. His mother was dead and buried but the arrival of this will made it feel as if, through some sort of miracle, his mother would appear. As if she was suddenly back in the room with him.

'She said she had her reasons,' the lawyer answered. 'Listen, Emilio, we have a little bit of time but not much. Probate must happen within the year, so we need to move quickly.'

'I hear you. I will be in touch.' Emilio ended the call, tossed his phone onto a stack of papers and ran his fingers through his hair.

The vineyards. They had meant everything to his mother. As a young boy in Perlano, Emilio would beg his tutors for a break just so he could run down to the vineyards and help her tend to the grapes, despite the legions of workers they had. Emilio was certain he'd been more of a hindrance than a help, but his mother would smile down at him and praise his hard work.

An ache formed in his chest, so intense that it had him gasping for air. He missed her gentle yet fierce love for him, for the vineyards. Everyone knew just how much she had loved them. Just as everyone knew that their father's condition in giving them to her was that upon her death they would go to Enzo, so the *conte*'s estate would be whole once more, as it was meant to have been through centuries of tradition. Legacy.

Those grapes were precious—not just to the family but to his mother. Of course Emilio wanted them. He wanted to hold onto any part of his mother he could. And the fact that his mother had chosen him over Enzo to trust with something so precious…

A smile formed on his face. It was a balm over the shattered, scarred parts of his soul from his father's rejection and his brother's indifference. His brother, who would be expecting to have the business with the vineyards settled soon. Emilio ought to call him, let him know of this development. But, even as his thumb hovered over his brother's contact in his phone, he stopped himself.

He and Enzo did not call each other. They didn't speak of anything private. They barely talked at all. Work was the only reason they kept in contact and even that was seldom. They avoided each other as much as they could help it. The only option he had was to go through the family lawyers.

And that wouldn't be the smart play. The moment that Enzo knew, he would do everything in his power to stop Emilio from having what was, it now turned out, rightfully his.

Emilio wouldn't tell anybody yet. He would go to Italy, visit Perlano and Vozzano and see for himself what the state of things was. He'd get all the information he could gather. Once he let the family lawyers know about the new will, there would be all-out war, of this he was certain. But he wasn't going to run from it. He was just going to be smart about it. He loved his mother, more than Enzo ever had, and he was going to fight for the thing that had been closest to her heart.

He was so engrossed in poring over the rest of the document that he almost didn't register the office door opening again. But he snapped his attention back to the present to find Rachel standing on the threshold, hand still on the door handle.

'Apologies for interrupting, Emilio,' she said, 'But there's a woman here who insists on seeing you urgently.'

'Who is it?' Emilio couldn't think of a single person who would urgently need to see him right now. He could barely think about anything when his mother's will was still clutched in his hand. The door opened further, unveiling the last person he expected to see.

'Jasmine,' the woman said, walking in with confident strides.

Emilio hadn't been able to stop thinking about her, about their night when they'd met at Boulevard. He still remembered his utter disappointment when he'd woken up and found that she had left. Gone without so much as a, 'That was fun.' He didn't usually feel that way about his casual hook-ups, and part of him had wanted to look for her. New York was a big city, but it wouldn't have been hard for Emilio De Luca to pull some strings...

Except, *she* had left. Snuck away while he slept. He'd taken it as a sign that she'd truly wanted the passion they'd shared to last for one night only. He could understand that. It was what he'd wanted too. But he'd been less sure ever since.

Something about Jasmine had messed with his sensibilities. Memories of her had haunted him. The feel of her skin. Her taste. It was all imprinted in his mind. He remembered every little thing about her. The softness of her curls. The touch of gold in her eyes.

The document in Emilio's hand slipped to the desk as he stood and went round the desk. The woman in front of him now looked the same, and yet completely different from the one he'd known so intimately.

The night they'd met, Jasmine's golden curls had hung low on her back; now they were pulled back, mercilessly pinned. Not a strand out of place. Then she had worn a daring dress he couldn't take his eyes off; now she was in a charcoal power suit, ruthlessly tailored to fit her body perfectly. The strappy heels that had made her long legs even more tempting had been replaced with shiny pumps, the leg of her trousers falling at the perfect height for her shoe.

The Jasmine he had met had been fun. A free spirit. This woman was tightly controlled. She'd paid attention to every minute detail. If it weren't for the blood rushing to his groin, or the way his heart sped at the very sight of her, Emilio would have sworn this must be a twin.

'I have *asked* her to make an appointment.'

'It's alright, Rachel,' Emilio replied, not looking at his PA at all. Despite the maelstrom of hope, grief, longing and fierce determination brought on by the arrival of the will, Emilio was still glad to see Jasmine. But that didn't mean he wasn't suspicious of her sudden appearance. Even as the sight of her took his breath away, unease crept in his belly. For two months he'd heard nothing from her, so why now?

'Have a seat,' he said, pointing to the chair in front of him.

'Thank you,' she replied, every bit as elegant as he remembered.

Emilio didn't say anything in response. He simply watched her, his head cocked to the side, studying every movement of her body. The way she crossed her legs and set her clasped hands on her knee. There was a twitch in her arms that told him she would have preferred to cross them against her chest.

'I don't know how to say this,' she said at last, 'So I'm just going to come out with it. I'm pregnant and you're the father.'

That unease in his stomach turned into a stone. He watched, nearly paralysed, as Jasmine placed a sonogram picture on his desk. He looked at it as if it were a venomous snake poised to attack. There was no way this was happening. Not today.

'Mine?' he heard himself say. 'I hardly think so.'

'It's yours, Emilio.'

'Am I just to take your word for it? A woman I knew for a few brief hours? You'll have to do better than that.' The shock was making him antagonistic, but he couldn't help it. He couldn't control it, which only further frustrated him.

'I'm not the type to sleep around,' Jasmine said. The huskiness in her voice turned into a near growl. Anger flared in her eyes.

'And yet is that not exactly how we met?'

'Look, I don't care what you think of me, but I haven't been with anyone other than you in nearly five months.'

Idiota.

Emilio had white-hot anger pouring through his veins—anger at himself, for yet again failing to control his impulsiveness. This was *exactly* like him. He had been impulsive with Gia and he had been impulsive with Jasmine. He hadn't even gone out seeking company that night, but he'd seen her and lost all sense.

Enzo's voice rang in Emilio's head, the anger in it barely contained. *'I fixed this mess, but know that, you and I? We're done. You never think, Emilio. Not about anyone, and I'm sure not even about yourself. You can't ever see further than the nose on your face. And one day your impetuousness is going to cost you, and it's going to cost this family.'*

Yes, he was guilty of messing things up, but not this time. He wouldn't let that happen again. He took one look at the will still sitting on his desk and realised he needed to compartmentalise. This truly couldn't have happened at a worse time. The first thing he needed to do was protect the legacy.

What if Jasmine was attempting to run some sort of scam on him? He didn't know her. She could have faked the sonogram picture. He picked it up regardless, remembering his PA putting up her sonogram picture next to her computer. After years of trying, she'd been so excited and anxious about it that he had told her to take two days off. She hadn't realised he hadn't counted them as leave until she'd seen her pay slip. He remembered a lot from Rachel's journey, and a quick mental calculation in his head gave him a rough idea of how far along Jasmine must be…if she wasn't lying.

'So you're telling me that you're about ten weeks' pregnant with my child,' Emilio said emotionlessly. He was going to come at this as he did with all his business dealings—with cold logic. 'That means we should be able to do a paternity test immediately.'

Jasmine exploded. 'I'm sorry, what?'

'You didn't think I would just take your word for it, did you? I don't know you and, more importantly, I don't trust you.'

'You seemed to know me, to trust me, enough to take me to a hotel room.' A vein had begun to throb in Jasmine's temple. That was fine. She could be angry if she wanted to be. Emilio had too much to protect to worry about manners right now.

'Yes, and as I recall we both took great pleasure from that.'

'I didn't say otherwise. I'm merely pointing out that you claim you can know and trust me perfectly fine to have sex with me, but not enough to believe me when I come to you bearing the consequences.'

'Good. You understand.'

Jasmine's face flamed red. Her eyes looked more green than usual in her anger. Emilio didn't take pleasure in this, but he never went into a negotiation blind or emotional. That was why he always came out on top.

Yes, the possibility existed that the baby was his. If it was, he would take care of it then. Step one was to determine whether Jasmine was lying. He lifted the receiver of his office phone and hit the direct extension for his PA. 'Rachel, I want Dr Silver in my office asap.'

'Yes, Emilio.'

'You would task your PA with something as sensitive as this?' Jasmine questioned with a cocked brow.

'My employees are fairly compensated to ensure their compliance and discretion, I assure you. You will wait here for Dr Silver to arrive. He will draw blood for the paternity test.' It was an instruction, and Emilio wouldn't budge.

'Who the hell do you think you are to order me around? I don't work for you, Emilio. You can't instruct someone to perform invasive tests on me without first securing my consent.'

'True. And if you fight this,' he said calmly, 'I will know you're lying and this supposed child is either not mine or non-existent.'

'How dare you?' Jasmine demanded, enraged.

'I dare because I don't know you. I haven't seen you or heard from you in two months and now here you are with this grand announcement, no doubt after finding out my name.'

'I don't want anything from you,' Jasmine said through gritted teeth.

'Then why are you here?'

Jasmine dropped her head, letting out a humourless huff. 'Why am I here?' she said softly, as if to herself. Then she looked him in the eye. Her expression was defiant; she was utterly unfazed by who he was. 'I don't know. I guess because I thought it was the right thing to do. I don't need anyone, or trust anyone. Certainly not a *man*. I'm fine doing this on my own.'

Certainly not a man? What was that about?

'I came here to inform you,' Jasmine said, slinging her handbag over her shoulder. 'And now I have.'

She rose from her seat. Just as she did, the office door opened and in walked a middle-aged man in khakis carrying a black medical bag.

'Dr Silver from our in-house health care; Jasmine...?'

'Hall,' she finished for him.

Jasmine Hall. The siren finally had a name. Despite how much he had wanted to look her up, he hadn't, and he couldn't name the feeling that was settling over him as the knowledge sunk in.

'Well?' he said. 'Are you staying or are you leaving? It's entirely up to you how this goes. If you're not lying, what have you got to lose—a vial of blood? But, if you leave, I'll have no choice but to assume—'

'I'm *not* lying, Emilio.' She turned to face him. 'You know what?' She dropped her bag on the seat, shuffled out of her jacket and folded up the sleeve of her blouse. 'Do it.'

Emilio watched the procedure. Jasmine wasn't nearly as acrimonious with the good doctor as she was with him. Once the vial was filled, Dr Silver placed a sticker on the bottle and asked Emilio to take a seat, then he removed a long swab from a sterile tube.

'Open.'

Emilio obeyed the doctor's instruction and felt the textured tip rub along the inside of his cheek.

'The results will be ready tomorrow,' Dr Silver said, placing the buccal swab back in its tube.

Emilio pointedly cleared his throat.

'Tonight,' the doctor amended.

'That's better.'

The doctor quickly collected his things and left the office. There was nothing left to do now but wait. Yet, Emilio didn't have the time to sit around waiting for results that could change his entire life. He desperately wanted to get back to the will, but he didn't want to let Jasmine out of his sight.

And it wasn't just because he didn't trust her. That tugging connection between them was still there, and Emilio had to be honest with himself. He didn't want her to leave for the very same reason that he had wanted to seek her out that morning two months ago when he'd awoken alone.

'You will wait here where I can keep an eye on you for the results,' Emilio said.

The gall of this man! He was the most overbearing, high-handed ass Jasmine had ever met. Comparing him to the man from the club was like comparing Jekyll with Hyde.

'I really don't care what you want, Emilio. I have already made one concession for you.' True, they hardly knew each other, so demanding a paternity test was sensible...*in theory*. But the way he had gone about it had made her want to explode. She couldn't be with him another minute, or she would likely strangle him. She pulled out a business card from her bag and slammed it down on his desk. Infuriatingly, even that hardly seemed to move him. 'I have a business to run, so I will not be catering to your whims.'

She'd already been through that with Richard. A man who had wanted to control her. Who'd been threatened by her. So much time had been wasted trying to appease him. She wasn't out to make herself palatable to anyone any longer.

She shrugged her jacket back on and marched to the door, pausing just long enough with a hand on the door handle to fire over her shoulder, 'You can find me there when you're ready to stop being an ass. I came here to tell you that we bear a consequence from that night, and I have accomplished that. Goodbye.'

She slammed the door behind her before he even had a chance to respond. She wasn't interested in anything he had to say. Not until he received those results proving her right.

CHAPTER SIX

It was dark outside, New York lit up like shining jewels on black velvet. The streets snaking along in golds and silvers. Inside, the light over Rachel's desk had long been switched off; what little leaked from Emilio's office cast dim shadows.

He was the only one still working on the floor. Not working. No. More like rueing.

Emilio sat with the paternity test result. There was no doubt. He was the baby's father.

'Cazzo,' he swore under his breath.

'One day your impetuousness is going to cost you, and it's going to cost this family.'

Enzo's words haunted him. He wondered if his brother would celebrate being right. They were all that was left of the De Luca line and they could barely tolerate each other. The legacy had already been in jeopardy for many years: Enzo would never attempt to marry again because of the mark Emilio had left on him by sleeping with his fiancée. By Emilio's betrayal. That much was obvious. Emilio himself had no intention of subjecting himself to a path that could only end in rejection and regret.

But now there was an heir—his child, not Enzo's.

His child.

The word terrified and—to his great surprise—excited him in equal measure. That was ridiculous. He didn't want children or family.

Didn't want, or resigned yourself to not having?

Emilio pushed away from his desk and went to stand at the window, unwilling to go down that path. Excited or not, a child born of a one-night stand with a woman he'd picked up at a club would be a scandal he couldn't afford. A scandal that was entirely his fault. For being impulsive, yet again.

Impulsive, yes, but he was not, had never been, irresponsible. He wouldn't be the CEO of one of the most respected financial companies in America if he were.

Emilio had taken responsibility for his actions in the past. He had worked so hard to control that impulsivity in him. He'd made drastic changes to his life because he could never allow himself to forget the damage he could do if he let that side of him out. Enzo's hatred of him would always stand as the proof of that damage. Emilio had used it, used his mistake with Gia, as motivation to act responsibly for the company—to ensure he always took the best decisions for his employees, the legacy and the family.

He would do the same now. He turned around, picked up the manilla folder on the corner of his desk and opened it to view a fact file on Jasmine. As soon as she had left the building, he had called one of his fixers, asking for everything they could find on her. They hadn't disappointed.

Pacing his office, Emilio read through it: excellent schooling; an impressive scholarship; ownership of a thriving start-up. Its year-on-year growth surprised even Emilio. She was intelligent—but that had been evident from the moment he'd met her, even if they hadn't been much interested in each other's intellects at the time. He skimmed the section on her personal life. She had been raised by a single mother, no father in the picture and…

The next line gave him pause.

There had been an engagement announcement, but the marriage hadn't happened yet. When he saw the date set for the wedding, he cursed yet again. Well, that would explain why she had been drinking alone that night at the club.

He had seen enough. He tossed the file on his desk, picked up the results and left his office. He knew exactly what he needed to do and how to propose it.

'Wait here,' Emilio instructed his driver as he exited his Maybach. It had been a short drive from the financial district to downtown Manhattan. Now he stood outside an older, somewhat industrial building that had seen some careful modern restoration. He went inside, taking the lift up to a loft-style work space with whitewashed walls that exposed the brickwork. Open work stations stood in careful, practical clumps, with only a few enclosed spaces dotted around the floor—and, even then, the walls were made of glass, with black metal frames. On one wall in large black letters were the words 'Style on Point'.

Jasmine, as she had been this morning, fit in here perfectly. The woman from the club? He couldn't see her at all.

Emilio walked through the darkened work space—here too, everyone had clearly already left for the day—towards the only office still brightly lit. Within it sat Jasmine, frowning at her screen.

It would take all his charm and power for his plan to work, because this woman was not afraid to challenge him. But Emilio was okay with that. So far nothing in his life worth having had come without a fight. He wouldn't be swayed.

He knocked on the open door, obviously startling her. Perhaps she'd thought he wouldn't come. He watched as the surprise faded and she quickly put up her guard.

'Can we talk?' he asked.

'If you're going to act like a civilised human, then yes.'

It took a great deal of restraint not to smile at her tone. Damn this woman! The pull she had on him was frustrating.

And he couldn't help but admire how completely immune she was to his name. When she had arrived at his officer earlier, there'd been no hint of intimidation. It took a brave soul to barge into a De Luca's office like that. When he looked at her now, he could see all that strength.

He took the available seat at her table, arranging his thoughts before he began. 'I apologise for my behaviour earlier,' he said. It would be best to get her attitude towards him to soften before they talked further. 'The news came as a shock.'

'Yes, because I was fully prepared for it,' Jasmine sniped.

'That's fair.' Emilio placed the test result on her table. 'But we need to get past this unpleasantness. We are going to have a child and I plan on being part of their life.'

'I'm glad to hear it,' she said. 'And I agree, maybe we should start over—*honestly*, this time.'

There it was again, a cryptic hint about trust and honesty that unsettled Emilio. He had broken trust before. Destroyed it absolutely, in fact. But he wasn't going to think about Enzo and Gia when he was here to do the right thing for his child and his family.

'I'd like that.' He extended his hand. 'I'm Emilio De Luca.'

'Jasmine Hall,' she said, shaking it. It was as if her touch burned. Scalded him to his marrow. He wanted to let go and keep holding on at the same time. Judging from the way she looked at him, she felt it too—and quickly let go, not giving him the choice.

Emilio shut down the disappointment; he still had to achieve what he came here to do.

'About the baby...' he said. 'You're carrying a De Luca heir.'

'What does that mean?' He could hear the apprehension in her tone.

'It means they will have the De Luca name,' Emilio said

plainly. Jasmine was an impressive woman, a self-made entrepreneur, but her heritage didn't bring with it any power. His did. His child would inherit centuries' worth of history and prestige. His name would open doors that Jasmine couldn't imagine in her wildest dreams. Most importantly, this child was *his*. They would be denied nothing.

Including the vineyards.

The realisation hit him like a physical blow. The vineyards meant twice as much now: not only had his mother loved them, but one day his child would inherit them. Emilio was willing to fight for both those causes. For everything his child deserved.

'I have no reason to trust you,' Jasmine said. 'If you stick around, we can hyphenate.'

'Not happening.' He wasn't about to relinquish the De Luca name to Enzo by hyphenating. *His* child would be the next De Luca heir. 'They *will* have my name; it's not negotiable. But that's not all—you will have my name too. We will be getting married.'

'What?' Jasmine was on her feet in an instant.

'You heard me.'

'No, no, I'm certain I heard wrong.' Emilio could see her using that tone in a boardroom. He was certain anyone else would have been back-tracking right about now, but he wasn't just anyone.

'I said, we will be getting married.' He could tell his calm tone was further inciting her anger.

'You're out of your mind, Emilio! I'm not marrying you!' She looked around the office, searching for who knew what; when she looked back at him, her hazel eyes were vivid with repressed rage. 'It's the twenty-first century, Emilio. We don't have to get married just because I fell pregnant. We can co-parent. Come to a satisfying custody agreement. There is a myriad of options that don't include marriage!'

Absolutely not! Emilio wasn't going to miss out on any part of his child's life the way his father had removed himself from his. Shared custody would mean he would have to go days, maybe weeks, without seeing or living with his child. No way was that happening. He wanted every moment. His child would not wonder where he was, would not question why they weren't enough for his attention. They wouldn't grow up with that pain.

'Together, we can give our child a better future, Jasmine. A better life. Surely you want that for them?' She had grown up poor; that had been clear from the fact-file. 'If we share custody, they would be bounced from house to house, having to unpack a suitcase just to turn around and pack one again the next week. They will have more stability if we marry.'

Jasmine planted her hands on her desk and leaned towards him, a vein throbbing in her temple. 'You mean you can avoid a scandal if we marry.'

Emilio didn't want to lie to her, so he said nothing.

'I know how it works with old money, Emilio,' she said through clenched teeth.

'Surely you would agree that growing up in a two-parent household is better than the alternative?'

'You utter bastard!' Jasmine pushed off the desk, her nostrils flaring. He saw her hands clench into trembling fists as she tried and failed to contain her outrage. 'You looked into me, didn't you?'

'Of course I did. You have to know that a man in my position can't operate on blind faith,' Emilio said calmly, still seated in his chair. But what he wouldn't say, wouldn't show, was that he knew a little about how Jasmine felt. He'd never know what it was like to struggle for money, but to be raised by a single parent... That he understood.

Jasmine's father had abandoned his family for a new life in a new town; Emilio's father had stayed. He had lived with them, slept in the same bed as Emilio's mother, showered attention upon Enzo. But he had still abandoned Emilio—just him. His father had removed himself from Emilio's life. There'd been no conversations with his younger son, or concerns about his well-being. Not even a word for him at dinner.

Emilio knew exactly how it felt to sit alone and question what could be so wrong with him that he deserved to be unloved.

He didn't want that for his child. He would give them the attention—the affection—that he'd never once received.

Emilio had infuriated her, and he was being ridiculous, and—worst of all—the maddening urge to climb him like a tree hadn't abated. But, despite all of that, Jasmine had to acknowledge that he was right. If the roles had been reversed, she would likely have been suspicious too. And she had to admit that, now the paternity had been confirmed, Emilio was here taking responsibility.

She was fully capable of providing for her child, but she knew what it was like coming from a single-parent background. She would move heaven and earth for her baby, but it still might not be enough. How would her child feel when she had to prioritise work over something important to them? That would happen, inevitably, because she would need SOP to thrive more than ever: her child's livelihood would depend on it. And how would they feel without their father's constant presence? She knew how *she* had felt growing up: the anger and hate and questions. What about when her child found out that they could have had a complete family, but Jasmine had been the one to say no? Would they grow to resent her for making that choice?

She walked to the open door and scanned the floor of vacant desks. Every one of those symbolised an employee, another responsibility. She had worked so hard to be a success.

The goal had always been financial stability, then marriage and then children, in that order. Her father leaving was a big reason for that. She had thought Richard was going to be her partner through that journey, but his secrets and lies had just left her with greater wounds, and wasted the years she had spent trying to make herself fit into a mould for him.

'You're working on a Saturday! Are you trying to prove that you're more ambitious than me? Is that it? You need to prove you're better?'

She'd allowed Richard into her head. Tried to work less around him, tried to make him comfortable. Now she had replaced him entirely with SOP and was happier for it, but her lifestyle meant that both she and her child would have to make sacrifices. On her own, there would be sacrifices, no matter which way she looked at things.

It might not be the way she would have chosen for her plan to come to fruition, but Emilio was offering her everything she had wanted, and he seemed sincere in his desire to be a father for this child.

'You're right,' she said reluctantly, still not looking at him. 'A home with two parents to love our child would be better.'

She turned round to find Emilio giving her his full attention. His face was a perfect mask of calm. That rationality would make what must come next a much easier discussion.

'We need to set some ground rules for this marriage.'

'I'm all ears.' Emilio gave nothing away. There was no twinkle in his eye or smile on his lips. His leg was crossed over his knee, elbows on the arm rests, fingers knitted between each other. This was a negotiation.

'What happened between us at Boulevard was meant to be just for a night. I don't know you and I don't trust you. We will not be sharing a bed.' It was best that she remove any temptation to grow close to Emilio. Physical intimacy could lead her to grow feelings for him, to rely on him. Her trust had been broken, shattered too many times to risk that again. Last time, she'd lost her fiancé and her best friend. It was always safest to go through life depending on no one but herself.

'You don't trust me yet, Jasmine, but I'm hoping that with time you will. That said, I agree with you.'

She hadn't expected him to agree so readily. Especially when it was clear to her from that night at the club that he was someone who revelled in female company. Her doubt must have been written on her face.

'I don't require sex to live, Jasmine. It's not that important in my life. What's your next rule?'

She found that hard to believe, and not just because she was disinclined to believe anyone's words any more. He had *clearly* enjoyed himself during their encounter. Despite her thoughts, she continued.

'The second thing is that I am happy for you to be involved with the baby and provide for our child. But you will not be doing the same for me. What is our own will remain so.'

'I will have a pre-nup drawn up immediately and sent to you for approval. You can look it over tomorrow morning. I will arrange to have the ceremony in the afternoon.'

This man was insane.

'No.' She moved to perch on her desk. Emilio's unhappy gaze followed her.

'What do you mean *no*? You already agreed to be my wife. I have urgent business in Italy that I need to attend to.'

'Then attend to it. I have a business to run. Nothing will change in the time that you're gone.' What was the need to marry so urgently? The baby wouldn't be here for nearly another seven months.

'With every day that we delay, we risk word getting out. We need to come out ahead of it, control how it gets out. You have a start-up with investors, Jasmine; you can't risk your judgement being called into question any more than I can. We bear a lot of responsibility.'

'Yes, I understand that, Emilio,' she said irritably, 'But I am not showing yet and will likely still not be by the time you get back from Italy.'

'No,' he refused stubbornly.

Jasmine had to take a deep breath. 'How about a compromise?'

'Continue.'

'While we make the arrangements to marry, we can take our time, appear as a couple, be spotted strategically. Then it won't matter if I start showing before the wedding.'

'That timeline isn't acceptable to me,' Emilio said firmly. 'But there is value in your suggestion. Here is my counter: we can have two weeks, during which we will be seen publicly. Then we marry. That's all the time I'm willing to allow.'

Jasmine could sense the urgency from him, but she still had no idea why.

'Fine.'

What was the use in arguing about timings? It wasn't as if she was in any danger of falling in love with the man, be it now or later. She just had to adjust her goals somewhat: falling pregnant then marrying and then having a child. Just because her wedding with Richard had fallen through didn't mean the plan was lost altogether, as she had thought that night at the club when she'd been determined there would never be marriage or family. With Emilio she would still have the stability and the family without any of the unnecessary emotional vulnerabilities that came with a traditional relationship.

It would be all her goals finally realised, just in a way she'd never imagined. With a man who made her pulse race, who held secrets and who she could never fully trust.

CHAPTER SEVEN

Emilio stood on the pavement, leaning against the door of his Maybach. He checked the time on his watch. Any minute now Jasmine would leave her brownstone and find him waiting. When her driver had arrived in her black SUV, Emilio had instructed him to leave. Jasmine had raised a valid point: they needed to be seen strategically before their marriage. After all, a short courtship would look better than none.

So here he was. The doting fiancé, just waiting to take his beloved to work.

Soon the door opened and out stepped Jasmine, just as prim and proper as she had been the day before. Today she wore camel trousers, a white blouse and a heavy coat—not a crease in sight, not a hair out of place.

And, the instant Emilio saw her, all blood rushed south. He fully intended to obey her ground rules—he had the restraint—but he couldn't pretend to be unaffected by this attraction. It was as if his body craved hers.

'Emilio? What are you doing here?'

'Taking you to work, of course.' He grinned. He pushed off the car so he could open the door and stand aside.

'Where's my driver?' Jasmine asked with a hint of irritation.

'I sent him away. I thought your fiancé should have the honour of escorting you to work.' Despite knowing that he shouldn't, Emilio found riling her up highly entertaining.

He suppressed a laugh as he watched her internally debate the merits of ignoring him completely. But he knew that *she* knew that appearing together in public had been her idea, and that making a scene in the street would be completely counterproductive. Who knew who could be watching?

With a huff of annoyance, she walked towards him, heels click-clacking on the pavement and, with a long, unimpressed look, climbed into the car. He followed her in. The moment they pulled out into the road, Jasmine fished her phone out of her bag and ignored him.

'Are you going to be annoyed by everything I do?' Emilio teased.

'When you're being high-handed, yes,' she answered, not looking away from her phone screen. 'I prefer to go to work alone. I like the quiet, and it gives me a chance to catch up on my emails.' Her fingers flew over the screen, rapidly tapping away.

'You can have quiet, but you are going to have to get used to this. We have a certain appearance to uphold.'

She didn't respond but Emilio didn't need her to. Yes, he was doing everything he could to save his family name and the company any scandal, but it was more than that. This woman was carrying his child. If taking care of both of them meant ferrying her from home to work every day, then that was what he would do—even though it annoyed her. He wouldn't be denied.

Making their way through the rush hour traffic took a while. Neither said a word to the other, opting instead to work in peace. Still, Emilio felt her presence so acutely that it was a struggle to concentrate. She was right there. All it would take was the smallest of movements to brush against her arm, reach over and pull her to him. Kiss her like he had months ago. And he was certain she was feeling it too. He caught her sneaking a few peeks at him.

The silence didn't help. Without conversation to distract him, he could think of nothing but her. Even his phone—usually so busy—wouldn't ring to give him an escape. So when he saw the SOP building drawing closer, he was both relieved and disappointed.

As soon as the car stopped, she had the handle in her hand. Emilio stopped her. 'No. Let me.'

He exited the car first and held open the door, allowing Jasmine to climb out elegantly. She stopped in front of him, something on her lips. But whatever the words were—a thank you?—she caught herself before she could say them, turning on her heel instead. Emilio caught her wrist and brought her closer. He couldn't let her leave just yet. He needed to be a convincing fiancé. A chaste kiss on her lips would be sufficient evidence for the world.

But, as he leaned in, his eye was caught by movement on the steps of SOP. Most people were entering the building; one person was leaving.

Jasmine followed his gaze, and whatever softness had crept into her expression was replaced by hard, unyielding anger. It was written in every line on her face, in the tension in her shoulders.

The woman noticed Jasmine, looked away towards a car on the kerb, hesitated, then started walking towards them. A moment later a blonde man with sharp blue eyes in suit trousers and a white shirt, both of which had to be uncomfortably tight in a classless show of physique, joined her.

The hand that had been resting in Emilio's palm gripped at him like a vice.

'I told you that you were no longer welcome here,' Jasmine said icily. Emilio thought back to the anger Jasmine had shown him the day before, and her annoyance that morning. Both paled in comparison to the effect these people's presence had on her.

'I just came here to fetch—'

'I don't care what you came here to do, Zara. Stay away from SOP and stay away from me, or I will make you.'

Emilio could feel the tremble in her body and stepped closer. He was ready to jump in at any moment but guessed that Jasmine wouldn't appreciate that. He would wait until he was certain it was the right thing to do.

'You can't do that, Jasmine,' the woman—Zara—said hotly. 'I have friends here.'

'And how will you betray them? Sleep with their fiancés too?'

Emilio's body turned cold.

Cazzo! This cannot be happening! His stomach roiled at the words.

No wonder Jasmine was so distrustful. Now he understood why that wedding hadn't happened. Why she had been at the club that night. How vulnerable she must have been. Emilio was horrified. How could the one person he was so attracted to, the one person he *needed* to trust him, have been the victim of the same crime he was guilty of having committed against his brother? Every day Emilio tried to be better than the person who had made that terrible mistake. How could fate be this cruel?

His pulse raced. His mouth turned dry. *Certainly not a man...* Now that comment made sense. One had walked out on her and the other had cheated on her. He knew the kind of scar that left, the devastation it wreaked. He could still see it on his brother's face when he closed his eyes. It tormented him. A necrotic wound on his soul that he'd inflicted upon himself. Upon his family. They'd never been whole again afterwards. There'd never been another family meal.

He had done that.

And it would happen again to the family he was creating. Jasmine would never even tolerate him once she knew his past. He would lose the privilege to be in his child's life. That couldn't happen. He wouldn't let it. He wouldn't lose his baby!

If Jasmine was ever to trust him—and she *must*, for the sake of their child—then she could *never* find out about Gia.

Jasmine had always considered herself stronger than most. Her mother had raised her to be, and her father had taught her never to rely on men. What she hadn't realised until it was too late was that she should never rely on *anyone*. Everyone had the capacity for cruelty.

She would have done anything for Zara. She'd trusted her so much that she'd started SOP with her, worked with her until she'd run off with her fiancé. It had been hard for Jasmine to buy Zara out and cast her from her life, but she'd done it. She'd rid herself of everything that reminded her of Zara and Richard. She had even given Zara her garish engagement ring as she'd pushed her out of the door, confident that she wouldn't have to see her again. New York was a big place, after all.

But here they were. And Jasmine had *never* felt weaker. She was hurt and angry and whatever peace she had managed to find was gone.

'That's enough,' Richard said, coming to Zara's defence. He had never done that for Jasmine. He was the one who'd forced her to make herself smaller, over and over. It was only once he was gone that she'd seen how much she'd shrunk around him. The realisation hurt more than she could express.

'We all need a Zara in our lives.'

Jasmine felt a burn behind her lids, but she wouldn't get emotional. She would not give them the satisfaction.

'I agree,' a smooth, deep voice said. Emilio wrapped his arm around Jasmine's shoulders, pulling her flush against his side. 'That is enough from the two of you.'

Then he turned to Jasmine. *'Belleza,'* he said, sliding his palm against her cheek in a touch that cleared the despair from her mind. He turned her face towards his and she let him. Looking into his dark-brown eyes and forgetting about the people who had hurt her so badly even as they stood just two feet away. 'Would you like me to call security?'

He was usually so high-handed. Now, in front of Richard and Zara, he was giving her the choice. Showing them that she controlled this situation.

'That's not necessary,' she managed.

'As you wish, *amore mio*.' He kissed her on the forehead, a small, loving yet possessive touch. It was all for show, but she felt it everywhere in her body.

'Who are you?' she heard Richard ask.

'Emilio De Luca.'

Jasmine saw both Richard's and Zara's eyes widen. It would have been comical if it hadn't been so satisfying. Maybe that was petty, but Jasmine didn't care. She was just grateful that Emilio was with her, lending her the strength that had gone missing when she'd needed it most.

And the fact that she was grateful for his strength was supremely disappointing. It made her want to pull away from him to prove to herself that she could deal with this on her own.

Almost as though he could hear her thoughts, Emilio's hold around her waist tightened fractionally. The power in his body undeniably a comfort.

'When did this happen?' Richard demanded, as if he had any right to ask. As if he hadn't been the one sleeping with her best friend for *months* prior to their wedding.

How should she answer, in any case? Should she tell the truth or should she be vague? They were supposedly engaged, but she didn't have a ring on her finger. She settled on saying exactly what she felt. 'You don't get to ask me that.'

'Jasmine, can't we at least be civil?' Zara asked pleadingly.
The nerve!
'No,' Emilio said. 'I suggest you leave, and I strongly urge you to reconsider any thoughts about coming back here.'

Jasmine was certain that tone had most of the world bowing to Emilio's demands. And it looked as if Richard and Zara were no exception.

Before the pair had even had a chance to turn and walk away, Emilio's focus was on her. 'Are you okay?' he asked.

'I am,' Jasmine said softly.

And then he leaned down and kissed her. And, just like the first time, the moment their lips met she was consumed. Transported away from this place or time. She existed only in this plane where Emilio granted her pleasure, and she pressed her body to his, wanting more.

This is why you don't want to be physical with him. But there was a battle within her between what she wanted and what she *needed*. The problem was that she couldn't tell which was which. It was only the band of Emilio's arm dropping away that made her finally put some space between them, force herself to step back.

As she did so, she spotted Richard's car driving by. Both he and Zara were watching her.

'Let them look.'

How did Emilio keep reading her mind?

'I will be back this evening to take you home,' he said.

'You know I can get myself home. I've been doing so for years.' The hint of annoyance audible in her voice was welcome. It made her feel more like herself, less shaken from the interaction with her ex.

'I know you can, but we will have a few things to discuss. I'll see you later.'

Jasmine didn't respond. There was no point.

She walked away, feeling utterly conflicted. She didn't

have anyone in her life who came to her aid quite like Emilio just had. While it felt good to be part of someone's team, she was also royally irritated that she had liked leaning on him. And why must he make her body come alive with the simplest touch?

Her mood didn't improve much throughout the day, because Emilio was never far from her mind. And, while her office was usually a great escape, he had been there too. There was no reprieve!

When she finally left the office that night, she found Emilio's Maybach parked out front. This time it was his driver who held the door open.

'Thank you...?'

'James, ma'am.'

'Thank you, James.' She gave him a small smile and entered the car, where Emilio was seated with a velvet box in his hand. She settled in the seat, closed her eyes and took a deep breath.

That didn't help. The space smelled like him. Like his light, airy cologne. It made her think of vast oceans and open meadows—a tranquil scent. Ironic, because that was far from the effect he had on her.

'What? No "hello"?' he teased.

'Please, Emilio, I'm not in the mood.'

'Very well.' She heard the snap of a box which had her opening her eyes. 'Give me your hand. This morning made me realise that my fiancée cannot be without a ring.'

They must have been thinking the same thing during the altercation with Richard and Zara: a ring would make it so much easier to explain their relationship.

She pulled her hand back to examine the jewel in the light. She had never quite seen anything like it; the emerald-cut stone changed colour between a bluish green and a purplish red. Little sparkling diamonds were set around it and all along the platinum band. It was the most beautiful ring she had ever seen, and she couldn't help but think that it looked so much better on her finger than the one that had sat there previously.

'It's beautiful.'

'I'm glad you like it,' Emilio said, and she believed him. 'You should know, my team will be taking care of the paperwork, and we will appear together to get the marriage licence. Thereafter, a court judge can marry us.'

'A court judge?' And the moment was gone.

'Is that a problem?'

Jasmine didn't answer. She looked out of the window at the city passing by, trying to make sense of her thoughts. Before Emilio had come along, she had planned a wedding, a beautiful ceremony. She'd got so close to walking down the aisle. She'd wanted her mother there—she would have been the one to give Jasmine away. But it had never happened. She'd been denied.

She still wanted that. Even if this marriage was nothing but a union of convenience for the sake of their child, Jasmine didn't want to give up that dream.

'I want a wedding,' she said calmly.

'We don't have time for that, Jasmine,' he replied, matching her tone. 'There is no need.'

'It's not that important. We can get married in the court house, for all it matters.'

She didn't want to marry another Richard. This morning the two men had been like night and day, but right now Emilio sounded so much like him. It made her determined not to give an inch.

'We either have a wedding or we don't get married at all,' she said defiantly, staring him down. 'What is the basis of your opposition?'

She noticed a flash of emotion in his eyes before he swallowed, but she couldn't decipher it.

'Time.'

'That's easily fixed. I can arrange it. You simply have to be there.'

'No.'

'Emilio.'

'Fine. I will take care of it, Jasmine. I give you my word. You will have your wedding. And, once it is done, you will move in with me.'

Her rage flared again. 'Don't you pull this alpha bullshit on me! You don't get to dictate to me, Emilio. If you want to have a discussion, I will be willing to listen, but I will not obey. I won't leave *my* home because you ordered me to. Besides, I don't even know where you live. It could be some dark lair, for all I know.'

'I will not be living in some frilly townhouse either.'

'Where do you get off—?' Jasmine stopped herself before she could burst an artery and took a deep breath, and then another, until she could trust herself to speak calmly. 'This marriage is never going to work if we are both unwilling to compromise.'

The car came to a stop, and she saw that they were outside her home. She grabbed the handle and opened the door before Emilio could react, internally celebrating at the unhappy look on his face.

'Think on it.'

She closed the door and walked away. It would be interesting to see if he could compromise at all.

CHAPTER EIGHT

EMILIO SAT IN his office. He'd read and re-read the document in his hand several times over but he just couldn't get himself to focus on the words. His inability to concentrate these days was utterly maddening. And it was entirely Jasmine's fault. He found himself thinking of her at the best of times, but it wasn't just her beauty or their connection that was on his mind right now. It was her demand for a wedding.

She was so focussed, so driven and logical that he'd taken for granted that she would see reason and realise a wedding in their circumstances was utterly unnecessary. But didn't most people *want* a wedding? A special day on which to tie oneself completely to the person they loved?

Emilio wasn't one of those people.

But Enzo was. And you took that away from him.

Emilio dropped the page and pushed away from his desk, scrubbing his hands down his face.

That was exactly why Emilio didn't want a wedding. It would bring too much back from the past. It reminded him of all the ways in which he was truly loathsome. Of the worst thing he'd ever done. Of the grand wedding in Perlano fit for a *conte* that Gia and Enzo had been planning eight years ago. The wedding Emilio had ruined. The rejection that had followed.

After what Richard had done to Jasmine, Emilio had rather hoped that she'd feel similarly about weddings. That she wouldn't want to face it. But he supposed he should have planned for this possibility. There were two very different sides to Jasmine. As buttoned-up as she was now, the woman from the club was a part of her too. It just made the Alexandrite ring he'd bought her all the more fitting: two colours for the two sides of her.

Well, at least one side of Jasmine expected a wedding, and he had to deliver on that promise. He picked up his phone and called his PA.

Rachel walked into his office carrying a notebook and pencil mere seconds later.

'Have a seat, please. I have a special task for you.' Emilio crossed his legs and placed his hands on the arm rest, forcing himself to look like a man who was relaxed. Who was completely unbothered by the idea of impending nuptials.

'What is it?'

'I need you to plan my wedding.'

'Really?' Rachel's eyes shone with excitement. It was one of the very few times she had ever broken through her absolute professionalism.

'Yes.' Emilio forced himself to smile.

'Okay, do you have a preference for a theme or venue?'

'It will take place on my roof top, but I have no preferences other than to make sure there are some pink oleander in whatever you decide to do.'

His mother's favourite flower. He didn't know how Valentina would have felt about what he'd done. Would she have forgiven him for sleeping with a random woman and getting her pregnant, as she had forgiven all his past transgressions? He hoped she would have seen that he was trying to do the right thing by marrying Jasmine, and he knew in his heart she would have loved her grandchild. The only thing in the world he wanted at his wedding was a reminder of the one person who'd loved him unconditionally.

'You have complete freedom to do whatever you want. I trust your judgement and your discretion.'

'Of course, Emilio. Also, everything regarding the marriage licence is done. I've put your appointment at the city clerk's office in your calendar.'

'Thank you, Rachel.' Before he could say anything further, his phone began loudly vibrating on his desk.

'Congratulations.' Rachel smiled and left his office.

He picked his phone up to see Jasmine's name flash across the screen.

'What are you doing tonight?' she asked without so much as a hello. Pleasantries lost time and that was inefficient. The thought made him smile.

'Hello, Jasmine. I'm well, and yourself?'

'Emilio, stop being aggravating.'

But it was so fun to draw these reactions out of her, when she seemed so comfortable with him. When she treated him like Emilio and not the De Luca spare. But he also wanted to draw out the other side of her. He wanted to tell her that it was okay to let go every now and then.

But look how that turned out.

'Are you available or not?' Jasmine demanded.

'I can make myself available for my fiancée.'

'Great. Dinner at my place. Seven.'

After what he'd said about her home—something he'd kicked himself for afterwards—he was surprised she would invite him into it. Perhaps it was an olive branch, and if so he would be a fool not to take it.

'I'll be there.'

'Thank you,' she said in a gentler tone and hung up.

He was on the door step of her brownstone at precisely seven. He rang the doorbell and waited. Perhaps she would be willing to discuss moving into his penthouse after an amiable dinner. After all, his fiancée couldn't be seen living apart from him, and after their display in the street the day before, and the ring she was now wearing, it would be obvious to everyone that she was engaged and to whom. His plans to save the company and family legacy from scandal were falling into place. He just needed Jasmine to be less stubborn about this one detail.

She answered the door wearing jeans and a knit sweater pushed up to her elbows, her feet bare and her hair down—just like when he'd first seen her. As much as Emilio respected the level of control she had, he couldn't help rejoicing at the sight of that fun, free Jasmine peeking out just a little.

'Exactly on time,' she greeted him. 'Come in.'

He stepped into the foyer and his words from the day before came back to him: *some frilly townhouse*. This was far from frilly. Black and white photographs hung on bright white walls above dark wood floors. They were lit softly from above, beckoning him inside. An invitation into the rest of the home.

'Can I take your coat?' she offered.

He shrugged off his suit jacket and handed it to her, taking a look around. Even the wall leading upstairs had photos on it; he first thought they were gallery prints, but on closer inspection they turned out to be pictures of Jasmine with what he assumed was her mother. The looks on their faces made him ache for his own.

'I should probably tell you now,' Jasmine said behind him, 'My mother is joining us for dinner. She's here to meet you.'

So it wasn't an olive branch. So much for honesty and compromise. 'What is this? Some sort of test?'

'What? No.'

'Then why would you withhold information?' He was angered that she would do so. He was trying to fix his impulsive mistake by considering every angle and following a carefully calculated path. Now he'd been dropped into a situation Jasmine had deliberately ensured he was unprepared for.

'You didn't think I would get married without my mother there, without her knowing, did you?'

Had he factored Jasmine's mother into all of this? He realised he hadn't.

'Would you?' she questioned.

Would he? The answer was an immediate no. He'd spent so much time with her growing up, just the two of them. Even when he had moved to New York, he'd still gone back to Perlano as frequently as he could. Towards the end of her life, he had worked from the estate just so he could be close to her right to the end. He wouldn't have hidden this marriage or his child from her.

'No,' he conceded. 'Lead the way.'

Emilio followed Jasmine into a large open-plan lounge and dining area. There was so much art on the walls. There were huge windows that must have let in so much light during the day. A large fireplace with a small fire crackled within. The whole space was furnished in browns, whites and blacks. It was modern and warm. Not at all *frilly*.

It felt like a home, and in that moment he craved that—somewhere warm and inviting to return to at the end of each day. His expensive penthouse was cold and stark in contrast—a showroom for an interior decorator. He'd hired the best, but that didn't change the fact that it was just a glossy place to sleep and wait out the hours between work and emotionless visits to the club. How empty his life truly was.

'You must be Emilio,' a woman said, drawing attention away from his thoughts. She was considerably shorter than Jasmine, but he could see the similarity in their faces, in their hazel eyes. 'I'm Angela.'

'*Buonasera*, Angela,' Emilio said, respectfully shaking her hand.

'I look forward to getting to know you.' There was a twinkle in her eye that made Emilio like her immediately.

'And I, you.'

'But I will reserve judgement until after dinner.'

'That sounds fair. I better make a good impression.' He caught Jasmine rolling her eyes and all annoyance from earlier evaporated. How could he have thought to exclude Jasmine's mother? Perhaps Jasmine would have been more forthcoming about the visit if he hadn't been so combative.

Another trait he had picked up as a child. It had been easier back then to snap at Enzo rather than have another memory of being ignored by his father. But he wasn't nine years old any more. He had to do better.

He rolled up his sleeves. 'Put me to work. What can I do?'

'You?' Jasmine laughed.

'You don't think I would be handy in the kitchen, *belleza*?' A mocking smile curled Emilio's lips. The way he sauntered over to stand before her made Jasmine think of the man from the club: predatory and fun; laid-back. Over the last two days she hadn't been able to see that man at all, but tonight he was peeking through again.

'I don't.'

He narrowed his eyes and everything below her waist coiled. 'Care to bet on it?'

'You've never washed a dish in your life.' It would take nothing at all to close the small space between them and kiss him. And she wanted to. Just as she had wanted to in the club and as she had wanted to outside SOP.

'I don't need to,' Emilio replied. 'I don't know if you heard, there are machines for that these days.'

'So you're telling me you can cook.' Disbelief was clear in her voice, a smile tugging at her lips. She always tried to be so in control, but around Emilio everything was heightened.

She smiled more, laughed more, grew impossibly angry or annoyed. He didn't let her feel anything in small measures. Not even pleasure.

'I can cook you anything you'd like.'

'Yeah, right.'

'Who do you think feeds me?'

'I thought you just grew satiated on wine and the suffering of the little man.'

'I'm going to make you eat those words.'

'Or maybe one of you could lay the table so we all could eat?' Her mother reappeared in the kitchen, holding a Dutch oven. Jasmine had completely forgotten she was even there. She was taken back to that night at the club when she'd forgotten about the dancing bodies and loud music. It had all faded into nothing around Emilio.

'Let me take that,' Emilio said hurriedly. He took the Dutch oven over to the table while Jasmine quickly set down plates and cutlery. Behind his back, her mother gave her a nod of approval.

'It's nothing fancy,' Angela warned Emilio when they all sat around the table. He had moved his place setting from the end of the table to beside Jasmine.

'It's perfectly fine, Mom.' This simple dish—sausage, spiced rice and a mish-mash of vegetables—was part of who Jasmine was. She wasn't going to hide that from Emilio, and she wanted to know now, at the start, if he would have a problem with it. Growing up, her mother had magically turned inexpensive ingredients into delicious dishes that Jasmine would ask for again and again. It hadn't mattered how cheap the food was when it had made her mother smile to hear her daughter ask for it.

'You don't have to eat that way any more, Jasmine, and I certainly don't want to. Let's take your mother to a nice restaurant instead.'

Jasmine didn't want another Richard. She had been so blind to so many of his flaws during their relationship. Hidden parts of herself to make him comfortable. She didn't want a repeat.

She watched Emilio serve her mother first, then her and lastly himself. When he finally ate a morsel, he didn't complain.

'This is delicious, Angela,' he said. A warmth spread in Jasmine's chest at his words.

'You think so?' Angela beamed. Jasmine knew that it hurt her mother that, no matter how hard she'd tried, Richard had never liked the food she prepared. In just a few minutes, Emilio had put a smile on her mother's face in a way her ex-fiancé never had.

'Yes.' Jasmine could have sworn that Emilio looked almost wistful for moment before he turned his attention to her and placed a warm hand on her back. 'Are you okay?'

'Yes.'

'Then why aren't you eating?'

Because she was comparing him to Richard and feeling guilty about doing so when he was nothing like him.

'I could make you something else if you're feeling unwell,' Emilio offered. Jasmine felt her heart skip a beat. In that moment she had no doubt she could ask for whatever she needed and Emilio would see that she had it. She caught a warm look in her mother's eye that told her Angela thought the same.

'I'm fine,' she said hastily and put a forkful into her mouth.

Her mother's smile didn't fade. 'Do you like to cook, Emilio?'

'I do. It makes me feel closer to my mother.' That wistfulness Jasmine had seen before was back, but this time he didn't attempt to hide it.

'Is that something you do together?' Angela asked. Jasmine was surprised by how happy it made her to watch them interact, see the tender way Emilio conversed with her mother. How comfortable her mother seemed. Dinners with Richard had never been this easy, this light.

Maybe this was a test, but so far Emilio was passing with flying colours.

'We used to before she passed.' Jasmine could sense the longing wafting from him. Then he smirked, lightened his tone. 'Perhaps I could teach you,' he said to Jasmine.

'I agree. *If* you're the one making pasta and I get to watch,' Jasmine said, hiding her smile behind a sip of non-alcoholic wine.

'That could be arranged.' He grinned back at her.

His attentiveness continued throughout the meal. He topped up her mother's and her glasses, ensuring they had seconds, enthusiastically participated in her mother's stories. There was a genuine warmth in the way he interacted with Angela. It told Jasmine something: Emilio was a caretaker. Some of what she'd taken for highhandedness made a little more sense now. She felt herself thaw just a little more towards him.

The Emilio she'd seen recently had been him in crisis mode—her own fault, she thought guiltily. She'd been the one who'd begged him not to stop that night. Here—with dinner cleared away and his arm resting along the top of her chair—he was relaxed. The real him had come out. And she'd never been more sure that marrying him for the sake of their child was the right thing to do.

'I like you, Emilio,' Angela said finally, pulling Jasmine from her thoughts, 'But I can't advise my daughter to marry you.'

Jasmine had fully expected her mother to say that, but the tingle of disappointment she felt at the words was a surprise. She looked at Emilio for a reaction—anger, disappointment? But he just sat there patiently awaiting her mother's judgement.

'That said,' Angela went on, 'I trust my daughter's judgement.'

'Angela, I assure you, I will always take care of Jasmine.' Emilio moved his arm, taking Jasmine's hand in his own and placing them on the table. A show of intent.

Her mother noticed, and kept looking at their joined hands as she went on. 'Having met you and spoken to you, that isn't my concern. I'm sure that you will. But will you love her, and will she love you?'

'Mom…' Jasmine started but her mother cut her off.

'I know it was difficult for us, Jasmine,' Angela said kindly, 'But you are not me.'

Jasmine opened her mouth, but Emilio beat her to it.

'Angela, I'm aware that your daughter could successfully raise our child alone. But I want my child to grow in a home where their parents are always present for them. I won't be a part-time father, nor will I abandon Jasmine or my child.'

Emilio's words were gentle, but there was that look in his eyes again, the one that Jasmine couldn't decipher. Was there another reason he was so adamant that they should marry? It was yet another question she would need an answer to. Not that the answer would affect her decision. They were getting married for their baby; she just needed some transparency.

Angela reached over the table and placed her hands on theirs. 'You are both adults, so I can't tell you what to do,' she said, 'And I greatly admire your integrity, Emilio. But just consider the type of love you both deserve and if you could live happily if you should never find it.'

'I have considered that,' Emilio replied.

Angela smiled, something sad in it. 'Then, I guess…welcome to my family, Emilio.'

'Thank you, Angela.' He smiled.

Later, when he left, Jasmine walked him to her front door.

He paused on her doorstep and turned to face her. 'I'm willing to compromise.'

'I'm listening.'

'We can live here after the honeymoon. Until then, you will move into my home. My fiancée has to be seen living with me.'

Jasmine thought about it. It was a fair offer, really. Maybe when Emilio was in his own home she would see more of the man she'd seen tonight. A man who, it seemed, was capable of compromise. Of putting their baby's and her comfort ahead of his own. A man who held so much power but was willing to hand some of it over to her. Who didn't seem threatened by her making a long-term decision for them.

There was really only one right choice. 'I accept.'

CHAPTER NINE

JASMINE STOOD BY the window of a guest room in Emilio's penthouse while her mother did up the buttons on the back of her wedding dress. She glanced out at Central Park, a view she had woken up to for the past two weeks.

Emilio had helped her move in the morning after the dinner. She'd been surprised by how little she hated his home. Sure, a lot of it seemed impersonal. There was so much white here. White walls. White marble in the kitchen and bathrooms. But the décor was just right. The bedding in every room was perfect. His kitchen was a dream for any foodie—which, it turned out, he was. With all the light that poured in through the walls of windows, it all felt so airy. As if he'd invited the outside in.

That didn't stop Jasmine noticing how little of himself he put on display. Apart from a singular frame on the mantelpiece holding a picture of a beautiful older woman who must be his mother, there was nothing of him in here. Not even in his bedroom, which she'd seen once, during the full tour he'd given that first evening. She knew he had a brother, but there was no evidence of the other De Luca heir in Emilio's home. It was strange. If she had a sibling, she would at least have had a picture of them up.

The man himself was warm, charming, arrogant and the most infuriating person she had ever met, but his home was just a beautiful canvas. The only place that felt different was the rooftop terrace. Emilio had created an Eden in the middle of the city with trees, flowers and hedges. A pathway wound through it to a greenhouse filled with various plants. Jasmine found herself drawn there every evening, and looked forward to her new ritual of taking a cup of coffee and sitting in there where it was tranquil and beautiful.

And that was where she would be married today.

'How are you feeling, sweetheart?' her mother asked.

'I'm not sure.' While Jasmine was coming to know Emilio a little bit more, she was certainly not in love with him. How could marrying a man she didn't love be anything but disappointing? But she was excited about what this marriage would mean for her baby.

'Are you nervous?'

'Not really.'

'You know, you can still back out of this marriage,' Angela said.

'I thought you liked Emilio.'

'It's not that. I know you always think everything through so carefully, but you don't know each other very well. I worry what will happen later on if you don't marry for love.'

'Love is a myth, Mom. You just need to make the best choice with the information presented.'

'And Emilio is the best choice?'

Jasmine turned and took her mother's hands in hers. 'He is.'

Angela was right: they didn't know each other. But Jasmine was learning there was so much more to Emilio than he let anyone see. Would she ever find the man beneath the playboy? If she should care to.

'I know he wants to be there for his child, but that doesn't mean—'

'It does. Being married to him will give this child things I could only ever dream about.'

'Was it really so bad for you growing up?' Angela asked in a gentle voice.

Jasmine could have kicked herself. She didn't want to hurt her mother; she was only doing what she knew would be best. 'No, it wasn't. But we had some tough years, Mom. I can provide for our baby—I know I can—but I can't give them what a father can. I can't give them what Emilio can. It's not a bad idea to marry Emilio when I'm doing everything I am for my child's future.'

'Okay,' Angela said with a sigh. 'I'll see you upstairs.'

She turned to leave, but Jasmine halted her with a word. 'Mom.' She hurried over to the only person she had ever been able to rely on, to trust, and hugged her fiercely. When she let go, her mother's lashes were damp.

With a small smile and a hand on her cheek, Angela rushed out. Jasmine turned to the mirror, adjusting her hair. She'd worn it down, one side pinned back with a sparkling crystal grip: a gift from Emilio. Everything she was wearing had been a gift from Emilio, in his usual heavy-handed way. Diamond earrings. Designer heels. A new dress.

Even though she hadn't got married in the dress she'd picked before, Jasmine had impulsively decided she wanted something different, untainted by the idea of Richard. And she'd been prepared to get it herself; Emilio hadn't even wanted a wedding, after all. But he wouldn't hear of it. He'd arranged for Jasmine to be taken to a renowned designer after hours without him, and had arranged payment for whatever Jasmine wanted, insisting she indulge. So she had, even though she wanted nothing from him, even though she'd reminded him of their rules. He had simply stated that she'd made no rule against a wedding gift. So she'd grudgingly accepted and picked the dress purely by gut feeling.

Now she was glad this dress was different from her first one. And how different it was! The dress Jasmine had meticulously picked for her first wedding was long-sleeved, whereas this had no sleeves at all. The old one was thick and heavy; this was made of the finest tulle and lace. And, when she moved, the light caught all the floral, hand-made lace that covered the skirt. This dress, with its corset-style top, mermaid silhouette and short train, fitted her statuesque body in a way the old one never had. This one felt good. It felt right.

Jasmine didn't want to think too much about that. How could an impulsive reaction to a momentary lapse in judgement feel so much better than a carefully controlled plan?

'That's it! No more thinking,' she told her reflection. 'Let's get this over with.'

She went up to the terrace that had been made over in the few hours since she had seen it last. A long white runner had been laid over the path, and her mother met her at the head of it.

'Ready?' Angela asked.

'Yes.' Jasmine linked her arm with her mother's and down the aisle they walked, under newly erected white arches covered with flowers and vines. Down she glided, towards the greenhouse, where Emilio stood with the celebrant. Rachel must have been there too somewhere, to act as their second witness. But Jasmine couldn't tear her eyes away from her groom.

Emilio, standing there in a light tan suit, a gold pin twinkling in the centre of his tie. A pink flower in the lapel of his jacket. He looked incredible, but it wasn't the fancy three-piece suit or the spectacular garden that carried her towards him. It was the look in his eye: ravening, predatory, just like when she had first met him. A look that said he wanted her. A look that had her questioning her sanity.

Was she right to deny their chemistry? It was potent, what they had. It took away sense and left only hunger in its wake. And, she wondered, would she always have to battle this attraction? Would she be able to?

* * *

Emilio could scarcely breathe. His fingers twitched by his side, aching to feel those curls—worn down, just like on that fateful night they'd met. That dress...white and pure, but eliciting filthy thoughts. Thoughts that were only fuelled further by the fact that he already knew how she tasted. He knew, and he craved it, but had agreed to her rules. To deny them both.

But, when he looked into her green and gold eyes, so magically illuminated in the sunlight, he could tell she felt this need too.

Then she was in front of him.

Angela placed Jasmine's hand in his with a knowing smile, and that feeling every time he touched her was back. Flame licked up his skin, consuming him with her very presence. He wanted to kiss her, but he couldn't. He wanted to touch every inch of her skin, but he couldn't do that either.

'*Belleza,*' he said instead, and she smiled at him. A smile that gripped his heart.

'Shall we begin?' the celebrant asked.

Emilio nodded without looking at him. Without looking at anyone but Jasmine. He had hoped that the two weeks they'd spent together would ease the effect she had on him. That he would develop some kind of immunity. But the opposite had happened. He was aware of her all the time, and when she left a room her perfume lingered to drive him insane instead.

So here he was, marrying the most beautiful woman he had ever encountered, barely able to keep his libido in check.

'Marriage requires selflessness,' the celebrant began. 'The promise to trust and support one another. The promise to future children of raising, educating and supporting them in all aspects of life.'

That was exactly why Emilio was marrying Jasmine. He wondered then if his father had ever made such a promise to his mother and, if he had, why he had only kept it for his eldest son. Had Emilio not been worth his father's time, his promises, from the moment of his birth? Or had he decided to cast Emilio aside even before then?

Unaware of the thoughts in Emilio's head, the celebrant went on.

'Now, I shall ask of the both of you: do you, Emilio Luciano De Luca, take Jasmine Sophia Hall to be your wife and partner, forsaking all others?'

'I do.' Emilio slid a platinum wedding band onto Jasmine's slender finger, seating it firmly against the ring he had given her only two weeks ago.

'And do you, Jasmine Sophia Hall, take Emilio Luciano De Luca to be your husband and partner, forsaking all others?'

'I do.'

He watched her place the ring on his finger. His days of medicating with partying and one-night stands were over. This ring was a reminder to be what his family needed, what his child needed. Everything his father wasn't. But it was also a symbol of irony. Marriage and love weren't for him. Once upon a time, when he'd briefly thought maybe it would be possible with Gia, Emilio hadn't considered a marriage to be anything like this, with ground rules and deliberate separation. That wasn't what he'd wanted, yet look at him now.

'I hereby pronounce you man and wife. You may now kiss the bride.'

Emilio hadn't kissed Jasmine since that morning they'd run into Richard and Zara. He'd scrupulously adhered to their agreement to avoid physicality. But this kiss…there was no escaping it. There was no denying how much he wanted it. So he placed her hands on his chest, cradled her face and brushed his lips against hers in a desperate bid to make this last. This feeling of utter intoxication. He did it again and then took her lip between his, trying so hard not to lose control. Not to turn this into something hard and bruising like the passion inside him begged.

But, when Jasmine's tongue met his, any control he had disappeared. She angled her head, allowing him to kiss her deeper. His heart was pounding against his rib cage. He could feel her rapid pulse in her neck. They were lost, lost to each other.

The only thing that brought them back was Angela clearing her throat with amusement.

Emilio looked at his wife. Her pupils were blown wide. A flush coloured her cheeks. The air around them was thick with want. Keeping his distance from her was going to be far harder than he could ever have anticipated.

CHAPTER TEN

Normally, when Jasmine travelled, Jenna booked her in business class. And, while she enjoyed the luxury, the priority status, she was still just another person.

Not Emilio.

A large private jet stood waiting for them on the airport tarmac. Their luggage was already loaded, without any instruction. When the driver opened Emilio's door first, he stepped out and offered Jasmine his hand. She took it.

She had been the one to say there would be no physicality, but she found herself not minding his touches all that much. In fact, after each one she would only crave the next. It was frustrating. She kept reminding herself that they were only marrying because of the baby. They didn't feel anything for each other—apart from an irresistible, devastating attraction. Like moths drawn to a flame.

But, with Emilio's power and influence, she was likely to be the moth and she would not allow her wings to be singed by him.

Seeing him in front of his private plane now, in a dark suit and a pair of aviators, drove home just how far removed the two of them were, despite Jasmine's success. It was confirmation that she had been right to marry him for the sake of their child, but that she could never trust or rely on him, because Emilio could destroy her more utterly than anyone else.

I shouldn't be going on honeymoon, she thought as they

climbed the stairs into the plane. *I should stay here and build SOP.*

But she couldn't leave.

Emilio was still holding on to her hand. She understood why he'd done it outside: they needed to look like a real couple, a growing family. But in here, when it was just the two of them and his driver, all it did was needlessly torture them with a passion she wouldn't allow.

She looked around her, taking in the smell of expensive leather and the vast array of seating. A polished wooden wall stood at the back, obscuring her view.

Emilio saw her looking. 'The bedroom is back there.'

The bedroom—as in, singular. After an entire day spent in close proximity to Emilio, after kissing him and drowning in that kiss, if they shared a bed Jasmine wasn't sure that she would be able to fight this thing between them.

She needed to sit alone, or she needed to leave.

Emilio could see a mess of thoughts in Jasmine's eyes. It was why he'd kept hold of her hand. He didn't know how she would react to such a show of his wealth. If she would want to flee.

As soon as the doors closed, she pulled her hand from his and moved to one of the single seats towards the front of the plane which forced James, his trusted driver, to sit all the way at the rear. Like a sentry at the bedroom door. She was still trying exceptionally hard to maintain their distance, then. Of course, if that was what she wanted, he would respect it. That didn't mean he had to like it.

He settled into the seat closest to hers, swivelling them both so that he could see her. Waited for her to voice her thoughts.

'I don't see why we need to go on a honeymoon,' she finally said. 'Why are we even bothering? The wedding is over;

we're married. Everyone in New York knows I'm Jasmine De Luca now. We live together. I don't see why we need to play this game any more when we could just go about our lives.'

'You're right, everyone knows we're married. And the expectation is that newlyweds would have a honeymoon. It would be particularly strange for *us* not to have one.'

'I'm not buying it, Emilio. We're both busy people; it wouldn't be out of the realm of possibility that we would be too busy to have one. So what's the real reason?'

The real reason was that Emilio needed to visit the vineyards. He needed to deal with his mother's will. And he wasn't going to leave his pregnant wife alone while he did so. He didn't know exactly when his father's indifference for him had started but, having seen the way his parents lived, he was sure his father would not have been attentive to his mother during her pregnancy.

He'd still been young when he'd noticed how separate their lives were. Nobody had ever acknowledged it—he wasn't sure his brother had even realised it—but once Emilio had spotted the divide it had been obvious. His father hadn't allowed the *contessa* into the affairs of Perlano. She'd had no say in De Luca and Co, despite how much she'd loved the vineyards. She'd never gone to his father with any matters concerning her own businesses. She'd insisted they ate together as family, but that had come about *because* it was the only time they were a family.

Even then, Emilio's father had barely looked at him.

The life Jasmine had laid out for them, the rules he had agreed to, meant there would be so much distance between them too. They would be leading separate lives. Just like his parents.

Emilio wanted to be a better man, be everything his father wasn't. And, even though there was no love in this marriage, there was respect, there was attraction. Jasmine was his wife. And he would do everything in his power to make up for that distance between them.

Which meant he had to start being open with her, where he could.

'We're going to Perlano.'

Jasmine didn't say anything for a moment. A crease formed between her eyebrows, and he knew she was trying to piece things together. It would be interesting to see what she came up with.

'You said this baby is a De Luca heir. Are you taking me there to show me what they'll inherit? Because I already know about the estate.'

Emilio gave a bitter laugh. 'How much research did you do on me?'

'Enough.'

'You don't know anything, Jasmine,' he said gently.

'Then tell me. I want us to be honest. I want us to know each other better. We're going to be a family. We can make life or death decisions for each other; surely, we need honesty and trust?'

Emilio took a deep breath. 'You're right. And you're partly correct about Perlano. I was born there. My father was Conte di Perlano. He died eight years ago, and the title and estate were passed down to my brother.'

'Enzo.'

Emilio nodded.

'Our family legacy is hundreds of years old. The companies, estates, and wealth all belong to the *conte*.'

'Wait,' Jasmine said, sounding shocked. 'Are you telling me you get nothing?'

'Yes. That is, until recently.'

'What happened?'

'It's a long story, Jasmine.'

'We're forty thousand feet in the air, Emilio, we've got nothing but time.'

This was too much. Telling Jasmine about the will would mean revealing so much more about his childhood, his family. He'd never been this vulnerable with anyone. Not since Gia. But he knew Jasmine wouldn't stop until she knew. And she had a right to push: this included their child.

It was the comforting hand she placed on his thigh that finally made him speak. No partner, Gia included, had offered him that before.

'When we were younger, much younger, my father gifted the vineyards to my mother. Everyone knew how much she loved them. In fact, for years I suspected that the only reason she stayed married to my father was because of them. Growing up, we all knew there was a condition attached to her ownership—that upon her death Enzo would receive them.'

'That way the legacy would be whole again,' Jasmine guessed.

'Yes. When she died, her will was read. She had honoured my father's wishes.'

'So what happened?'

'The day you came to my office, I had received a different version of her will, a later version. Her lawyer says it's valid. In it, she has left the vineyards to me.'

Understanding dawned on Jasmine's face. 'And our baby will inherit them.'

Emilio nodded.

'There's more you aren't telling me… What was in the wills—both your father's and mother's?'

'My father left everything to my brother.'

'And nothing to you. Like, at all?' Jasmine was outraged and it filled him with a bitter sort of happiness to have someone upset for him.

He shrugged. 'In death as in life.'

'What does that mean?'

'It doesn't matter.' Emilio appreciated her concern, but it wouldn't fix anything. It wouldn't heal the hurt from his childhood. It wouldn't make him any more worthy of love now. He was who he was, the sum total of all the rejection he'd experienced. 'My mother left everything to me. I think it was her way of trying to balance things.'

'Is this why you're being so pig-headed about being there for our child?'

'I know what it's like to have a father around and not have him care.'

'And I know what it's like to watch a father walk away. That doesn't mean we would ever do those things.'

'I know we won't, *belleza*, because I won't let that happen.'

Jasmine leaned forward, taking Emilio's hands. He wanted to pull her off her seat and onto his lap, but he couldn't. Not without breaking his promise to her.

So, as he did every day, he fought his impulses.

Jasmine knew there was so much Emilio must be leaving unsaid, but for once she was happy to allow it. He had already revealed so much, especially about his father. How ironic that the man she found most irresistible had had a disappointment for a father too.

Emilio wouldn't be like that. She could see how much he was trying to be there for their child. After this conversation, even his insistence that she move into his home looked a little different. Had he been difficult? Yes. But the way he spoke of his mother and of wanting to fight for his child's inheritance told her that the move hadn't just been for appearances.

'Can I ask you something?'

'Anything, *belleza*,' Emilio replied.

'When you insisted we move in with you, was it so you

could keep an eye on us?' She placed one hand on her stomach, her tiny bump. 'Take care of us?'

Emilio looked out of the window, refusing to answer. But it was answer enough for her.

'I thought so. You're a good man, Emilio.'

'Don't.' He closed his eyes tightly, as if that would erase the words' existence.

Why wouldn't he hear them? Jasmine was determined to find out. To seek out the real man he had buried away.

CHAPTER ELEVEN

JASMINE WASN'T SURE what to expect when she arrived in Perlano. During her research on Emilio, she'd been too focused on the man himself to spare many glances for the postcard-worthy images of the De Luca vineyards. Now, as James drove Emilio and her through the massive gates, she realised exactly how impressive his family's legacy was.

The beauty of this place, the scale of wealth, was unimaginable even for her. As she got a clearer look of the house, she thought it barely a house at all. It looked like some sort of boutique hotel, or a resort amongst the vineyards.

'You're very quiet,' Emilio said as the tyres beneath them crunched on the gravel path.

'So are you,' she replied. The closer they'd got to this place, the more subdued he'd become, until he was completely silent, a frown etched on his forehead. 'Is there anything I should know before going in?'

She could handle herself in any company, but Emilio came from a seriously old-money family. In New York that meant different traditions and norms; Jasmine could only imagine the same would be true here.

'Only that we will be sharing a room.'

'*What?* Emilio, we have rules in place.' Jasmine was already way too attracted to her husband. Sharing the same space with him in their private moments would only weaken her resolve. She didn't need that.

'And I plan to honour them. But we are in my family home. You are my wife. It would be strange to sleep apart. It'll be fine. Just trust me.'

Could she? After a lifetime of being let down by men who should have been there for her, Jasmine wasn't sure. It would take a lot longer for Emilio to earn that.

'Then give me a reason to. Tell me why we're sharing.'

Emilio was silent for a moment, his teeth grinding together. Just when she thought he wouldn't take that step she needed, he answered. 'The head of the household staff here is incredibly loyal to my brother. I don't want her to think our marriage isn't strong, or not what it seems—or to pass that suspicion on.' He glanced at her, his voice taking on a tone of resignation. 'I haven't forgotten the rules, Jasmine. If we have to share a bed, we'll find a way to make it work, but I will look for a solution that respects your boundaries first.'

'Fine.'

'Does that mean you trust me?' He gave her the smallest of smiles, but it was half-hearted at best. It was as if Emilio had lost his colour, his vibrancy, here.

'I wouldn't push it.'

This time, Jasmine waited for him to open the car door for her. After what he had said on the plane, she figured it wouldn't have been easy for him to be back here so soon after his mother had passed. And, with her gone, she could only imagine the other memories that would haunt him. She understood how a mother's love could keep the worst memories at bay.

Emilio took her hand and led her to the door. Before they reached it, it opened and out stepped an older woman, her black hair streaked with grey and tied back in a bun.

'Emilio?'

'*Buonasera*, Isabella.'

The old lady smiled at him and it seemed as if she was

about to reply, when Jasmine saw her eye catch their linked hands. The rings.

'Emilio,' Isabella said, voice full of concern, 'What did you do?'

That was an odd question—no congratulations? Was it because he'd married *Jasmine* or was there something else going on here?

'Make sure my wife is comfortable.'

'Of course.'

'Jasmine.' Jasmine extended her hand. Isabella took it, shaking it with warmth in her eyes, and Jasmine was relieved that the very obvious coolness in the air was not intended for her. It just made her more curious to know what had transpired.

'Welcome to Perlano, Jasmine,' Isabella said, in heavily accented English.

'Thank you.'

'I'll show you to our room,' Emilio said, before they could say any more. He hadn't let go of her hand during their entire interaction with Isabella, and now he led her through the house. It was somehow even more spectacular inside than out. Parts of it seemed historic—Jasmine had no idea how old—while others seemed modern, carefully styled to fit with the rest. She wondered how much of it had been altered over the years. Wondered what it would be like to be part of a history like this.

She stuck close to Emilio as he led her up a flight of stairs. She could feel the heat of his body radiate through his suit, the warmth that she was growing so accustomed to.

Their room was situated in the corner of the house and painted in a dark green. There was a sturdy carved four-poster bed against the one wall with dark wood accents. The air of masculinity in this room was unmistakeable, but Jasmine could see how the man who'd dreamt up this room would have such a wonderland of a garden in New York. And, when she walked to the window, she could see the gardens were just as stunning, with a hedge maze and a breathtaking fountain.

'This is where we will sleep,' Emilio said. 'I'll bring in our luggage. You can get comfortable.' He was out of the door before she even had a chance to ask him if he was okay. She wanted to go after him, but if he had left it meant he wanted a moment to himself and she had to respect that.

And, after all, weren't her rules in place to prevent her from becoming emotionally attached to him?

That didn't mean she didn't want answers. She was curious about so many things. Who Emilio really was. What had happened in the past. What his family was like. And she had never in her life stayed anywhere as old as this place. So, despite Emilio's words and her own exhaustion, what she really wanted to do was explore. She hadn't been told she wasn't allowed to…and, as a De Luca herself, surely she now had the right?

She left the room and made her way along the top floor, opening doors and peeking inside. Many seemed to lead to guest rooms, but there was only one that she thought could rival Emilio's room for the best view. When she looked out of the large window, she saw rolling hills of vineyards, all lush and green. The bed was positioned in such a way that whoever lay there would be able to see them lying down.

She continued exploring and found a library and an office which also had a view of the vineyards. Every wall had some sort of painting; some looked ancient.

Finally, she came upon a small staircase—probably intended for staff. Eager to see where it led, she went down the winding stone steps that led to a door that was slightly ajar. Beyond it, she could hear voices. One of them was unmistakeably Emilio's.

'Does Enzo know you're here?' A woman said—Isabella, Jasmine realized—just as she was about to step through. Something made her pause to stop and listen. 'With a wife, no less!'

'Lower your voice,' Emilio instructed. 'And, no, he doesn't know, and you won't be telling him either.'

Jasmine was torn. She wanted to know what was being kept from her, but also knew she shouldn't be caught eavesdropping either. Quietly, she turned and retreated upstairs, her heart racing and a tingling in her chest. Why wasn't Enzo to know they were there? Why had Isabella, who'd seemed genuinely welcoming to Jasmine, twice now spoken to Emilio without that same warmth? Surely Emilio couldn't keep their presence in Italy a secret from his brother? Prior to their wedding, being seen in public had been the plan.

None of this made any sense.

She paced the room, wringing her fingers. There was very obviously a secret being kept from her. Another man withholding information. Another man she shouldn't trust. A man she was having a baby with, whom she was married to.

She had been understanding enough, but no more. Emilio was going to tell her the truth.

When he walked into the room carrying their luggage, the words were out of her mouth before he could even close the door. 'What's going on, Emilio?'

'What do you mean?' He closed the door with a soft click.

His calm infuriated her even more. A stiffness formed in her neck. 'I heard you and Isabella,' she said in a sharp tone. 'Enzo doesn't know about me or that we're here.'

'Were you eavesdropping on me?' His eyes flashed. As if she should be the one ashamed of their actions, when he was the person keeping secrets! Just like Richard. Just like Zara.

'I was exploring and overheard you, then came straight

back here to give *you* the opportunity to be honest with me,' she said lowly, barely able to keep the growl out of her voice.

'It's nothing you have to worry about,' he said, placing the bags on the tufted ottoman at the foot of the bed.

'Like hell it isn't!' Jasmine had to take a breath to stop her temper taking over. 'You've dragged me across the world for a "honeymoon" that isn't happening. I could have been home working. It's a sacrifice for me to be here, Emilio, so I demand answers. What *was* that between you and Isabella? Why shouldn't Enzo know we're here?'

'Jasmine.' Emilio pinched the bridge of his nose. His shoulders slumped. When he looked at her, his eyes appeared haunted.

In that moment, he seemed so weary, so tormented, that it almost took the wind out of Jasmine's sails, but she still had a right to know. Otherwise, she would leave. She'd had enough of disappointment, of secrets. She couldn't be lied to again.

'What. Is. Going. On?'

'I don't want Enzo to know we're here. I don't want to give him a reason to come here.'

She remembered their chat on the plane, and why they were in Perlano. How Emilio's father had left nothing to him. He'd clearly favoured Emilio's brother.

'In death as in life.' It wasn't easy having a disappointment for a father; Jasmine knew that. She tried hard to calm herself, to push through her anger and annoyance so she could understand his actions. 'Why? Is it because of the will?'

'Yes. As soon as Enzo finds out, he will do what he can to see it doesn't happen.'

'Why would Enzo fight you for the vineyards if your mother has left them to you? You both run the company anyway, so what does it matter? Wouldn't he want to respect her wishes?'

'Enzo and I have a…fractious relationship. We don't talk

unless it's about work, and even then we avoid it where we can. Since my mother's funeral, we haven't had any contact at all.'

Jasmine could only imagine how painful it would be to lose the only loving parent and then have no one to help with the grief, despite having a sibling. And one day, she realised, she might be in that position.

It was a sobering thought. She put aside her irritation and walked over, taking Emilio's hand and pulling him to sit with her on the couch in front of the large fireplace. She had to ignore the feeling his touch constantly awakened in her; any distraction was not welcome right now.

'I need more than that, Emilio,' she said, deliberately keeping her voice gentle.

It looked as though he was struggling to voice his thoughts, so she waited patiently. Allowing him the moment he needed but showing him she would not settle for anything but the truth.

'Enzo and I didn't have the same childhood,' Emilio said at last. 'He got to enjoy the affection of both our parents. Had everything handed to him, purely for being born first. Meanwhile, I had to endure being treated like an afterthought by our father, even though I worked hard for all that I have, all that I accomplished.'

Jasmine nodded, urging him to continue. She was trying not to rush to any judgments, but she couldn't help the flare of anger towards his father.

'My father showered Enzo with attention and praise, and Enzo *worshipped* him. He would always follow his word as law, and I suppose he had no reason not to. So he believes the estate should be whole and in the hands of the *conte*. He's possessive, and if anything is taken from him—or chooses to leave—he will ensure that no one can have it. That is just who my brother is. So you see, it's imperative that I deal with this will quickly. That Enzo remain in the dark. For our child's sake.'

'I'm sorry for what you've had to deal with, Emilio, but I can't shake the feeling that you're leaving something out. Tell me the rest of it.' She placed her palm on his cheek, offering comfort. Trying to convince him to trust her. 'Please.'

'I can't, Jasmine,' he said, removing himself from her embrace with a shaking hand. 'Because, if I do, you'll hate me too. You'll hate me as much as I hate myself.'

What did that mean?

'Emilio!' she called out, reaching a hand out to him, but he was already out the door.

Emilio rushed outside, needing a moment to clear his mind. He understood that Jasmine wanted to know everything. The buttoned-up side of her had to be in control of every aspect of her—and, he suspected, their baby's—life, but he couldn't tell her this. He couldn't tell her why Enzo hated him so much. Everyone else might have moved on from the Gia scandal, but Emilio never would.

It had revealed to himself the kind of person he truly was. Impulsive. Selfish. Unlovable. Worth a good time, a meaningless night, but nothing more.

From this spot in the grounds, he could see the spire of the church where his mother was buried.

'You made a mistake.'

His mother had been right.

It had been a mistake that night, all those years ago, when he had indulged Gia.

'You can't make a girl drink alone. Where's your chivalry?' Gia said, shaking a bottle of wine at Emilio from where she was sitting at the bistro table on the balcony of his room.

'We were supposed to have our cake tasting today. On the drive, Enzo said he's feeling the pressure of living up to your

father's legacy in the company and, when we got there, he kept checking his phone, then he got a call and had to leave. The driver brought me back here afterwards. Look at me. Am I not beautiful enough for him to ignore the company when he's with me?'

'You're more than. He's a fool,' Emilio said, taking a seat.

'He is. But at least I have you. You'll always be there for me.' Gia smiled one of those smiles that always punched him in the gut. A smile that was reserved only for him.

'Always. I know what it's like to be ignored by my brother. I don't want that for you.'

Gia cupped his cheek. 'I know. No one cares for me like you do, Emilio.'

He more than cared. He was falling in love.

It had all been a mistake and now, standing where he had approached his brother eight years ago to ask if they could talk, glancing over his shoulder at the house behind him, at the window of the room that had once belonged to Enzo, the room where he'd made his confession, Emilio was thrown back to that day.

'What is it, Emilio?' Enzo asked with a hint of impatience when they went to his room to speak privately. He was likely late for something but the grounds weren't the right place for this conversation. He was always rushing somewhere since taking over De Luca and Co. There was always some business to attend to. Emilio knew both Gia and his mother were feeling his absence. That was why Gia had been drinking the night before.

'Like I said, we need to talk.' Emilio's heart was racing. His hands growing clammy as shame washed over him. 'It's about Gia.'

Enzo's face morphed from impatience to concern instantly. 'Has something happened? Is she okay?'

'She's fine...but something has happened. I want you to know this was never my intention.'

'Out with it, Emilio,' Enzo said, growing angry.

'Last night Gia came to see me. She was upset that you'd left her again—'

'I have a company to run and people to look after. There was an emergency!'

'It doesn't matter, Enzo. She needed you and you left her.'

'She had to choose cake, for heaven's sake.' Enzo straightened. 'But that's not what you want to tell me, is it?'

'No, it's not. She was upset and getting drunk, and asked me to drink with her so she could talk.'

A nerve started throbbing in Enzo's temple. 'What did you do?'

'I got drunk,' Emilio admitted and steeled his spine, forcing himself to say the next words even as they gouged him raw on the inside, like blades carving his betrayal into his soul. 'And we slept together.'

He watched, horrified, as Enzo's face slackened, losing all trace of anger, as if he was numb. Then he saw it—the flash of devastation in his brother's eyes. The hurt that Enzo couldn't conceal. Emilio wanted to vomit. His brother—big and proud and a source of so much heartache for Emilio—stumbled back until his foot caught the leather arm chair and he fell into it. Heavily.

The thud reverberated in Emilio's head. He had never intended to let his attraction to Gia get this far. He'd never intended to hurt Enzo like this, even if his brother constantly hurt him by bragging about all he'd got to do with their father over dinner during all the years they'd grown up.

And yet a small part of him also wanted to ask his brother how it felt to be rejected—and Emilio knew right then the loathsome person he truly was. And he hated himself just as much as everyone else did.

Emilio turned away from the house and looked out over Perlano. There was no love lost between Enzo, the perfect son, and him, but that day haunted him still. From the moment he'd met Gia, they'd had a connection. At first, he'd foolishly thought it was friendship. She would tell him everything: what she'd done, things she'd looked forward to. Things about Enzo: how Enzo had feared he would never live up to their father. How Enzo had worried that he wouldn't leave a lasting mark, like all the *contes* before him had. Emilio and Gia had never had a secret, and with her he could be himself. Could be vulnerable. He hadn't needed walls or to hide his pain.

But falling in love with Gia had never meant that Emilio intended to act on their attraction. Except he'd got drunk, lost control and done just that. He should have pushed Gia away that night, told her that they needed stop.

But his self-loathing hadn't diluted the hate he'd felt when Enzo had paid Gia to leave, or when she'd taken the money. That had hurt most of all.

Emilio turned his face up to the sky. The last of the day's rays did nothing to warm him. Not when he felt so empty inside. He'd foolishly thought they'd had something special.

'He's forcing me to leave.'

'What do you mean? What did he do?'

'He paid me.'

'He paid you to leave?' Emilio was incandescent with rage. *They'd made a mistake, but paying Gia? An insult against her integrity like that was beyond the pale!* *'I'll come with you. I'll leave all of this behind. We can start over somewhere else, just the two of us.'*

'I wish that were possible, but I don't want to jeopardise all that I have been given, Emilio.'

The words were a slap in the face, sobering. *'Is the money worth more than me?'* *She stood there in all her poised beauty, silent. 'Answer me, Gia. Do you want fame and fortune more than us? Than me?'*

She looked him in the eyes. Unwavering. Certain. 'Yes. It was a fantasy, Emilio. I deserve more. It's over.'

All alone outside, Emilio laughed humourlessly at his own idiocy. It truly had been a fantasy to think Gia would choose him. She must have seen the same thing within him that his father had—something rotten, unlovable. Of course she'd tossed him away to keep chasing the limelight. Not that much had come of that for her. Wasn't it ironic how his brother had worried about leaving his mark and yet that was something Emilio had done so thoroughly in the worst way?

And now he was married. Emilio toyed with the new ring on his finger, reminding himself that he could never expect love from Jasmine. A woman who would never have married him if it hadn't been for the baby. She hadn't chosen him. She was just a good mother.

She wasn't his.

This time he would do the right thing and keep his distance.

Even though it was harder than it had ever been with Gia.

Jasmine searched for Emilio all over the house until she ran into Isabella. 'Have you seen Emilio?'

Isabella smiled knowingly. 'Come.'

She led Jasmine outside to a place near the gardens Jasmine hadn't spotted from their window. And standing out there, like a lonely beacon, was her husband.

'They will never admit it, but these two brothers are more alike than they realise,' Isabella said. She squeezed Jasmine's hands gently and left.

Jasmine slowly approached Emilio, eyes on his still form. The white shirt-sleeves were pushed back, exposing his forearms. One hand was in his trouser pocket, and the other hanging by his side, the thumb rubbing his wedding band.

This man, so focussed on doing the right thing that he had married a near stranger for it. He had the world at his feet. He had money, power, good looks, all of which allowed him to have his way. Yet he hadn't used that to make his problem—Jasmine and their child—disappear as she would have expected of someone in his place. Instead, he'd chosen to bring them into his life.

What could a man like that have done to make him hate himself? And why did he think it would make her do the same? How bad could it be?

'You don't have to bear it alone...whatever it is that's made you hurt so much,' she said, coming to stand next to him. 'You can talk to me.'

But he remained stoic.

So Jasmine spoke instead. 'When we hooked up that day, I was left at the altar.' She chanced a look at him. While he still gazed out at the horizon, she could tell he was listening. 'Before that, I hadn't been intimate with my fiancé in three months.'

He looked at her then, a frown dawning on his face.

'Just as I was meant to walk down the aisle, the wedding co-ordinator gave me a letter from Richard. He said he couldn't marry me. Apparently, I'm controlling...tightly-wound. He said that he loved Zara, and had already been with her for five months—my maid of honour. *She* wasn't stifling to be around. *She* didn't suck the joy out of life.'

Jasmine huffed a chuckle. She had become the cliché. Had been humiliated for months. 'All that time I thought he was just too busy to make time for us to be together. His work was stressful, so I understood. I poured all that extra time into SOP. Meanwhile, he was spending it with my best friend, who was helping me plan my wedding.'

Jasmine remembered the pain, the anger. It didn't burn as brightly any more but it hadn't faded completely. 'So I left my wedding dress there, went home and changed into the most scandalous dress SOP stocked and ran off to Boulevard, determined to have a good time and ignore the world…and then I ran into you.'

Emilio was watching her closely. Now that Jasmine had started talking, she didn't want to stop, so even though she kept her gaze straight ahead she moved closer to Emilio, just as her body always wanted to do. Had done, from the first moment they'd met.

'I should have seen it coming, seen the signs. After all, my father had given me a great lesson in that. I was five and I still remember him walking out the door, remember asking him where he was going. If I could go with him. He just walked out and closed the door, ignoring me. My mother ran out after him in tears. When she came back in, she was broken, sobbing on the floor. I curled around her, holding her until she could stop.'

Jasmine turned to face Emilio then. She needed him to understand. 'So, you see, I have little incentive to trust—especially to trust a man.'

'Do you still love Richard?' Emilio asked, his voice low, even.

'No. I was angry. I guess I still am a little. I was hurt. But I wasn't sad. Not about him anyway. I didn't even miss him afterwards. Maybe I never loved him. Maybe it's complicated. Maybe I don't believe in love at all at this point. All I've seen it do is hurt and destroy and disappoint.'

They fell into silence. Jasmine's mind was a flurry of memories, hopes, fears—everything that pushed her to be independent at all costs. To be successful. To meet and exceed every goal.

'Have you ever heard from your father?' There was a note of caution in Emilio's question.

'No.'

'Do you want to?'

'You know where he is.'

Emilio nodded.

A small spark of surprise flared and died. Emilio's file on her probably detailed her entire ancestry, but she didn't care. She had the chance to get answers, but those answers would come from a man who had looked at her without a smile and left without a goodbye. Had left her mother devastated. Shattered. She didn't want anything from a person capable of such immense cruelty. 'No, I don't want to know. Some things are best left in the past.'

'That's true,' Emilio agreed.

'Whatever you're shouldering, Emilio, it's not just in your past. It's affecting your present. How much power are you going to give it?'

'Belleza.' He swallowed hard. His dark eyes reflected so much hurt and remorse that Jasmine wanted to take him into her arms, but she didn't. 'I can't tell you.'

And there it was. That was why, no matter how good a man he was, no matter how much she wanted to help him, she still couldn't trust him.

CHAPTER TWELVE

EMILIO LAY ON the leather couch, a blanket tossed over his body, staring at the patterns in the ceiling of his bedroom. He traced every crystal in the chandelier with his eyes. He had barely slept. He kept thinking of everything Jasmine had said. How she couldn't trust men. Couldn't trust him, until he opened up.

Emilio couldn't allay any of her fears. He didn't want to lie to her, and he couldn't tell her the truth. Being honest with her about Gia would only lose him any hope of having his child in his life, because he knew she would leave.

He couldn't have that.

And keeping something from her wasn't the same as lying. Jasmine was able to make a clean break from her past, but Emilio's followed him. He might hate his brother for everything Enzo had taken from him—his father's affection, Gia—but he would always be in Emilio's life. Emilio had worked too hard for his position in the company to leave, and once the issue with vineyards was settled there would never be any escape.

He reached for his watch and in the sliver of light leaking through the curtains saw that it was still very early. Jasmine wouldn't be awake for another few hours, but he could get up and start his walkthrough of the vineyards.

He tossed aside the blanket and crept to the bathroom as quietly as he could, trying not to disturb her. But he couldn't resist looking at her. So peacefully asleep. Her curls wild, falling over the pillow like a halo of gold. She was so utterly beautiful, and she was married to him. But she was not his. She was so close but beyond his reach.

How would he survive this marriage? How could he wake up to her every morning and see her every night and not lose his mind to this longing, this constant ache? Every single time he saw her he had to fight the urge to kiss her senseless. To lose himself in her. He had felt her around him once and craved to feel it again—and wished in equal measure to have it wiped from his mind. At least then he wouldn't know how perfectly they fit in passion.

'Emilio,' she mumbled in her sleep and his heart rate notched up a beat. Was she dreaming of him? Were her dreams anything like his?

He forced himself into the bathroom and turned on the shower. Hard, and lusting after his wife, he took himself in hand, thinking about her taste. About Jasmine's lips on his. Her lips around his hardness. The euphoria of plunging into her over and over. Then, with her name on his lips, he was spilling into his hand, his release washed away in the current of water. It cleared his mind a little, but not enough to rid himself of this need for her.

It was always there.

Emilio dried off then dressed in a suit. He'd intended to walk out of his room without a backward glance but found himself lingering, going over and tucking her in firmly. It put a small, content smile on her sleeping face, a softness she wilfully kept at bay when awake. That fun, devil-may-care Jasmine was in there somewhere. Maybe one day she would trust him enough to let him see her again.

Trust you without you telling her about Gia?

Maybe not.

Emilio left the room and headed outside.

The sun was low in the sky and there wasn't a soul out in the vineyard yet. He hadn't seen it this quiet in a long time. Before his mother had died, he'd spent every moment he could spare with her. In fact, he hadn't even come out here the last time he had been to Perlano. But how well he remembered running around here as a small boy, brandishing his tiny tools.

'I want to help, Mamma! See, I brought my shovel!'

'Very good, piccolo re. Are you ready to get dirty? There's a lot of mulch here and I need a very strong helper.'

'I'm strong!'

'The strongest, mio figlio.'

'Emilio!'

The memory of his mother in her sun hat and gloves dissipated like smoke. He wasn't five years old now. He had to keep his mind focussed.

'I wasn't expecting you.'

Emilio turned towards the voice. '*Buongiorno*, Marco. How busy is your morning?'

Marco managed production here from seed to cellar, so Emilio suspected the answer was 'very'. But he'd make time for the head of De Luca and Co's North American empire.

'It depends.'

'I need a full tour.'

'Of course,' Marco replied, attaching a stylus to his tablet. 'Where would you like to start?'

They walked amongst the rows of lush green plants, Marco talking about current projects, changes they'd implemented, the health of the plants and expected harvest dates. He emailed copies of reports to Emilio from his tablet, which Emilio skimmed on his phone as they spoke.

'How often would my mother come out here?'

'Before she became ill, most days. Afterwards, whenever she could manage. Even then we kept her abreast of operations. When she was well, she would do a full walk-through and inspection every quarter, but she kept a close eye on the plants through each stage of growth.'

Emilio lived in New York and would have a baby soon enough. How would he manage to keep a similar schedule?

'It wasn't necessary. I assure you, Emilio, production is well in hand.'

That was beside the point. His mother had trusted him with her most prized possession. He couldn't let her down. But he couldn't let his family down either. Jasmine would be fine without him, but he didn't want to be away from his child.

Truth be told, he didn't want to be away from Jasmine either. No matter how maddening her presence was.

'I'm certain it is. Show me the rest.'

Jasmine was awake and working in the kitchen when he returned. For a moment, he couldn't speak, couldn't think. The sunlight fell over her and, with her curly hair loose, she radiated gold. He found himself being carried to her—unsure of what he would do when he reached her, only knowing that he needed to touch her, to feel her sun-kissed warmth against him.

'Emilio, what are you doing back so soon?'

He stopped before he could reach her, the spell broken. Why did this woman affect him so? 'What are you talking about?'

'Isabella said you were gone before breakfast. She said not to expect you until much later.'

Sometimes it was easy to forget how well Isabella knew him. Especially considering how cold she had turned after Emilio had slept with Gia. He had been so close to her, and he felt the loss acutely. Gone was her pet name for him: her *peluche*. After that, he'd become nothing but Emilio.

'I was able to get what I needed done quickly. We don't have time to waste. Make sure you're ready to leave this afternoon. We're going to Vozzano.'

***

Jasmine buckled herself into the back seat of a gleaming black saloon as Emilio shut the door. She looked in the mirror, watching their luggage being moved from the plane to the boot of the car. Once it was in, she watched Emilio round the car and join her, slipping in elegantly.

'How are you feeling?'

He had been so attentive since leaving Perlano. She could see some of the Emilio that she had been growing accustomed to in New York come out again. He clearly loved the place, but it dimmed his light.

'Still fine,' she said. He had asked her the question when they'd left Perlano, on the plane and now again. She had to admit, the attention felt good. While she wasn't relying on him, he was choosing to take care of her. And, even though she didn't mean to, her brain automatically compared him to Richard. A man who would be chivalrous to a point in public but not when they were alone. Emilio was the same person all the time.

When Jasmine had woken that morning, she'd found herself so comfortably tucked in that she had slept far later than she usually did. And, even though they'd had to share *his* room, he hadn't pushed her to ignore her boundaries for him. Emilio had made sure she was comfortable before he'd slept on the couch.

Jasmine hadn't anticipated feeling guilty about that. Hadn't considered that she might want him next to her, might crave his warmth and that open-sea scent. Or that she'd be so acutely aware of his presence in the dark that it would take a long time for her to fall asleep. When she had slept, she'd dreamt of his hands on her body, his mouth trailing her skin. She'd awoken with his name on her lips.

She'd wanted to see Italy for so long—the landscape, the fashion. But she'd been so focussed on SOP that she hadn't been able to take a holiday in years. And yet now, she didn't look out of the window in wonder. She watched Emilio. She took in the relaxed posture of his body, the suit that fit him so deliciously. A suit that belied the power hidden beneath. She had seen that body. Felt it. It still haunted her dreams.

'Why are you staring?'

She startled. 'What?'

'I can feel the way you're looking at me, *belleza*. It's distracting.'

Jasmine laughed. 'I would have thought you'd be used to it.'

'I'm not used to it from my wife.' He turned to her and winked. Such a small action, but still it got her heart fluttering.

She rolled her eyes at him, pretending to be unaffected, but the smile on his face told her she was fooling no one.

'We're not far from Vozzano now,' he told her. 'I'll take you to the house and get you comfortable, then go check on the vineyards here.'

Jasmine thought about how desolate he had seemed when they'd spoken the day before and how agitated he'd been when he'd returned from the vineyard earlier. She didn't want him to face this alone. He was the father of her baby, after all. His wellbeing was a concern to her.

Is that all? You're lying to yourself, Jasmine.

'I'm going with you,' she said.

'No, you're not. You've been working all day, even on the plane.'

Only to give her something to concentrate on that wasn't Emilio, who'd seemed to be controlling her libido telepathically.

'And there will be a lot of walking to do. You need to rest.'

'I'm pregnant, Emilio, not an invalid.' She meant to snap at him but even she heard the lack of bite in her words. This was the man she was likely to spend the next twenty years with—a long time to constantly skirt the truth—so she chose honesty. 'I'd like to be there for you. I've seen the difference in you here. Allow someone in your corner.'

He looked at her. In that split second she saw both longing and rejection building, but then he clenched his jaw, took a breath and said, 'Fine.'

It was a small step, but a step nonetheless.

They arrived at a hilly estate, covered in rows and rows of vines. At the very top sat a stone house with a muted red roof. In fact, 'house' was way too understated a word for the structure. Broad-leafed trees and tall conifers stood around it. Sunlight fell in broad beams over the whole estate, creating sharp shadows and a rainbow of shades. It was utterly spectacular. She loved it even more than Perlano, and she hadn't even been inside yet.

'Wow...' She breathed.

'I love New York, but nothing beats this place,' Emilio said.

'I would miss this. How do you manage to stay away?'

'I have little business here usually. I miss it occasionally, but I don't have room in my life for indulging that kind of impulse.'

Emilio certainly didn't strike her as impulsive. He was calculated. It was as if his entire life was a chess board. He didn't move the pieces without thinking five steps ahead. The only impulsive thing he'd done in their acquaintance was sleep with her.

'Do you ever take time away from work?' The irony of Jasmine asking that question wasn't lost on her but, unlike her, Emilio had safety nets.

'I suppose I did when my mother passed.'

'That doesn't count. You were doing your duty.'

'I always am.'

That statement seemed loaded with things he didn't want to talk about, but Jasmine wanted to know. Every time she dug a little deeper with Emilio, she found more questions. It only made her more curious. But she didn't want to have to ask. She wanted him to *want* to share with her.

The car drew to a stop outside a building that looked like something from a postcard.

'I need you to understand the trust I am showing you by allowing you in here,' Emilio said. 'One day the vineyards will belong to our child, but—'

'Emilio, I understand. This is your family legacy.' She waited for him to open the door for her, and this time she took his hand in hers, offering whatever support she could.

She watched him shrug on the mask of indomitable CEO as they began their tour of the Vozzano winery. Throughout his questions, she never retracted her hand, and neither did he. When the sun finally started to sink, they stood amongst the grapes alone.

'Do you think they'll tell Enzo you've been here?' Jasmine asked, still awed by the view.

'They have no reason to. They don't know why I've been here. Even so, we need to be cautious.'

Jasmine watched the way he glanced out at Vozzano, a faraway look in his eye. She wanted to know what he was thinking. Wanted him to take her through his memories,

'I want to see something,' he said, and they began the walk back up towards the buildings. When they got there, he stopped at an old tree and ran his fingers over his name carved in the wood. 'My mother did this.'

Jasmine stepped closer to examine the bark and saw a jaggedly etched *Emilio*, deep enough to withstand the years.

'We came here for a few days—just the two of us and my tutors. On our last evening here, after I had helped tend to the grapes, she carved my name into the tree. She said a piece of me will always be here.'

Jasmine wrapped her arms around Emilio. There was so much grief in his voice, it broke her heart. There had clearly been so much love between Emilio and his mother. She couldn't imagine the pain he was in. Especially since, from the terms of his will, it seemed that his father had had no interest in him. It surprised Jasmine how angry that made her.

'You two had a special bond.'

Emilio didn't respond. Jasmine wasn't sure he could, considering how hard the muscle in his jaw was feathering. She didn't want Emilio trying to hide what he felt. Keeping his vulnerabilities to himself. She wanted to see them. Help him bear them.

'Tell me, Emilio,' she urged. 'Tell me the words you're trying to swallow down.'

'I could never express to you exactly what it means that my mother left this to me. The vineyards... It means more than everything else she had because they weren't hers for good. She loved something that wasn't hers to love—selflessly. I don't want to let her down.'

He turned to Jasmine then and she could the sincerity in his expressive eyes. 'I don't want to let you and our baby down either, by travelling back and forth between here and New York all the time. Leaving you both when you need me.'

'Emilio.' She cupped his cheek and he instantly leaned into the touch, which made her close the distance between their bodies, surrendering to the gravitational pull that had existed between them from the first moment she'd caught a glimpse of him in a crowded club. 'We'll make it work. I promise.'

With the golden setting sun between them, Jasmine reached across the small space to Emilio. An inch away from his lips. His breath ghosted over hers. Myriad emotions swam in his fathomless eyes. A hunger for her. His hands curled into the fabric of her blouse at her waist. His resolve was weakening. Exactly what she wanted. What she needed.

'Kiss me,' she whispered. Begged. Instructed.

In a heartbeat, his lips were on hers and it felt so right. This was where she wanted to be: tasting him, feeling him, bathing in his warmth.

'Jasmine,' he said. A prayer. And then he was worshipping her. Every slide of his lips on hers was a veneration. The last rays of the day fell over their embrace like an ancient blessing. And she sighed. She sighed from the power of this kiss that she felt in every part of her. She never wanted to stop. She pressed her body against Emilio's, wrapped her arms around his neck. Felt his tighten around her back. They were connected by nearly every inch. And, when she traced his tongue with hers, he let out a choked sound. His hardness twitched against her.

She wanted to feel him again. To hell with her physical boundaries—she could look out for her independence *and* succumb to this passion.

'*Belleza*, we should leave here while I'm still capable of thinking straight.'

'Do I affect you that much?'

Emilio pressed his manhood even harder against her. 'You know precisely how badly you affect me.'

Jasmine grinned. 'Then let's go.'

CHAPTER THIRTEEN

EMILIO OPENED THE door to the grand house that sat at the very top of the estate. The heavy wood swung inwards with barely a creak. He loved this place and now he would be sharing it with Jasmine.

Jasmine, who stood behind him. Jasmine, whose kiss had brought him out of the spiral he'd been falling into at the vineyard. Whose body called out to his.

He turned around and carried her bridal style over the threshold and into the grand foyer.

'What are you doing?' She laughed.

'Something that was a little overdue, don't you think?' He set her on her feet and watched her look around. Nothing had changed. The large wooden console table still bore a huge bouquet of flowers to greet all who entered. The same herringbone wooden floors covered the expanse of the entire house. The same chandelier hung above—the one his mother had wanted to change, but his father had always overruled her. The one his mother had preferred had eventually found a home in Emilio's bedroom in Perlano.

'After you.' He urged Jasmine into the rest of the house, still watching as she looked up at the vaulted ceiling and ran her hand over the venetian plaster that covered the walls.

'It's quiet here,' she said.

'That's because we're alone.' Enzo couldn't keep his distance any longer so he walked up behind her and wrapped his arms around her waist, kissing the side of her neck.

'No staff?' He loved how her voice changed when he touched her. It became breathy and soft. As if she was allowing him past that assertive barrier she always held in place.

'No. I've instructed them to take the week off. The staff quarters are down by the lake anyway,' he said against her skin.

'There's a lake?'

'Mmm-hmm. So it's just us, *belleza*.' A proposition that both excited him and terrified him. Especially when he felt as desperate for her as he had after their very first kiss.

'Alone in this big house...' She breathed. Her head was thrown against his shoulder. He could feel her pulse flutter, her chest heave as he dragged his hands up the front of her blouse. How easy it would be to unbutton her shirt. To slide his hands over her bare skin and see the goose bumps rise in their wake.

'Do it, Emilio.' He halted his roving touch. 'I can hear what you're thinking.'

'Are my thoughts that loud?' he asked as she turned in his arms.

'Only because they match mine,' she admitted.

Joy.

It overwhelmed him, pure and consuming, at the knowledge that she was as affected as he was. That she wanted him as much as he wanted her. The spell was woven and he couldn't break it. Not when she looked at him like that: begging...pleading for him to kiss her. It was what he wanted too, so he did. Not softly or gently, or in any way slowly to savour her, but hard and desperate. As if she was the first breath of air after he'd spent so long suffocating.

He grabbed her beneath her thighs and lifted her onto him. Jasmine wrapped her legs around his waist, anchoring herself to him, the curtain of her curls falling in a golden waterfall over his shoulder as she bent down to kiss him.

Dio! She's intoxicating.

He walked them over to the large couch that stood before a behemoth of a fireplace. It was magical in the winter; he wished he could transport them in time so he could lay her on the fur rug, with a crackling fire warming them both as he took her.

'Emilio, don't make me beg.'

He wanted her to. He wanted her to beg for him and only him. Wanted her to look at him as though he was worth something.

She did look at you like that. In the vineyard. It was true. And here he was, laying her on a couch, about to have his way when she deserved so much more. This rush to pleasure... it was what a hook-up was like. Jasmine was far from that. There was something morphing between them. She had been out there supporting him today. What would happen after they had sex? Would they go back to separate rooms? Live separate lives? Would she need to re-establish her boundaries?

I don't want that.

He wanted to nurture whatever this change was. He wanted to feel the way he did around her all the time. This drunken spell... it was how they had behaved that first night. Impulsively. That wasn't the man he'd vowed to be with Jasmine.

He didn't want to ruin this...whatever this was.

He cradled her face and broke the kiss.

'*Belleza*, it's been a long day. You must be tired.'

'Are you?' Her breath came in little pants that puffed over his lips and he wanted to kiss her again.

Don't ruin this, Emilio.

He brushed the back of his fingers along her cheek and over her hair. 'I'm going to run you a bath and, when you get out, I'll have dinner waiting.'

'That sounds nice.'

Not quite ready to let Jasmine go, Emilio carried her up the wide flight of stairs. She hadn't argued once. Whether she meant to or not, she was letting him see the softer, more laid-back side of her, and that felt momentous.

He took her through the master suite and into the bathroom, a marvel of marble and antique luxury with a chequerboard floor, and sat her down while he filled the tub large enough for two of him. Once the water was deep enough, he held out a hand. Jasmine took it and let him draw her to her feet. There, he slowly undressed her. Her gaze never strayed from his face. Instead of surrendering to the lust within him, he kissed her gently on the lips, then picked her up and placed her in the hot water.

'I'll see you soon,' he said and turned to leave, but she caught his hand.

'No,' she said. 'Join me.' It was a soft command.

'Jasmine...' Emilio looked down at her naked body. Being in that water would drive him insane.

'Please.'

One word was all it took to convince him. He shed his clothes and stepped into the bath, settling behind Jasmine and pulling her against his chest.

Jasmine placed her hand over his, linked their fingers and moved his hand over her skin, over her breast, then let go: silent permission for him to touch her. And he did, up her chest and over her throat. When he tightened his fingers ever so gently, Jasmine leaned her head back against his shoulder, lengthening her neck.

'Dove sei stato tutta la mia vita?' he said in a low voice against her skin. *Where have you been all my life?* Because this, right here—he and Jasmine, skin to skin—felt right in ways he couldn't express.

He moved his hand down, down, down over her ever so

slightly swollen belly. Only recently had she started showing. He had noticed in the two weeks leading up to the wedding and every day since. Jasmine was growing his child. His flesh and blood.

His miracle.

He walked around with the sonograph picture in his wallet, a constant reminder to make the right choices. A reminder that the vineyards were not just for him, but their future. His wife and child's.

With each day he felt more drawn, more connected to Jasmine. But it felt like the most intimate they had ever been, lying in this tub together. Even more intimate than the physical release of sex. This calmed his soul. This was spiritual.

She placed her hand on his. 'You've gotten quiet.'

'Don't worry about it, *belleza*, I'm just thinking.'

'What about?'

'Our baby.'

'Do you think we could bring him here?'

'Him?'

'Just a hunch.'

'We can bring her here as often as you'd like.'

Jasmine laughed. 'Do you have to disagree with me?'

'I just think that she will be like her mother.' He didn't want to curse his child to be anything like him. They would be sweet and good and pure, like Jasmine. 'And she will love running around this place.'

'Did you?'

'Yes…and no.'

'Tell me, Emilio.'

'What do you want to know?'

'Everything. Tell me what it was like growing up here and in Perlano.'

Emilio wanted to brush off the question, but he remembered how much she valued honesty. Hadn't he just decided he would make the right choices for his child? But it was more than that—he *wanted* to tell her.

'It was wonderful and it was terrible,' he admitted. 'Since I was little, my father had almost no interest in me. It didn't matter what I did or what I tried to achieve, it meant nothing to him. So I acted out. I partied.'

'With lots of women,' Jasmine added.

'Guilty.' He chuckled briefly. 'And still he didn't care. My mother had a rule—that we would have dinner together every night, and if both my parents were around it happened without fail. During those meals my father wouldn't speak unless he spoke to my mother. If he had a word to spare, it went to Enzo. Never to me.'

Jasmine's hand tightened over his own, but she said nothing.

'That didn't sit well with my mother.' Emilio smiled then, his cold heart warming with happier memories 'While Enzo was taken to work and on trips by our father, she would take me with her into the garden and the vineyards. It didn't matter what happened inside these houses because outside we could be happy.'

'What was she like?'

'Valentina De Luca was a fierce woman. People listened when she spoke. When she went away on business or to come here, she would bring me and my tutors along. Enzo may have learned all he knows from my father; I learned from my mother. She raised me alone. Clothed me. Educated me. Loved me. I may as well have had no father.'

'We're the same,' Jasmine said. 'We owe a lot to our mothers. Women who had to be far stronger than it was fair to expect.' She toyed with the ring on his finger. 'What about Enzo?'

'What about him?'

'What was your relationship like?'

'Prickly,' Emilio answered in a matter-of-fact way. He regretted hurting his brother. He should never have betrayed Enzo the way he had, and he still hated himself for it, but there'd never really been any love between them, no brotherly bond. Enzo had had everything Emilio wished he had: two parents who'd loved him; memories of both of them; his father's approval. Emilio would have settled for simply an acknowledgement of his existence.

'My father could do no wrong to Enzo, and Enzo saw nothing wrong in how I was treated. Or maybe he didn't care. Either way, he said nothing and, seeing as he was away with my father so much there really was no point in pursuing a relationship. And, as we grew, he looked down at me and how I lived with contempt.'

'And the resentment grew into hatred.'

'Something like that.' Emilio couldn't tell her the rest. She would leave and take this peace, this feeling, she nurtured within him. He would lose his baby. He would lose everything.

'Why was Enzo so favoured over you? Why were you treated so badly?'

'Because Enzo was his heir. I was an insurance policy in case anything happened to Enzo. Beyond that, I don't know.'

She kissed his hand and he felt something new—treasured, comforted. He had never felt that with Gia. She had never taken care of him. He'd always been the one offering her comfort.

'I'm sorry you went through that,' Jasmine said. 'Your father was a fool.'

Emilio said nothing. No words could change the past.

'It sounds to me like he didn't love either of you. Enzo seems more like an investment than a son, and you deserved none of that neglect.' Jasmine turned round in the water, holding Emilio's gaze, her green and gold eyes alight with indignation. 'You deserved so much more.'

He tucked a lock of hair behind her ear. 'You did too, *belleza*.'

She smiled. 'I know.' She turned back round and leaned against Emilio's chest once more. 'Have you considered… that perhaps you want the vineyards not just for our child, or what they meant to your mother, but also to have Enzo back in your life in some way?'

'No,' Emilio replied instantly. There was no way that was true. Enzo had his life and Emilio had his.

But, once you have the vineyards, the two of you will be bound permanently.

No, he told himself. No, it couldn't be. Too much had happened between them…hadn't it?

No. He was done thinking about this.

'I think that's enough talking.' He removed his hands from her hold, moving one up to her hair to turn her face towards him; the other slid down her body, his fingers parting her core. When she gasped, he kissed her. And kept kissing her until she clearly forgot all thought, became lost in pleasure. Consumed by him alone.

CHAPTER FOURTEEN

THE NEXT MORNING when Jasmine woke up in Emilio's bed, she found him standing at the window, bare-chested, grey sweatpants hanging low on his hips. He was serene, the picture of tranquillity, as he surveyed the vast estate. It seemed as though the playboy, the high-handed CEO she'd seen in New York, had been cast away to reveal the real him. A little calmer, with a much purer smile than the smirks of the charmer.

Despite his mixed memories of this place, he clearly loved it here. Jasmine wished she could give him this peace all the time. But how? They lived half a world away. She wasn't sure what this marriage was turning into. She had been the one to say she would not sleep in his bed but here she was, waking up to his scent on the sheets. She couldn't lie to herself. There was something brewing here that was more than chemistry.

She burrowed further under the covers, Emilio's scent enveloping her, and the movement attracted his attention.

'Buongiorno, belleza.' He moved away from the window and walked to the bed, giving her flashbacks of the night before, when he'd prowled towards her and taken her lips in a ravishing kiss. But, still, he hadn't pushed to sleep with her.

'I wish I had a camera,' she said.

He reached over, picked up his phone from the side table and handed it to her as he sat on the bed.

'One that would do you justice,' Jasmine amended. She

saw the look of confusion on his face and continued. 'To capture the way you looked when you stood there.' She nodded towards the window.

'Ah, you were watching me, were you?' His conceited smirk made her laugh.

She ran her fingers through his hair. It was always so soft. 'You love it here.'

'I do.'

Jasmine thought maybe there was a way she could allow him this feeling a little while longer. 'I have a suggestion.'

'What's that, *mia regina*?'

Jasmine barely understood two words of Italian, but she was growing to like it when he used it on her. She didn't care about the meaning when the words fell like silk upon her.

'Let's stay in Italy for a few weeks more. You love it here and so do I.'

'What about work?' Emilio asked. Jasmine wasn't surprised; she had made it perfectly clear that SOP and their baby were *all* she cared about. But maybe that was losing some truth.

'The Internet is a thing, Emilio,' she teased. 'Besides, neither one of us has had much of a vacation in the last few years.'

Maybe with Emilio she could let go just a little bit, enjoy the life she had built for herself. That she was still building. What use would it be to achieve all that she wanted if she didn't let herself enjoy it? Even Emilio, with his massive weight of a legacy, found time to enjoy himself. That was how they'd met, after all.

That life wasn't filled with enjoyment. He was escaping, just like you.

'Are you sure?'

'Unless I've read this wrong, and you don't want to spend this time with me.'

He took her hands from beneath the covers and kissed them on the knuckles, sending sparks skittering along her skin. 'I would take all the time you gave to me and still want more.' She watched him study her before he said, 'I would very much like that.' He paused. 'But I don't want to go back to Perlano. We'll stay here.'

'That's fine by me. I'd like to see more of Vozzano anyway. You still have a lake to show me.'

'Mia vita,' Emilio whispered, caging her in his arms and kissing her. Lightning sang through her. If this was to be her very first holiday since starting SOP, she was glad it was with her unlikely husband.

A few days later, while Emilio was unsuccessfully trying to teach Jasmine how to make a ragu—honestly, he was shirtless in the kitchen while cooking and feeding her little samples to taste; how was she expected to concentrate?—her phone rang loudly on the stone worktop.

'Hi, Mom.' Jasmine suddenly realised she hadn't spoken to her mother since she'd arrived in Italy. She never went that long without calling to check in. She looked at Emilio, who was concentrating on the pot in front of him. Had she relaxed so much because of him?

'What did you do, Jasmine?'

'I don't know. What did I do?' Alarm bells went off in her head. Had something happened to her mother? To SOP? Did she need to leave for New York? She was halfway out of the kitchen when what her mother said next stopped her in her tracks.

'You didn't have to buy me a house!'

Jasmine spun around and looked at Emilio. He'd stopped stirring the contents of the pot and watched her impassively. 'Mom…'

But Angela continued without letting her get a word in.

'And I could have moved myself in. You didn't need to go through all this trouble.'

Jasmine could hear how close to tears her mother was and it made her own eyes well up. 'I've always wanted to take care of you.' She wasn't sure if she was saying that to herself, her mother or Emilio, but the words hung in the air.

'I love you so much, Jasmine.' Angela was crying now. Jasmine could hear it. Could hear her mother's watery voice and sniffles.

'I love you too, Mom.'

'I'll let you get back to your honeymoon, but I just have to say something: he's special.'

'I know.' Jasmine hung up but stayed where she was. A lump was forming at the back of her throat that made it hard to speak. 'You did this. You bought my mom a house.'

'I did. I know you've wanted to take care of her...'

He knew because he'd wanted that too, to take care of his own mother before she'd passed.

'So I bought her a house close to ours.'

Ours. Her brownstone, that he'd promised to move into even though it wasn't nearly as fancy as his penthouse. A promise he'd made so they could both be there for their child and he could be the father he hadn't had. Jasmine was seeing him so much more clearly now.

'When you say close...'

'A street over. I thought you would want her close by as this pregnancy progresses. Would need her support when our daughter is born.'

Jasmine laughed despite the tears running down her face. When had anyone cared this deeply for her? Cared for her so much that they respected her goals, took care of her family? Richard had wanted more space from her mother. Emilio understood why she needed Angela.

Emilio was beyond special. And he'd finally begun opening up to her. True, nothing he'd said quite explained his behaviour in Perlano; there was something, she was sure, that he was holding back. But...

Maybe it didn't matter. How bad could his secret be? His actions spoke volumes: he was good and kind and everything she could hope for in a partner. So unlike the last man she had promised herself to, who had found her controlling. Maybe Richard had had a point. She did try to control everything. What if, in her pursuit of this secret, she pushed Emilio too far and he left too?

She would lose the perfect father for her child, and she couldn't do that to her baby. Maybe it was time for her to let go of the barriers and allow him to tell her in his own time. Maybe she could make peace with not knowing. Maybe she should.

She crossed the kitchen and kissed him. Kissed him with everything she had, and he held her tightly to him, kissing her back, returning her passion. The affection she couldn't name.

'Are you happy?' he asked, resting his forehead on hers.

'You have no idea.'

That kiss had turned Emilio's world on its head. He'd felt Jasmine's feelings for him shift in the kitchen but he wasn't quite sure what it meant. What they meant to each other. The only relationship he could compare this to was what he'd felt for Gia, and he didn't want to do that. He had already made a commitment to Jasmine for their child, but he wanted this to be the start of something more. And that would start with being there for Jasmine. He hadn't been around when Jasmine had learned of her pregnancy, or for the very first scan of their child. He couldn't change that, but he could be better.

After dinner, and after Jasmine had fallen asleep in his bed, he sat in an arm chair in the corner of the room and did as much research as he could. He sat there until his eyes began to droop. He did it every night for a week and then some.

Jasmine was in the window for the baby's genetics testing and nuchal translucency scan—things she would easily have made an appointment for in New York. But, out of her generosity to him, they were staying on in Italy, so it was his responsibility now to ensure she received the care she needed.

Over the past weeks, she had let go so much, relaxed, but Emilio knew she still needed control. Both were key parts of her personality. Having the doctor of her choice around would give her that control, even when they were away from home.

So he called her OB-GYN and had him on the next available flight to Milan.

'Thank you,' Jasmine said on the drive to meet with him.

'Of course.' He laced their fingers, kissed her hand then placed it on his thigh. He liked the way it looked there. As though she had ownership of him.

Jasmine didn't protest when he took her hand as they walked to the doctor's room in the medical centre, and he was especially glad that she didn't let go when the doctor performed the ultrasound.

'There's your baby,' the doctor announced.

The pulsing sound of his child's heartbeat wasn't something Emilio was prepared for. Yes, he had expected it, but to see this tiny living thing that was part him and part Jasmine filled him with wonder.

Jasmine looked at him with tears in her eyes and a tender smile on her face. He was happy—a happiness he wasn't sure he had ever experienced. And he'd found it with Jasmine, a random stranger he'd met in a club, but Emilio was certain that fate had intervened, because there was no other reason someone so perfect should be in his life.

There was something real, something tender, between them, something he'd never experienced with Gia. She'd taken everything he could offer but she hadn't cared about him. He'd been young and stupid and thought he'd fallen for her, but it hadn't been true.

He knew that now. Everything before Jasmine was lifeless. *This* was love. This was home.

Once the doctor was done, he took some blood and left the room. Emilio helped Jasmine wipe off the gel and straighten her clothes, even though he knew she was fully capable of doing it herself. Once her appearance was as impeccable as ever, he kissed her.

'I know none of this happened as you had planned, but I'm grateful it did.'

Jasmine smiled at him, glowing brighter than ever. 'I am too.'

During the entire drive back to the Vozzano estate, Emilio kept replaying the sound of the baby's heartbeat in his head, over and over. It was the sweetest music. His baby had been a tiny shape on a screen, and he couldn't comprehend just how much he loved them already. More than ever, Emilio couldn't understand his father at all. How could he have witnessed such a thing and remain unmoved? All Emilio knew was that he was done with wasting time.

'Get some rest, *belleza*. I have an email to send and then I will bring you some tea.'

'Thank you.' She caressed his cheek and he left her to go to his study.

Inform the De Luca lawyers about the will, he typed. I want this dealt with swiftly.

Everything that was his mother's was his and his child's. He had no doubt that it all would be resolved quickly—he probably wouldn't even have to deal with Enzo.

His attention now belonged to his wife.

CHAPTER FIFTEEN

JASMINE STOOD AT the window of their bedroom.

Their...? When had she started thinking of Emilio's spaces as theirs? Oddly, it didn't feel uncomfortable. She'd been so adamant she would never rely on him, never trust him. She still didn't *want* to do those things with anyone, but she couldn't lie to herself any longer. Not after the moment they'd shared earlier, seeing their baby together for the first time. Seeing the awe and love for his child on Emilio's face. There was no denying the fact that Jasmine *had* trusted Emilio. She'd trusted him to take care of their child. She'd trusted him enough to embark upon this journey. Part of her must have trusted him to take responsibility, even at the start, otherwise why would she have gone to his office?

And there was no denying that she felt something for him. These past weeks had been wonderful. Wrapped in a bubble in Italy. It was idyllic here. It felt like a real honeymoon... well, almost. But it certainly felt as if they were a family, and she couldn't deny how much she enjoyed waking up in his bed every morning, the serenity she felt in his presence. The calm his scent brought.

And now he was off 'sending an email'. She knew exactly what that was about. In the weeks they had been staying in Vozzano, Emilio hadn't mentioned the will or Enzo. He'd been fully present in every moment they shared. But today? Today was a reminder of what he was fighting for. It was obvious how much he'd loved his mother and Jasmine understood how devastating it would be for him to know that Valentina would never meet his child. This was one way he could pass that love down to their baby.

This email was important. She couldn't rest until she knew Emilio was alright.

'Why aren't you resting?'

She hadn't heard Emilio enter, and jumped at his voice. How did he always read her thoughts like that? 'Does it only qualify as resting if I'm lying down?'

'No.' He was carefully holding a tea cup and closing the distance between them. In an impressive show of strength, he pulled her against him and sat them both in the arm chair, sweeping her onto his thigh. In the other hand, he still held the cup. Not a drop had spilled. 'There, you're resting and not lying down,' he said, lips twitching with a deliberately repressed smile.

'Maybe I don't want to rest.' She twisted around a little more and took the cup from him, placing it on the small table beside them. 'Maybe I want to do something else.'

'Like what?' He smiled with darkening eyes. A smile that went straight to the heart of her and made desire rapidly course through her.

God! This man is beautiful. And she wanted him. She didn't just want the pleasure he offered. She wanted it all. So she leaned in and brushed her lips against his. Pulling away as he tried to kiss her. Teasing him. Challenging him. Wanting him to stop being so careful with her.

'*Belleza*, this is a dangerous game you're playing,' he said, voice low.

Jasmine grinned. 'I know.'

'You're a siren.'

'Then stop resisting.'

Emilio pulled away, searching her face. 'Do you really want this?'

'Yes.' She was never more certain of anything. 'Do you?'

'Every moment I resist the urge to be with you is torture. *Il mio cuore vuole il tuo.*'

She loved how his perfect English disappeared when he was overcome. The deepening of his accent, the words, all indicated just how lost he was.

Emilio took her breath away. Made her desperate. She needed to show him how desperate, so she crushed her lips against his, pouring every ounce of this maddening, intoxicating, exhilarating feeling into the kiss, but he threaded his fingers in her hair and took control, slowing this frantic kiss into something sensual. Erotic. Tender.

Every slide of his lips on hers sent a flurry of sparks through her core. It rendered her breathless and, when he tilted her face, trailing kisses along her jaw, Jasmine sighed.

'Emilio…'

She felt his teeth on her skin then, as if he was trying not to devour her, and she wished he would.

Emilio had never felt so owned, so at anyone's mercy, as he did when she said his name. She had his heart and now she had sunk her teeth into his soul. Emilio knew he would never shake her from his being. Every slide of her lips, every taste of her tongue, every touch of her skin on his was imprinted on his mind. He was Jasmine's, and he wanted her to be his, despite how unworthy he was of her. Emilio had never wanted anything more than for Jasmine to want him in every way. Heart and soul. Passion and lust.

He turned her round and made her sit her between his open legs. Her back was against his chest, his hardness trapped between them. He wanted her to feel it. To know what she was doing to him. And he was about to make her feel the same.

With one hand on her throat, he held her against him. Soft, gold, curls pressed against his shirt and he kissed her. There was reverence in every swipe of his tongue, while his other hand travelled along the front of her shirt, slowly unbuttoning her satin blouse. Her breathing grew ever more rapid with each one. He slid it off her and dropped it to the floor, exposing her milky skin. The small bump of her belly that just made him even more possessive of her.

Emilio took deep breaths, trying to control his body and how badly it wanted to rip off the rest of her clothes, but that wasn't what this was. This wasn't sex. This wasn't a hookup. This was how he showed Jasmine what she meant to him. How he would treat her. Worship her.

Biting and sucking on her shoulder, he removed her bra. The strapless garment fell away and instantly his hands were on her breasts. Cupping, kneading, caressing. Jasmine mewled, a sound that had his heart thrumming, and he could take it no more. He placed her on the chair and knelt in front of her, holding her gaze. Making sure she could see in his eyes what he was about to do to her.

He took her nipple into his mouth, making her moan out loud while he undid her trousers. And, sliding his hands under all the layers of fabric, he pulled them away, leaving her naked and panting. Her arousal glistening on her skin.

Emilio trailed kisses down her undulating body, taking his time. Tormenting them both. Savouring the wait, because it would only make his reward that much sweeter. And it was *his* reward, because pleasuring Jasmine like this was a blessing. A privilege. A prize for some good deed he must have done in a previous life. Certainly not in this one.

He kissed the little freckle above her belly button and then lower and then lower still. *'Sono tua,'* he said, and then he kissed the heart of her: *I'm yours*. Her taste flooded his mouth. He would always crave it and never be prepared for it for as long as he lived.

'Emilio!' Jasmine cried out. He barely heard it but still it registered even though he was completely at sea with the pleasure this brought him. That sound would find him no matter how lost he was. He lapped at her slowly, taking that little bundle of nerves at the apex into his mouth. Sucking. Kissing. He never wanted this to end. She cantered her hips against his face desperately and it made him chuckle.

'Please, Emilio,' Jasmine begged.

'I love it when you beg for me.' It made him feel powerful to have this powerful woman put aside her strength in a show of absolute trust. That she trusted him—a man who was unworthy. Unlovable. In these two words she showed that they could be the pieces they each needed. That she could let go and he could be worth someone's trust.

So he would show her that that trust was, just this once, well placed.

He slid her legs over his shoulders and hooked his arms around her hips, licking, sucking, kissing until her body was flushed and writhing, her chest heaving. One of her hands tightly gripped his hair while the other gripped her own. Breaths and moans became more frantic until she couldn't even say his name. Couldn't say anything in any existing language, but he still understood her; understood her pleasure and how close she was. Then her body arched. Her legs tightened on his shoulders as she crested the wave of her pleasure, and he drank down every drop of her release. And still he couldn't stop until she was begging and pulling on him.

But he wasn't done. They weren't done.

Emilio picked Jasmine up and placed her in the centre of his bed. Then he slowly stripped off his clothing. It was as if each shed piece revealed more of himself to her. His true self. The Emilio who hid his vulnerabilities with partying and planning and strict discipline. The Emilio who could never quite be enough for anyone but so desperately wished to be. Except that had changed. He only wanted to be enough for Jasmine.

He placed his hand on the handle of his bedside drawer and looked down at it. He needed to earn her respect, give her choice and control, even when he was the one forcing her to let go.

'Do you wish me to use protection?'

A soft smile appeared on Jasmine's face. 'No.' She shook her head. 'No, I want all of you.'

More trust.

So Emilio climbed on the bed and lay beside her.

'Take control, *belleza*,' he said. The broad, wicked smile on her face was everything to him.

He steadied her as she climbed over him. She hovered above his hardness that was weeping with anticipation. He swallowed hard and closed his eyes, waiting to be transported to heaven.

'Look at me,' Jasmine instructed and he obeyed. 'Eyes on me, Emilio.'

As if he could look anywhere else.

She lowered herself onto him and it was far beyond heaven. Beyond anything he could think of.

'Oh, Dio, si.' He groaned. The feeling of her was incredible; watching their bodies connect, divine. And, once she had taken all of him, he was completely overwhelmed. The first time they had slept together, Emilio had changed because nothing had ever come close to that feeling. But this? This made even that first time pale in comparison. 'Give me a moment, *amore*.'

'I thought I'm in control, Mr De Luca,' she said with a cocked brow. She was, so he relinquished control. Gave in to the feelings she brought out of him as she began to move her hips. 'I love making you desperate.'

'Siren...' he tried to say but it came out breathless and strangled, making her laugh some more. It was a sound so joyous, it healed the broken parts of him like some sort of emotional *urushi*. His soul turning into a piece of *kintsugi* art. The gold did not hide his damage but showed the beauty of healing despite it.

He grabbed her face and pulled her down, kissing her hard. His ardour was obvious. He hoped she could feel his love even though he couldn't quite say it. Not when those were the last words he had said to his mother. He had only just put himself back together. He couldn't risk saying the words that could shatter him again. Not when Jasmine hadn't indicated an affection that had grown as strong as love for him.

Emilio couldn't let go of her and so, when her rhythm started to fail, he took over. His pistoning hips driving them both further and further towards their peak as he held her against his body. Her moans mingling with his. Their breaths becoming one. And, with cries in complete sync, they shattered through that pinnacle barrelling into the infinite Eden of their pleasure.

'*Sei la vita mia,*' he whispered in the aftermath of his release, his forehead against hers: *you are my life*.

She was. This was. What they'd created. What they were creating: the family life he had never had.

Jasmine kissed him sweetly. 'Emilio, I'm not done with you. I want to taste you.' Light fingers danced on his hip, teasing, demanding. Perfect. So close to where he wanted her touch, where he ached for it. An ache he had come to understand would never go away.

'I can feel how much you want me,' she said.

The sun was going down, casting a spotlight into the room and catching Jasmine's back. Leaning on her elbow, hovering above him, she looked angelic, with a golden aura around her. '*Belleza*, torment me.'

Jasmine grinned.

Her smile lit a lamp in the darkest parts of his soul. Her happiness felt like his own. Seeing her here, happy, unguarded, was the greatest gift and he wondered what it would be like when they returned to New York. Would he kiss her and send her off to SOP, as the in-charge woman he admired, only for her to return home as the laid back, uninhibited Jasmine he got to see in private? Because that was what he wanted.

A lifetime of this.

He watched with a held breath as Jasmine moved down his body. She had briefly teased him with her mouth that night at the club and he'd never forgotten it. He played that moment over in his head when he lay in his bed alone, when he showered. The memory even popped into his head unbidden when he could do nothing about it. When he was at work. In a meeting.

This woman had got into his blood from the first moment.

'Look how hard you are for me.'

'Jasmine,' he said in a strangled voice that made her chuckle. He closed his eyes and pushed his head back into the pillows. 'You're wicked.'

And, as if to prove him right, she licked him in a long stroke from base to tip. Desire exploded in his body and, when she took him into her wet, warm mouth, pleasure coiled in the base of his spine and stole his breath. He needed to look but was unprepared for the sight of his erection disappearing between her lips. No fantasy compared to this sight. To this feeling.

Emilio grabbed onto the covers, curling his hands into fists, seeking some relief from this onslaught of wicked pleasure. But then Jasmine took his hand and placed it on her head; he sunk his fingers into the soft curls, and was struck by the importance of this moment. Of course Emilio had done this with other women—it had come with his hard-partying lifestyle—but there had never been emotion in it. It had always been about the end. With Jasmine, he was willing to be vulnerable with her. To let her lead, and she trusted him enough to be at the mercy of his lust.

'I have little incentive to trust.'

He fought for control then. Fought to honour that trust.

'Let go, Emilio.' Jasmine looked up at him, hazel eyes shining. 'Let go with me. You're safe with me. I want this.'

'I...'

'Let go,' she urged, and then her mouth was back on him, giving him no choice, so he gave in. His hips bucked and she made a noise of approval that only made his passion burn brighter until his body was pulled taut for an eternal moment, before shattering into a release so powerful it robbed him of his vision. A sound that was entirely guttural, animalistic, leaving his lips.

And, before he could even open his eyes, he was pulling Jasmine up and kissing her deeply. He was irrevocably in love with her. He was immutably hers. Even if all she ever did was trust him this much, the truth of it would never change. Emilio had loved before without being loved back; he could do it again, because this time it was with the mother of his child, and simply being in her orbit was a privilege he couldn't squander.

'Non posso vivere senza di te,' he said softly. He knew she didn't understand Italian, but he had to say the words, even if they were just for him: *I can't live without you.*

But you don't deserve her either.

That was true. He didn't. But he had to hold onto her because she would leave...she would never choose him if she found out about Gia. He knew Jasmine wouldn't forgive him for keeping a secret, but she also wouldn't forgive the secret he kept. Not telling her was the lesser of the two evils. It would allow this paradise between them to live on, so he would take the risk. He would take the secret to his grave.

'I have a question for you,' he said.

'What's that?'

'Have you ever been to Venezia?' Emilio was aware that they would have to return to New York soon, but he wasn't ready to let go of this dream just yet.

'I haven't been to any other part of Italy,' she replied.

He could rectify that. 'How would you like to go to a gallery opening tomorrow?'

'I'd love that.'

CHAPTER SIXTEEN

Emilio waited at the foot of the staircase for his wife, impatiently waiting to see what she would step out in. If everything went to plan, this would be a night she wouldn't forget soon.

Once they reached Venice, they'd be attending the opening of an art gallery. He'd wanted to surprise Jasmine with a breathtaking outfit of his choice but had realised that wouldn't be respectful—not to the woman who'd single-handedly been responsible for the success of Style On Point. Instead he'd told her to pick out whatever she wanted from a personal shopper's catalogue and that it would be paid for. She had fought him at first but then graciously accepted.

It wasn't long before he heard her heels click-clacking towards him and he buttoned up the jacket of his black suit.

Jasmine appeared at the top of the stairs with a broad smile. Her hair pinned back. Her long neck emphasised by a pair of long, bold, black earrings. One shoulder bare, the other covered in a strap of black fabric. Her legs looked delectably long in the monochrome jumpsuit. Her wrists were adorned with black bracelets that glittered exactly as her earrings did. On her feet were strappy sandals with a shorter heel than he had seen her wear in New York.

'Bellissima,' Emilio said.

'Grazie.' She smiled. 'Before you get too excited, that is the extent of my Italian.'

Emilio laughed. He couldn't remember a time when he'd felt so light. 'I have plenty of time to teach you.' He kissed her cheek and pulled away before either of them could succumb to temptation. 'Ready?'

Jasmine nodded and he led her out to the grounds, where a helicopter stood on a private helipad. He helped her into her seat, working to tighten the belts until he was satisfied. Then, for the next hour and a half, he basked in the wonder on Jasmine's face as she looked at Italy glittering in the darkness.

When they landed, he ushered Jasmine into a waiting runabout bobbing in the water, then smoothly navigated the canals, bringing them to a dock where a uniformed man moored the boat. During their short walk to the gallery, his hand never left the small of her back.

The gallery itself was a vast open space with a maze of floating walls. Around each corner was a collection of art installations and an array of sculptures.

'I love it here,' Jasmine said, beaming. 'Thank you for bringing me.'

'Anything for you.' He kissed her forehead. 'Lead the way.'

She took his hand and they moved through the space, ignoring the other patrons and even the waiters. Jasmine only had eyes for the art, lost in its beauty. But the only beauty he could see was her. They could have been in a cell with pure white walls and Emilio would scarcely have noticed.

'Whatever you want is yours,' he whispered in her ear.

She spun round. 'You can't be serious?'

'Of course I am.'

Jasmine laughed. 'Where would we put it, Emilio?'

'Where do you want it? The penthouse? I'll let you redecorate. Any of our other homes.'

'Our *other* homes?'

'You didn't think we just had New York, did you? We

could put them in Rome or Tokyo or Paris or London or Singapore. There are more.'

'*We?*'

'*Belleza*, my home is our home. Our child's home.'

'Emilio.' Her eyes welled up and, even though they were clearly happy tears, he didn't want to see her cry. He cupped her cheek. Just as he was about to kiss her, he heard his name.

His blood ran cold.

'Gia.'

He pulled Jasmine against his side, glimpsing the searching look in her eyes.

'I haven't seen you in eight years!' the familiar voice said.

'And I would prefer not to have seen you again.'

He felt the truth of the words to his very soul. Looking at Gia now, she hadn't changed at all, but he felt nothing: not anger; not sadness; not longing…nothing. He couldn't even remember why he'd thought he was falling in love with her. He knew now how love really felt. Love was what he felt for Jasmine. Jasmine, who was trustworthy and generous and kind. Gia was selfish and greedy, and he had never seen what they'd had more clearly. 'Have a good evening.'

'Don't be like that.' The woman batted her lashes. 'It's like fate!'

She was stunning. Brunette, and curvy in all the right places. Dressed in bright red—sophisticated, if conspicuous for a gallery opening, where the art was meant to shine. She was shorter than Jasmine by a head despite the pencil heels she wore. Jasmine disliked her instantly, and not for any reason other than the waves of hostility pouring off Emilio. A man whom she had come to know as caring. Friendly. Careful.

'No,' Emilio replied icily. 'Fate is how I met the most incredible woman in the world.'

Jasmine looked up to find him glancing down at her with softness and caution in his eyes.

The woman—Gia?—turned her attention to Jasmine now. 'And who is this?'

'My wife...' He placed a curious emphasis on the word. Something strange was going on here. Those doubts Jasmine had tried to ignore began rearing their heads. 'Jasmine De Luca.'

Jasmine's fingers were curled around Emilio's bicep, her engagement ring and wedding band on full display, and she watched the woman's eyes dip to them, then lower to Jasmine's belly. She extended her hand. 'You are...?'

'Gia Moretti.' She shook Jasmine's hand, a hair's breadth tighter than was friendly. 'By the looks of it you're expecting a little Emilio.' Her tone was pleasant but there was a sharpness there. 'I would never have thought you to be the fatherhood type, Emilio, but I guess life sometimes doesn't work out the way we plan.'

'I'm sure it didn't for you,' Emilio said evenly. 'How is that fame and fortune treating you?'

Jasmine had seen Emilio be antagonistic before, had experienced it when she had surprised him with the news of their child, but this felt different. The words were meant to wound. It only made Jasmine more anxious to know what was going on.

'Come now, Emilio, there's no need to be nasty. We had fun.'

The floor fell out beneath Jasmine's feet.

He was with women before you. You knew this.

But she'd never expected to be faced with the reality of it. Besides, her gut told her there was something wrong here, something more.

'I'd hoped we run into each other,' Gia continued.

'How did you know I was back in Italy?' Suspicion was clear in Emilio's tone.

'Come now, Emilio, you must know that you still get snapped, even when you're trying to fly under the radar.' Gia smiled. 'I thought we might have fun again…'

The audacity of this woman! Jasmine was just about to respond when Emilio's arm squeezed tightly around her. Maybe it was best just to observe, learn everything she could before she launched into confrontation.

'Why? Because you want back into the limelight?' Emilio laughed harshly. 'You're a selfish, toxic, greedy woman and I want you nowhere near my family.'

Jasmine saw the sneer that formed on Gia's face. The daggers in her pretty eyes when she looked at Jasmine's ring. Clearly this woman was used to getting her way and didn't take well to being thwarted.

'Has he mentioned me… Jasmine, was it? Did he tell you how we met?'

'Gia…' Emilio warned.

'Did you steal her from Enzo too?' she asked mockingly.

Jasmine looked at Emilio to find a thunderous expression on his face. His brown eyes, normally so warm, were like ice. 'Leave.' His voice was a low growl. Threatening.

'Oh, come on, you can't still be angry about what happened.'

'If you don't leave right now, Gia, I will take everything Enzo gave you and then some.'

Jasmine had had just about enough. She had had it with this woman. She'd had it with the secrets that Emilio kept. She'd thought she could live with it but, if this Gia was one of them, she wasn't sure she could. If Emilio was reacting this badly, Jasmine could only imagine how horrible his secret was—possibly as horrible as this woman. And why would he keep it unless he was afraid that it would affect her…affect their marriage, his plans? Jasmine fought a shiver. A chill ran right through her at the realisation that her trust was being betrayed again.

That chill was followed by the red-hot burn of rage. All of this reminded her so much of Richard and Zara. Her stomach roiled, but she wanted answers. She took a single step towards Gia, forcing her to look up. She didn't often use her height to intimidate, but right now she didn't care.

'Clearly you aren't wanted here, so I suggest you leave my family alone.'

'Oh, please!'

'I said, leave.' Gia must have seen something in Jasmine's face because with one last venomous glare, she turned on her heel and left.

Instantly, Jasmine rounded on Emilio. 'What was that about?'

'Jasmine…'

'What did she mean, Emilio?' she asked through gritted teeth, trying to control the hurt, anger, disappointment, forcing them into a box inside her. She had to be rational and she was fighting hard for that rationality.

Emilio sighed. 'I'll explain everything to you later.'

'No.' She crossed her arms. 'I want to know now.'

Emilio cursed under his breath and Jasmine knew whatever he was going to say would be bad.

'I'd rather have this conversation in private.'

'Then let's go.' She wasn't going to drop this. She realised if she'd been the old her, the person she'd been with Richard, she would have been so desperate not to make him uncomfortable or look bad, that she would have sucked it up and stayed the rest of the night at the gallery. She had made herself smaller for Richard in so many ways, but she was done doing that for anyone. Done being that person.

She wouldn't make this easy for Emilio. She would have

nothing less than honesty from him. She didn't care how controlling that made her seem. How difficult he found her.

Emilio took her hand, but she pulled it away.

'Please, Jasmine. Give me chance to explain before you reject me.' The defeat in his voice was like claws in her heart, but she had to remain strong. Stand her ground.

The journey to the hotel was tense and silent. She said nothing, even as Emilio checked them in, and stood away from him in the lift. She needed a clear head for what lay before her.

CHAPTER SEVENTEEN

JASMINE WAS IN the most beautiful hotel suite she had ever seen. She had always wanted to visit Venice. Now that she was here, she couldn't have cared less about any of it.

'I want answers,' she said as soon as Emilio closed the door.

'Can we not take a moment to—?'

'No.' She cut him off. She wouldn't be moved. She wouldn't be placated with sweet words or gestures. Wouldn't go to the bedroom or any other place where Emilio could distract her.

Gia's words had shaken her. They'd made her see sense. She couldn't put a plaster over their issues in the hope they could have something special. He was still lying to her, still hiding things.

'Talk, Emilio.'

She watched him run his hands through his hair. His distress was obvious on his face, in the stiffness of his body. He took off his jacket and tossed it over the back of an arm chair then rolled up his shirt sleeves.

'Who is Gia?'

'Enzo's ex-fiancée.' He pinched the bridge of his nose and took a deep breath, then walked over to her and placed his hands on Jasmine's shoulders, his eyes beseeching. 'I need you to know what I am about to tell you is not the person I am any more. At least, I have tried to be better.'

'Just tell me.' Part of her wanted to comfort him, because the pain on his face was clear for anyone to see, but a greater part, a part that protected herself, needed to know, and to hell with his feelings. So she stood in this awkward embrace, unmoved.

Emilio took the hint and stepped away from her. 'Eight years ago, before our father died, Enzo met Gia. Their relationship was romantic from the start. When he introduced her to the family, the two of us connected almost immediately. We were close. Became friends. She needed a confidante, and I would listen. Then, after our father died, she and Enzo became engaged. But my brother had always put duty above everything else. He was *conte* first and everything else second…'

Jasmine could understand that. After all, from what Emilio had said, Enzo had been groomed for the role. 'Gia was growing increasingly frustrated by that. She felt rejected when he would cancel plans for the company or Perlano, and it just got worse.'

'Of course; your father just died. Enzo would have had his hands full.'

Emilio shrugged. 'It doesn't matter. What matters is that he made her feel unimportant. One night when I came home, I found Gia on my balcony. She had been drinking; he'd run out of some wedding planning event and she was upset. We talked. She asked me to drink with her and, stupidly, I did.'

Emilio laughed humourlessly and walked to the window as though he were watching all this unfold in the distance. 'I never intended it to happen,' he said softly. 'I wanted to keep my feelings to myself.'

'Your feelings?'

'I was falling in love with her. Or I thought I was. I was twenty-one. Young and foolish. That night I got too drunk, too wrapped up in my feelings. She was upset and we made a mistake. Or at least, I did.'

'Oh God! Tell me you didn't…' Jasmine could feel the bile rise in her throat.

'We slept together.'

'Emilio…' Jasmine breathed, horrified. The trust she had for this man was cracking, then shattering…just like her heart.

'I regretted it immediately.'

'And Gia?' Jasmine was almost too afraid to know the answer.

'Nowhere near as upset as I was. That should have been my first sign. There were many signs,' Emilio said to himself.

'Signs of what?'

'The person she was. I hated my brother and still I couldn't look at myself in the mirror. She was supposedly in love with him, but she seemed fine with what happened. Glad for it. I misread that. I thought she might…return my feelings.'

Jasmine was stunned. She didn't know how to respond. Her throat burned but she didn't want to cry. Didn't want to be vulnerable. Not now.

'I told Enzo what happened the very next day. He was furious and hurt. And…and I knew.'

'Knew what?'

Emilio looked her in the eye, conviction in every line of his body. 'The kind of man I was. There was always a reason my father treated me the way he did, after all. He saw how loathsome I was before anyone else.'

Jasmine took a step towards him. 'Emilio.' *That* wasn't true, Emilio was kind, caring…but what kind of man did something like that? He'd betrayed his family. Jasmine knew exactly how that betrayal hurt. How much worse would it have been, coming from a sibling?

'Enzo broke up with Gia and offered to pay her to leave.'

'Why would he need to pay her?'

'To get rid of her. So none of us would see her again. I was angry, *belleza*, so angry. The insult of it—as if money could make her feelings disappear. But I was the fool.'

'What happened?'

'I offered to leave with her, and she rejected me. She wanted the money and fame. Between Enzo and I, she'd had everything she wanted. The passion and support from me, the power and wealth from him.'

Emilio's shoulders sagged and he moved to sit in the arm chair furthest from Jasmine. She hated that she was relieved by the distance. Her heart broke for him, but it didn't change the despicable thing he'd done. 'I was angry at Enzo for making her leave and angry at Gia for choosing the money. Angry at myself for what *I* did.'

'That's why Enzo hates you. Why you didn't want him to know we were in Perlano. We were in *his* home.'

'That was my home too, Jasmine.'

'*Was*, Emilio.' Rooted to the spot, Jasmine searched the room, as though the beautifully decorated walls could offer her some answers. She shook her head. 'What kind of man sleeps with his brother's fiancée?'

What kind of man sat in New York for years and never apologised to his brother? Was that the kind of man she wanted raising their child?

'Don't you think I've asked myself that same question?' Emilio snapped. 'Do you think it's easy to live with what I've done? I think about it every day, Jasmine. Every day! I work *so hard* to be better. Less impulsive. After that night, I never drank more than single drink at any time.'

'You ordered a second drink at the club.'

'Did I drink it?' he fired back at her.

No; no he hadn't. He'd played with it. He'd flirted with her. But he hadn't drunk it.

'I removed every temptation to be impulsive. I own no fast cars. I'm driven almost everywhere so I'm not tempted to speed. It's responsible if I choose to have a drink. I removed myself from the possibility of a partner and a family.

I leaned into a different lifestyle. One that I had initially chosen to act out against my father, but then I realised fleeting partners were a calculated risk that kept everyone safe. No relationships meant no one could be hurt by my actions, and I wouldn't have to deal with yet another person rejecting me.'

'So you were at the club on the prowl.'

'Not that night. That night I was there just for an escape. Then I saw you, *belleza*, and I couldn't look away.'

The day when Richard had left her for Zara: her fiancé and the woman who'd been as close as a sister to her. Closer, even. Two people she'd loved and trusted. It was amazing to Jasmine that she could have learned a lesson so thoroughly and yet still needed to relearn it.

'I should never have trusted you,' she said softly. 'You don't trust yourself! Why did you ever ask me to?' This time she couldn't stop her eyes from welling up. Especially when she thought back to how attentive Emilio had been. How he had stepped up for their child. Thought of the passion he ignited in her. But she couldn't forgive the lies. She couldn't forgive this lie.

'*Belleza*, please.' He tried to stand up from his chair, but she stopped him.

'Don't call me that. Don't touch me. I regret *everything*, Emilio. I regret walking into that club. I regret telling you about our baby because you...' Her breath caught in her throat, making her choke on the words. 'You made me think I could be wrong. You made think maybe giving you a chance wouldn't be such a bad thing. Never again! I will *never*. Trust. Again. And *you* did that.'

'Jasmine.'

'You knew about my father. You knew about Richard and Zara, and so you wilfully kept a secret for your own sake!'

Jasmine tried to steady her breath but she couldn't. What Emilio had done was horrible. He'd betrayed his brother and had never atoned. Maybe, if he had been honest from the start, things would have been different. Maybe she wouldn't have allowed herself to get so close. Or maybe she would have found it in her to work past it.

But that wasn't what had happened. He'd lied to her every day that they'd been together. He'd made that choice, knowing how important honesty was to her. He'd lied for his own selfish wants.

How could she be with someone like that? How could she trust him again?

'I'm done.'

Every word Jasmine said was a well-aimed blade into Emilio's chest. He deserved it. Emilio knew that. He'd never been worthy of her, having intentionally kept the affair from her. But he couldn't bear to hear the words leaving her lips now.

Jasmine was heading for the door. He flew out of his chair and caught her by the wrist, spinning her round and cradling her face. Her tears were a bludgeon to his soul. Everything he did to hold on to her and their child was backfiring.

'Please, Jasmine. We have something here. Something between us. I've never been in love, not truly. Not until—'

'Don't you dare say it.' The hurt in her eyes morphed and solidified into a burning anger. She pulled away from him and made for the bedroom.

'Where are my clothes?'

Emilio didn't want to show her. His heart was breaking. If she got her clothes, she would leave, and he needed her to stay.

'Jasmine, don't—stay. We can work this out. Just stay. Fight with me.'

She went to the adorned cupboard where several new sets of clothes hung up, all her favourites from the personal shopper's catalogue. Emilio had wanted to spoil her. How had it gone so wrong?

She pulled out a suitcase and began haphazardly packing the clothes into the bag. This wasn't her. She was meticulous about everything she did. He couldn't let her leave, if not for his sake, then for hers and their baby's.

'Jasmine, if you want to leave so desperately, I will see you to the airport myself in the morning.'

'No. I don't want to be around you.'

'I can't let you leave.'

She scoffed. 'And that's why you kept this from me—because you knew I would leave!'

His family was falling apart. He'd been so close to having everything and now it was slipping through his fingers.

'What about our baby? I won't lose my child.' He didn't want to lose her either.

'I will have my lawyers contact your lawyers. I'm sure we can come up with an agreeable custody schedule.'

Emilio could clearly read between the lines. 'And we would have no contact.'

'Not if I can help it.' She slammed the suitcase shut and turned to face him. 'And don't bother coming home either. It's mine, not yours.' She wheeled the suitcase to the bedroom door. 'I'll send you a cheque for the clothes.'

'*Per l'amor del cielo*, Jasmine!' He ran after her.

'Do not come after me, Emilio. I don't want to see you.' She didn't look back, slamming the suite door closed just before he could reach it.

He threw it open—but only made it a step. His soul cried out for him to heed his impulse to follow her. To bring her back. To make her understand where he was coming from. But the urgency of that need, the desperation, was exactly why he couldn't. He had trained himself for years to ignore his impulses, but he didn't want to now. He was losing his family, the woman he loved. But how could he turn his back on nearly a decade of control? How could he disobey Jasmine?

He was stuck. Stuck in this loop of who he should be and who he was. The man whose actions had driven his wife down the hallway and out of sight.

Gone.

Emilio's back met the wall and he slid down to the floor, his chest caving open. Where did he go from here?

In this moment of utter night, Emilio's phone began to ring. He didn't want to answer it, but what if it was Jasmine? What if she had paused for a moment and would allow him a chance?

A chance for what?

Anything! He'd take anything she offered.

'Jasmine?' he answered, without even looking at the screen.

'Emilio.' It was his lawyer.

His stomach sank. Not Jasmine. *She* never wanted to see him again. That fact hurt so badly, it robbed the breath from him.

He didn't want to talk to his lawyer now, but some rational part of his brain told him stay on the line. It was late—too late for this to be anything but bad news.

'What is it?' he managed to say.

The lawyer paused. 'Are you okay?'

No, he wasn't. He'd just lost his wife because of his own stupidity. 'Just spit it out.'

'If it's a bad time, I can call later or tomorrow.'

'If you didn't need me to know urgently, you wouldn't have called at all. Just tell me what happened.'

'It's about the vineyards.'

Emilio could hear the hesitation in the man's voice, and he tried to steel himself for whatever was coming next.

'I'm afraid you have no claim on them.'

'What?' That made no sense. They were his mother's and she had left them to him. It was simple. Those vineyards were his, and they would one day be his child's. His child, who would not be in his life every single day. Whom he would see only when Jasmine allowed it. He would have to make up for his absences. He would have to be worthy of them somehow. At least with the vineyards, he could give them a legacy that would always take care of them. Show them how much they were loved.

'Explain.' His gruff demand held none of the authority it usually did.

'They can't be bequeathed to you, because they were never your mother's to begin with. It turns out that the *conte* had never actually transferred them to her and, upon his death, they passed to his successor.'

'Enzo.'

'I'm sorry, Emilio. I know how fond Valentina was of them. If there's—'

Emilio cut the call. He couldn't hear any more. He clutched the phone in his fist. Fury at how badly his mother had been betrayed fought for space alongside the anguish of losing Jasmine.

Jasmine left because you betrayed her. Who does that sound like to you?

It sounded like his father. Funny how life turned out. Emilio had spent his whole life fighting his father, and had been adamant he would be different for his family. But, when it came down to it, he had lied to his wife to hold onto what was important to him. Exactly as his father had done with the vineyards.

Emilio dropped his head against the wall, pulling his legs towards his body. His flesh crawled. How had he ended up just like the man he despised?

CHAPTER EIGHTEEN

JUST GET HOME...
 Just get home...
 Just get home...
Jasmine didn't look back. She couldn't. Not when she was hanging on by a thread. Any sight of Emilio would have her dissolving in a mess of tears—of agony, heartbreak and disappointment—and she couldn't have that. She would not break here.

A water taxi took her to the airport, where she purchased a seat on the next flight out, boarding almost immediately. All the while she concentrated on the next step, and the next, to keep her mind focussed. It would only take one weak moment for her to crumble.

When she took her seat, she realised that her hell had only just begun. For the next ten hours she would have nothing but time to dwell on her shattered future with Emilio. On how much worse it hurt than any other betrayal in her life that Emilio had harboured this secret. On how wrong she had been to allow him her trust; how completely he had just shattered it.

Everyone had two sides to them, herself included. It just so happened that only one side of Emilio was worth her trust and respect.

For the first time, she understood how her mother could have fallen so deeply for her perfidious father. She understood her devastation when he'd left. Unlike her mother, at least Jasmine had been the one to walk away. She wasn't sobbing on the floor at the front door. But she *hurt*. She felt torn apart by the loss of the good in Emilio.

And Emilio's good side had been kind. Patient. Memories assaulted her—Emilio eating a cheap dinner at her table, her mother's fond smile—and she had to cover her mouth to stifle her sob.

Each day, he'd proved to be someone she wanted to lean on. Each day she'd allowed herself to hand over control to him just a bit more. But what had he done with that trust? He'd destroyed it. He'd done it with his brother and he'd done it with her.

Jasmine placed a hand on her belly. It wasn't just herself she had to think about. It wasn't just her he'd betrayed. Now her child would not have the home they had wanted to provide. And would Emilio break their child's trust along the way too? Would Jasmine have to protect them from their father, from the expectations he would allow them to have, only to fumble on his promises every time?

She closed her eyes, trying to will the tears away, begging her body to sleep so she could have some reprieve from the clenching in her stomach. From her constricted lungs. From the ache in her heart so severe, she was certain it would never be whole again.

She'd thought Richard's betrayal had hurt, but it had never felt quite like this.

Maybe because you were falling in love with him.

No! Absolutely not; it was a far jump from trust to love.

By her own admission, Jasmine wasn't sure what love really felt like any more. It *wasn't* love.

Jasmine, honey, please stop hiding.

Another text message from her mother. Jasmine wasn't hiding. She was trying to live with a gaping hole in her chest. Who would she be hiding from?

The world? Anyone you could possibly connect with.

Especially after she'd thought she'd seen Emilio outside her brownstone. But that had to have been her mind playing tricks on her because he would never have driven there, so she had turned her back on the sight and climbed into her own car.

Jasmine pushed away from her desk. She'd spent most of the past week and a half behind it, only going home to sleep, then returning to do it all over again.

When have I ever hidden?

When her father had left, she'd been there for her mother in the ways a child could. When Richard had betrayed her, she'd gone to the most exclusive club in New York. Yet, when Emilio had betrayed her, she immediately locked herself away in the office and stayed in there all day, every day.

'Enough!' she told herself, and grabbed her coat. She wasn't sure where she was going. All she knew was that she had to get out, to feel the sun on her face. To be somewhere, anywhere, else.

Not knowing where she was going or what she would do once she got there, Jasmine kept walking until she came upon a green space with benches and a small pond reflecting the blue skies overhead. It was a patch of tranquillity in the middle of the chaos of Manhattan. It called to her. Just as she approached a bench beside the path, she spotted two people walking towards her—two people she'd never wanted to encounter again.

It was too late to turn round. Richard and Zara had already seen her.

'Jasmine,' Zara tentatively greeted her.

Jasmine's left hand curled tightly. Her wedding and engagement rings—Emilio's rings—pressed into her skin. She'd tried to take them off several times, but she couldn't bring herself to. She didn't want to analyse why not.

Now they made her wish he was by her side, as he had been the last time she'd run into Richard and Zara. The memory made her miss him, the stifling hurt that had been present since she'd left Italy shifting.

Richard was sneering, of course. 'Where's your lover?'

Jasmine saw Zara wince and felt a small amount of pity for her. She would have to get used to that behaviour; that was who Richard became when he wanted control of a situation. Eventually Jasmine had found it easier just to allow him to feel as if he were in charge to avoid conflict. She hated that she had done that.

You never did that with Emilio.

'Did he see sense and leave?' he added.

It was amazing that she'd had put up with Richard's ugly side for so long. 'Why? Because I'm too controlling? Too tightly wound? Because it was stifling being around me and I sucked the life out of everything? I believe that's what you said.' The words didn't hurt. They didn't feel like anything at all now. 'Who'd want that?'

'I can't imagine anyone would,' Richard replied.

Visions of Emilio making love to her came to mind. The things he'd said to her in Italy.

'I would take all the time you gave to me and still want more.'

Emilio had run into the woman responsible for destroying his family and shattering his heart, but even in anger he hadn't been cruel. Antagonistic, yes; but cruel? No.

'Just because *you* need to control your partner to feel like a man, doesn't mean others do too, Richard.'

'Torment me.' The memory of Emilio's words still had sparks alighting in her belly.

'I thought I was in control, Mr De Luca.' Her own words. And Emilio had submitted to her. He hadn't *allowed* her control, as if it had been inherently his; he'd recognised that she had needed it and had surrendered to her. He'd been happy for Jasmine fully to be herself.

And she had been.

In a flood, it started coming to her: all the times Emilio

had given in to her desires. When she had been unwilling to budge, he had. When she'd wanted a wedding and he hadn't, he'd given her a beautiful ceremony. He'd taken care of it himself. Unlike Richard, who'd left her to do everything and then never showed up.

She thought about Emilio's reaction to a dinner meant to test him, and how he had been with her mother. How he had agreed to move in with Jasmine, despite owning a penthouse beyond her wildest dreams, all because he wanted to take care of her and their baby. How he hadn't forced her to be anything but herself even when he'd been hurting. When she'd stormed out of the gallery, he hadn't forced her to take his hand for appearances' sake. He had accepted her anger, her boundaries.

She thought about how relaxed she had been with him. She'd shown him a side that she had tried to smother, but he'd given her a safe space so that she could let go. Indulge her carefree side.

It all made her miss him. Made everything feel a little less bright. Made the sun feel less warm. Made her pine for the man who had looked so broken when she had walked away.

'Do you think it's easy to live with what I've done? I think about it every day, Jasmine.'

Of course he did, because the goodness in him wasn't a lie. His remorse was painfully evident.

Richard had never shown remorse for anything he had done in all the time they had been together. Suddenly, she found herself wishing she could magically manifest Emilio by her side. Wished they could talk.

She looked down at the ring on her finger, as if it could help her with these churning thoughts.

Zara followed her gaze. 'You're married.'

She was married…to a man Jasmine had compared to Richard time and time again. Now she felt guilty about it. Despite how badly Emilio had hurt her, he and Richard were nothing alike.

'I am.'

For now, she supposed. She would have to start divorce proceedings at some point. The very thought made her soul rip in two. Maybe afterwards she could bring herself to remove the ring from her finger… But even the thought of that was more than she could bear.

'Maybe you two will follow suit one day,' she said, looking at her former friend. 'After all, Zara, you already have experience planning weddings.' Zara's eyes widened and Richard glowered, but Jasmine didn't care. 'I'm glad you found each other,' she said sweetly. 'You deserve one another.'

And she meant it. They were out of her life. However briefly she had been with Emilio, he'd helped heal this hurt. He'd showed her how she wanted to be treated. Zara and Richard had no power over her any more.

Jasmine turned and walked away, feeling freed from a shackle, and yet her heart had never been heavier. Because now, she realised, what she had lost was love.

She had loved Emilio.

Scattered across the vineyards, in little fragments, were pieces of her heart that belonged to Emilio. When he'd bought her mother a house, when he'd flown her doctor over, when they'd seen their child, when he had taken her to bed afterwards, whispering sweet nothings in a language she didn't understand, she had fallen in love.

If only he'd been honest with her. If only he'd told her about Gia, maybe it would have been enough.

And now tears tracked down her cheeks. She was consumed by grief for what could have been, and the man she so desperately craved.

Emilio climbed into the driver's seat of his car. Not the Maybach, in which he was usually chauffeured everywhere, but a brand-new German SUV which he drove himself. A car that would be comfortably safe to drive his baby around in. A car that would give Jasmine and him some privacy to talk.

If he could get that far.

He set off determinedly towards Jasmine's brownstone. But, before he'd even crossed the bridge out of Manhattan, he found himself turning round and driving in the opposite direction, towards his office. Just as he had done every day for the past three weeks.

After the call with his lawyer in Venice, Emilio had tried to call Jasmine several times, but she hadn't answered. When he'd found out she had boarded a flight back to New York, he had made arrangements to leave as well. He'd landed only hours after her and had immediately bought the car.

The next morning, he was outside her brownstone waiting to take her to work. Waiting for a chance to talk to her. But he'd been denied. Her driver had been there earlier than usual, and Emilio had watched Jasmine walk down the steps, look at him then turn away. She'd got into her car and it had promptly driven away.

He'd wanted to be there for her, wanted to try and make her see why he had hidden the truth from her, but she'd rejected him. Just like everyone else. Except this time, it was entirely his fault. And when he'd seen her, as strong as she'd been the day she'd first walked into his office, as put together as ever, he'd known he was no good for her. She deserved someone better.

But that knowledge didn't make it hurt any less. Didn't stop him yearning for her or missing her every single moment of each day. For three weeks he'd sunk deeper into the pit of self-loathing and self-recrimination. For three weeks he'd grown more desperate for the love of his life that he'd let get away.

And, with Jasmine gone, he had no idea how his baby was doing. His child, that so completely owned his heart. But he'd lost the right to be there for them. Whatever life he'd get with them now would only be what Jasmine allowed him.

He had to stop trying. Stop attempting to drive to her home, the home that had so nearly been his. It was doing them both no favours.

That last little bit of hope that had been keeping Emilio together winked out.

Desolate. That was the only way to describe what he felt. As if part of him had just died and there would be no reviving it.

His phone rang. When Enzo's name flashed across his watch face, Emilio rejected the call. Enzo had attempted to call numerous times; each time he'd left a message just asking to talk, but Emilio had nothing left to talk about. He'd lost his family and the vineyards in one day. What would Enzo say—that his father had lied to them all for years and had never legally transferred the vineyards to their mother, and had been right not to do so? Emilio didn't need to hear that.

Walking into the office, he felt nothing. For the first time this job held no excitement for him. Perhaps he should leave. There was no reason for him to be at De Luca and Co. He had no De Luca legacy to leave to his child. Maybe his time would be better spent solely focussed on the interests his mother had left him.

'Mr De Luca…'

'Morning, Rachel,' Emilio greeted her emotionlessly, hurrying past. It was only when he opened his office door that he registered that she hadn't said 'Emilio' as usual.

There was the reason why: Enzo, in a perfectly tailored suit, sat in his visitor's chair.

Emilio closed the door. The soft click felt sonorous in his office. In the tense silence.

He wasn't sure what he felt first. Anger? Hatred? Shock? They hadn't been in the same room with each other since their mother's funeral. When they met online for work, Emilio always had time to prepare for his brother's presence. Today Enzo had given him no choice and no courtesy.

Maybe he was tired of you rejecting his calls.

Maybe Enzo deserved it.

'What are you doing here?' Emilio said, sliding his hands into his pockets. He stayed near the door. If he had his way, it would soon be slamming on Enzo's back. 'Have you come to gloat?'

'No,' Enzo said simply. 'I've come to give you something.' He stood. In his hand, he held a leather-bound book with an unfastened clasp. He walked to Emilio and handed it over.

Reluctantly, Emilio accepted it. It was odd to see their almost identical hands connected by this small object. Looking at Enzo was always like looking into a mirror. Apart from their eyes, they were so similar—the same height, similar builds—yet their lives had been so vastly different.

'What is this?'

'Mamma's diary.'

Emilio's eyes snapped to Enzo's in shock. Shock that part of his mother still existed. Shock that Enzo had shared it at all. And then he realised he had seen it on her bed that last day he'd spent with her.

'I've come for a few reasons, Emilio. The most important of which is to apologise. I just want to talk.'

Emilio wanted to say no. He wanted to send his brother away and never think of him again. But he had called and begged Jasmine for a chance to talk, to apologise, the night she left. It ate at him that she hadn't taken those calls. His conscience wouldn't let him get away with the hypocrisy of denying the same chance to his brother.

'Sit,' he ordered. To his surprise, his brother obeyed without question and without snarkiness.

'Will you join me?' Enzo asked with no hint of arrogance. 'Please.'

Emilio took a deep breath and sat in the chair next to Enzo's, turning it to face him.

'I meant what I said. I do want to apologise.' Enzo looked away. Looked ashamed. 'After Gia, and again when I found out you wanted the vineyards, I wondered why you were so set on ruining Perlano for me.'

'Did you ever consider that I just wanted to make some of it mine?'

'Not at first.'

'But then?'

'Then I met someone.' Enzo's face softened. He smiled so gently. Emilio understood what that feeling was like, and he ached all the more for Jasmine. 'She helped me see a lot of things more clearly.'

Enzo looked at Emilio then. There was sincerity in his eyes and Emilio noticed how open his usually closed-off brother was being. Enzo was usually cold; he'd been unmoved at their mother's funeral but he wore no mask now. 'And I needed the help, Emilio. I wasn't the brother you needed when you needed me. I didn't fight for you when you needed me to, and I'm sorry.'

Emilio didn't know how to respond. This was the last thing in the world he'd expected. Was he supposed to say everything was fine because of a few words?

We need honesty...

He heard Jasmine's voice, so this time he chose to listen.

'You'll never understand, Enzo.'

'Then explain it to me.'

Emilio laughed. How did he explain twenty-nine years of neglect?

Enzo shifted forward in his seat, as if he possibly wanted to offer comfort, but he held back and Emilio didn't know how to respond to that uncertainty from his brother. 'Emilio, I promise to listen. I will try to understand. I have many years to make up for, but we need to start somewhere. So, please, explain it to me.'

'You were never bothered that Mamma favoured me.'

'No, I never was.'

'You were so indifferent to me because you were so sure of your place. You had both our parents' attention, their love that you didn't even see the point of getting upset. I didn't have that. I spent every single day knowing I was invisible. Papa wouldn't even look at me at dinner. Do you have any idea what it's like to know that you would only ever receive attention if your big brother died?'

There was horror on Enzo's face. Tears welled in his bright-green eyes. 'No.'

'You have never had to earn anyone's affection, Enzo. You've never known what rejection is like.' Emilio couldn't remain seated any longer, not when everything was boiling up in him. He couldn't control what he felt now even if he'd tried.

'Did you celebrate?' he asked viciously, surrendering to the impulse to pace the office. 'When you learned of our father's deception? It got you everything, as usual. I was the one that was there for Mamma. I was the one that stuck around. I saw her die. I stayed for the funeral and comforted people who would never know how I felt.'

Enzo scrubbed his hands down his face and shook his head in denial. His eyes scrunched closed. It took a moment for him to collect himself and, when he spoke, his voice was low. Scratchy.

'Just because the vineyards are mine doesn't mean you have no right to them. We both have memories there, Emilio. It's equally in our blood. Look, we can't change the past, but we can choose a different future. Maybe we can start with you looking at that diary.'

'What?' Emilio didn't want to read the diary now, not in

front of his brother. He wasn't sure *when* he would be ready to reopen the wound of losing his mother.

'Not the whole thing, unless you want to. But look at the page I've marked.'

Emilio stared down his brother. Enzo could not possibly be serious, but it didn't seem that he was going to back down on this.

'What the hell? It's not like this day could get worse.'

'That's the spirit,' Enzo muttered, and Emilio smiled despite himself.

He opened the book to a page marked with a sticky note. He resumed his pacing as he read.

I signed my will today. Bennedetto made me create the first one all those years ago. Stood over my shoulder as I signed it. But I always knew I would leave the vineyards to Emilio. He never had his father's favour. And now there will always be something to tie Enzo and Emilio together. Especially when I'm gone. If Enzo takes the vineyards, there will be nothing to tie Emilio to the company; he'll leave and that will be the end for my sons. My death might bring them together...but that is probably wishful thinking. Maybe if they are forced to work together, they will talk. I'll talk to the lawyers, try to give them that time. They need to learn to be brothers again.

Emilio *had* been thinking of leaving; his mother had foreseen it. But this explained why there were two wills. Why she had instructed the lawyers to wait. The memory of those family dinners flashed across his mind. Perhaps she'd been doing the same back then. Perhaps those had been for the benefit of Enzo and him, not their father.

Their father...

He read the words again, anger curling in the pit of his stomach. 'Why would he do that? Why force Mamma to create a will for something he knew wasn't hers?'

'I don't know,' Enzo admitted. 'To keep up the appearance that he had given them to her? Perhaps it was a test. He was fond of tests.'

'Did he test you?'

'Constantly.'

Enzo seems more like an investment than a son.

Jasmine had been right yet again. Emilio felt a pang of sympathy for his brother. He thought of his own child who he loved so completely even though they were not yet born. Thought of how he wanted to give them the world, protect them from everything. He would never force his child to endure tests to prove their worthiness. The thought was horrifying.

'I didn't see anything wrong with it at the time,' Enzo continued. 'He was just training me to take over.'

'But now?'

'Now it's something else I was wrong about. I've been wrong a lot.' He smiled sadly.

That admission meant so much more than an apology. But maybe Emilio had been wrong too. He'd been angry at his brother all this time, but it was their father who'd put them both in that situation. As a soon-to-be father, Emilio wanted his child to love any future sibling. Would want them to support each other. His father hadn't cared.

From the moment Emilio had got the paternity test, he'd known he wanted to be a different type of father from the one he'd had. Now he realised that Enzo hadn't had a good father, a loving father, either. What power would Enzo have had over him anyway? Children weren't meant to fix their parents' mistakes.

Emilio moved to sit with his brother. For the first time, Enzo felt like one.

'Mamma thought she owned those vineyards. Do you realise how elaborate this lie must have been to fool her? Did she just trust him?'

'We all trusted him, Emilio,' Enzo said softly. 'Turns out he only cared about duty—to the vineyards and the company and the family name. Not to us, or Mamma.'

'I wanted him to feel something for me, Enzo,' Emilio confessed at the obvious pain in Enzo's voice. 'Hate me or love me, I didn't care. Either would have been better than nothing.'

'You should have had more memories with him, but I'm glad you don't, because those memories cost me time with Mamma. I'm happy you have those instead. Those can't be tarnished.'

That was true. Enzo's time with their mother had been limited, but he'd always revelled in their father's attention. These revelations were easier for Emilio to handle because he had always seen their father for the monster he was. Enzo, on the other hand... He would be questioning their whole lives. For the first time, Emilio's heart broke for his brother.

There'd been obvious affection in his voice when he'd spoken of their mother. Emilio thought of the vase of pink oleander beside her bed, the flowers that had never seemed to wilt, and felt guilty for years of uncharitable thoughts. That neverending supply of bouquets had been proof of Enzo's love.

'I'm sorry too, Enzo.'

His brother's bright-green gaze snapped to him. 'What for?'

'You're a victim in this too. And I made things worse.'

Enzo shook his head. 'Emilio, Gia wasn't right for either of us. She cared for only herself and what we could provide her.'

'That changes nothing,' Emilio said through gritted teeth.

Enzo frowned and leaned forward in his seat. 'I forgive you. When will you forgive yourself?'

'I don't deserve forgiveness.'

'Of course you do. Why would you think otherwise?'

Emilio couldn't answer. Couldn't tell his brother how ashamed he was, how much he'd changed his life after the affair.

'Emilio, I want you to listen very carefully to me. I was hurt and so I hurt you. That was wrong of me. I wish I'd handled things differently. I could have. We're *both* to blame for how the last eight years have gone. It's not all on you. You deserve forgiveness. So, ask me.' Suddenly, his bossy brother was back and the look in Enzo's eye said he wouldn't be dissuaded.

'Ask you what?'

'Ask for my forgiveness.'

'Enzo,' Emilio said brokenly. 'I can't'

'Yes, you can. You have to learn to ask for the things you need. So, do it.'

Could he do that? Could he ask his brother for his forgiveness after hurting him so profoundly?

What harm could come of it?

Nothing, Emilio realised. Things were already the worst they could be. He had nothing to lose.

'Enzo, will you forgive me for what I did to you? It's the very worst thing I have done in my life and I regret it to this day. I was stupid and selfish, and I can't fully express how sorry I am.'

'I forgive you, Emilio.' Enzo smiled.

Emilio hadn't been prepared for what he'd feel at those words. It was as if they stemmed the flow of a gushing wound.

'I have to atone.'

'You already have. Emilio, you need to know that you don't have to earn affection. You deserve to be with someone who deserves *you*. And, as I hear it, you have found someone.'

'Not any more.'

'What happened?' Enzo sounded genuinely concerned, and it occurred to Emilio that this was what he had craved from his brother growing up: this ability to talk, to share. And, when he hadn't got that, when he'd been jealous and angry, it had been so much easier to hate Enzo instead.

Have you considered...that perhaps you want the vineyards, not just for our child or what they meant to your mother, but also to have Enzo back in your life in some way?

Emilio should have listened to Jasmine from the start. His mother, in her infinite wisdom, was trying to bring them together from beyond the grave. Maybe he needed to stop being so stubborn.

He told Enzo everything.

'So you forced her to marry you?' Enzo asked with raised brows.

'Don't you dare judge me. I was doing the right thing.'

'The right thing for whom? That's your child, Emilio. They would have been family regardless of whether you were married or not. I wouldn't have judged you.'

Emilio scoffed. 'You wouldn't?'

'I have had time to reflect on a lot,' Enzo admitted. 'Jasmine needed a choice, a real choice. I have seen the damage forcing someone into marriage can do. I have destroyed someone for being guilty of it.'

'Destroyed...?' That was a strong reaction for someone as controlled as Enzo. It must have something to do with the person Enzo had said he'd met, and Emilio found himself wanting to know what had happened—not out of curiosity, but because he wanted to know what was going on his brother's life. 'I think you have a lot to tell me too.'

Enzo laughed. 'You have no idea.'

Emilio looked down at his wedding band, all that was left of Jasmine in his life. 'She said I don't trust myself.'

'Do you?'

Emilio only had to think of the things Jasmine had said when she was leaving to answer that question. 'No.'

'Then you have to work on that. It sounds to me like you both need each other. You allow her to be all of who she is, and she makes you want to be better. You just need to believe that better man is who you are. One bad action doesn't make you a bad person, Emilio.'

'How can you say that? If it weren't for me, you would have been married.'

'I would have, and I would have been miserable, but more importantly I would have missed out on Charlotte—and she is the love of my life. But, Emilio, that love was hard fought for. Do you truly love Jasmine?'

'With my soul.'

'Then fight for her. Has she sent you a separation agreement yet?'

'No,' Emilio realised. A small spark of hope bloomed in the darkness.

Enzo smiled. 'So all isn't lost. Get her back.'

Emilio had spent the last three weeks in a spiral of regret and heartache. He'd been so consumed with his angst that he hadn't considered the very thing that his brother had noticed in mere minutes: Jasmine hadn't started divorce proceedings. She hadn't returned the ring either. And she was always so on top of things that it couldn't mean nothing. Why hadn't he seen it weeks ago?

'I have to go.'

'Yes, you do.' Enzo grinned.

Emilio grabbed his keys off his desk and rushed for the door, leaving his brother in his office.

He stopped in the doorway, remembering things Gia had told him. Things Enzo had confided in her. The insecurities that Emilio was now certain no one had ever put to rest. 'Enzo.'

His brother looked up at him.

'You leave your mark on the people around you.'

CHAPTER NINETEEN

Tap tap.

The knock on the glass door to Jasmine's office was far gentler than Jenna's, and before she even glanced up a frisson of recognition ran down her spine.

Emilio was standing at the door. Every cell in her body wanted to leap into his arms. But she didn't. She stayed exactly where she was.

He was as beautiful as ever, but she noticed the dark circles under his eyes. His hair was mussed in a way that made her think he wasn't really taking care of himself. Clearly, she wasn't the only one suffering.

'Hello, Jasmine,' he greeted her softly as he opened the door.

'I don't want to see you, Emilio.' A lie, but she didn't know what to do with the truth. She still hurt.

'I need to talk to you, *belleza*. I'll wait all day if I have to.'

Hearing him call her that made her want to weep. Made memories of their time in Italy return in full force. She so desperately wished she could return there, but it was in the past. There was no regaining the trust he broke...was there?

But if he hung around her office all day it would be torture, not to mention a distraction for everyone. She doubted he'd make a scene, but still...

Her desk phone rang loudly, and she looked at the flashing light on the keypad. She was genuinely busy. She could ignore Emilio or send him away. But for weeks she had missed him. She *wanted* to talk to him.

'Not here.'

'Come with me, then,' he said softly, his palm outstretched. 'Please, Jasmine.'

She looked at his hand. Every cell in her body screamed at her to take it, but she couldn't.

She would, however, go with him. Hear him out.

'Fine.'

They made their way down to the street. The Maybach she'd expected wasn't there. Instead, Emilio walked up to a large white SUV and opened the door for her.

'You drove?' Emilio never drove anywhere. He didn't trust himself enough to do so and yet, when he opened the door, she spotted a child seat already fitted in the back.

She had seen this car before. It hadn't been her mind playing tricks on her that morning after she'd returned from Italy. It *had* been Emilio.

'I did,' he said cautiously—caution at her reaction, she realised. So she stepped forward and climbed into the car.

'Where are we going?' she asked when they pulled out into the traffic.

'Home.'

'Then you're going in the wrong direction.'

'We're going to mine. I didn't know if you'd want me at yours. And I need you to know that, no matter what happens after we talk, the penthouse will always be your home too.'

'Belleza, my home is our home. Our child's home.' That was what he'd said at the gallery, before everything had gone up in flames.

When they finally arrived and entered his penthouse, it felt as if no time had passed since she'd last been there. Since their wedding. She could still picture getting dressed in the guest room. Could see her mother witnessing their signatures as they'd stepped into the living room.

Jasmine swallowed thickly. No matter how badly she missed Emilio, she had to remain strong. 'Say what you need to then I'll leave.'

'Will you take a seat?'

'No,' she replied defiantly. She wanted to be here too much. If she got comfortable, she might not want to leave. 'Now, talk.'

Emilio didn't join her. He kept his distance, standing with the coffee table between them. She saw his hand twitch towards her but he stiffened his arm at his side. She knew how that felt. It was the same for her.

'I know what I did was wrong,' he started. 'Both when I was young and now, with you. Sleeping with Gia is the thing I am most ashamed of in my life. It's never far from my mind, and I know it can never be undone. I deserve to pay for it.'

Jasmine didn't disagree with him—what he had done to Enzo was awful—but she would be lying if she said she didn't hear his self-loathing in those words.

Emilio began pacing, as if it would help the words flow; Jasmine didn't comment on it, choosing instead to watch him. This honesty was what she had wanted from the start.

'For so long, I was jealous of my brother. I saw the relationship he had with my father, the manner in which he was favoured, and I craved it. Craved a relationship with him too, but when it didn't happen it was easier to hate him. But now, after talking to him, I realise that he was no better off than me.'

'You spoke to Enzo?' Jasmine was shocked.

'I imagine he's still in my office making a nuisance of himself.' Emilio huffed a laugh.

He was making jokes about his brother now... Was he making actual, healthy changes to his life?

You saw the car.

She had. That was a large part of why she was here right now.

'See, the thing is, I had no one to show me what life was really like for him. All I knew was that Gia was someone important to Enzo and she'd chosen me. However briefly, she'd chosen me.' His eyes scrunched shut.

Jasmine could tell the words were being ripped from deep within him. Could see the hurt and shame.

'You always want what you can't have,' she said, remembering watching other kids at school, kids whose parents used to take them on vacations and drop them off in fancy cars. Mothers *and* fathers in the audience during recitals. She'd known she couldn't have that, but she'd gone to bed thinking about it every night.

Emilio nodded. 'I was hoping to be loved and I think that's why I connected with Gia. Even though now I know how ridiculous it was. I didn't love her, and she certainly didn't love me.' He looked at the floor. 'I just wanted to be chosen.'

It sounded as if he was saying it more to himself than to Jasmine. Maybe he realised, because he cleared his throat and continued. 'But, after I slept with her, I knew no one ever would. I knew I wasn't good.'

He covered his eyes with his hand, but she could see the frown on his forehead. Could see the agony in his downturned lips.

'Maybe my father had always known that.'

Jasmine couldn't take it any longer. His pain felt like her own. Her eyes welled up. She went to him, pulling his hand away so he could look into her face.

'That's not true,' she said. 'I've seen the good in you.' It had all been good. Right up until the point it wasn't. She ought to step away, but she couldn't see him in agony. Her body sang when his was close.

She was torn.

'I don't want you to comfort me, *belleza*. I deserve to feel this. I just want you to understand why I couldn't tell you. I knew that I didn't deserve you—was convinced that, if you knew everything, you would never be able to care for me in any way. I already knew you couldn't love me, but I loved you. I *do* love you. I wanted to hold onto you despite all of it. And, even if you walk away from me today, I will go on loving you until my last breath. I will always be there for you and our baby.'

'Emilio.' She swallowed past the lump in her throat. 'That night in Venice… I didn't want you to tell me you loved me when I felt so betrayed, but I have come to realise I love you too…'

'You do?' Emilio cupped her face in his warm hands. Hope sparked in his brown eyes.

'Yes. But, if you could do that to your brother, how badly could you hurt me? Hurt our child?' Jasmine still felt stuck on that point. He had healed so much of her. He had such goodness in him, but had he changed enough? She put her hands on his chest, unsure if she wanted to push him away or clutch him tighter. 'I want to believe in you. God knows, I do. I'm just scared.'

As the words left her mouth, she realised that she still trusted him enough to put aside strength and show him her vulnerabilities.

'Then let me tell you who I am. I am a man who loved his mother, who was ignored by his father, who was jealous of his brother and unfairly hated him because of it. I've done two terrible things. I slept with my brother's fiancée— I have since asked for his forgiveness, which he gave to me. I don't understand it. And I hid my actions from the woman I loved—something I regret so deeply.

'It was selfish. I was scared of losing her, but I should have given her the choice to stay. I am a man who wanted so desperately to leave a De Luca legacy for my child, but that's impossible, because the vineyards were never my mother's. My father lied to her just like I lied. I have never been so disgusted at myself. I never want to be him.'

He'd lost the vineyards... Jasmine's hands fisted in his shirt. She wanted to comfort him but she stopped herself from saying anything, doing anything further, because she needed Emilio to continue.

'I am a man who wants to mend the relationship with his brother, and I am a man begging his wife, the love of his life, for a chance to show the real him. I'm flawed, Jasmine; I make spectacular mistakes, but I am not the person I was back then. I vow to be honest with you. To be worthy of you. To be someone you can trust—not just with your heart but with your worries and anxieties. I want to be the person you feel yourself with.'

'Emilio.' Tears streamed down her face. He wiped them away with his thumbs. All she had wanted was this honesty. For him to be open with her. 'Emilio, you already are that person. From the start, I was nothing but myself with you. It had been such a long time since I was able to do that, and the longer we were together the easier it became.' She looked at the ring still twinkling prettily on her finger, then into his eyes. 'All I ever wanted was for you be open with me. Just like this.'

'You make me a better man, Jasmine.'

'No, I don't. You were always good.' She felt the truth of it to her soul. 'You just did a bad thing.'

He rested his forehead against hers and, just like that, the weeks of agony lifted. It felt as if she belonged in his embrace.

'I'm scared too,' he said softly. 'I'm terrified that you'll reject me.'

'I don't want to,' Jasmine admitted.

'Then will you give me another chance?' Emilio whispered. 'Will you forgive me?'

'Yes.'

His lips were on hers in an instant, his kiss desperate. His relief palpable. And when she kissed him back his moan ignited her blood. Her arms went around his neck pulling him closer, and the embrace, already uncontrolled, became a storm of all their love. All their passion. His taste, his scent... they were so familiar. It was home.

'I couldn't let you go.' Jasmine breathed against his lips.

'You'll never have to. I promise, *belleza*. I'll be worthy of you. I love you.'

'I love you too.' She smiled, her heart lighter than it had ever been. There was nothing between them now. They could finally be together. Be a family. 'I really love it here, but what would you say to coming home with me?'

'You want me to move in?' He stiffened under her touch. She could tell he was holding his breath.

'I've had more than enough time without you. I refuse to do it for one more night.'

'*Amore*...we can go right now.'

EPILOGUE

Five months later

'WOULD YOU LIKE to hold her?' Jasmine asked from the hospital bed.

'Yes.' This was the happiest day of Emilio's life. 'Hold on.' He took off his finely pressed white shirt and laid it over an arm chair, then kissed his wife and took his daughter, holding her against his bare chest. With her wispy blonde hair and chubby little face, she was utterly perfect.

'I thought we could name her Francesca Valentina,' Jasmine said, her smile growing at the look on Emilio's face.

'Belleza!' He choked. 'Francesca Valentina De Luca,' he said to his daughter with unconcealed awe. 'She would have loved you.' Then he looked at his wife. Her curly hair was loose, her expression tired, and yet he had never seen anyone more beautiful. 'She would have loved you too.'

'As much as you?' Jasmine teased.

'No one could ever love anyone as much as I love you, *amore*. To think that is a crime.' He revelled in her laughter.

'I'm wishing I had a camera again.'

And, just as he had all those months ago in a bedroom in Italy, Emilio handed her his phone. He heard her snap a picture. When he looked over, she was still staring at the screen with a smile on her face.

'You have a message from Enzo,' she announced, handing the phone back. 'When will you be giving him your mother's ring?'

'When he comes to see Francesca,' Emilio replied. His brother was planning an elaborate proposal to Charlotte in Perlano and had asked if Emilio would be willing to part with the ring. He and Jasmine had agreed it would be a fitting way to share Valentina's affection, even if only symbolically. 'Would you mind if I called him?'

Jasmine shook her head and lay back against the pillows. With his daughter in one arm, and his wife resting by his side, Emilio video-called his brother. It would be late in Australia, where Enzo and Charlotte had made their home, yet, as always since their reconciliation, Enzo answered on the first ring. That had taken some getting used to, but now Emilio simply appreciated the ways his brother showed him that he was important.

'Meet your niece,' Emilio said delighting in the soft expression and gentle smile on Enzo's face. Before his brother could say anything, Charlotte pushed into frame.

'Let me see!' she demanded, and Enzo indulged her. 'Oh, she's beautiful, Emilio!'

'That she is. Just like her mother,' Emilio agreed, glancing at his wife. How had he ever got so lucky?

'We'll be there in two days,' Charlotte said excitedly. In the background, Emilio spied a tall Christmas tree, the bright Australian sun shining despite the hour.

'Yes, and we will have a lot to talk about,' Enzo added.

Talking was the last thing Emilio wanted to do when he was bursting with happiness. 'About what?'

Enzo and Charlotte looked at each other, then she nodded nearly imperceptibly.

'I've started the process to separate Vozzano from the holdings.' Enzo pulled a set of keys from his pocket. 'It doesn't seem right to have a set of keys to your estate.' He grinned at Emilio's complete shock.

'What?' Emilio was certain that his heart had stopped beating.

'I'm structuring it so that De Luca and Co still own the brand, but you own the property and vineyards. That way, the company will source the Vozzano grapes from you.'

Emilio was unable to speak. A lifetime of memories flashed before his eyes.

'You were right. You deserved to make some of it your own. This way, the De Luca legacy will take care of Francesca and any other children you choose to have.'

'Enzo.' His name came out strangled, but Emilio couldn't say any more than that. How could he express how much this meant to him?

'You can change that hideous chandelier now,' Enzo joked. 'I'll send yours in the post.'

Emilio still didn't know how to respond. 'Thank you,' he managed but the words didn't seem like enough.

'You never have to thank me, Emilio. I'm glad you never left the company. See you in a few days.' Enzo ended the call, but Emilio still held onto the phone as he processed the news. Slowly, it slipped from his grip, falling onto his lap.

Jasmine smiled. 'Congratulations.'

Emilio shook his head, reaching out to take her hand and kissing her knuckles reverentially. 'All that's mine is yours, *belleza*.'

'Is that so?' she questioned with a cocked brow.

'Including my heart and soul.' A truth that would never change.

'*Sono tuo*,' Jasmine replied, smiling broadly at the amazed smile on his face. 'I've been learning Italian. I was going to surprise you on your birthday, but I couldn't wait any longer.'

Emilio placed the baby in the cot and went over to his wife, kissing her fiercely.

'Tell me more,' he begged.

Jasmine laughed, her green-gold eyes shining. 'We have our whole lives.'

'Forever,' Emilio agreed.

* * * * *

If Pregnant Before "I Do" *left you wanting more,*
then don't miss the first instalment in
The De Luca Legacy duet, Strictly Forbidden Boss*!*

And why not explore these other stories
from Bella Mason?

Awakened by the Wild Billionaire
Secretly Pregnant by the Tycoon
Their Diamond Ring Ruse
His Chosen Queen

Available now!

MILLS & BOON®

Coming next month

TWINS FOR HIS MAJESTY
Clare Connelly

'The baby is fine?'

'Oh, the baby is fine. In fact, both babies are fine,' she snapped, almost maniacally now. 'It's twins,' she added, and then she sobbed, lifting a hand to her mouth to stop the torrent of emotion from pouring out in a large wail.

Silence cracked around them but she barely noticed. She was shaking now, processing the truth of the scan, the reality that lay before her.

'Well, then.' His voice was low and silky, as though she hadn't just told him they were going to have *two babies* in a matter of months. 'That makes our decision even easier.'

'What decision?' she asked, whirling around to face him.

'There is no way on earth you are leaving the country whilst pregnant with my children, so forget about returning to New Zealand.'

She flinched. She hadn't expected that.

'Nor will my children be born under a cloud of illegitimacy.'

Her heart almost stopped beating; his words made no sense. 'I—don't—what are you saying?'

'That you must marry me—and quickly.'

Continue reading

TWINS FOR HIS MAJESTY
Clare Connelly

Available next month
millsandboon.co.uk

Copyright ©2025 by Clare Connelly

COMING SOON!

We really hope you enjoyed reading this book. If you're looking for more romance be sure to head to the shops when new books are available on

Thursday 17th July

To see which titles are coming soon, please visit
millsandboon.co.uk/nextmonth

MILLS & BOON

FOUR BRAND NEW BOOKS FROM
MILLS & BOON MODERN

The same great stories you love, a stylish new look!

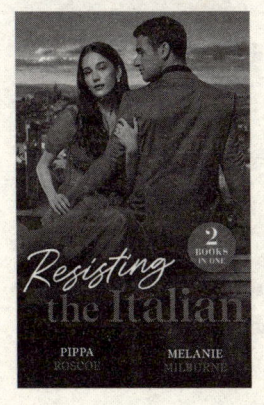

OUT NOW

Eight Modern stories published every month, find them all at:
millsandboon.co.uk

afterglow BOOKS

Afterglow Books is a trend-led, trope-filled list of books with diverse, authentic and relatable characters, a wide array of voices and representations, plus real world trials and tribulations. Featuring all the tropes you could possibly want (think small-town settings, fake relationships, grumpy vs sunshine, enemies to lovers) and all with a generous dose of spice in every story.

♪ @millsandboonuk
◉ @millsandboonuk
afterglowbooks.co.uk
#AfterglowBooks

For all the latest book news, exclusive content and giveaways scan the QR code below to sign up to the Afterglow newsletter:

SCAN ME

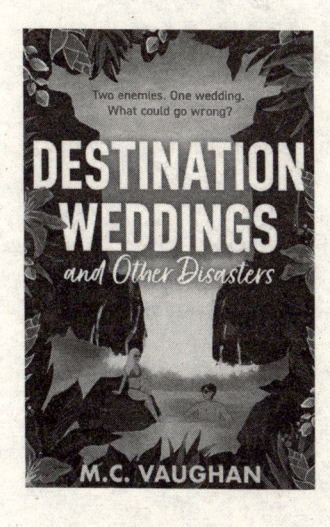

afterglow BOOKS

DESTINATION WEDDINGS and Other Disasters
M.C. VAUGHAN

Two enemies. One wedding. What could go wrong?

- ✈ International
- ♥ Enemies to lovers
- ((•)) Forced proximity

The Friends to Lovers Project
PAULA OTTONI

She has a plan. But he wasn't part of it...

- 👫 Friends to lovers
- ✈ International
- △ Love triangle

OUT NOW

Two stories published every month. Discover more at:
Afterglowbooks.co.uk

LET'S TALK
Romance

For exclusive extracts, competitions and special offers, find us online:

- **f** MillsandBoon
- **X** @MillsandBoon
- **◎** @MillsandBoonUK
- **♪** @MillsandBoonUK

Get in touch on 01413 063 232

For all the latest titles coming soon, visit
millsandboon.co.uk/nextmonth

OUT NOW!

Opposites Attract: Workplace Temptation

3 BOOKS IN ONE

CHRISTY McKELLEN
BARBARA WALLACE
STEFANIE LONDON

Available at
millsandboon.co.uk

MILLS & BOON

OUT NOW!

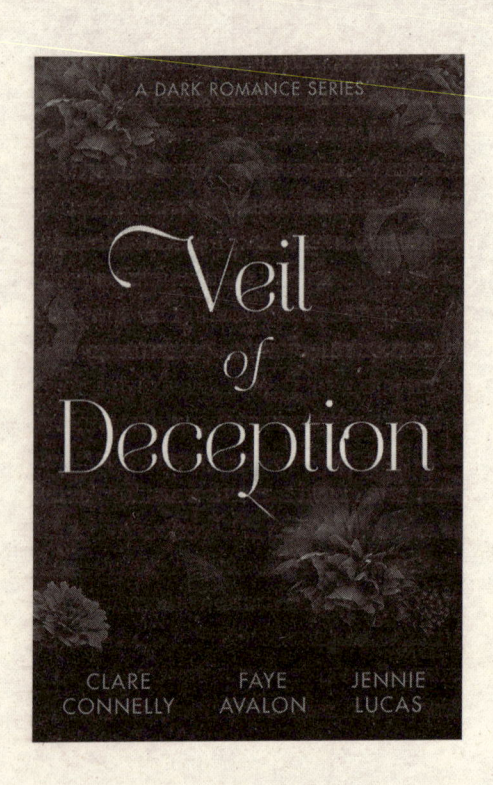

Veil of Deception

A DARK ROMANCE SERIES

CLARE CONNELLY · FAYE AVALON · JENNIE LUCAS

Available at millsandboon.co.uk

MILLS & BOON